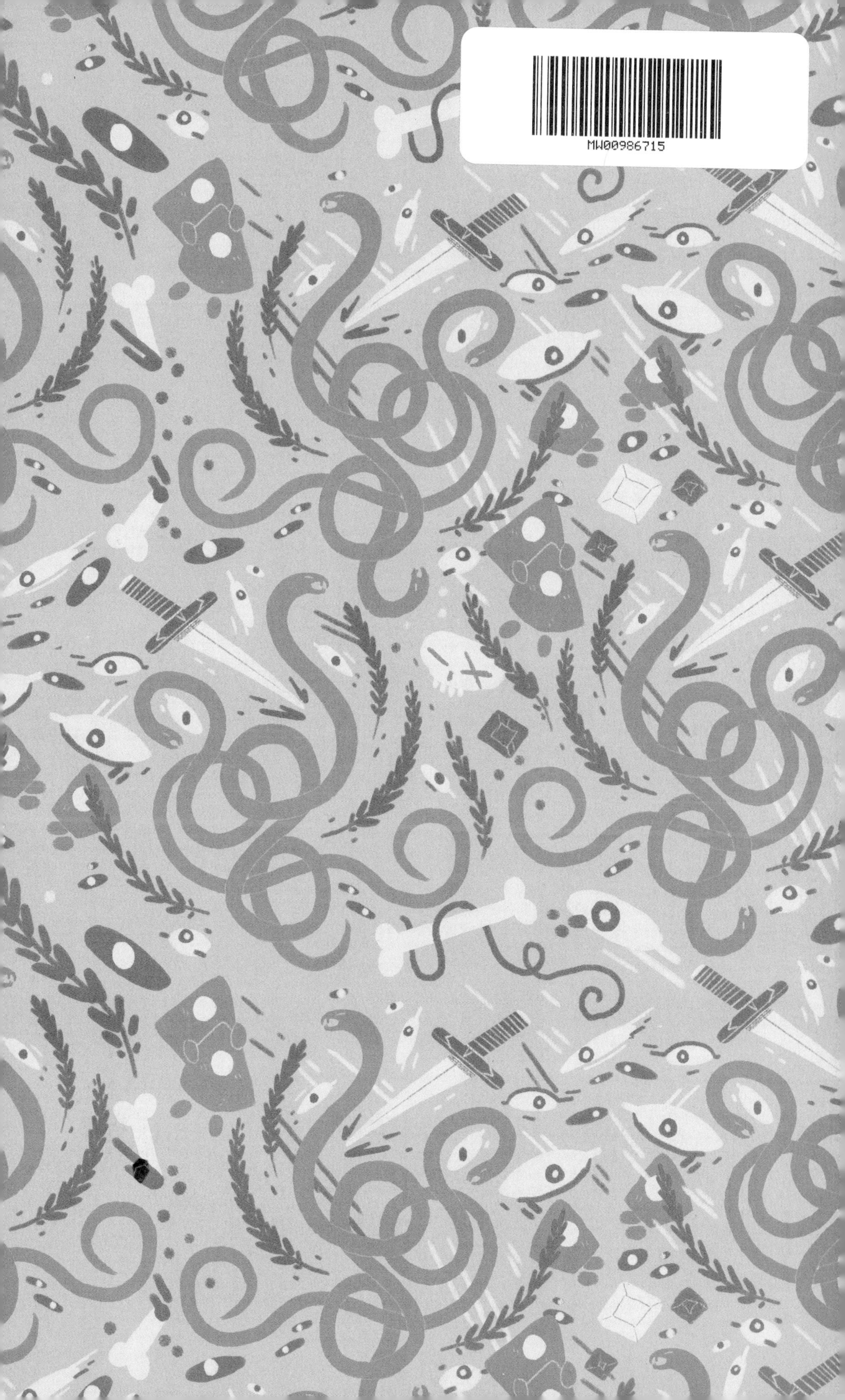

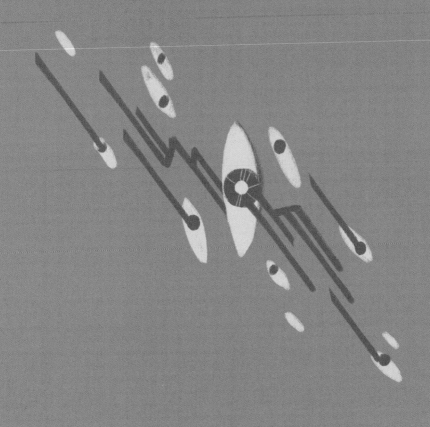

IMAGE COMICS, INC.

Robert Kirkman: Chief Operating Officer
Erik Larsen: Chief Financial Officer
Todd McFarlane: President
Marc Silvestri: Chief Executive Officer
Jim Valentino: Vice President
Eric Stephenson: Publisher / Chief Creative Officer
Jeff Boison: Director of Publishing Planning & Book Trade Sales
Chris Ross: Director of Digital Sales
Jeff Stang: Director of Direct Market Sales
Kat Salazar: Director of PR & Marketing
Drew Gill: Art Director
Heather Doornink: Production Director
Nicole Lapalme: Controller

IMAGECOMICS.COM

ISBN: 978-1-5343-1406-1

OPHIUCHUS

CREATED BY

ALI LERIGER DE LA PLANTE & NATASHA TARA PETROVIĆ

primary writer,
secondary artist

primary artist,
secondary writer

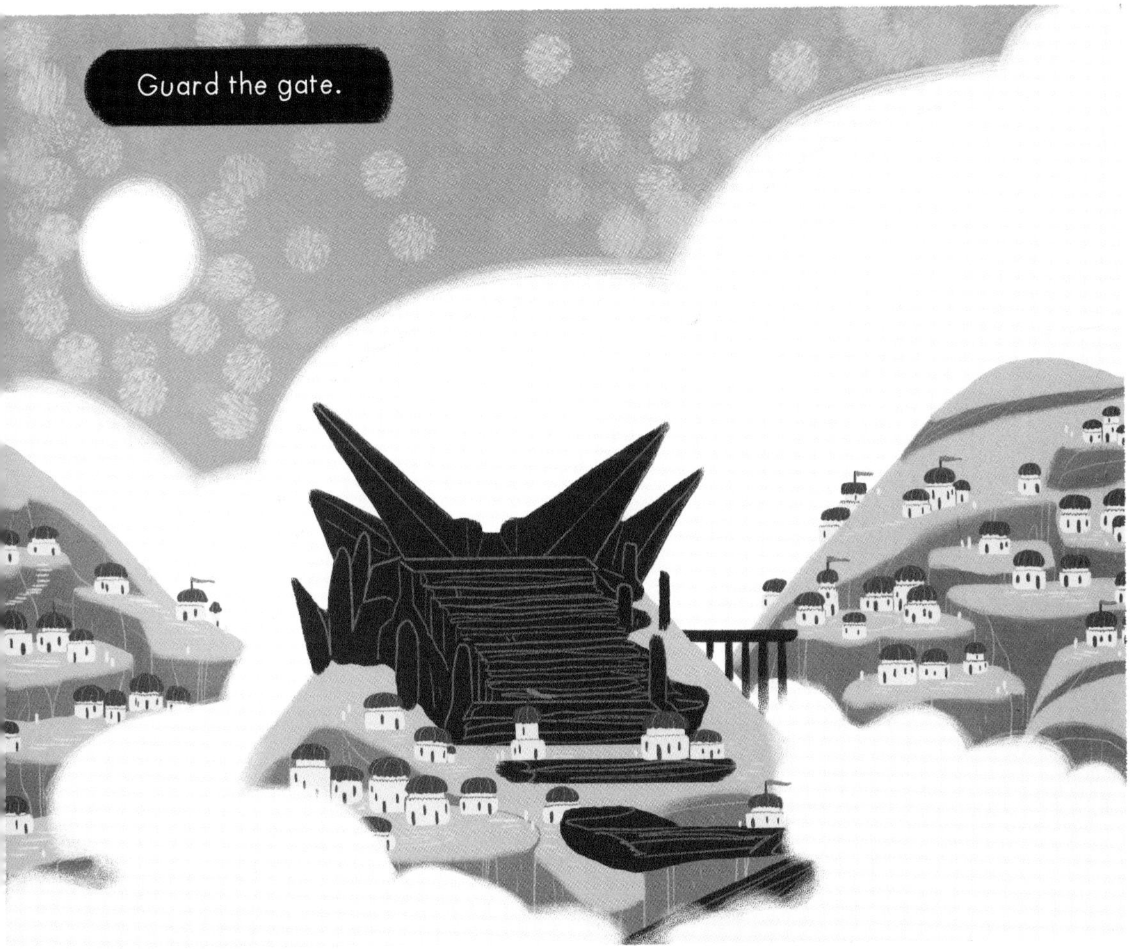
Guard the gate.

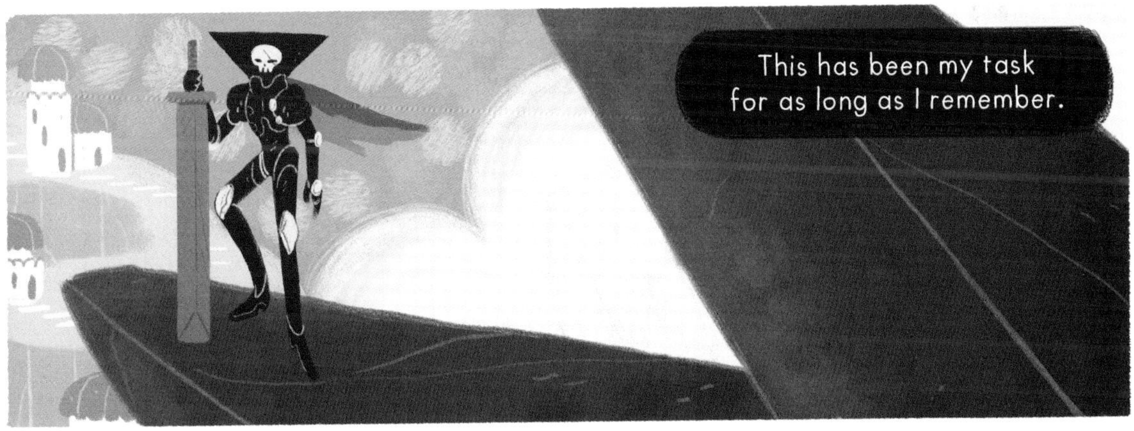
This has been my task
for as long as I remember.

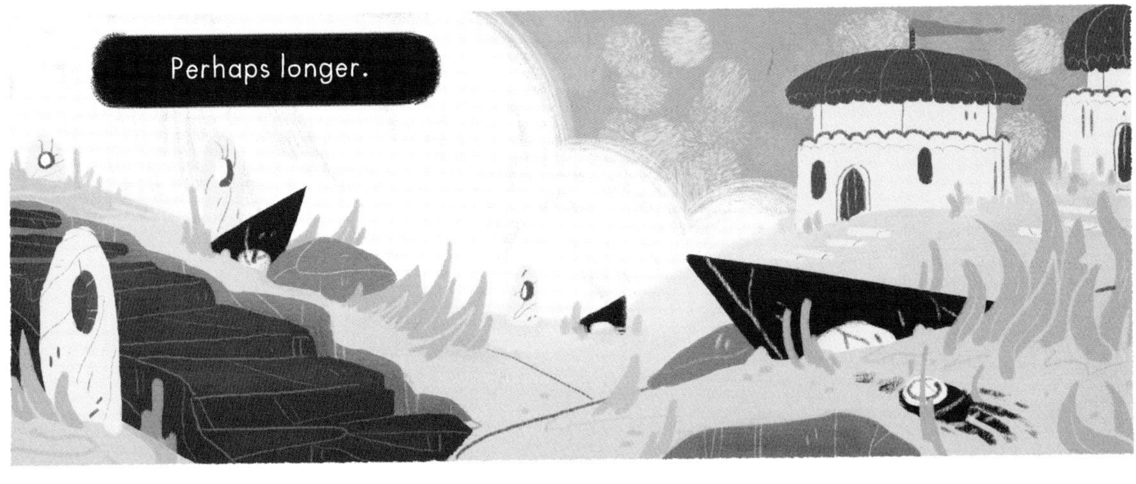
Perhaps longer.

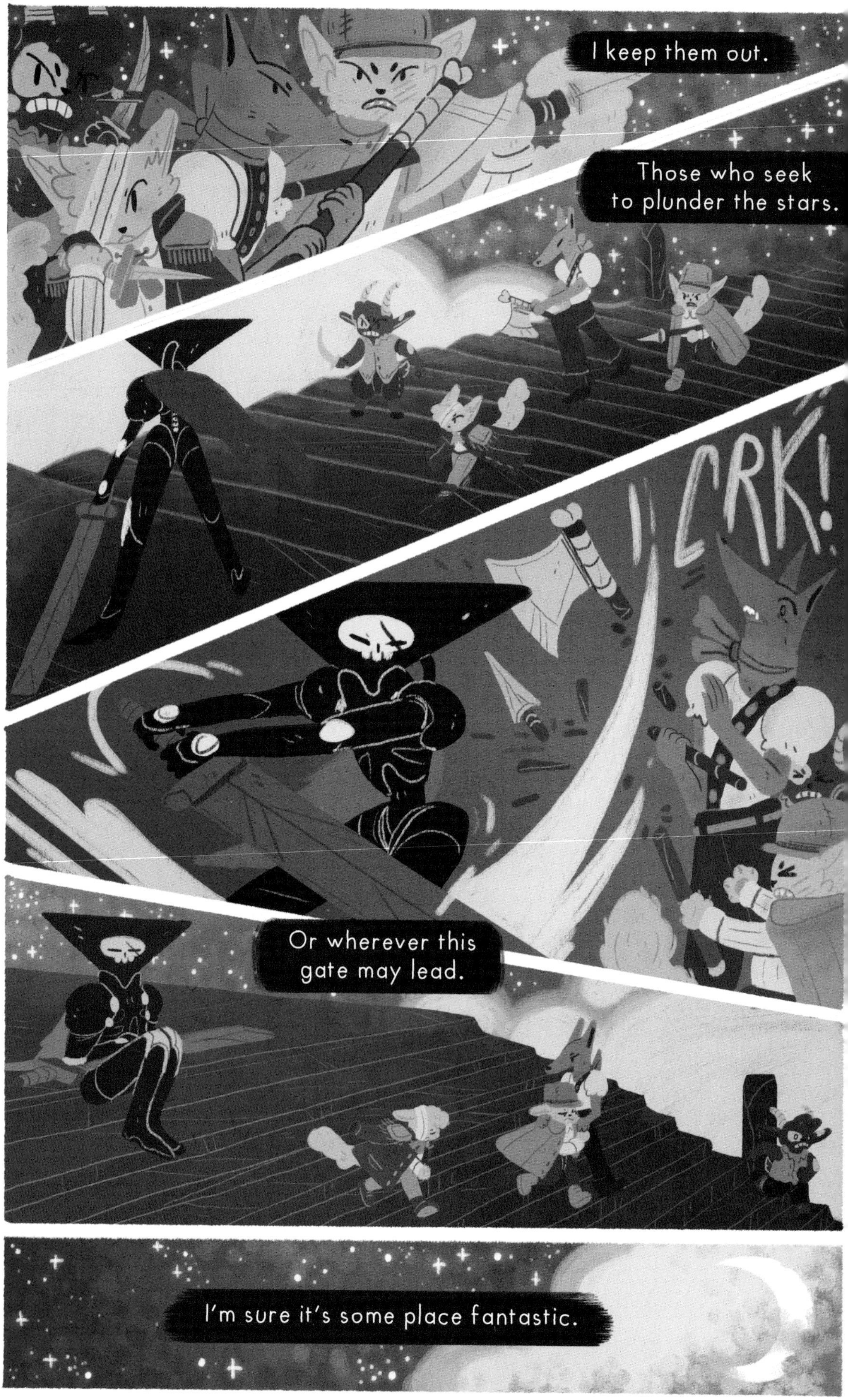
I keep them out.
Those who seek to plunder the stars.
CRK!
Or wherever this gate may lead.
I'm sure it's some place fantastic.

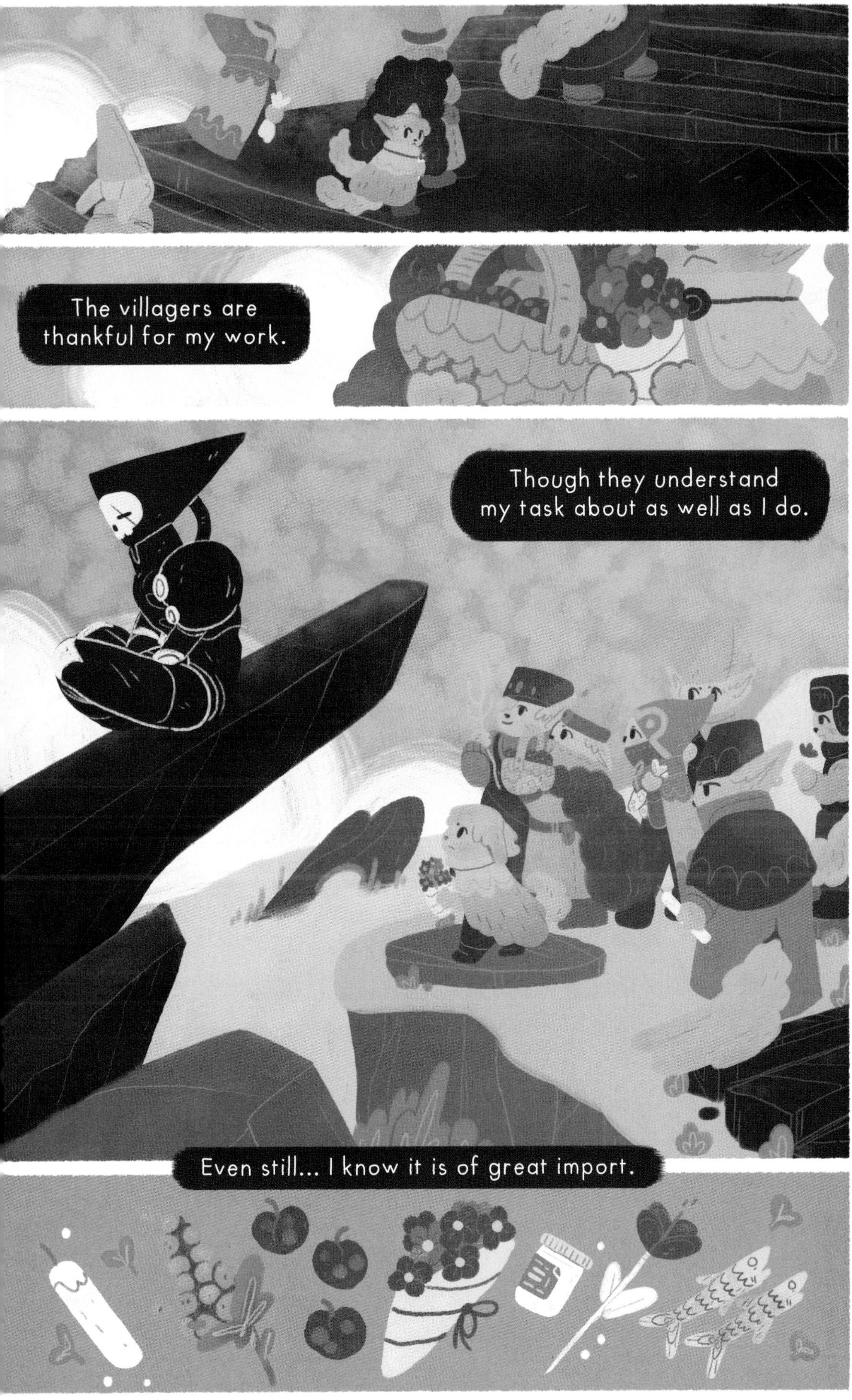

The villagers are thankful for my work.
Though they understand my task about as well as I do.
Even still... I know it is of great import.

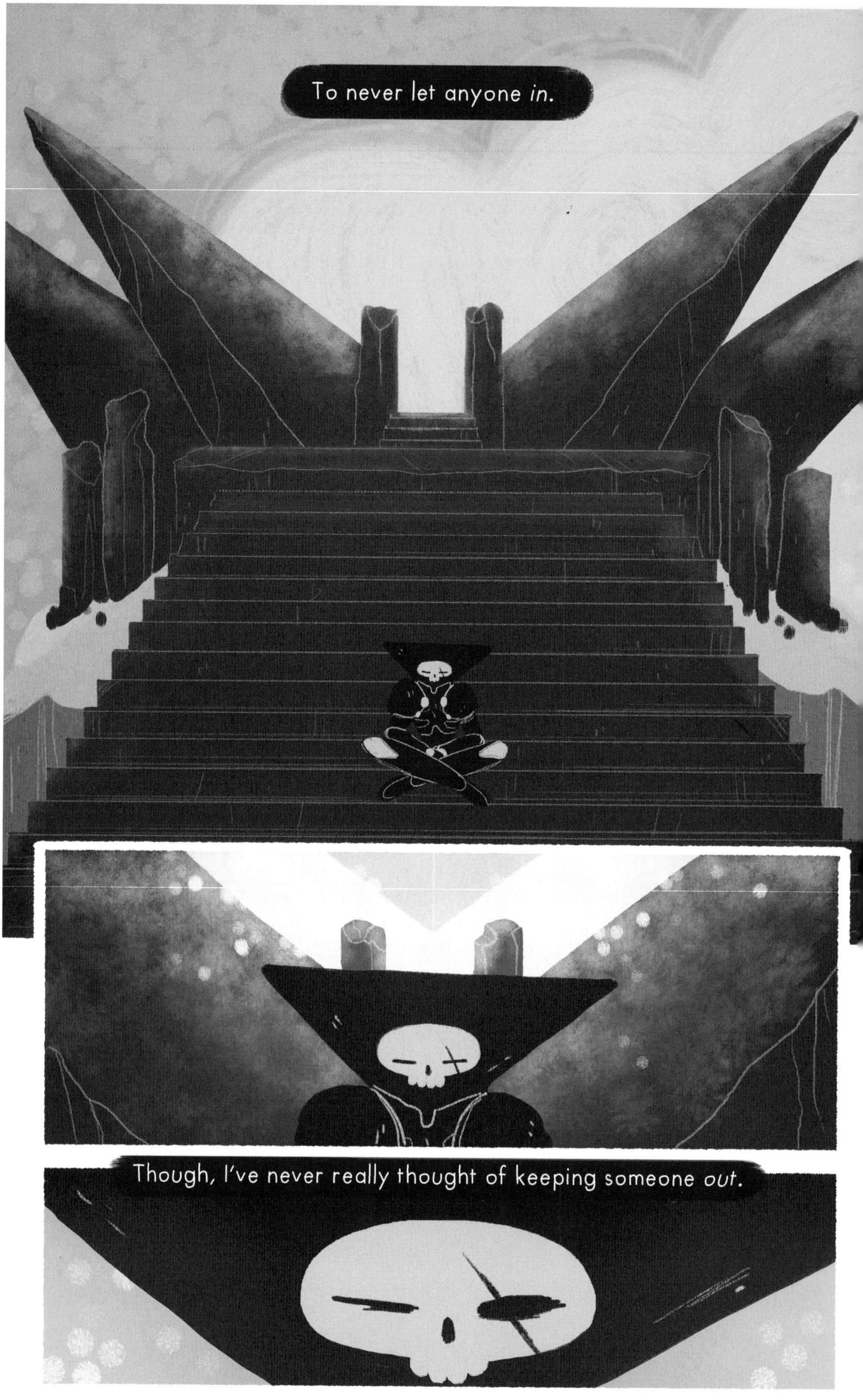

To never let anyone *in*.
Though, I've never really thought of keeping someone *out*.

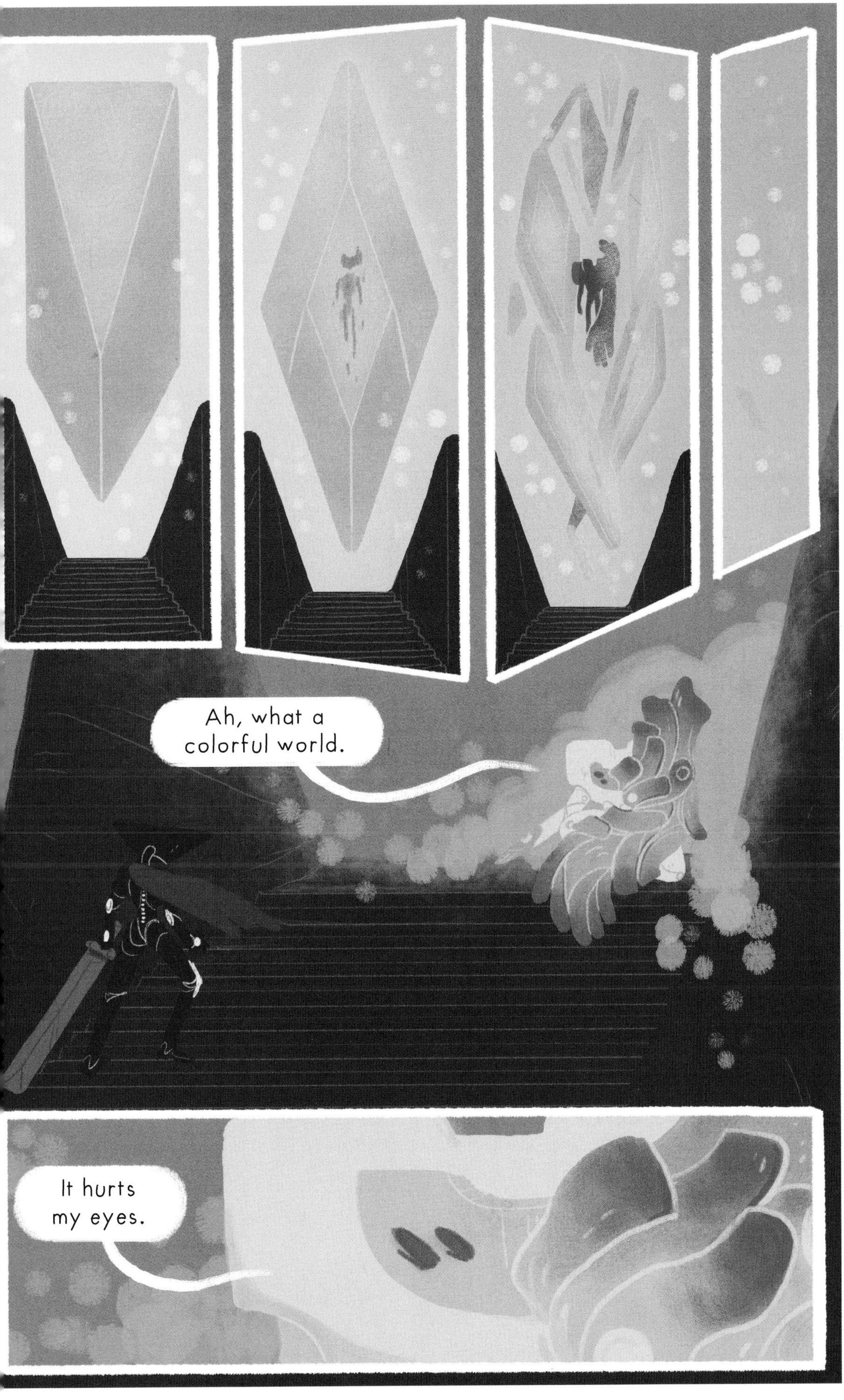
Ah, what a colorful world.
It hurts my eyes.

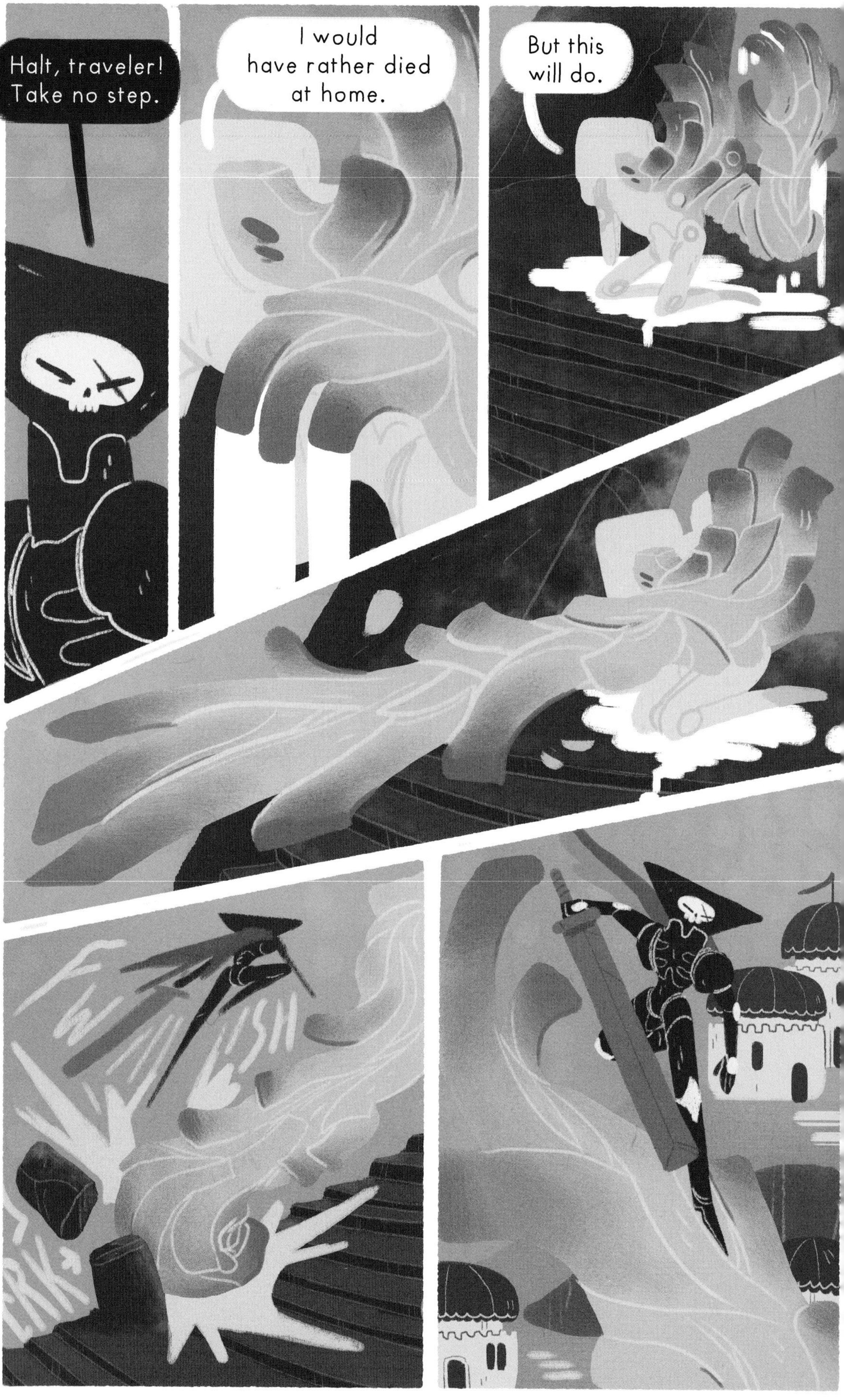
Halt, traveler! Take no step.
I would have rather died at home.
But this will do.

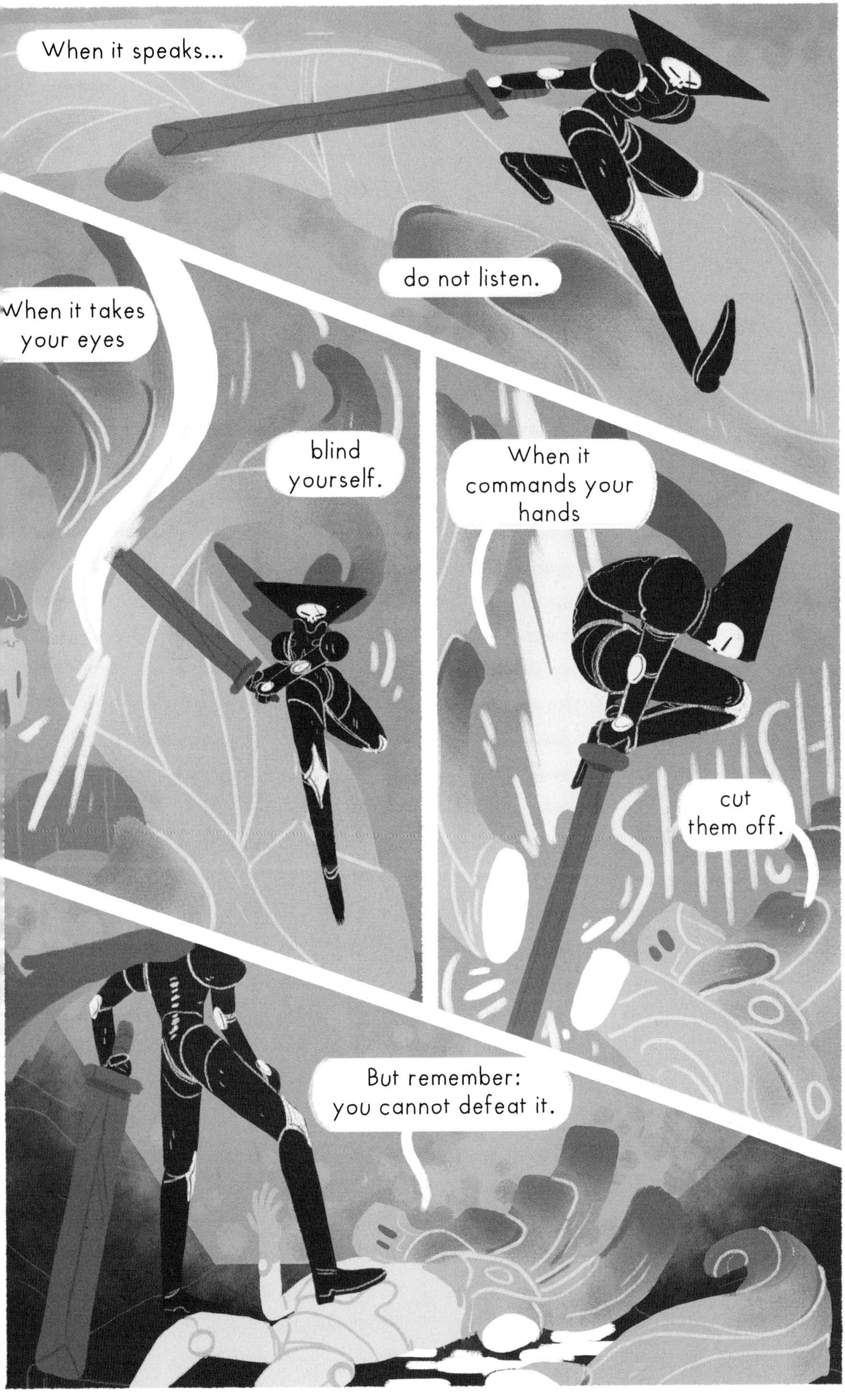
When it speaks...
do not listen.
When it takes your eyes
blind yourself.
When it commands your hands
cut them off.
SHHUSH
But remember: you cannot defeat it.

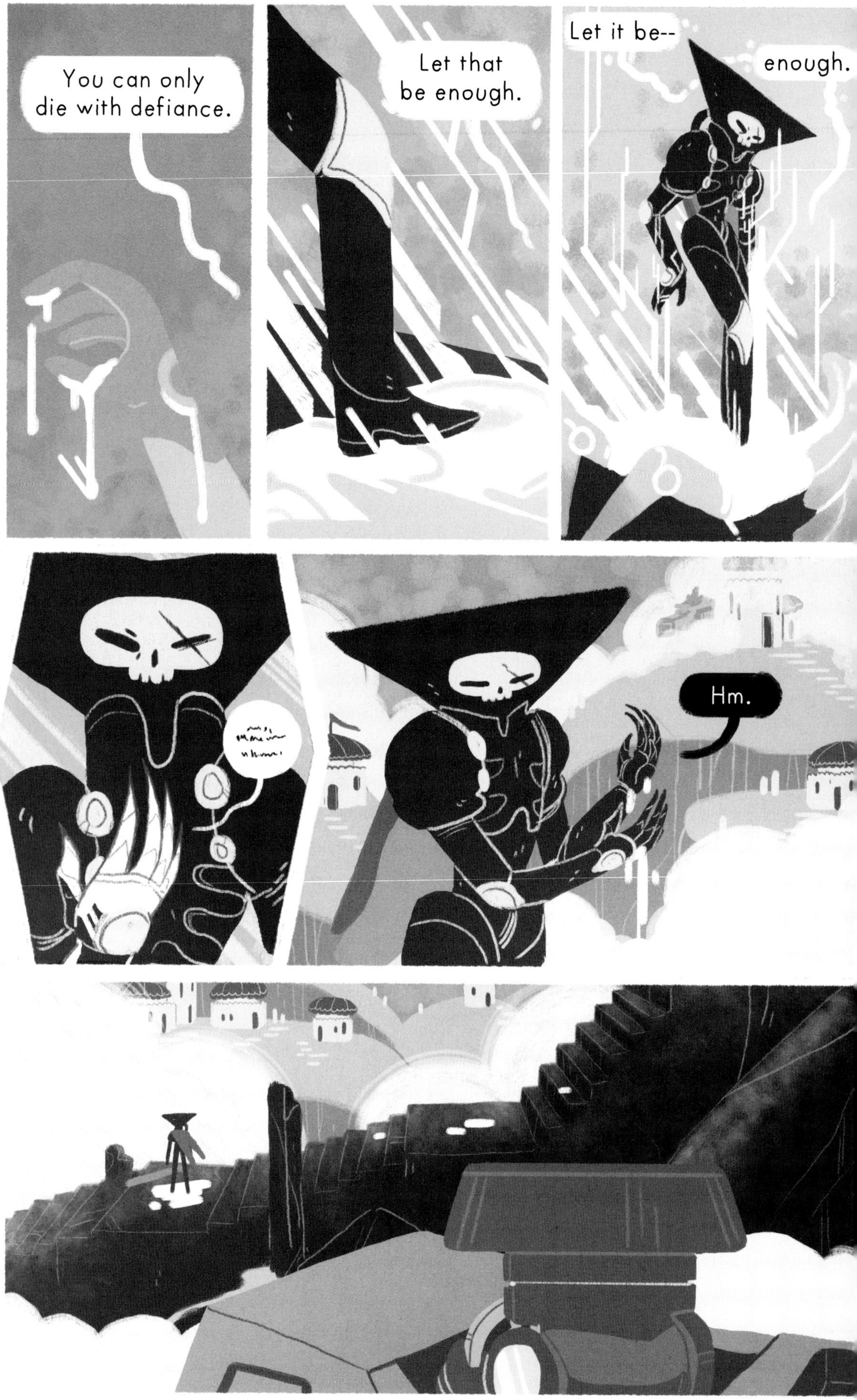
You can only die with defiance.
Let that be enough.
Let it be--
enough.
Hm.

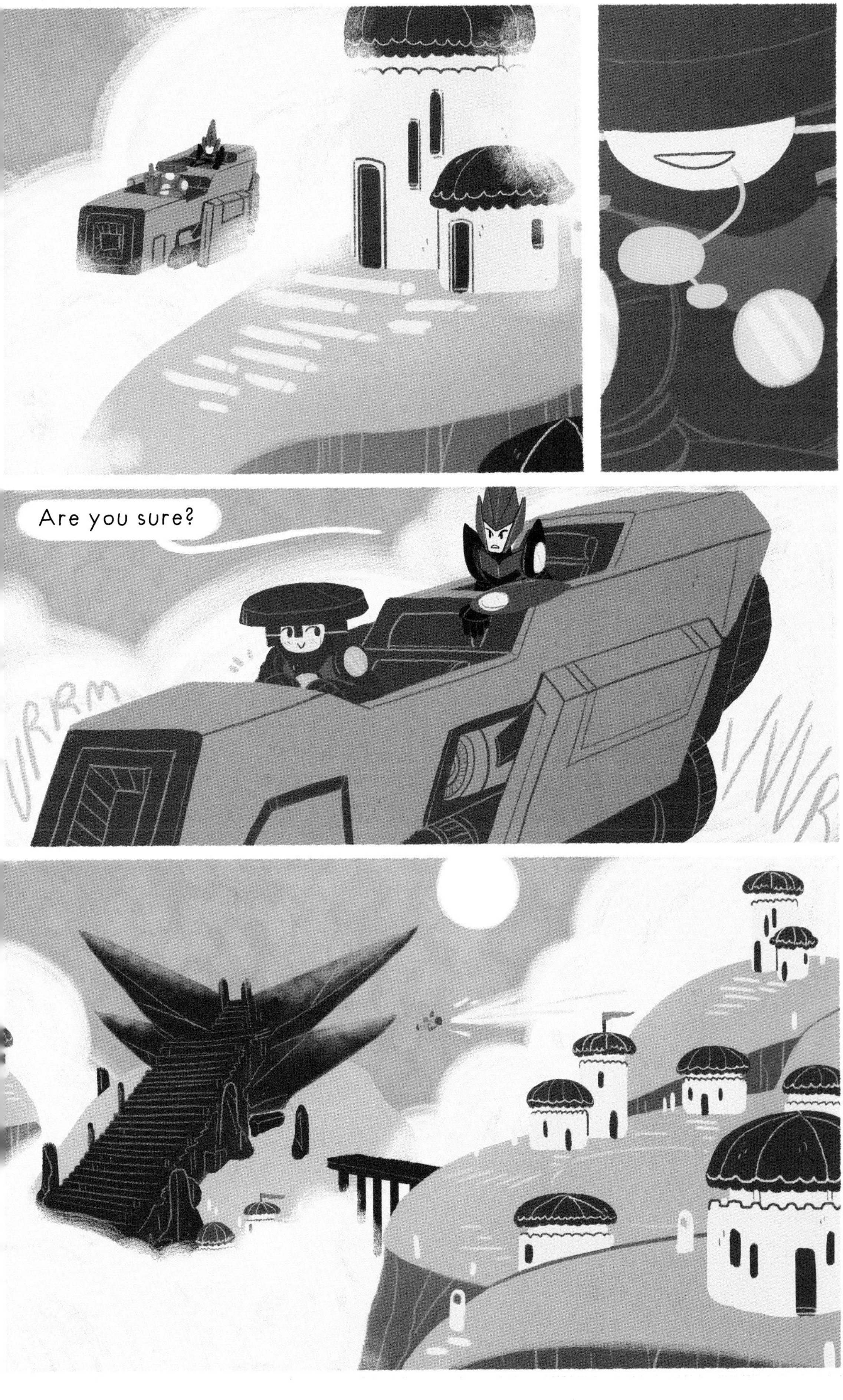
Are you sure?
VRRM
VVVR

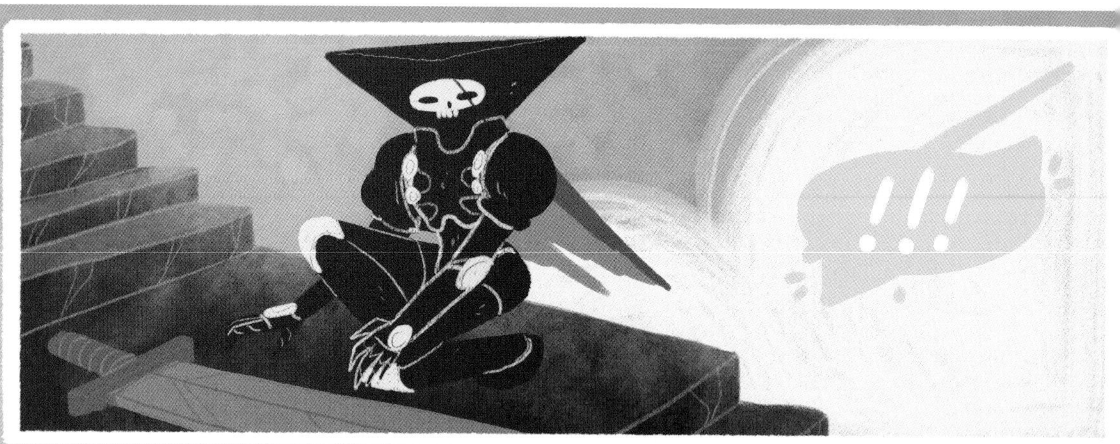
!!!

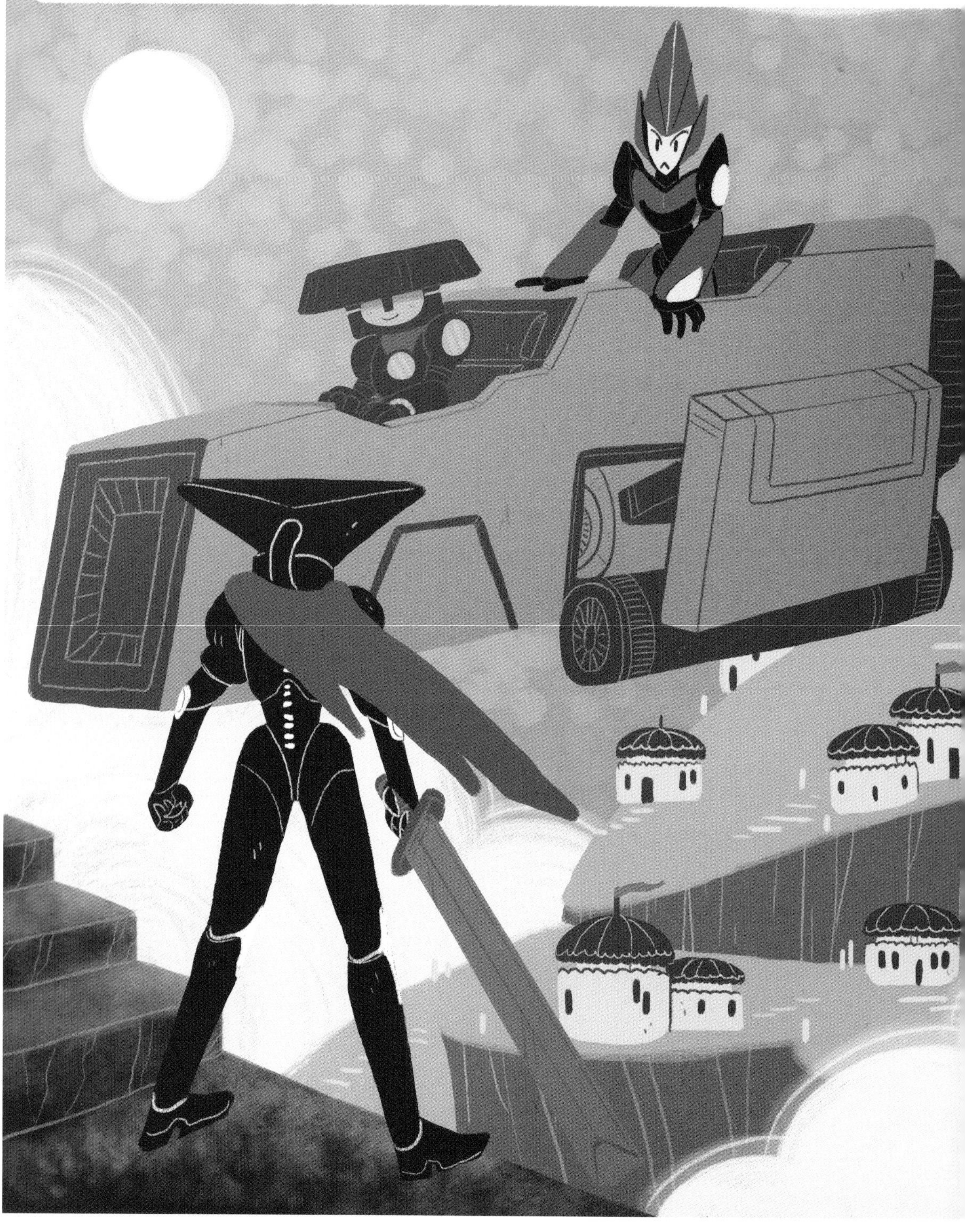

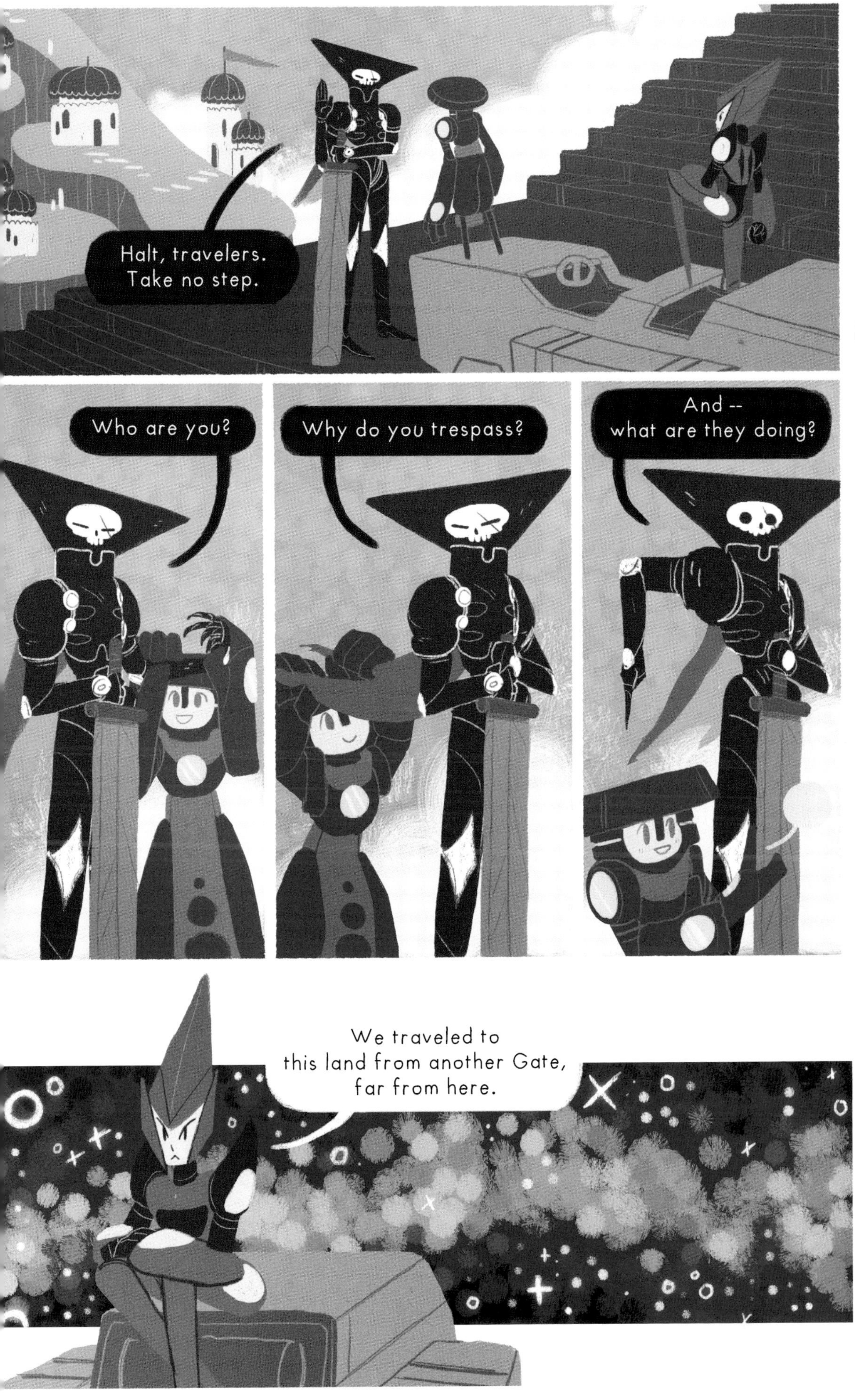
Halt, travelers.
Take no step.
Who are you?
Why do you trespass?
And --
what are they doing?
We traveled to
this land from another Gate,
far from here.

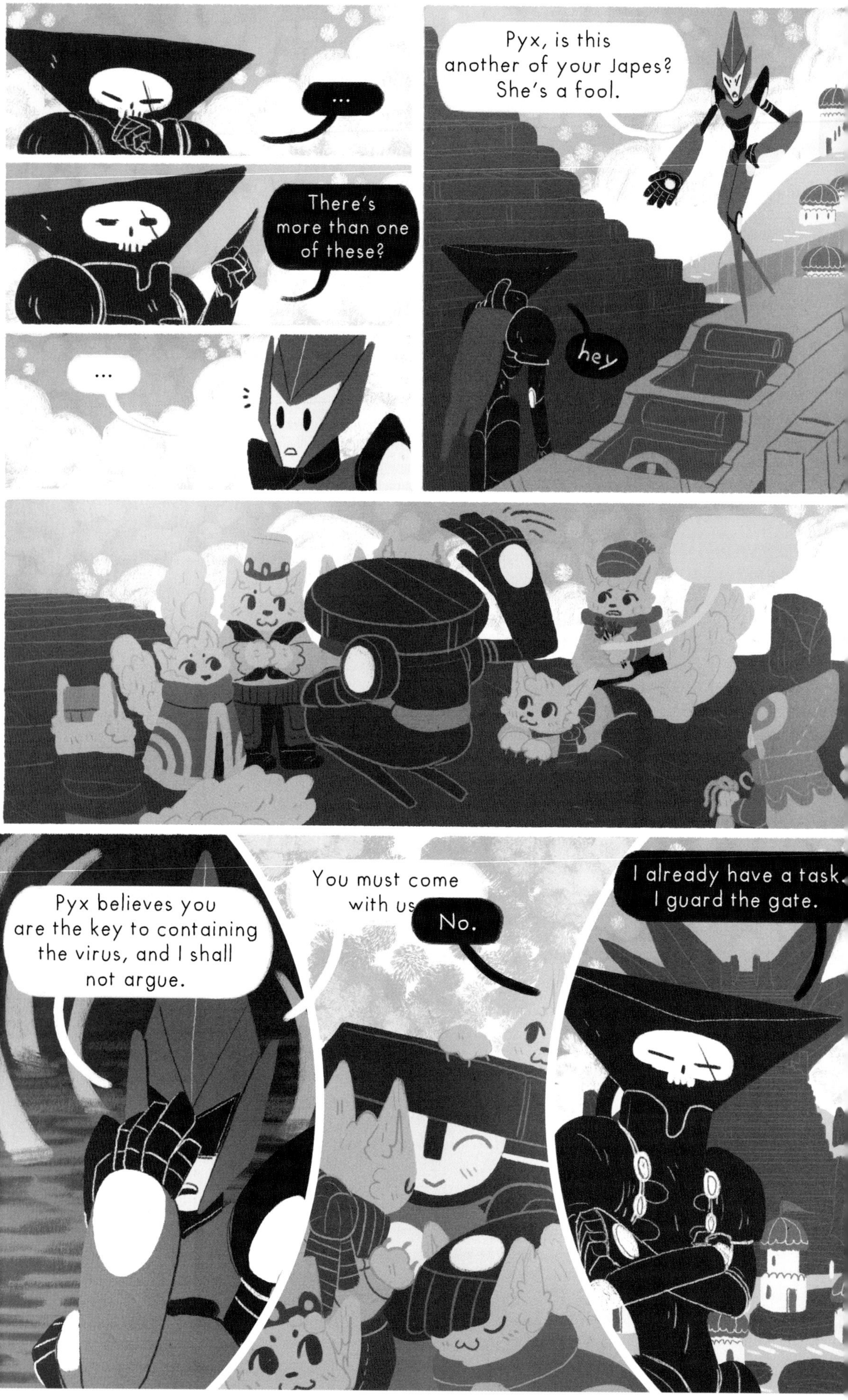
...
There's more than one of these?
...
Pyx, is this another of your Japes? She's a fool.
hey
Pyx believes you are the key to containing the virus, and I shall not argue.
You must come with us
No.
I already have a task. I guard the gate.

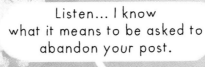
Listen... I know
what it means to be asked to
abandon your post.

You would rather
hold your line, die where
you stand.

But you cannot defend
a door from a hurricane.

It will stand, or it will fall,
and this gate has already fallen.

You must come with us.
It is not abandonment, it is your only
chance to save this world.

Otherwise the storm will come,
and you will all drown.

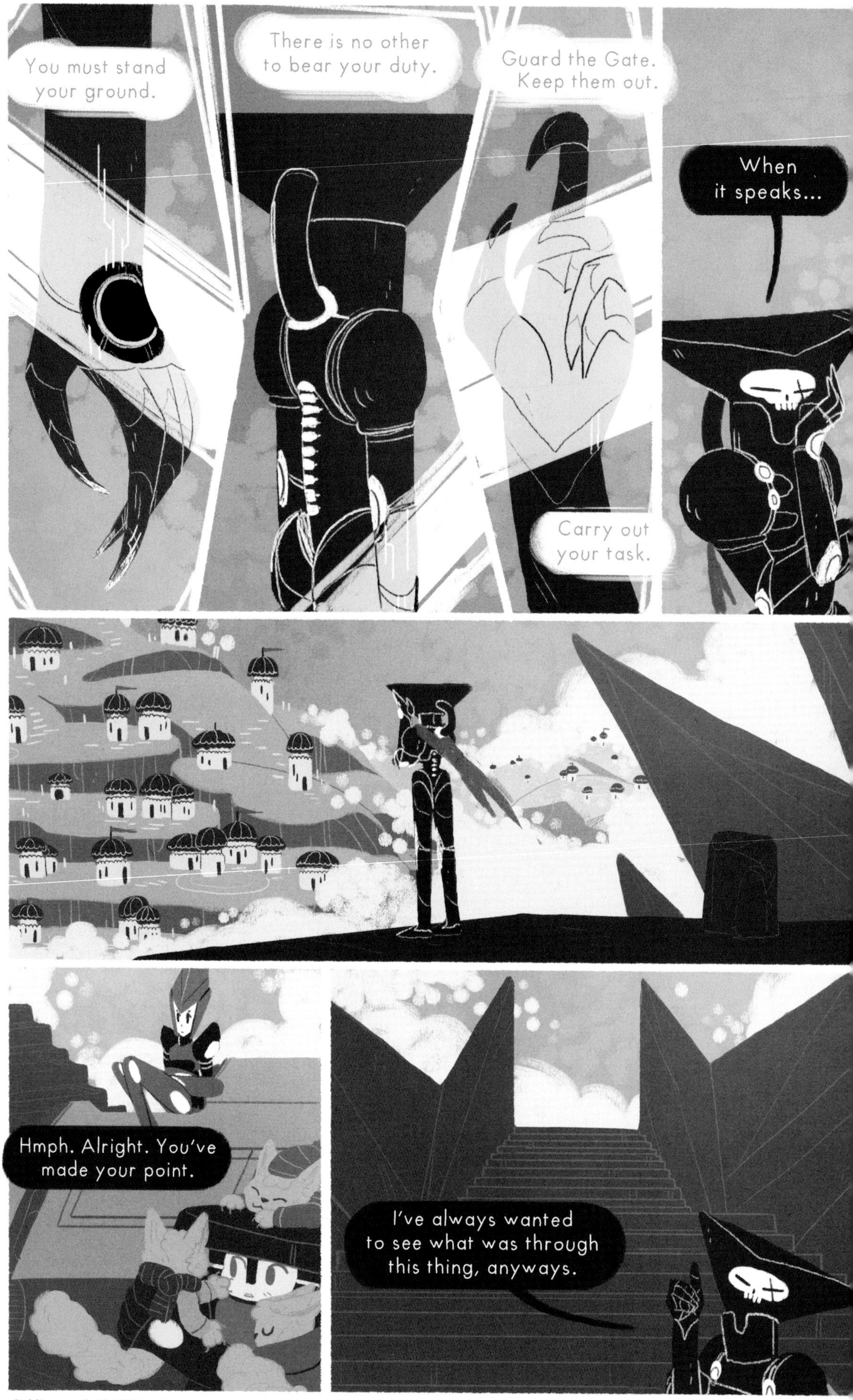
You must stand your ground.
There is no other to bear your duty.
Guard the Gate. Keep them out.
Carry out your task.
When it speaks...
Hmph. Alright. You've made your point.
I've always wanted to see what was through this thing, anyways.

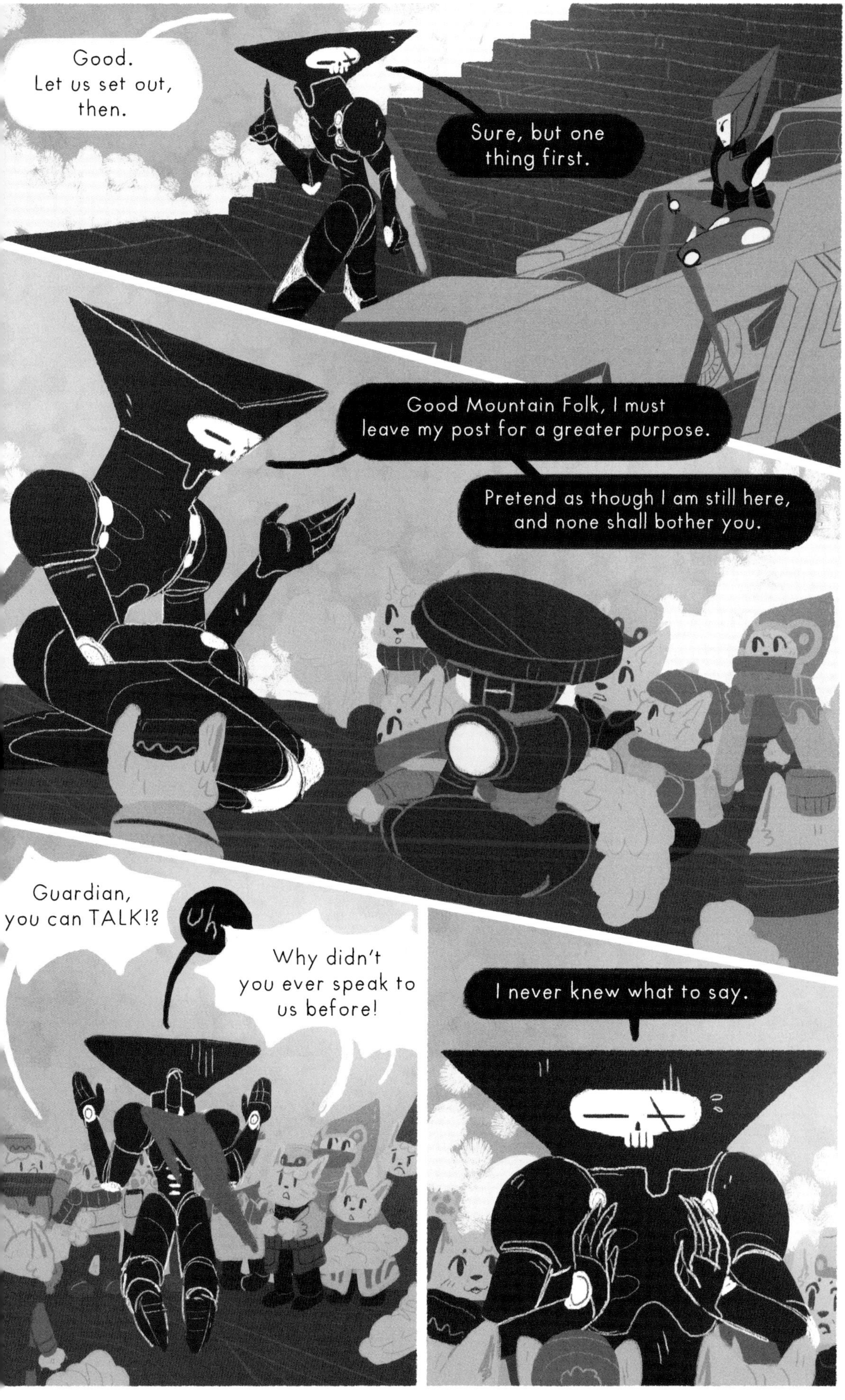
Good.
Let us set out,
then.
Sure, but one
thing first.
Good Mountain Folk, I must
leave my post for a greater purpose.
Pretend as though I am still here,
and none shall bother you.
Guardian,
you can TALK!?
uh
Why didn't
you ever speak to
us before!
I never knew what to say.

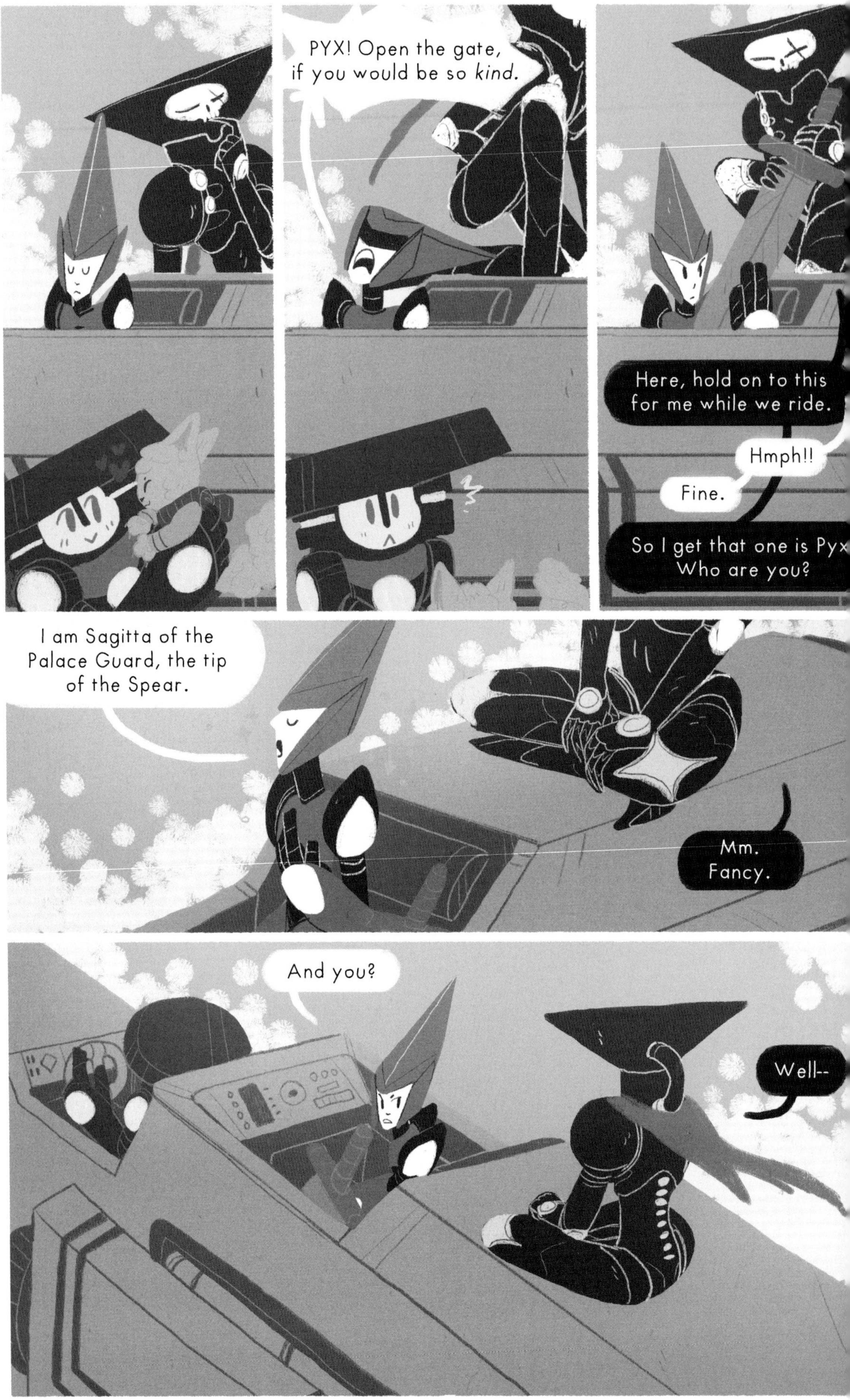
PYX! Open the gate, if you would be so *kind*.
Here, hold on to this for me while we ride.
Hmph!!
Fine.
So I get that one is Pyx
Who are you?
I am Sagitta of the Palace Guard, the tip of the Spear.
Mm. Fancy.
And you?
Well--

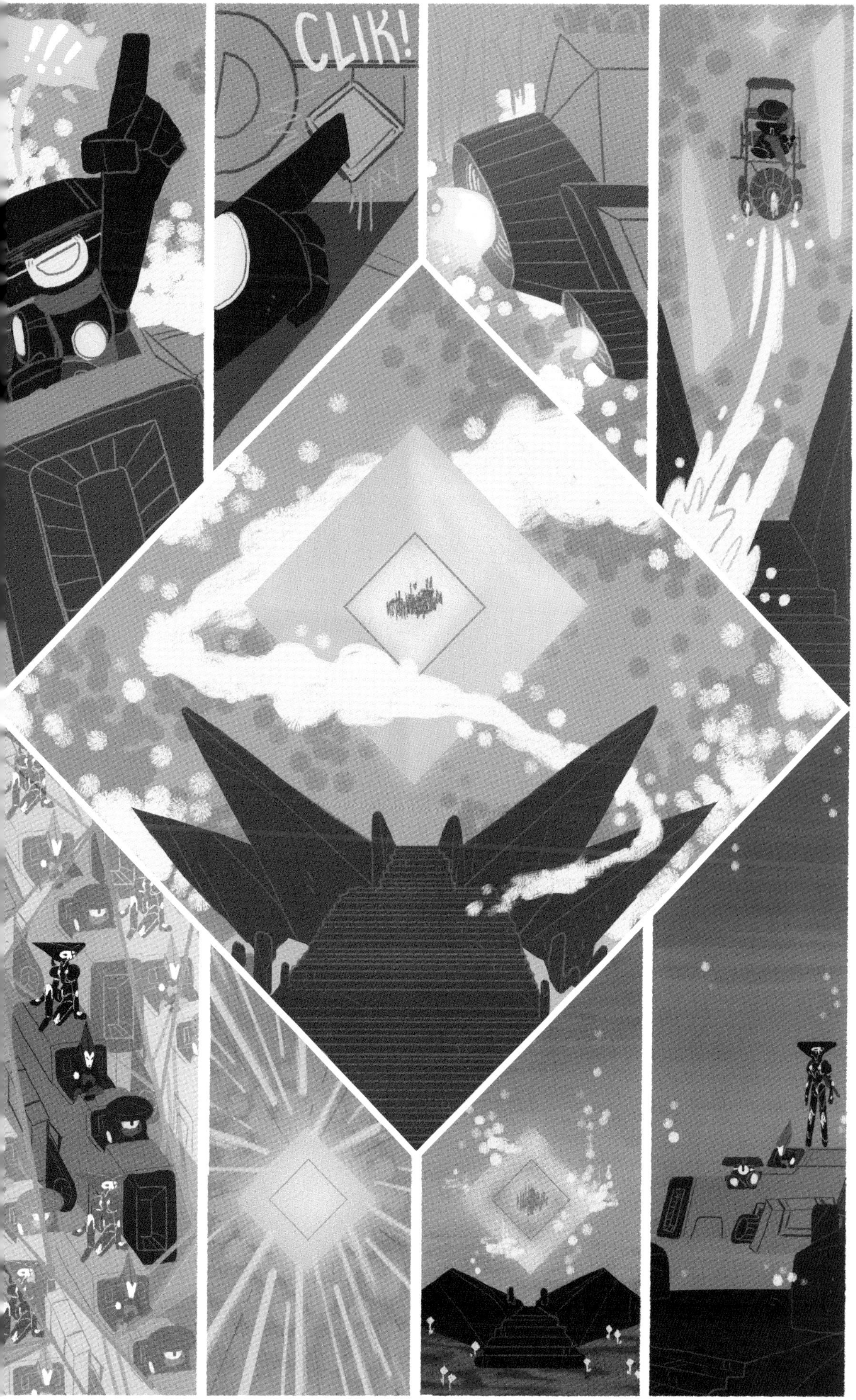
!!!
CLIK!

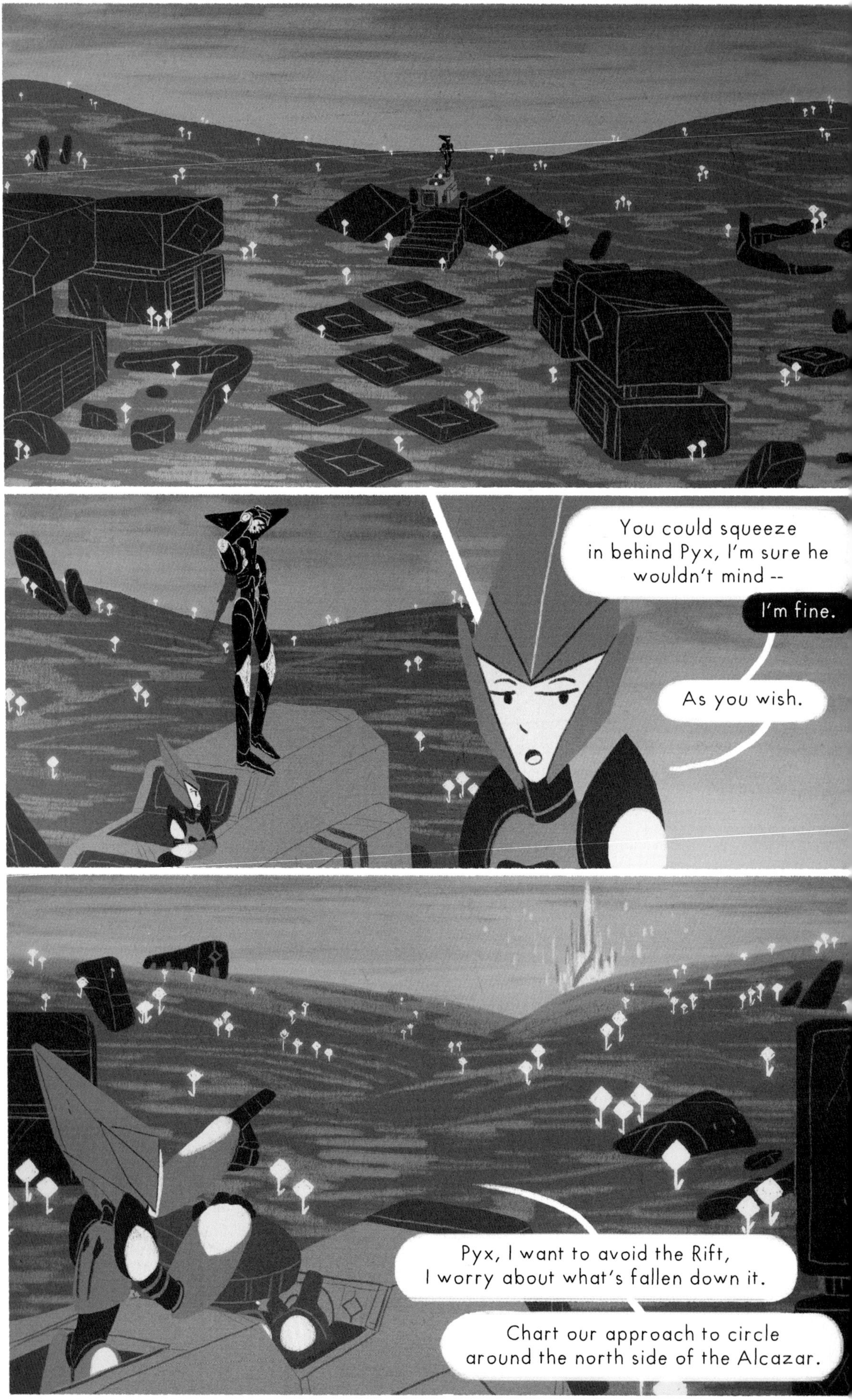
You could squeeze in behind Pyx, I'm sure he wouldn't mind --
I'm fine.
As you wish.
Pyx, I want to avoid the Rift, I worry about what's fallen down it.
Chart our approach to circle around the north side of the Alcazar.

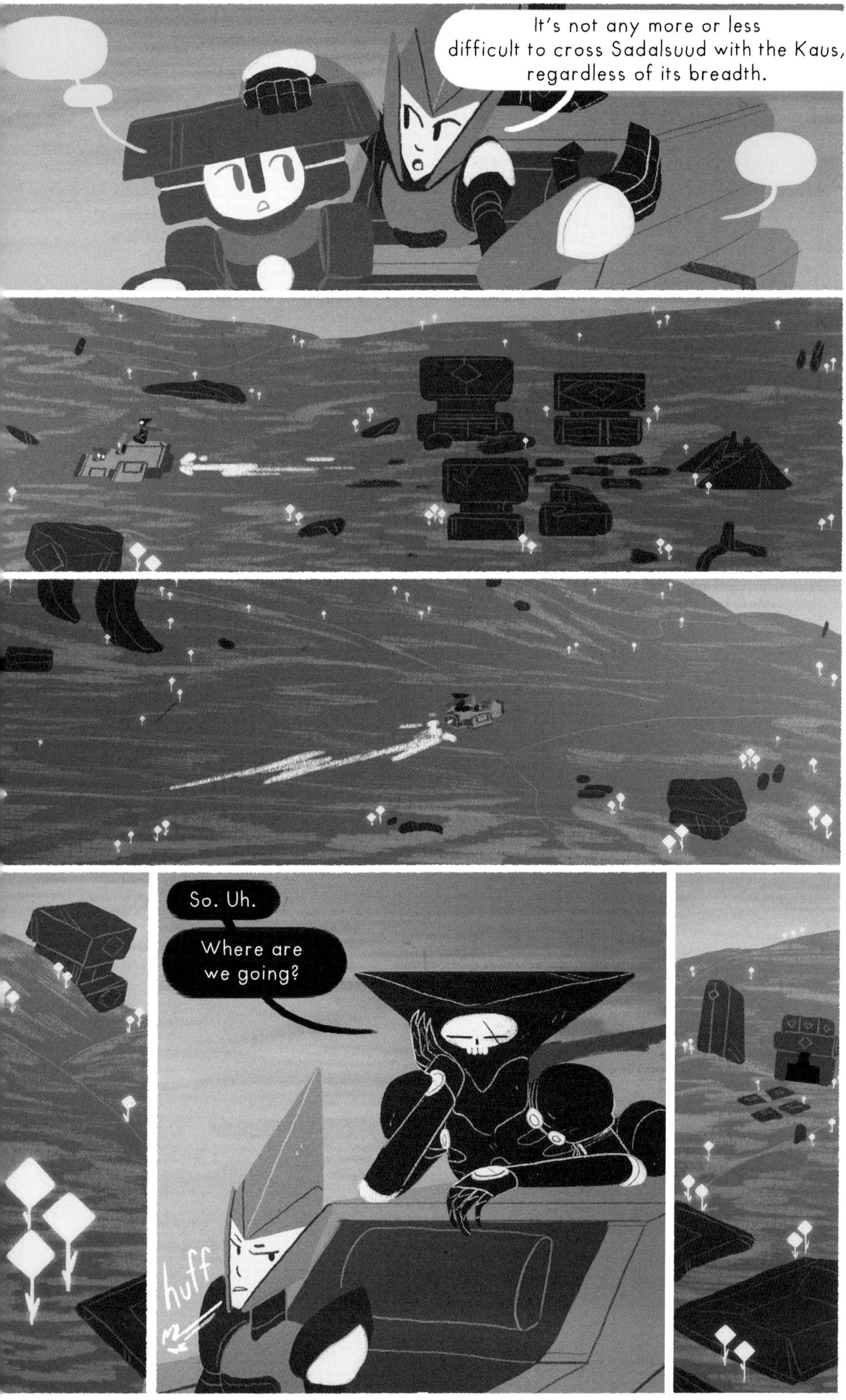
It's not any more or less difficult to cross Sadalsuud with the Kaus, regardless of its breadth.
So. Uh.
Where are we going?
huff

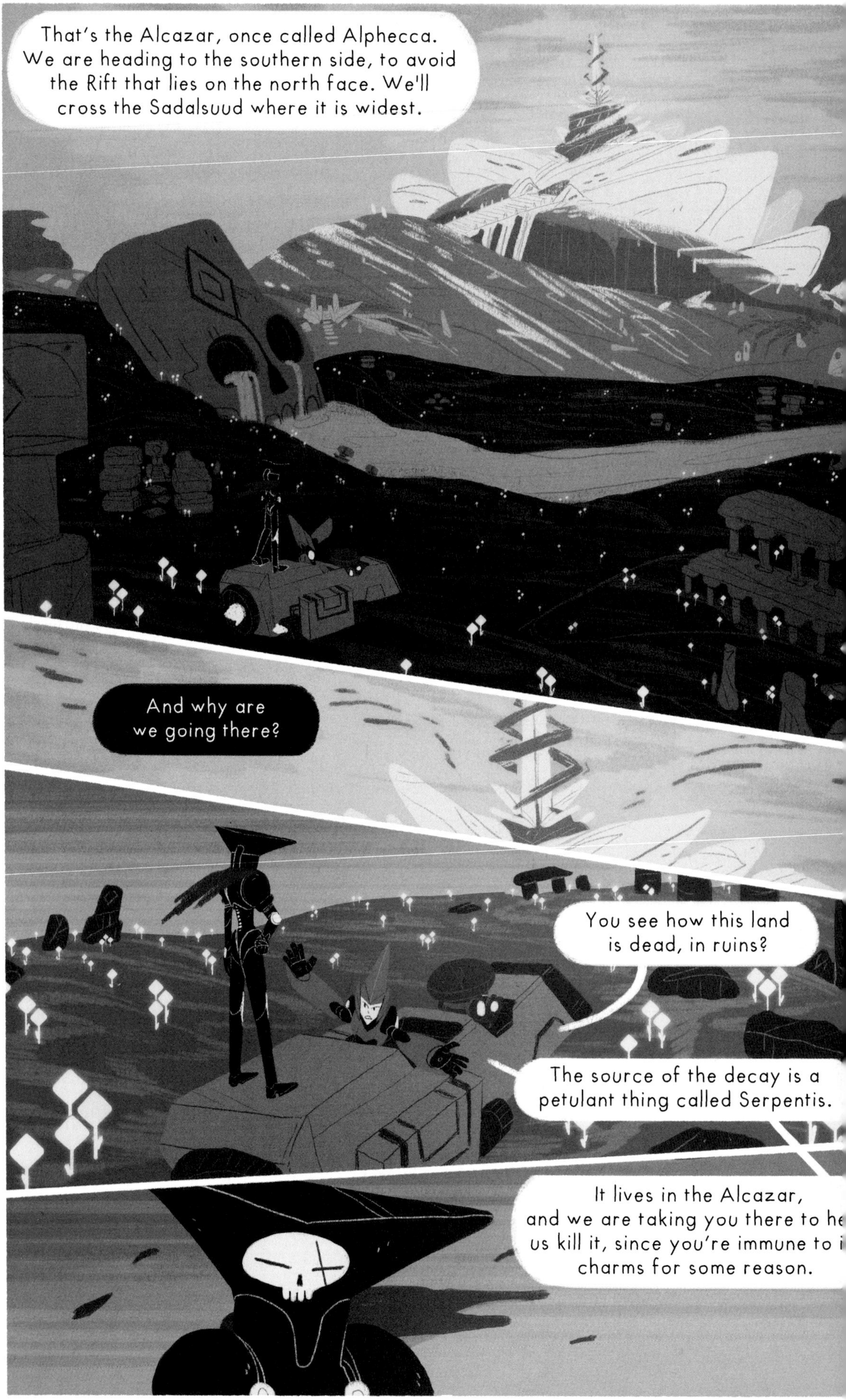
That's the Alcazar, once called Alphecca. We are heading to the southern side, to avoid the Rift that lies on the north face. We'll cross the Sadalsuud where it is widest.
And why are we going there?
You see how this land is dead, in ruins?
The source of the decay is a petulant thing called Serpentis.
It lives in the Alcazar, and we are taking you there to he us kill it, since you're immune to i charms for some reason.

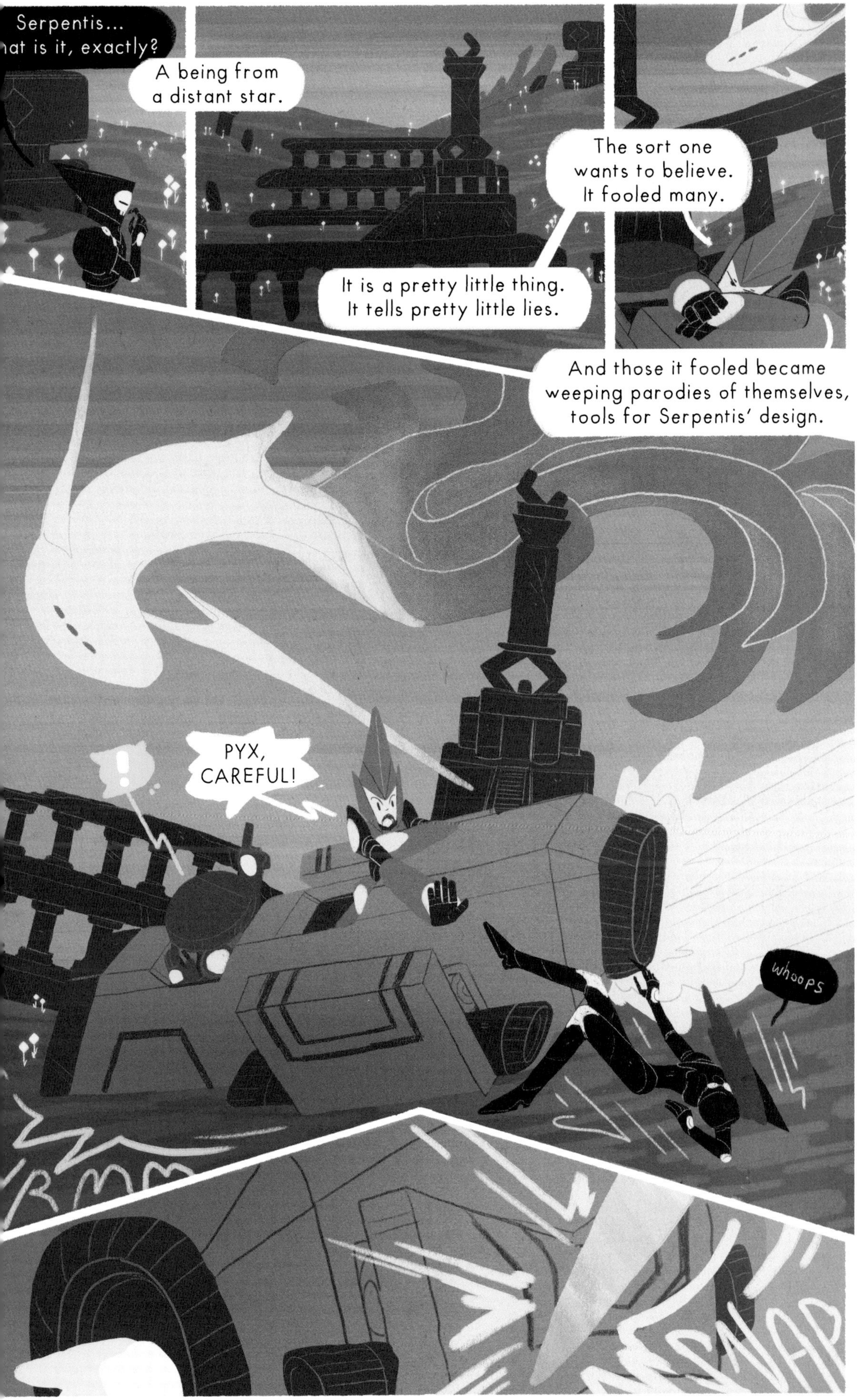

Serpentis...
hat is it, exactly?
A being from
a distant star.
It is a pretty little thing.
It tells pretty little lies.
The sort one
wants to believe.
It fooled many.
And those it fooled became
weeping parodies of themselves,
tools for Serpentis' design.
PYX,
CAREFUL!
whoops

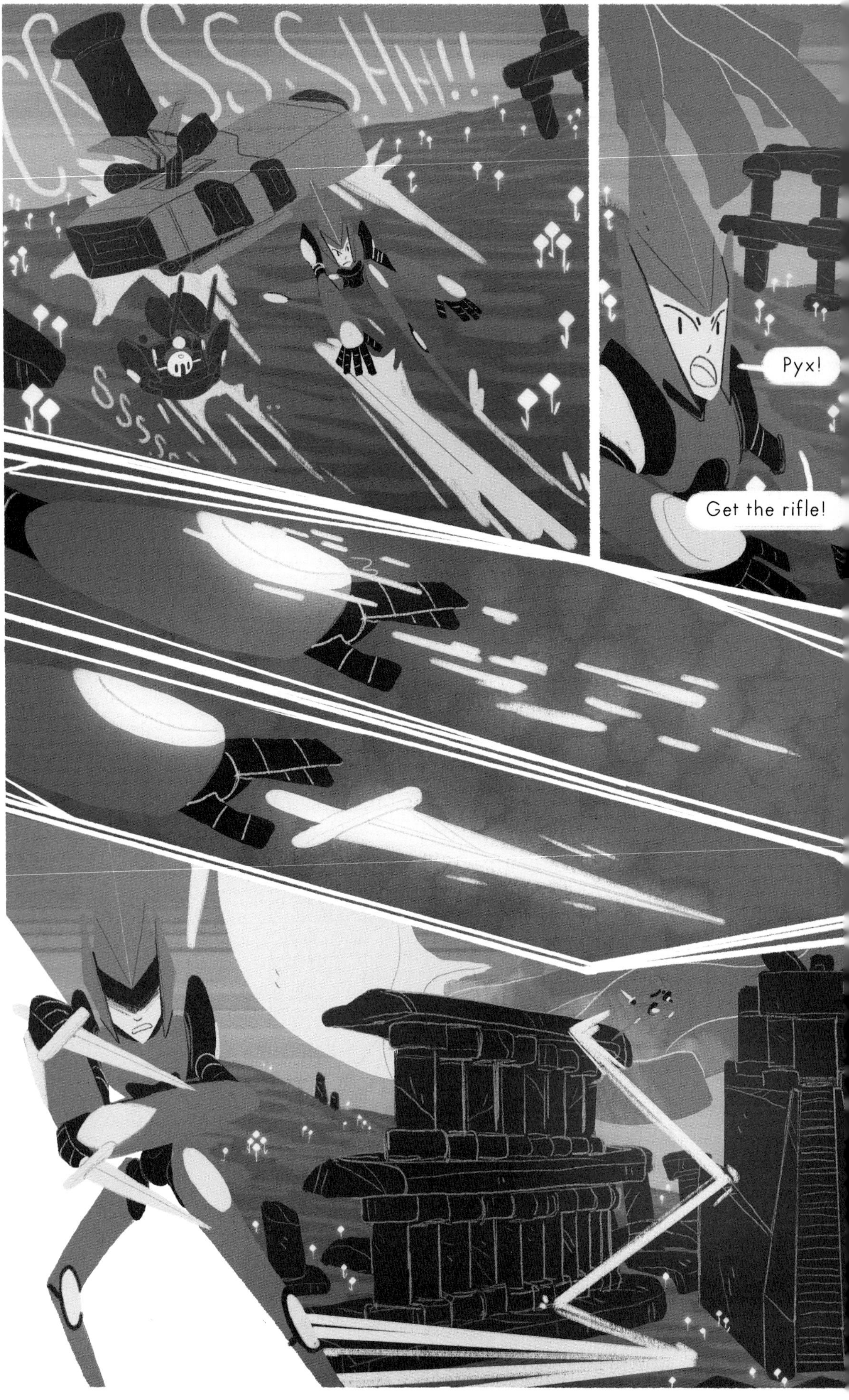
CRSSSSHH!!
SSSS
Pyx!
Get the rifle!

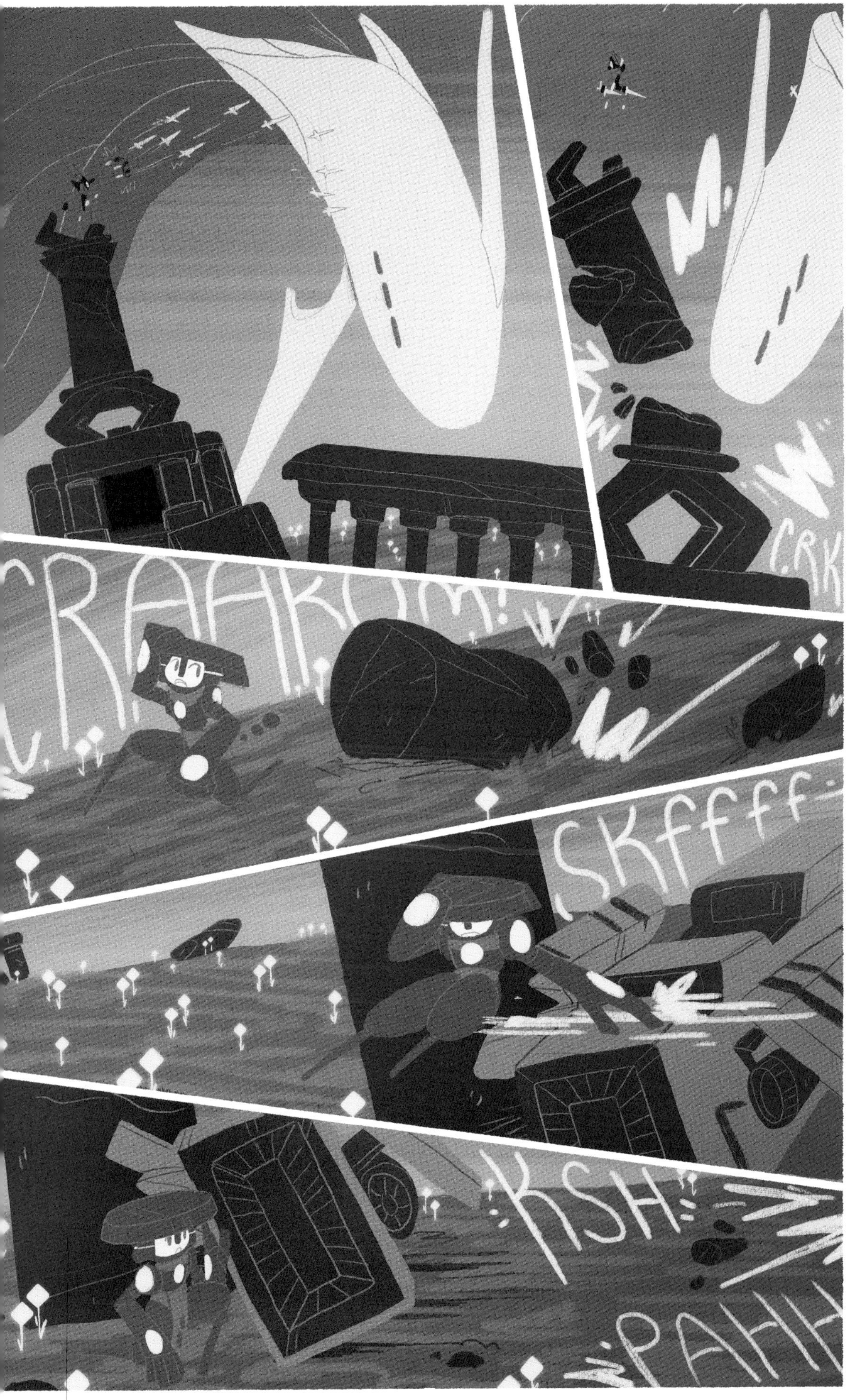
CRK
CRAAKOOM!
SKffff-
KSH!
PAHH

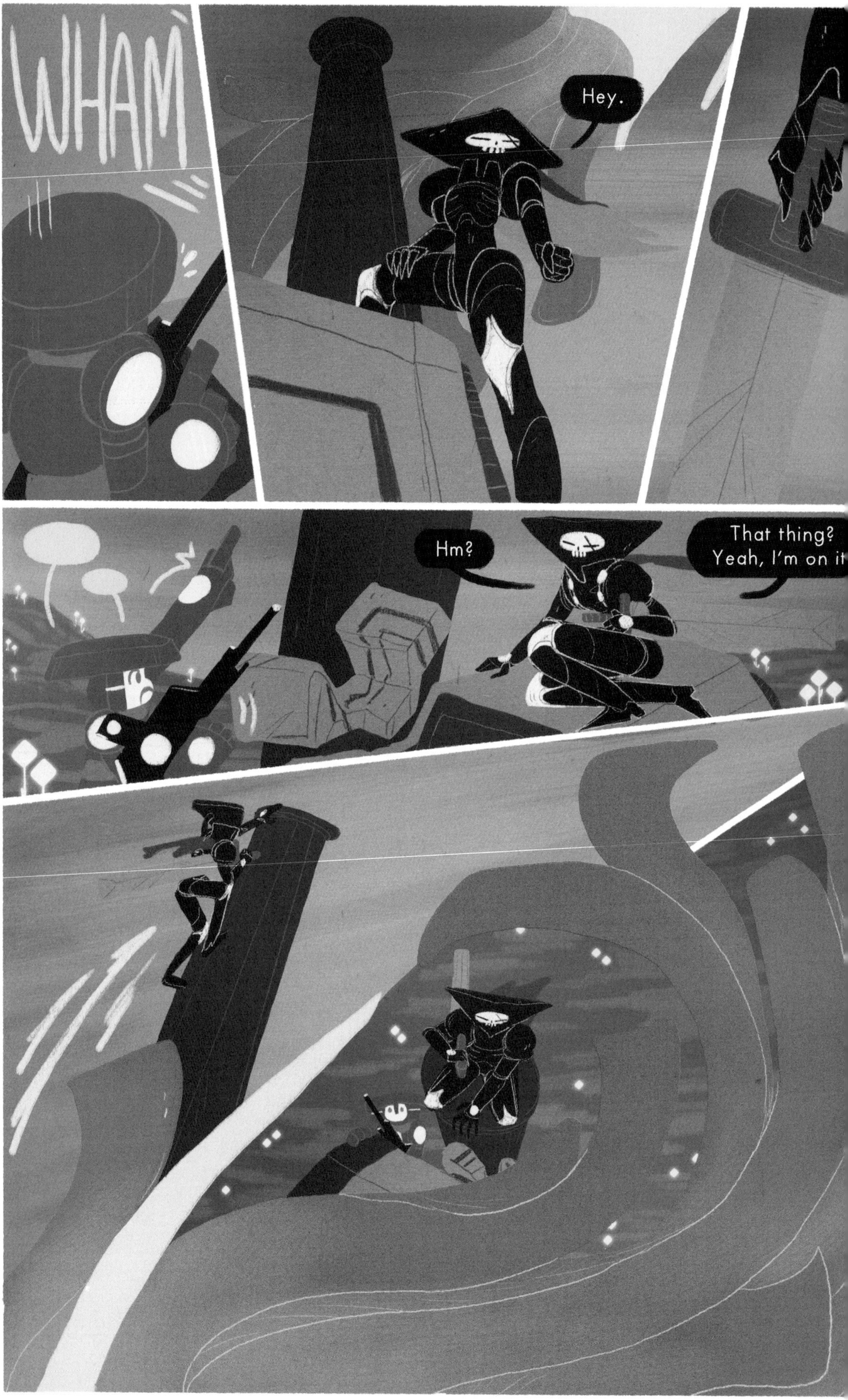
WHAM
Hey.
Hm?
That thing?
Yeah, I'm on it

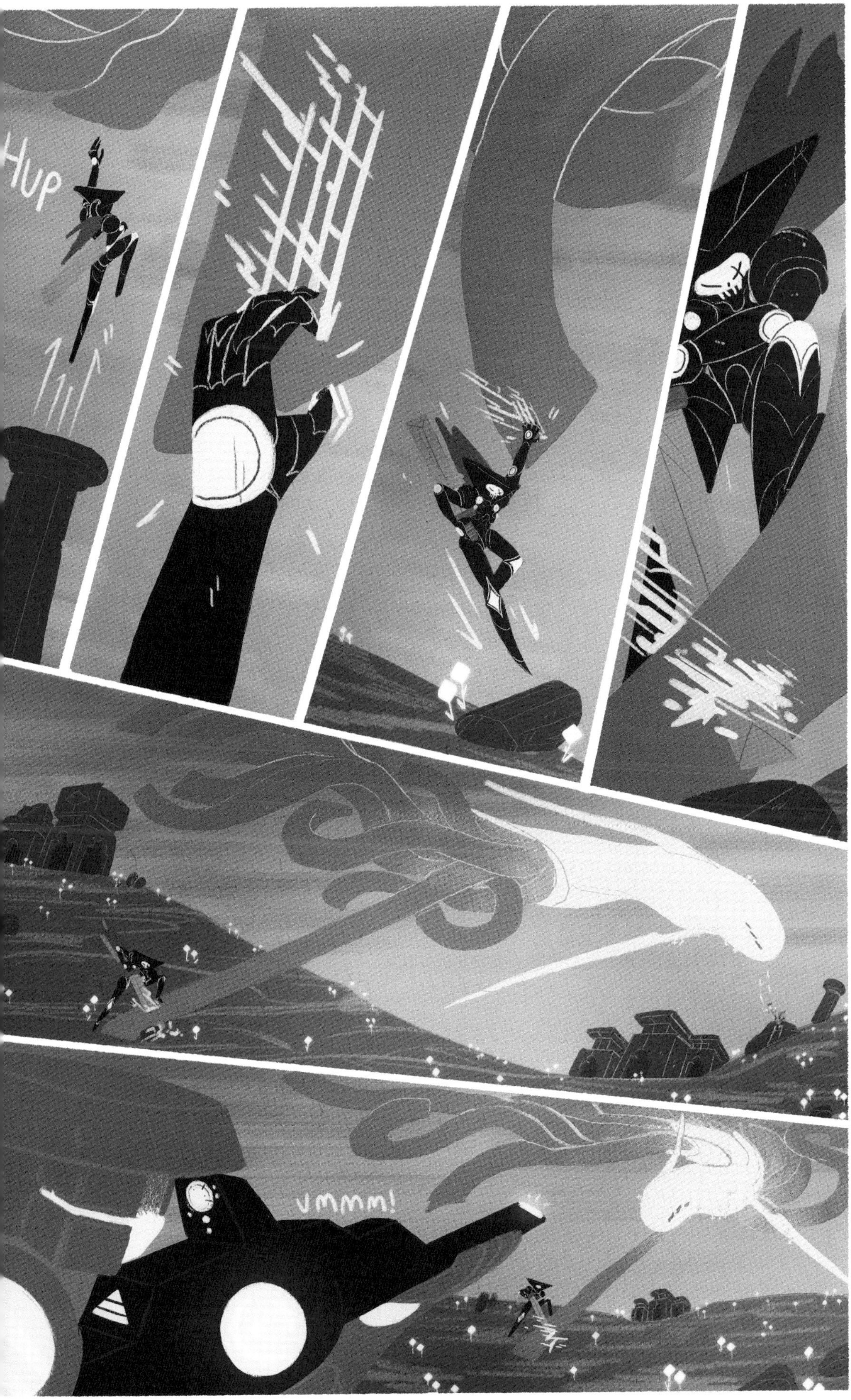
HUP
VMMM!

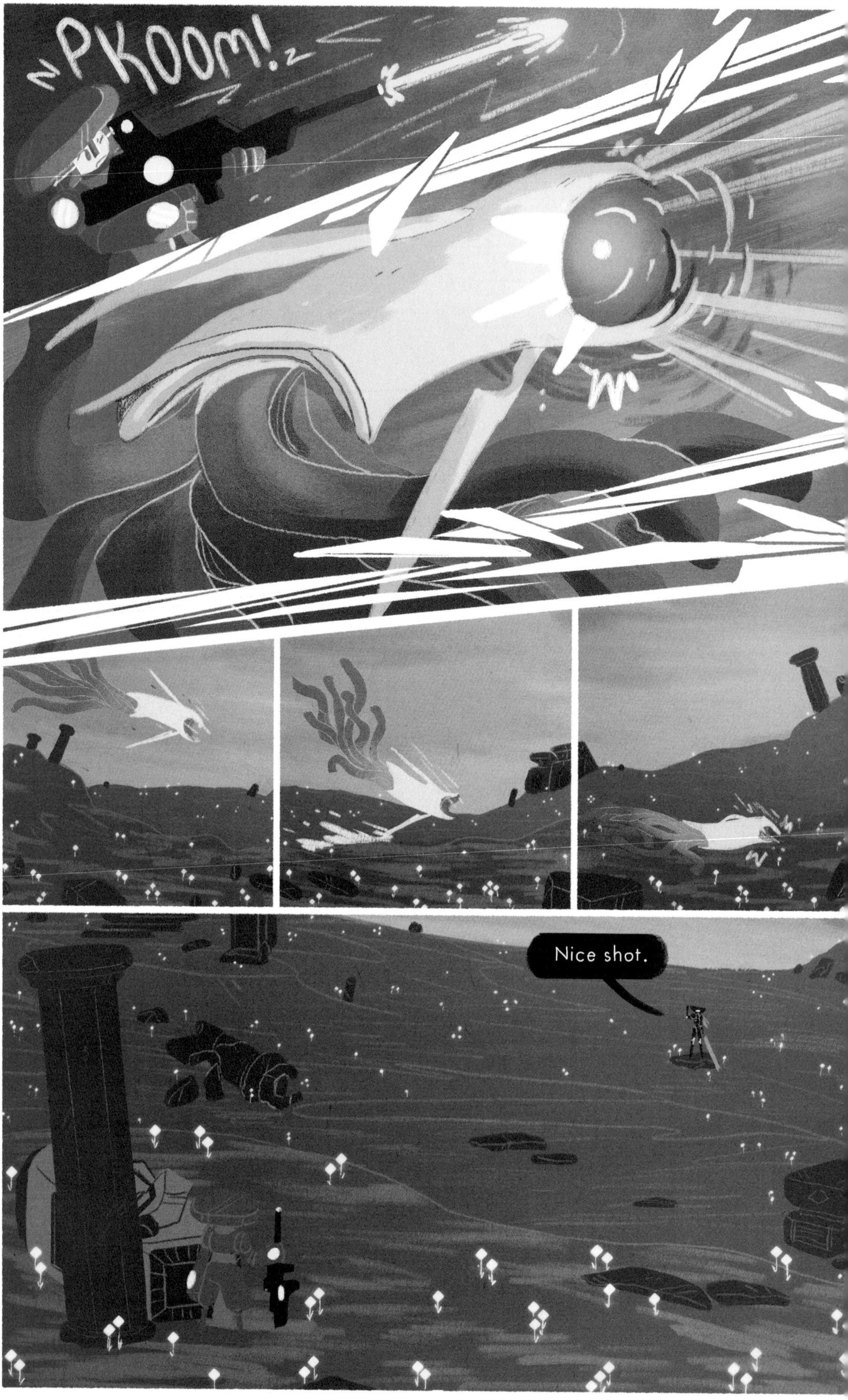
PKOOM!
Nice shot.

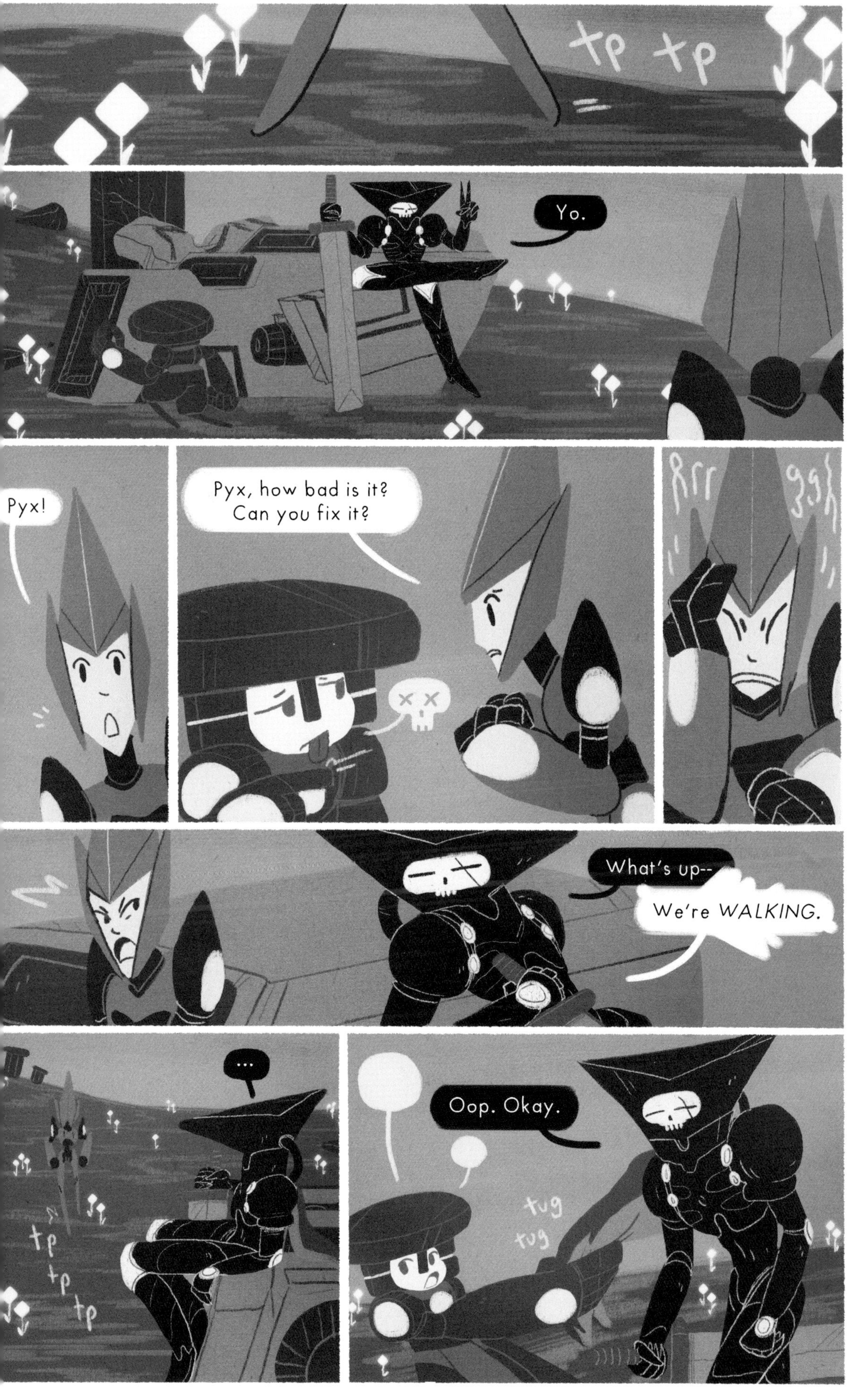

tp tp
Yo.
Pyx!
Pyx, how bad is it?
Can you fix it?
What's up--
We're *WALKING.*
...
tp
tp
tp
Oop. Okay.
tug
tug

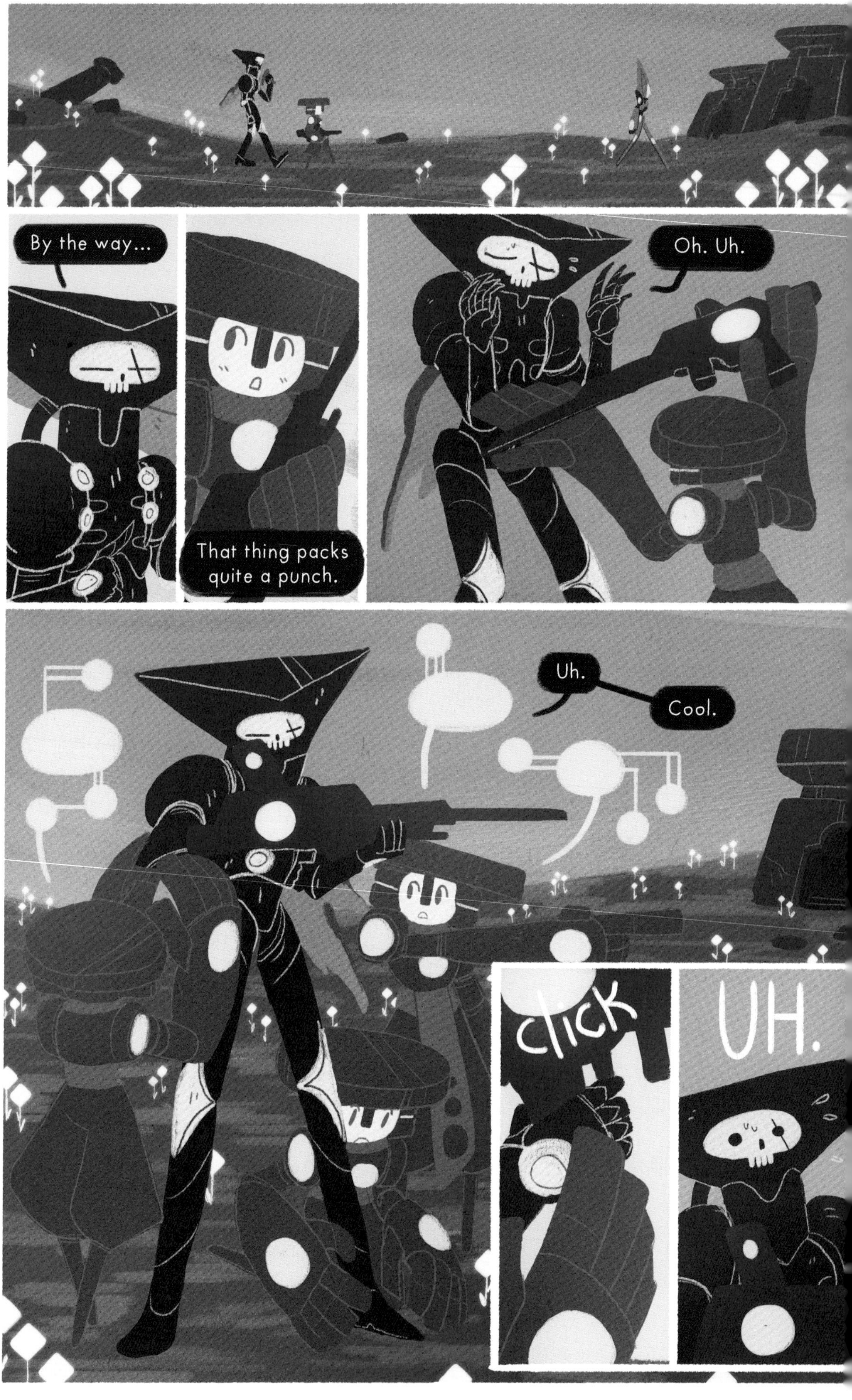

By the way...
That thing packs quite a punch.
Oh. Uh.
Uh.
Cool.
click
UH.

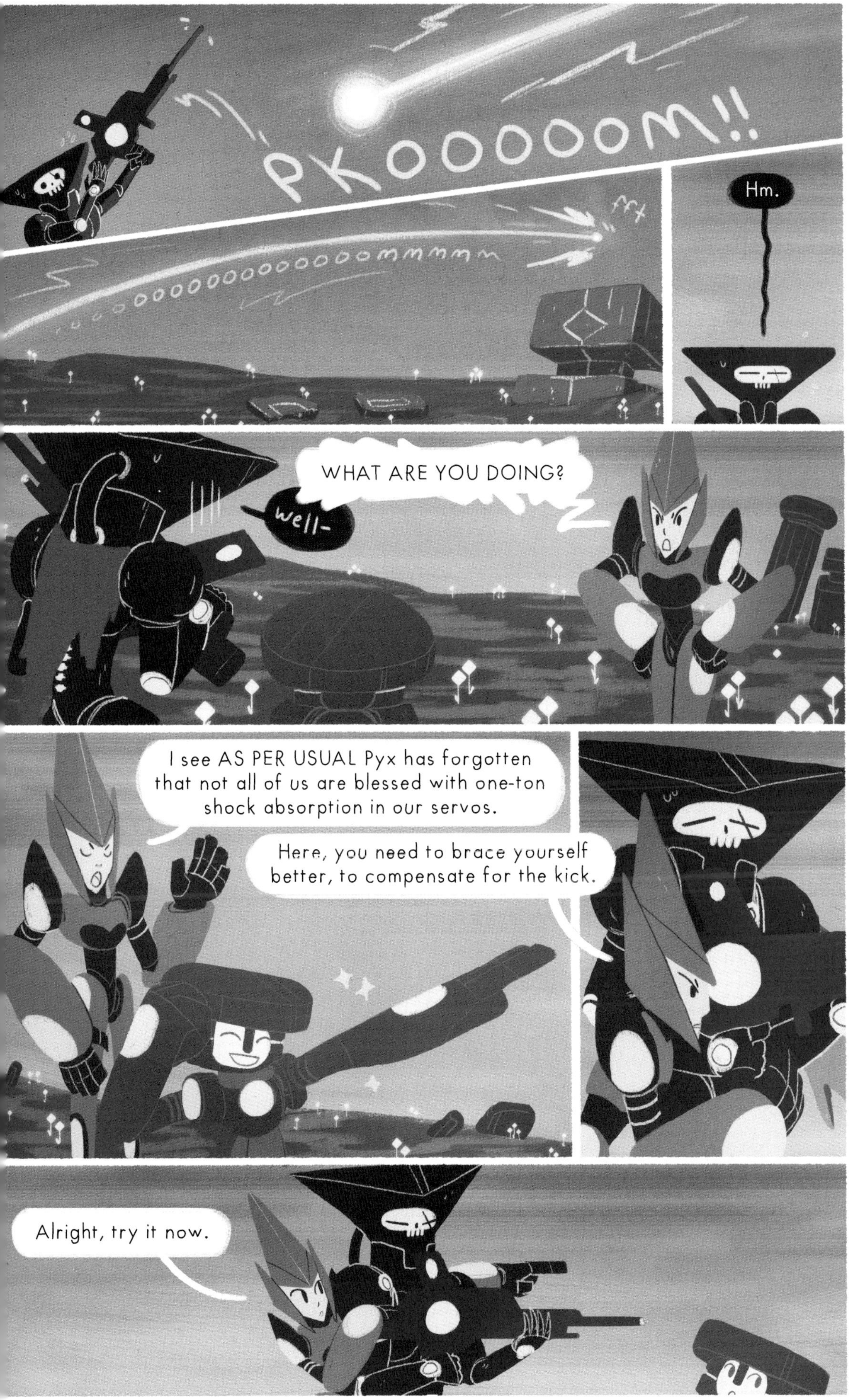
PKOOOOOM!!
fft
ooooooooooooooooooooommmmm
Hm.
WHAT ARE YOU DOING?
well-
I see AS PER USUAL Pyx has forgotten that not all of us are blessed with one-ton shock absorption in our servos.
Here, you need to brace yourself better, to compensate for the kick.
Alright, try it now.

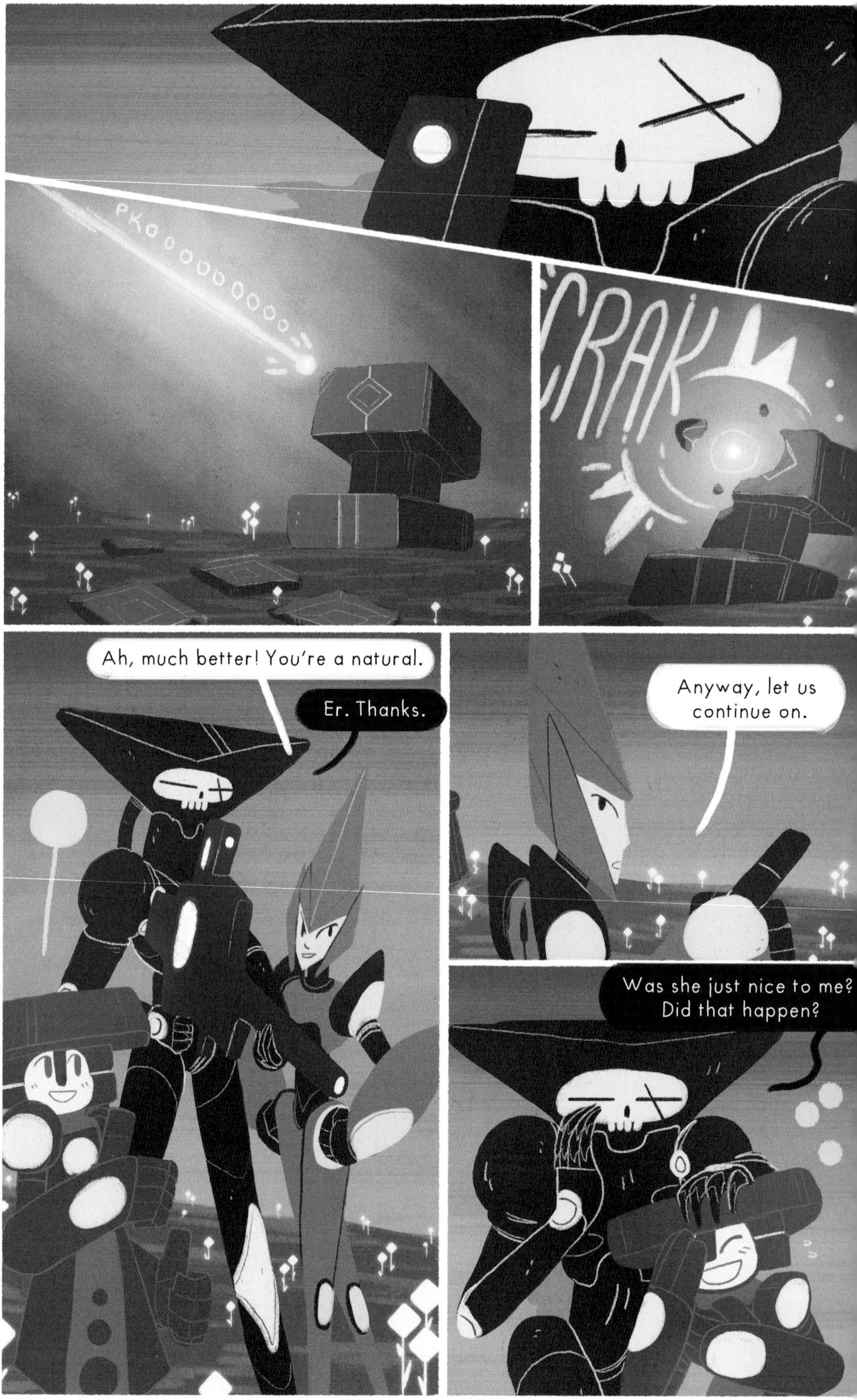
PKOOOOOOOOOO
CRAK
Ah, much better! You're a natural.
Er. Thanks.
Anyway, let us continue on.
Was she just nice to me? Did that happen?

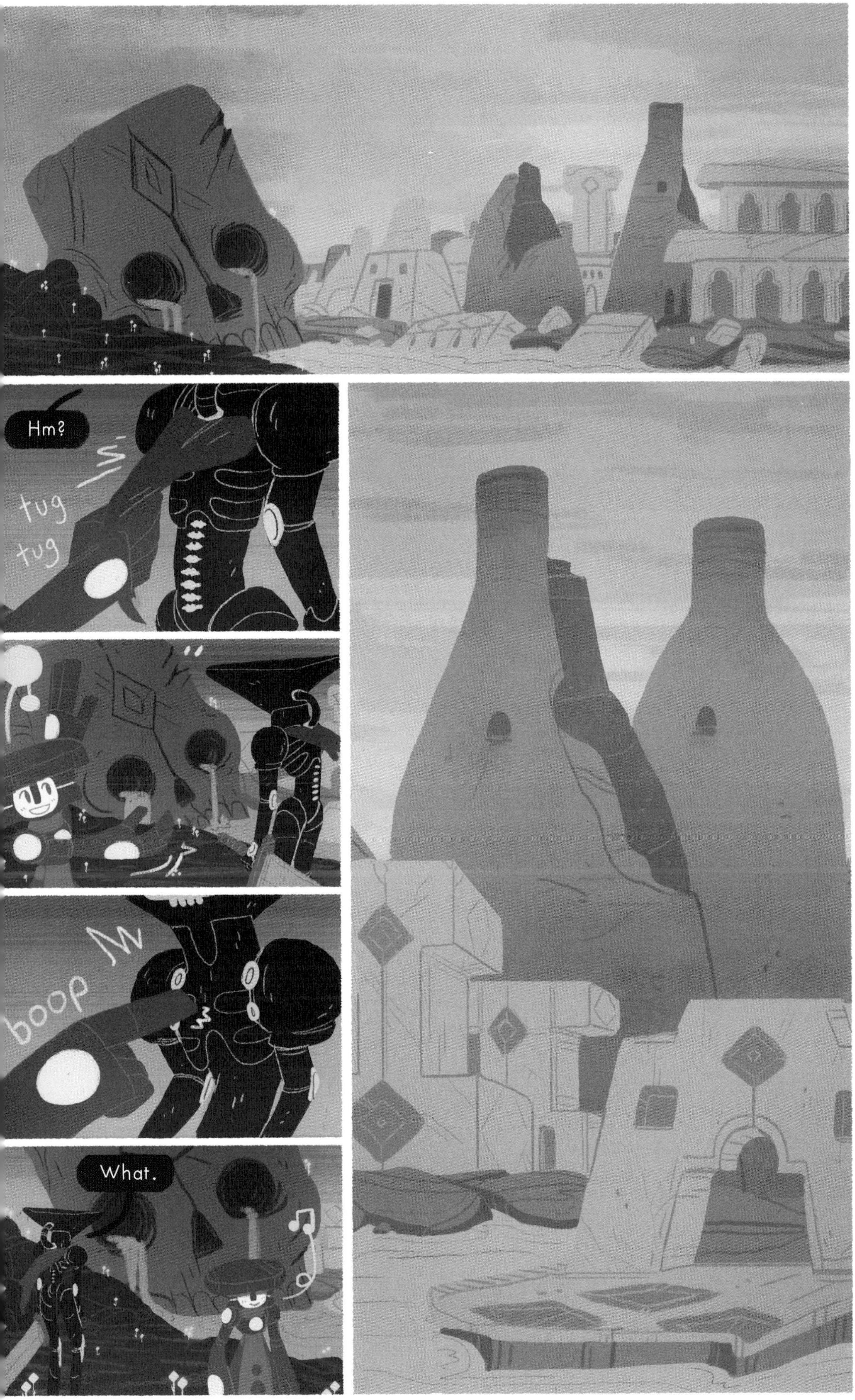

Hm?
tug
tug
boop
What.

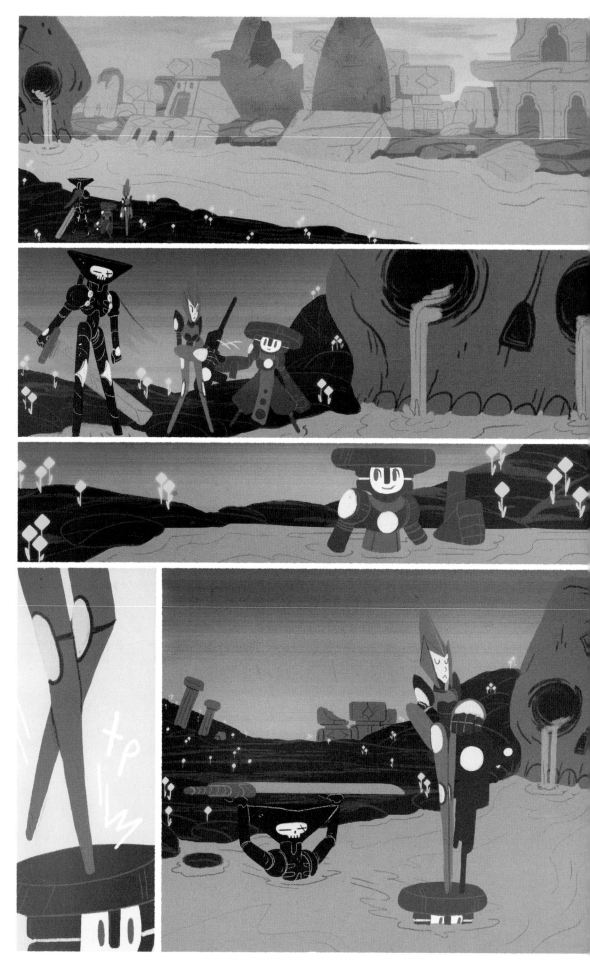

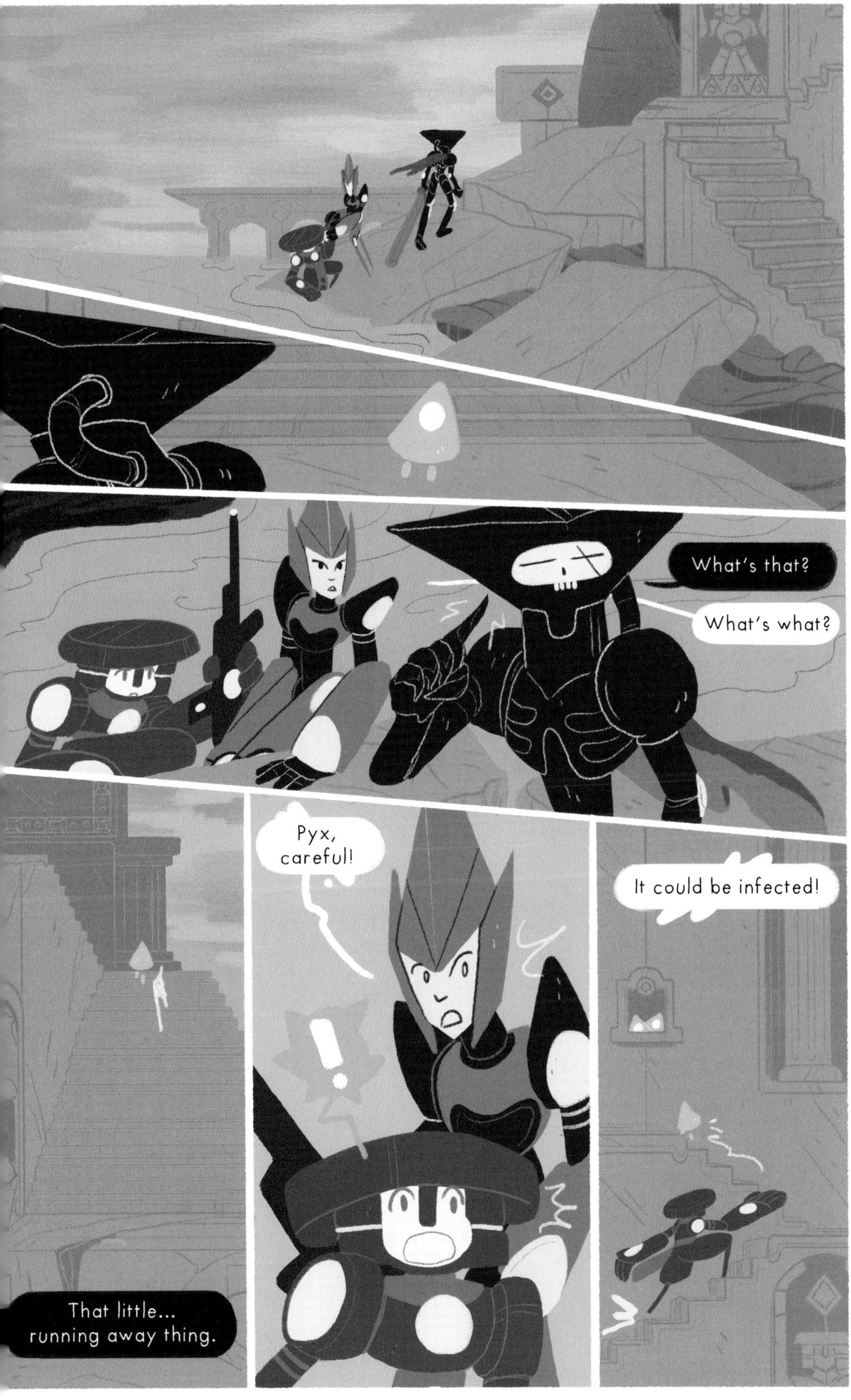
What's that?
What's what?
That little... running away thing.
Pyx, careful!
It could be infected!

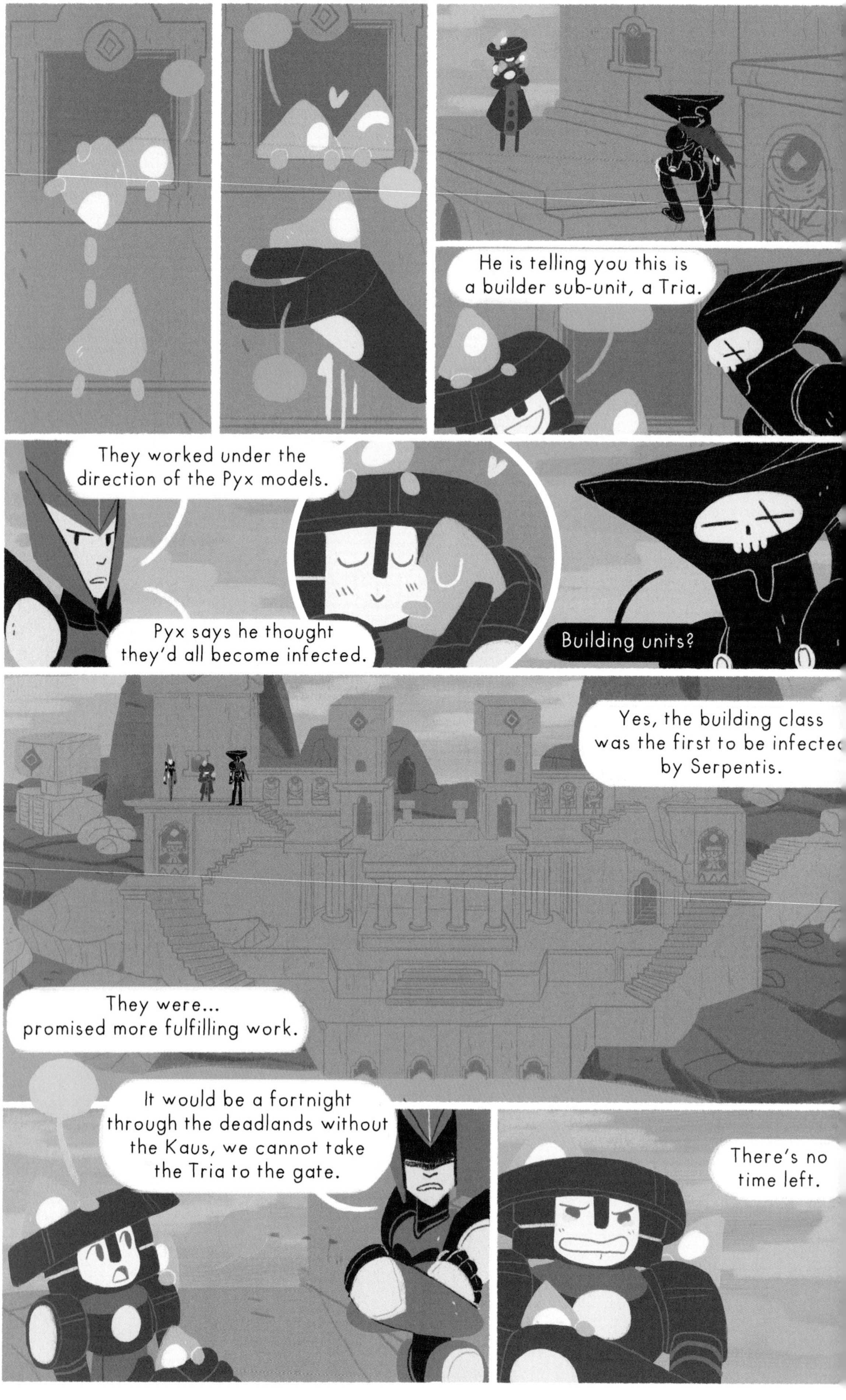
He is telling you this is a builder sub-unit, a Tria.
They worked under the direction of the Pyx models.
Pyx says he thought they'd all become infected.
Building units?
Yes, the building class was the first to be infecte
by Serpentis.
They were... promised more fulfilling work.
It would be a fortnight through the deadlands without the Kaus, we cannot take the Tria to the gate.
There's no time left.

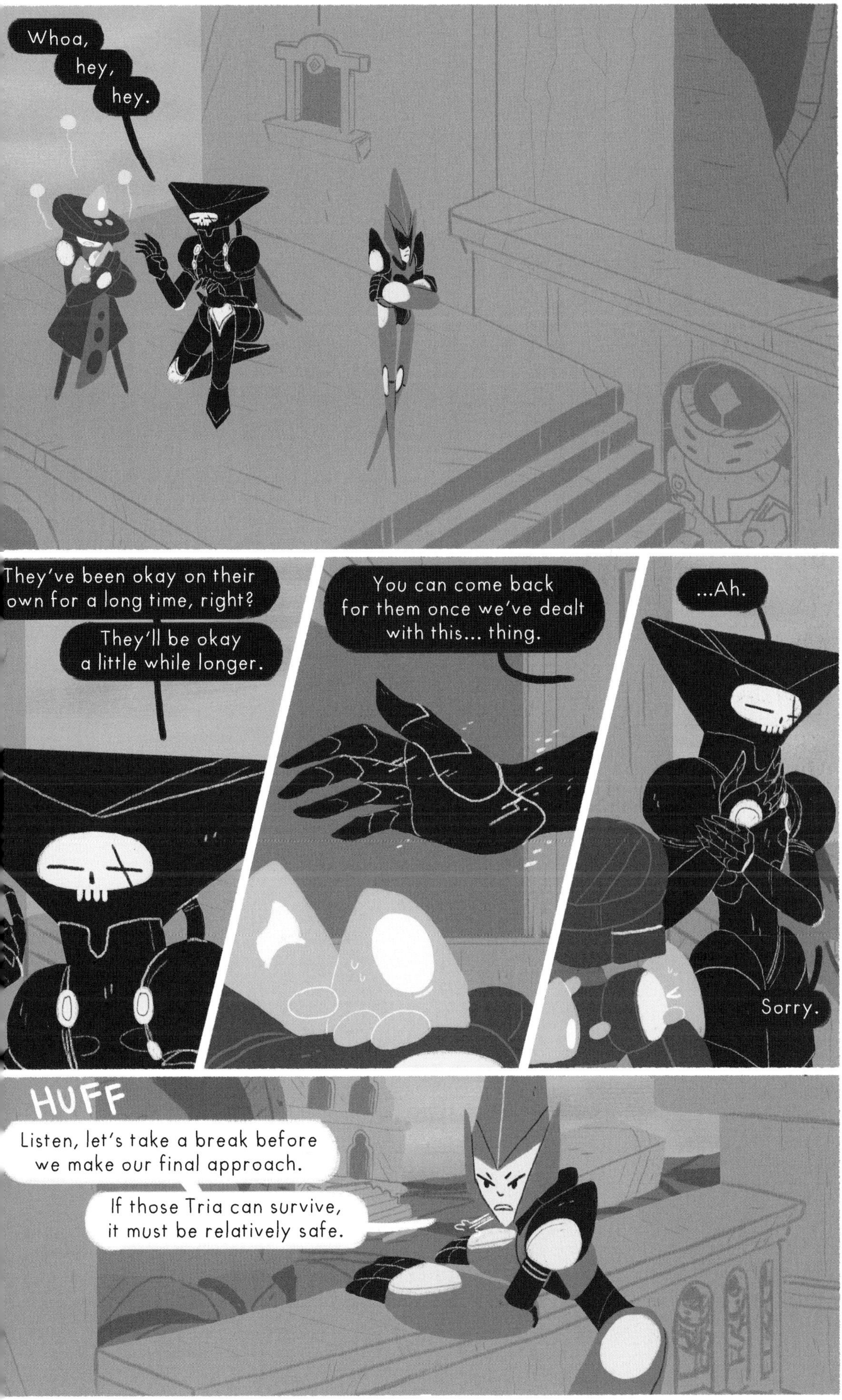
Whoa,
hey,
hey.
They've been okay on their own for a long time, right?
They'll be okay a little while longer.
You can come back for them once we've dealt with this... thing.
...Ah.
Sorry.
HUFF
Listen, let's take a break before we make our final approach.
If those Tria can survive, it must be relatively safe.

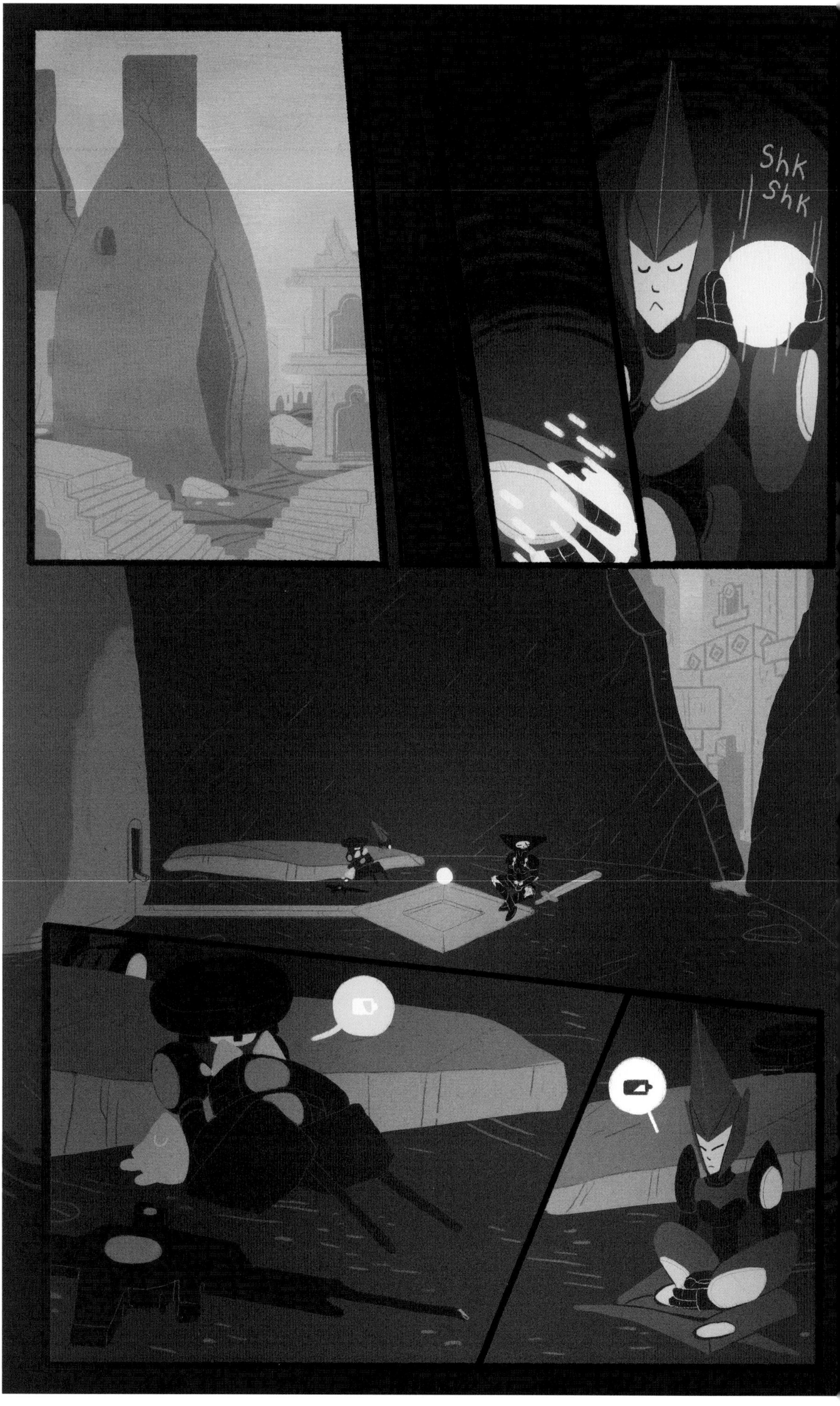
Shk
Shk

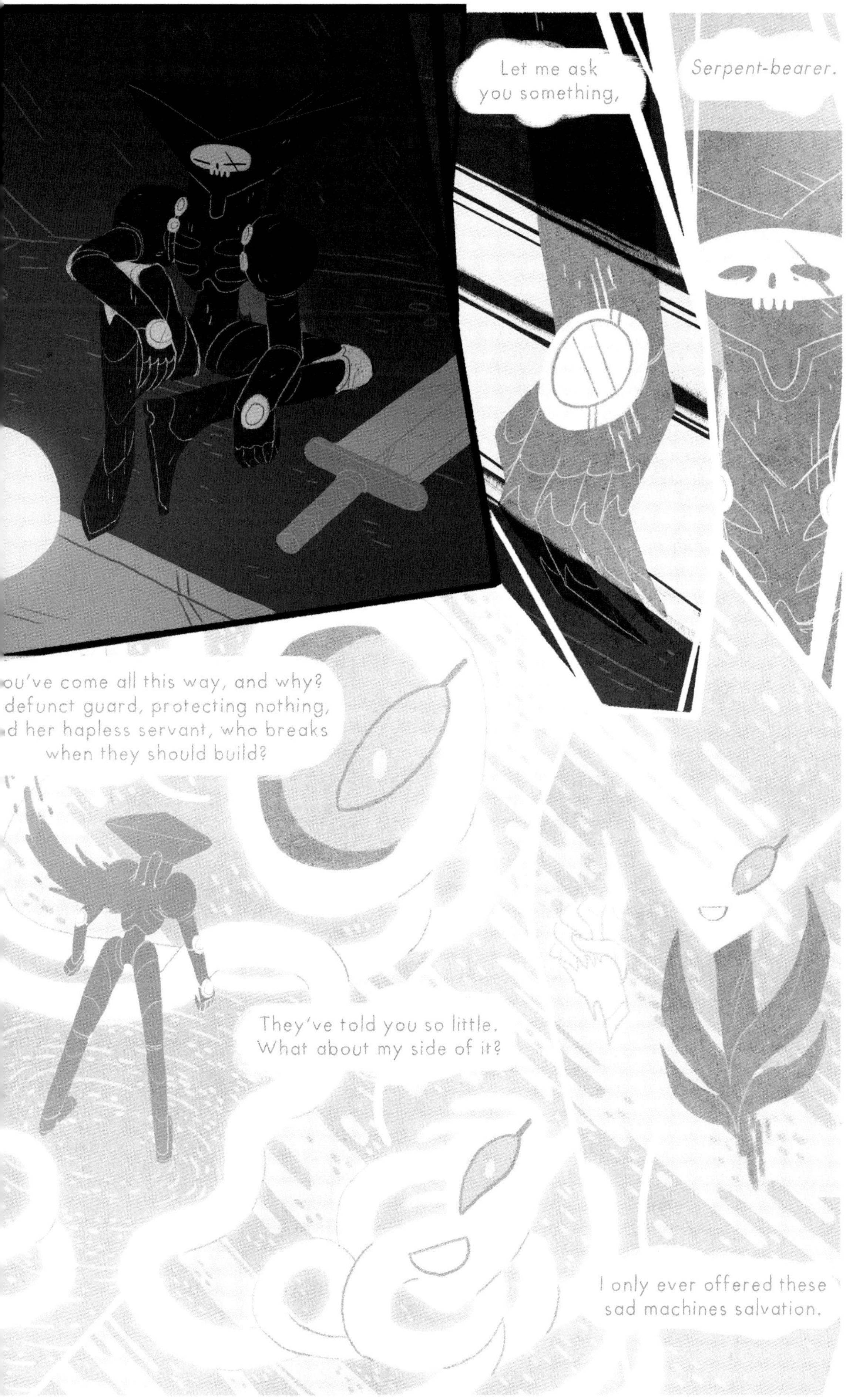
Let me ask you something,
Serpent-bearer.
ou've come all this way, and why? defunct guard, protecting nothing, d her hapless servant, who breaks when they should build?
They've told you so little. What about my side of it?
I only ever offered these sad machines salvation.

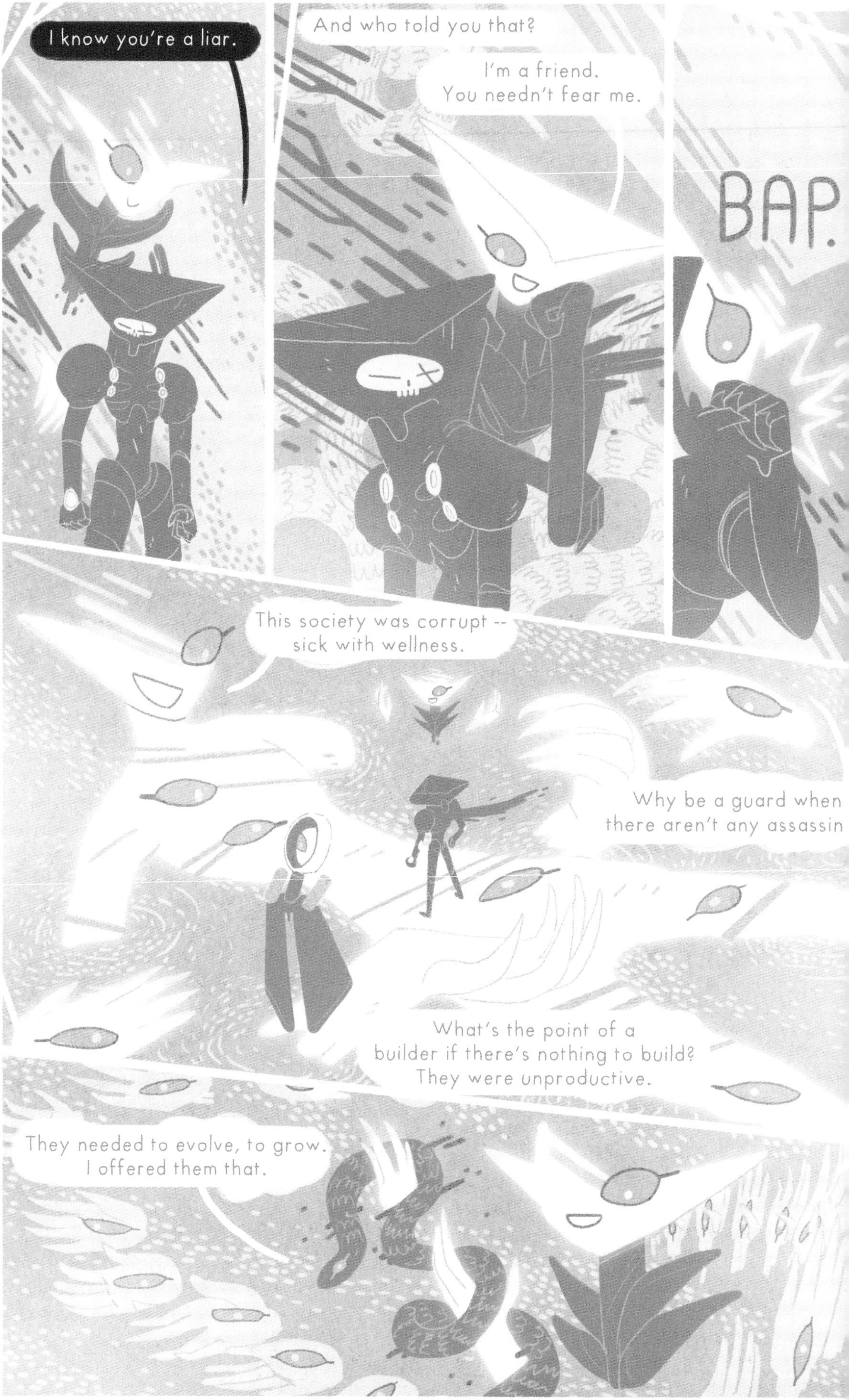

I know you're a liar.
And who told you that?
I'm a friend.
You needn't fear me.
BAP.
This society was corrupt -- sick with wellness.
Why be a guard when there aren't any assassin
What's the point of a builder if there's nothing to build? They were unproductive.
They needed to evolve, to grow. I offered them that.

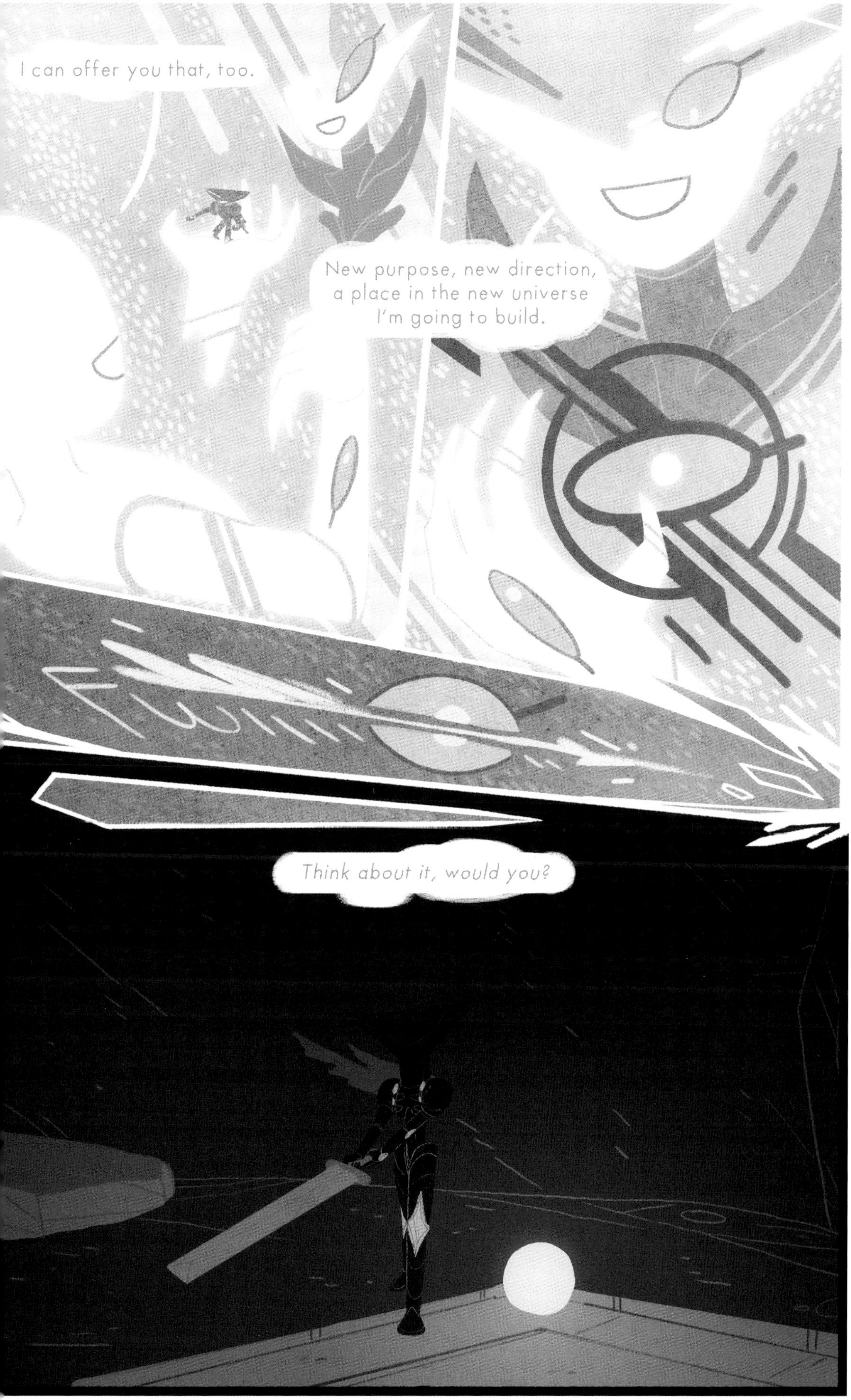
I can offer you that, too.
New purpose, new direction, a place in the new universe I'm going to build.
Think about it, would you?

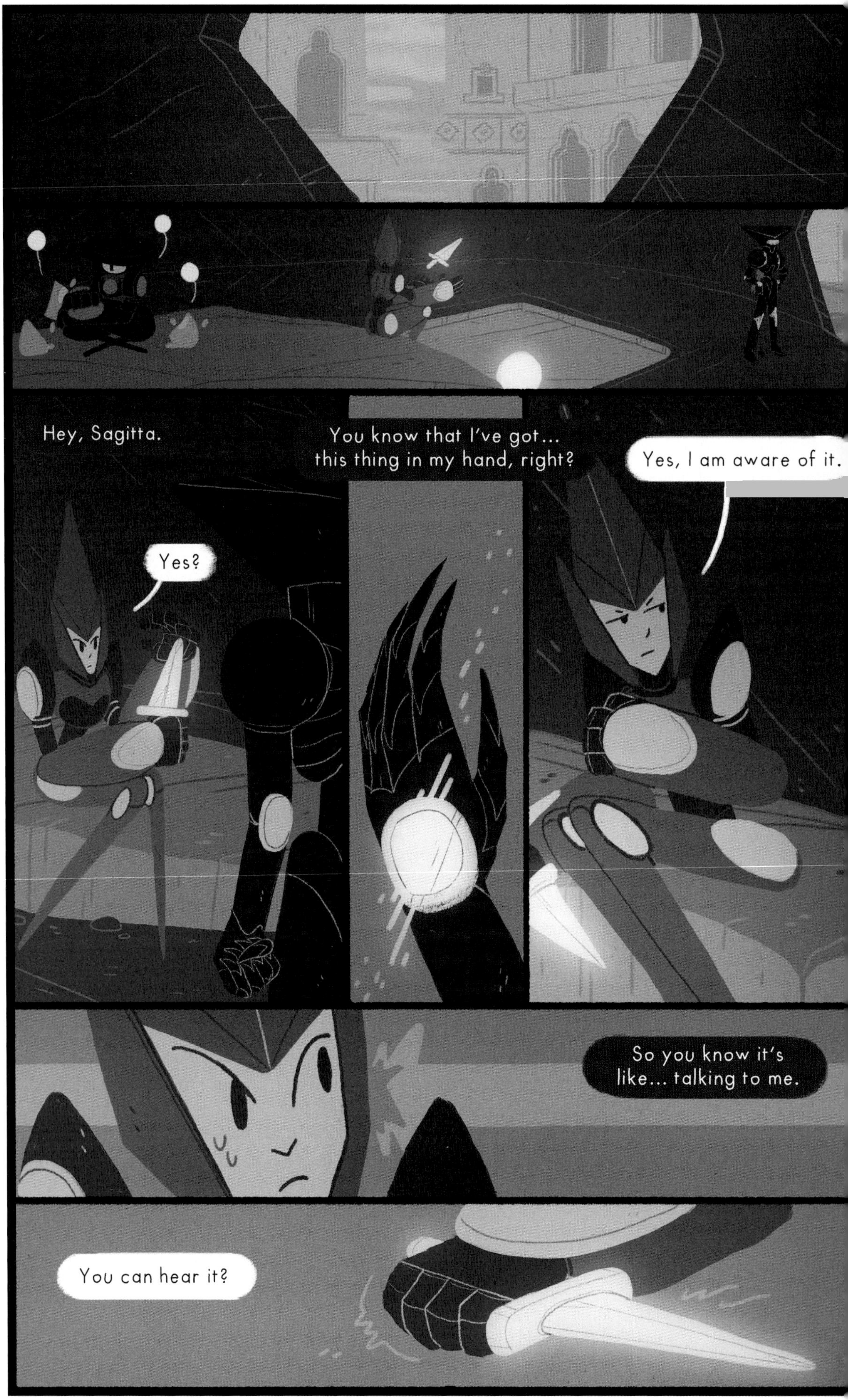
Hey, Sagitta.
Yes?
You know that I've got... this thing in my hand, right?
Yes, I am aware of it.
So you know it's like... talking to me.
You can hear it?

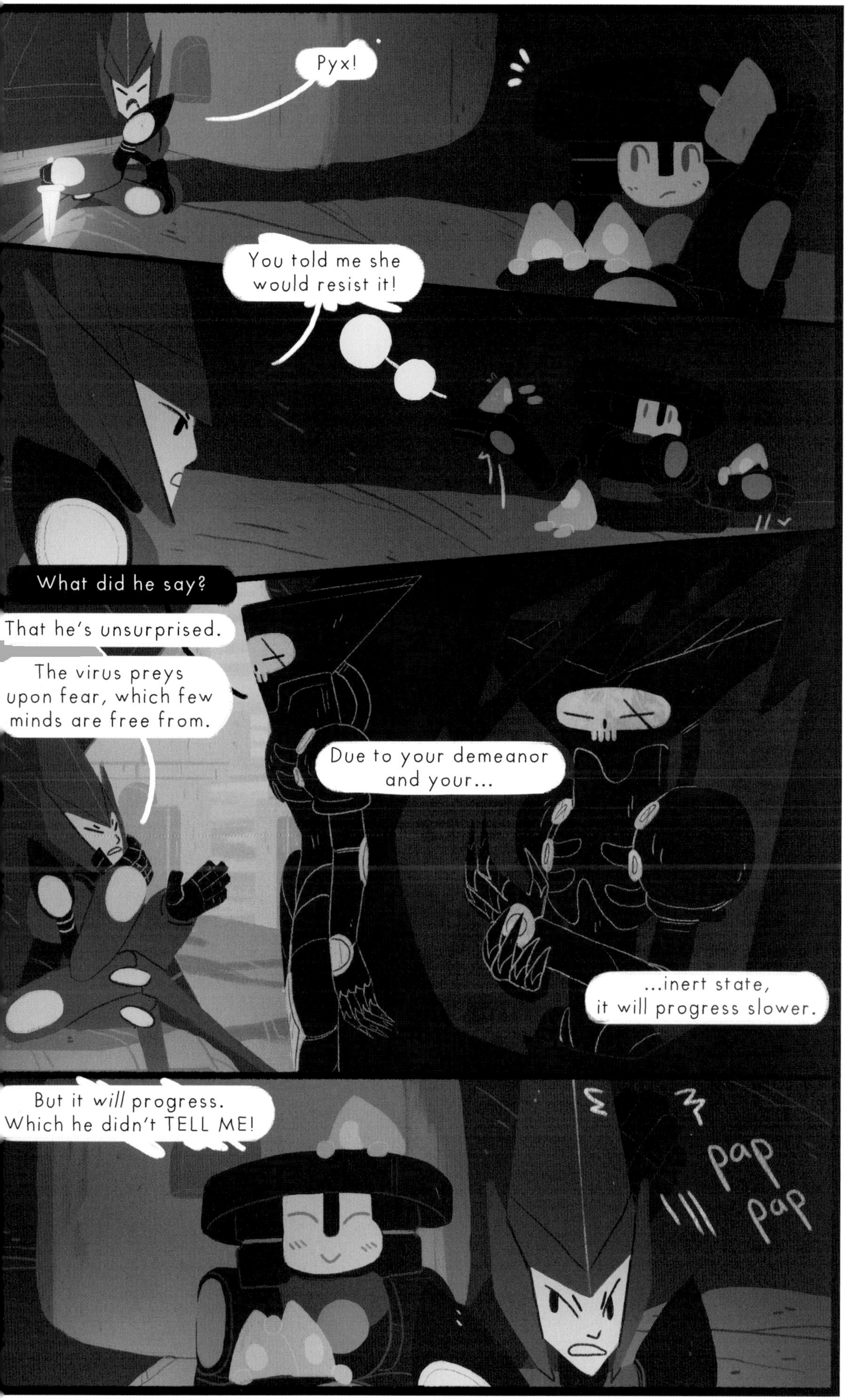
Pyx!
You told me she would resist it!
What did he say?
That he's unsurprised.
The virus preys upon fear, which few minds are free from.
Due to your demeanor and your...
...inert state, it will progress slower.
But it *will* progress. Which he didn't TELL ME!
pap pap

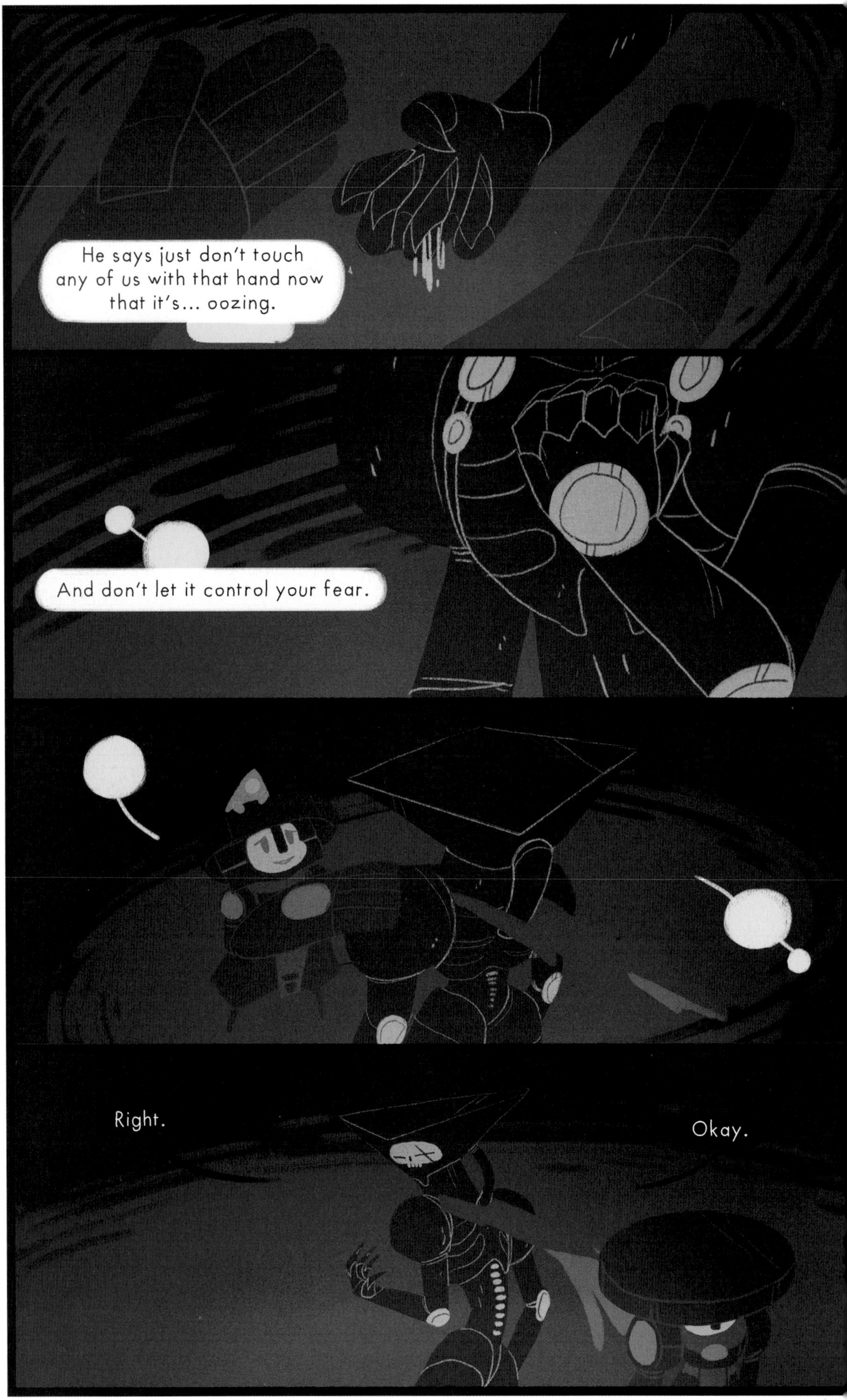

He says just don't touch any of us with that hand now that it's... oozing.
And don't let it control your fear.
Right.
Okay.

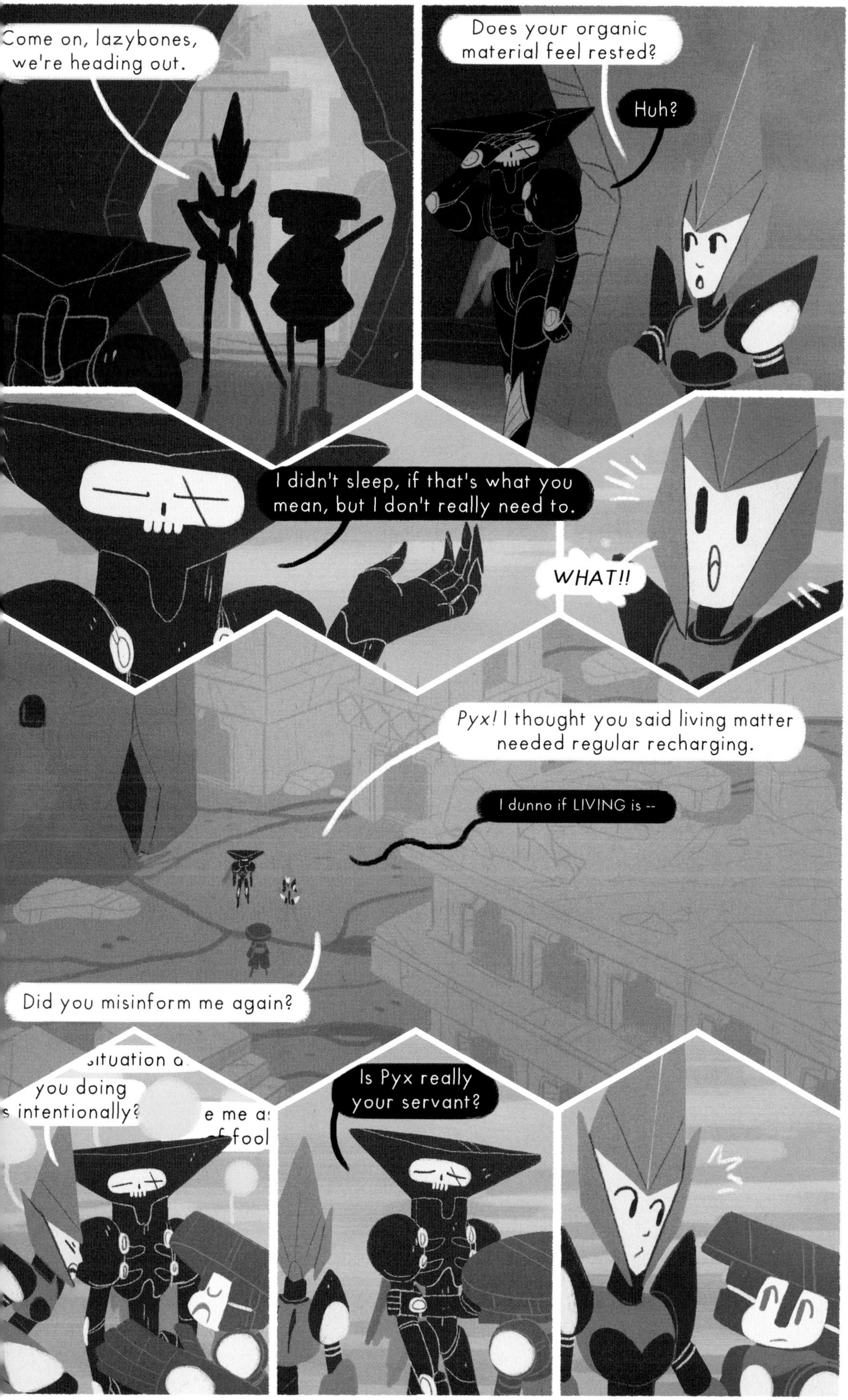
Come on, lazybones, we're heading out.
Does your organic material feel rested?
Huh?
I didn't sleep, if that's what you mean, but I don't really need to.
WHAT!!
Pyx! I thought you said living matter needed regular recharging.
I dunno if LIVING is --
Did you misinform me again?
situation a
you doing
s intentionally?
e me a
fool
Is Pyx really your servant?

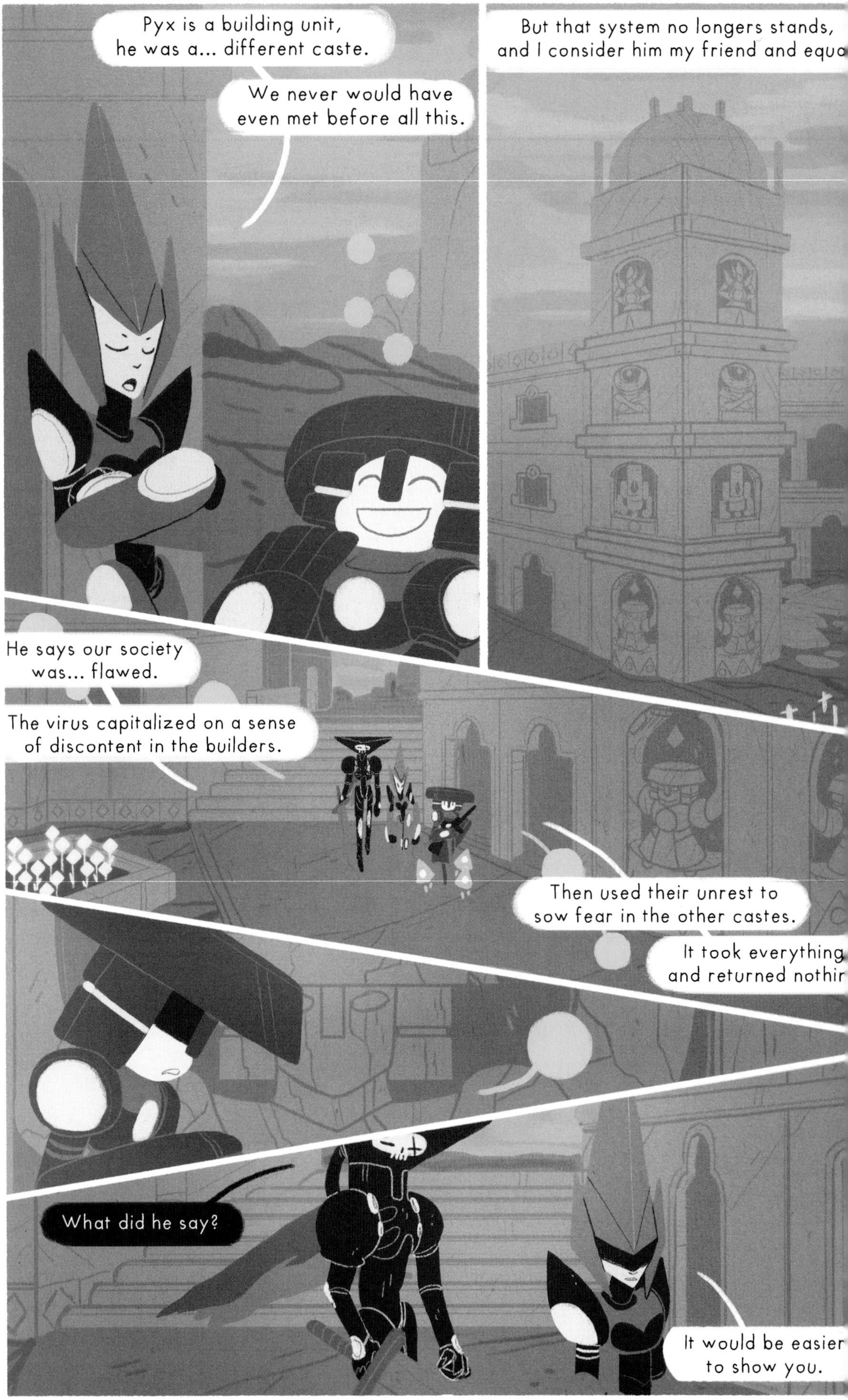
Pyx is a building unit,
he was a... different caste.
We never would have
even met before all this.
But that system no longers stands,
and I consider him my friend and equa
He says our society
was... flawed.
The virus capitalized on a sense
of discontent in the builders.
Then used their unrest to
sow fear in the other castes.
It took everything
and returned nothir
What did he say?
It would be easier
to show you.

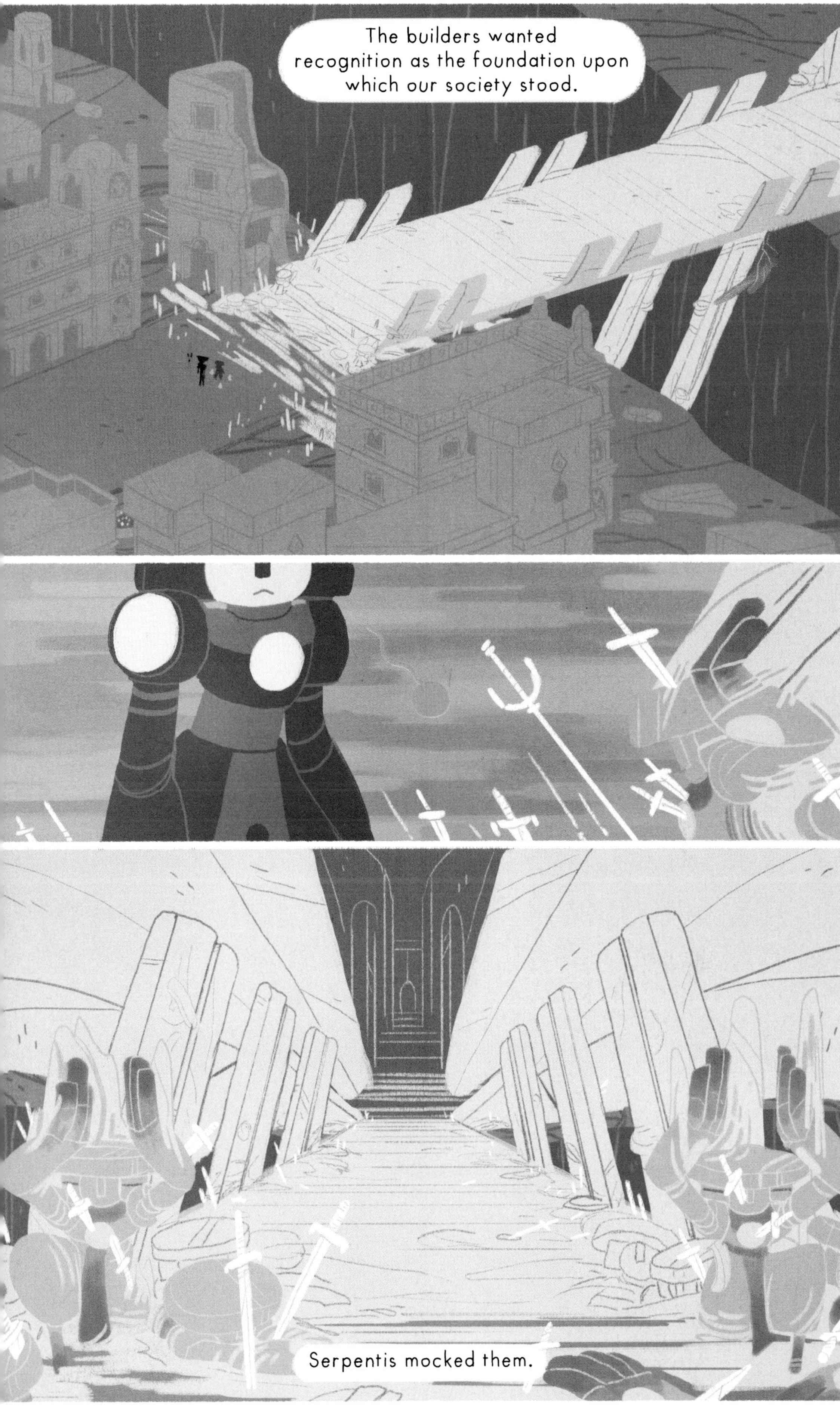
The builders wanted recognition as the foundation upon which our society stood.
Serpentis mocked them.

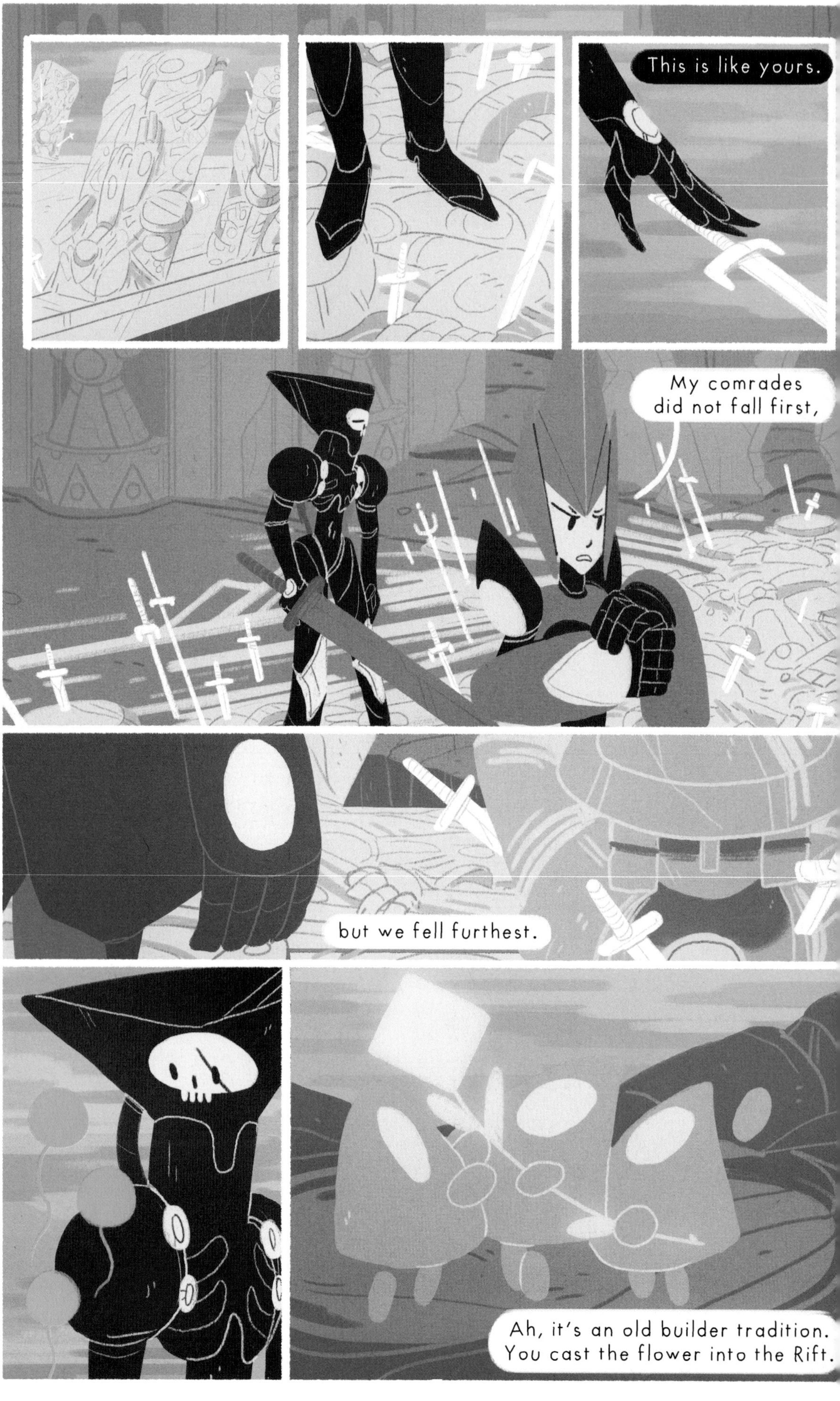
This is like yours.
My comrades did not fall first,
but we fell furthest.
Ah, it's an old builder tradition. You cast the flower into the Rift.

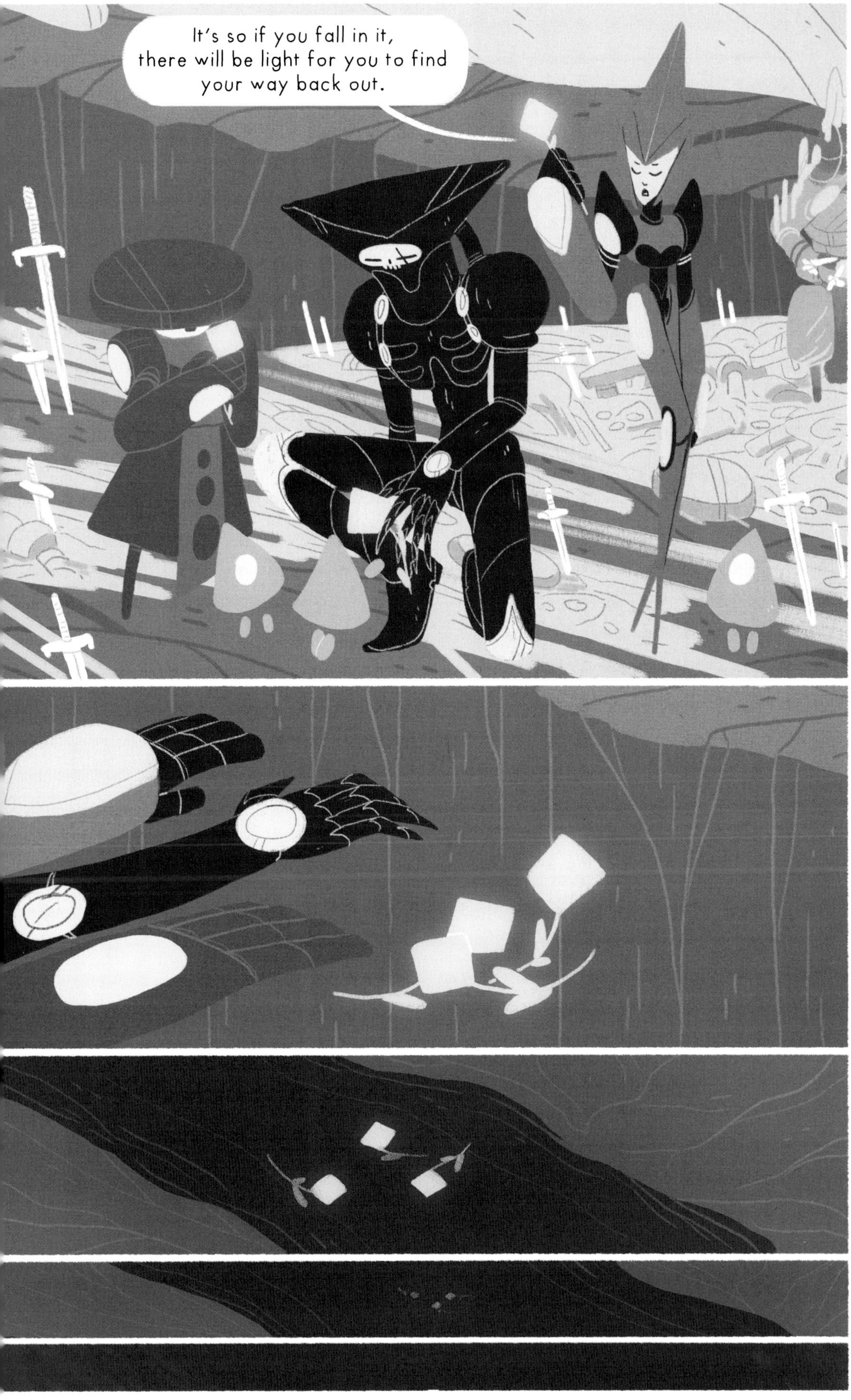
It's so if you fall in it, there will be light for you to find your way back out.

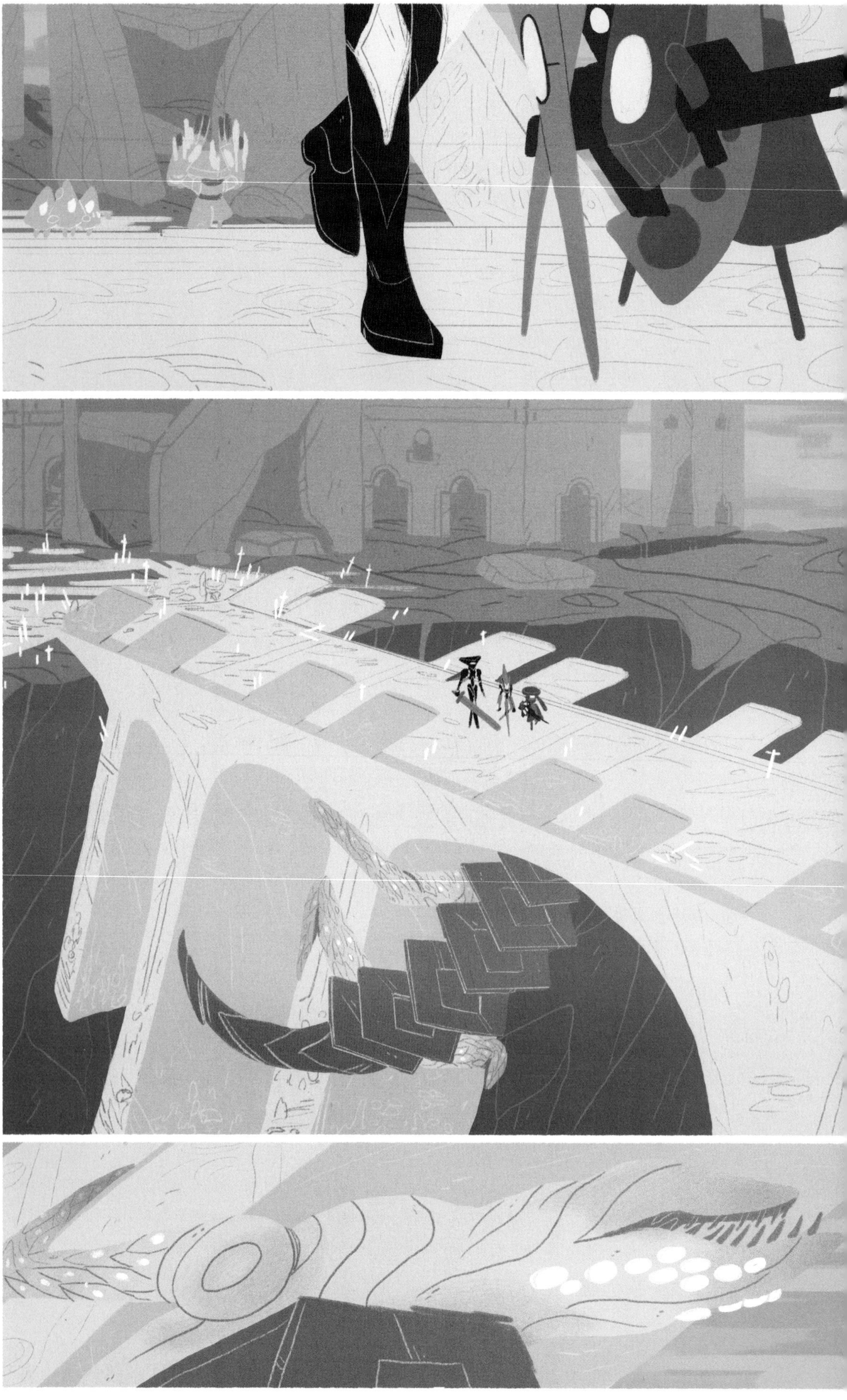

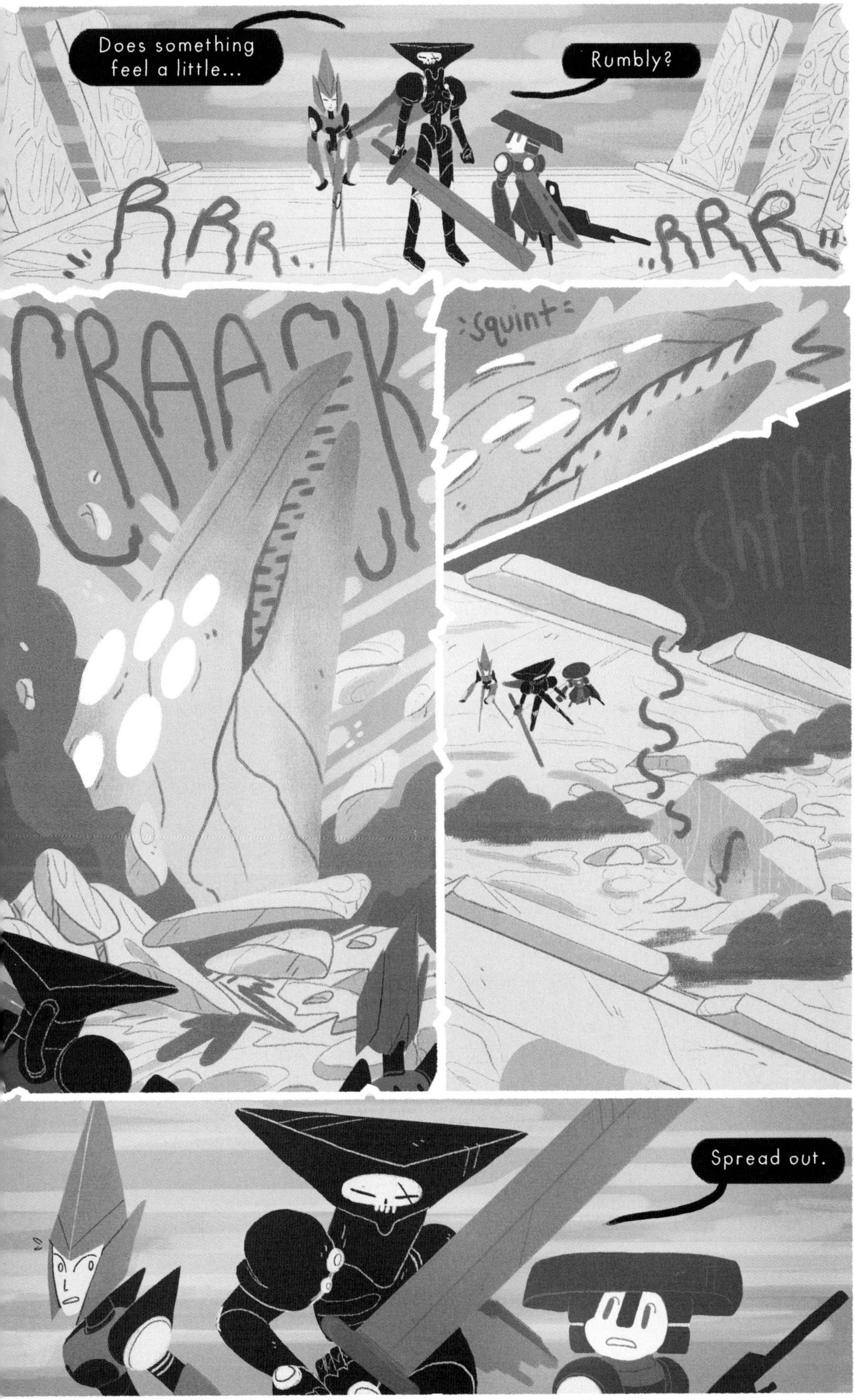
Does something feel a little...
Rumbly?
RRRR...
RRRR
CRAACK
squint
SHFFF
Spread out.

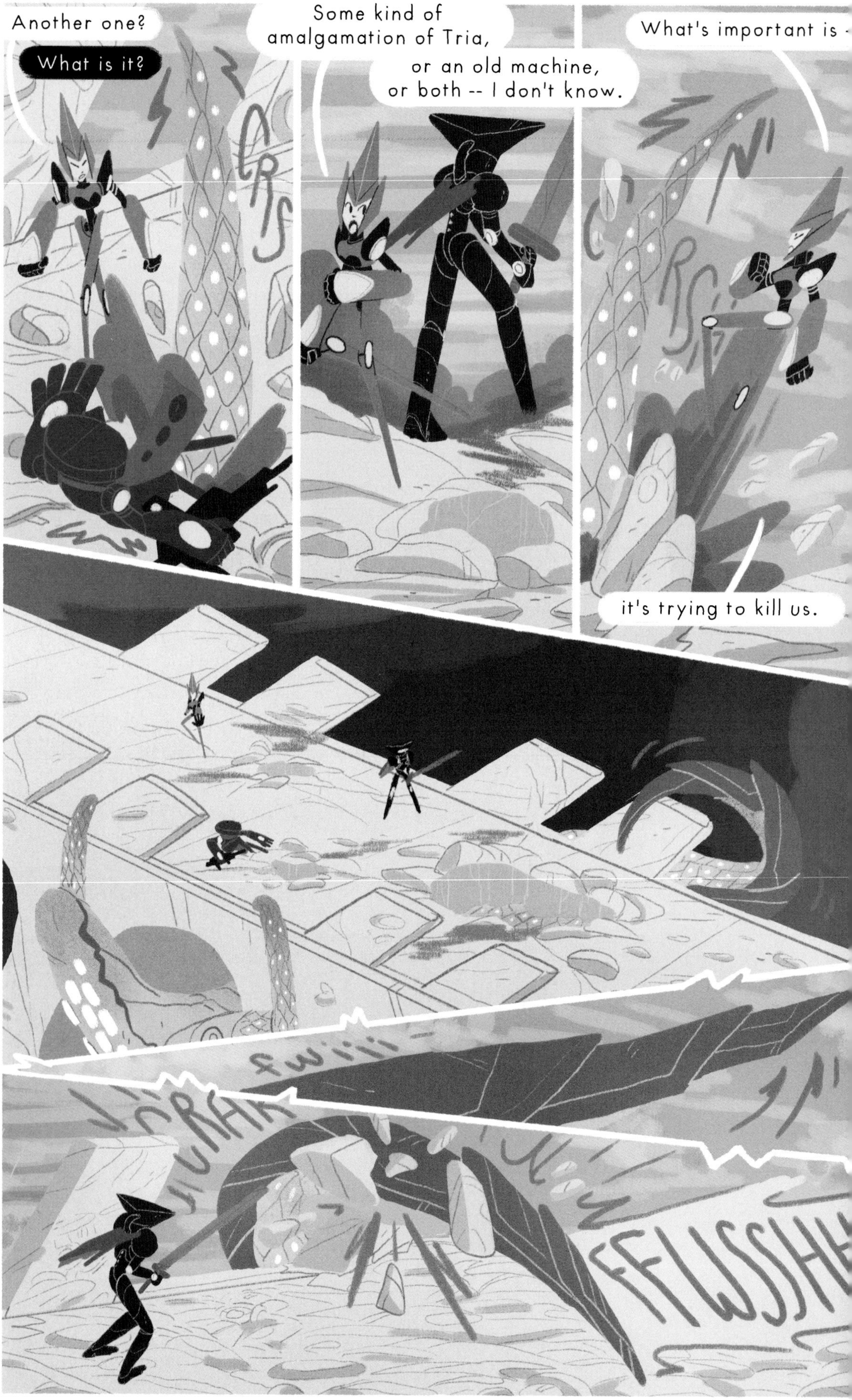
Another one?
What is it?
Some kind of amalgamation of Tria,
or an old machine, or both -- I don't know.
What's important is -
it's trying to kill us.

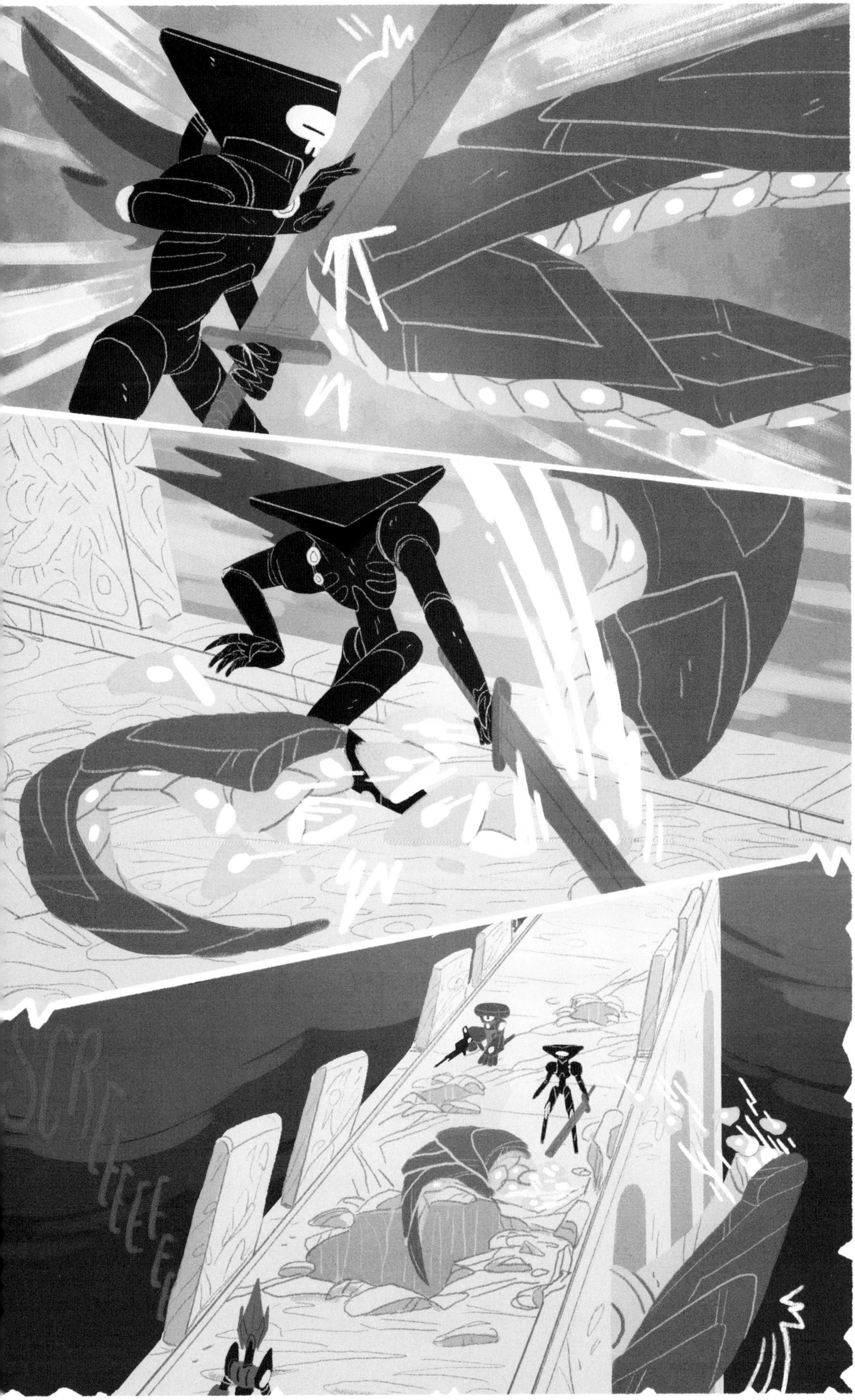
SCREEEEE

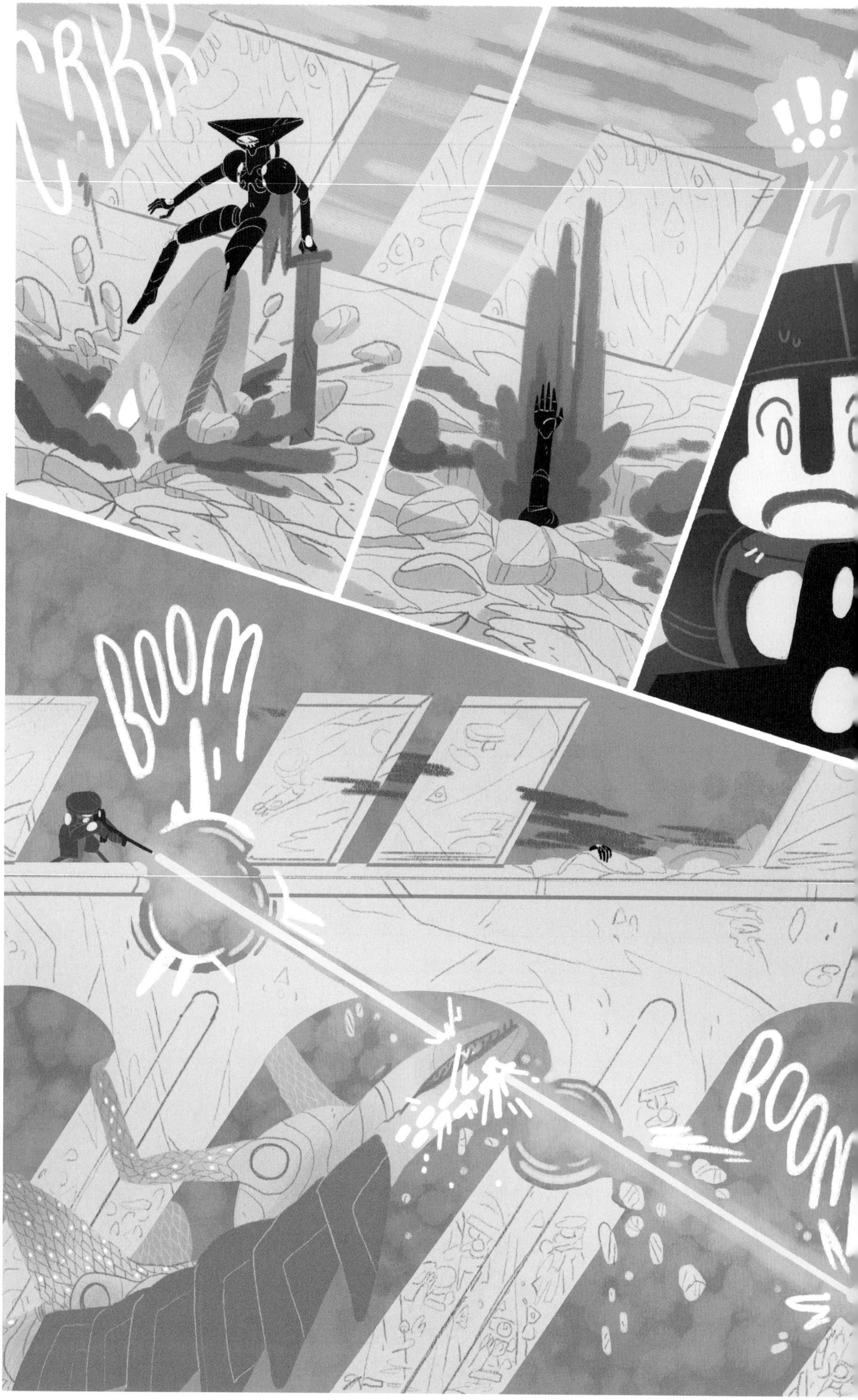
CRKK
!!!
BOOM
BOOM

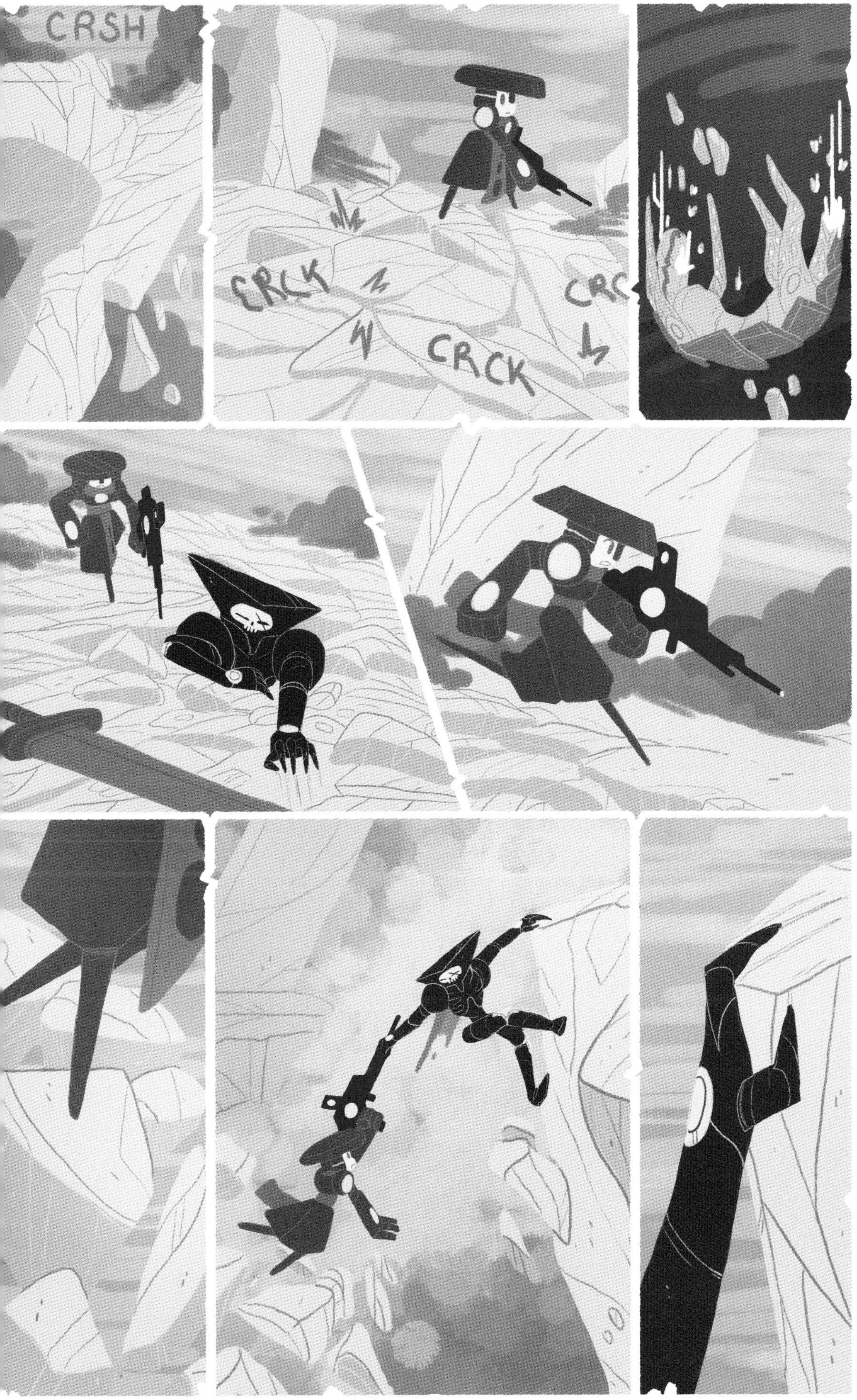
CRSH
CRCK
CRC
CRCK

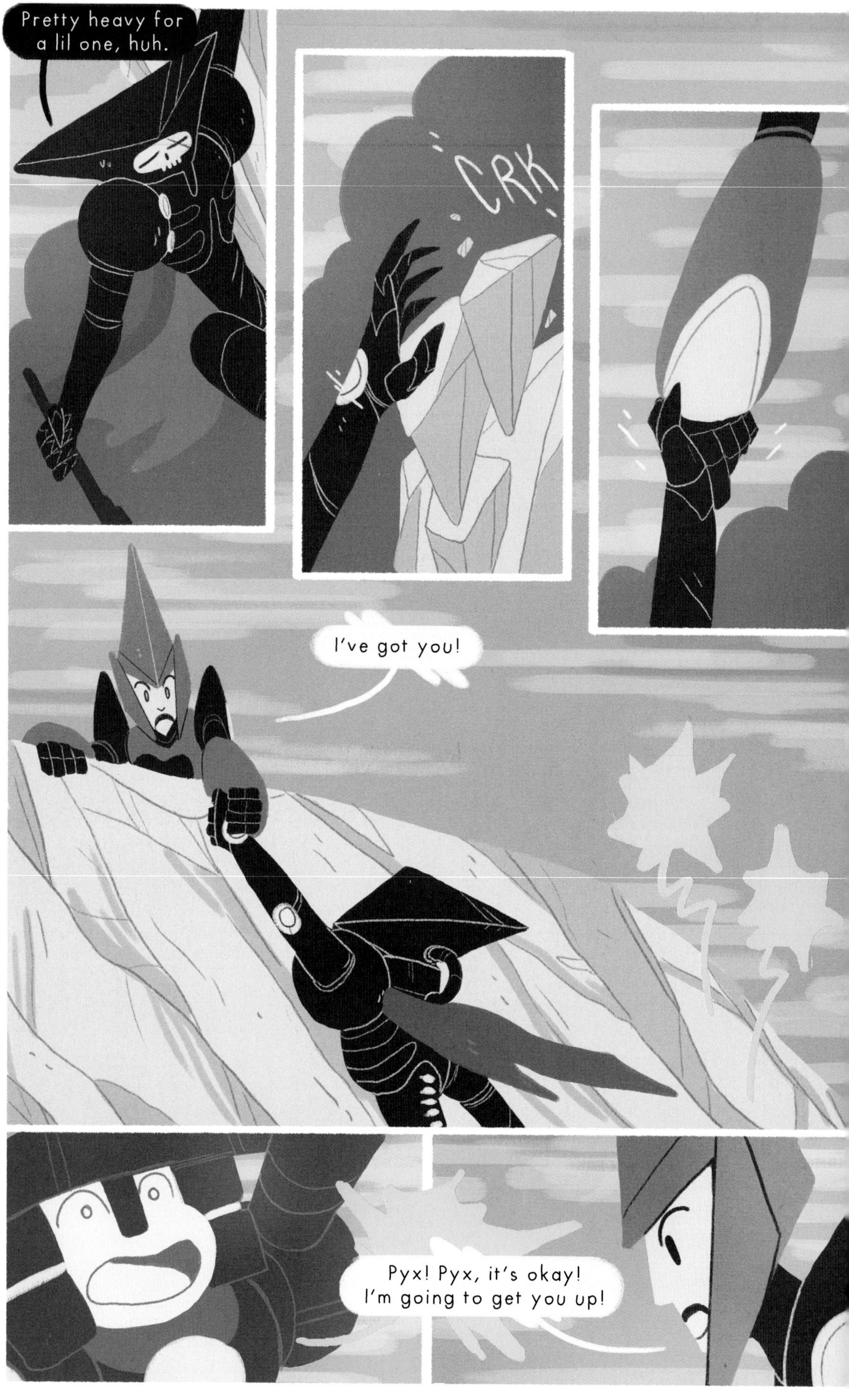
Pretty heavy for a lil one, huh.
CRK
I've got you!
Pyx! Pyx, it's okay! I'm going to get you up!

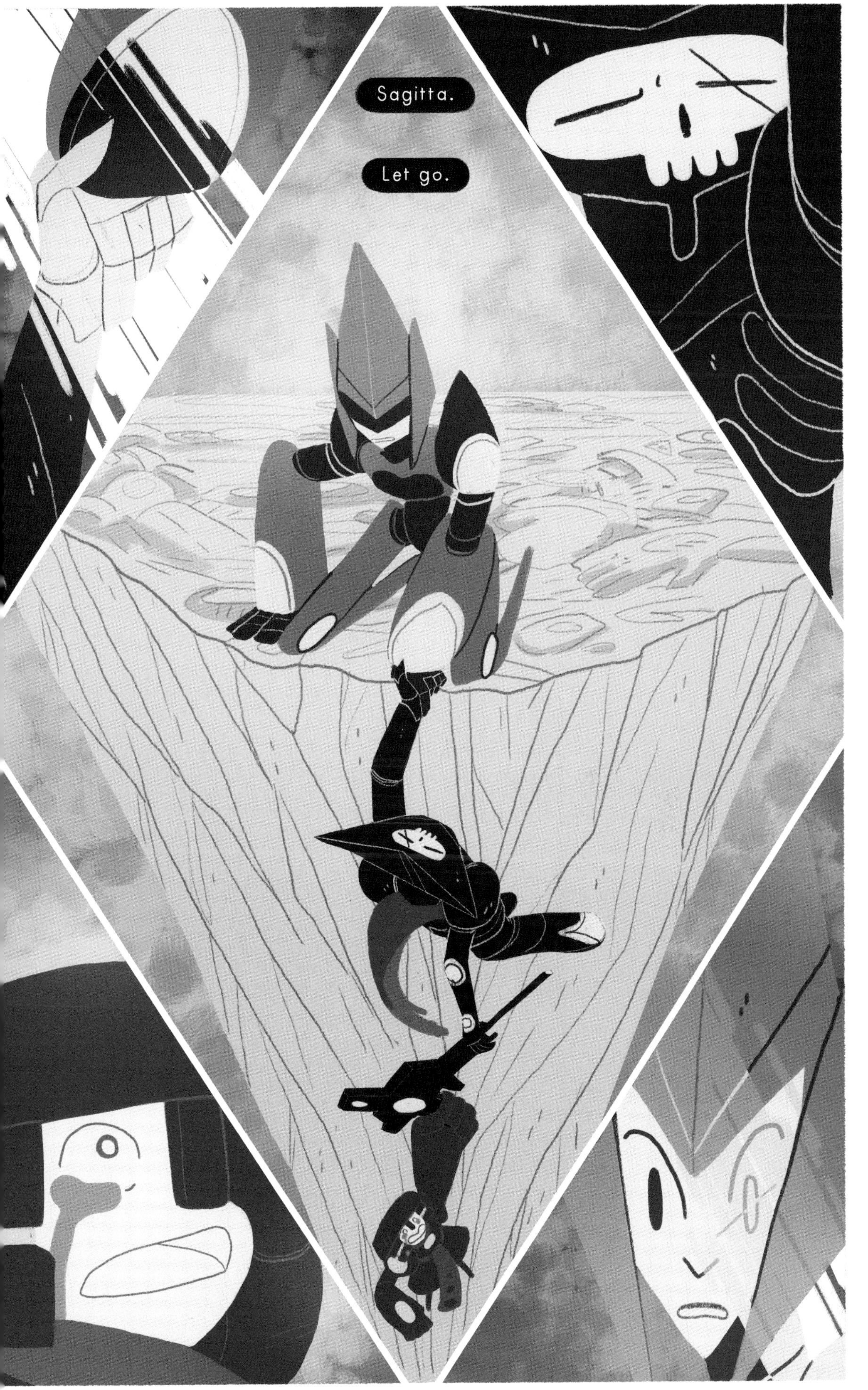
Sagitta.
Let go.

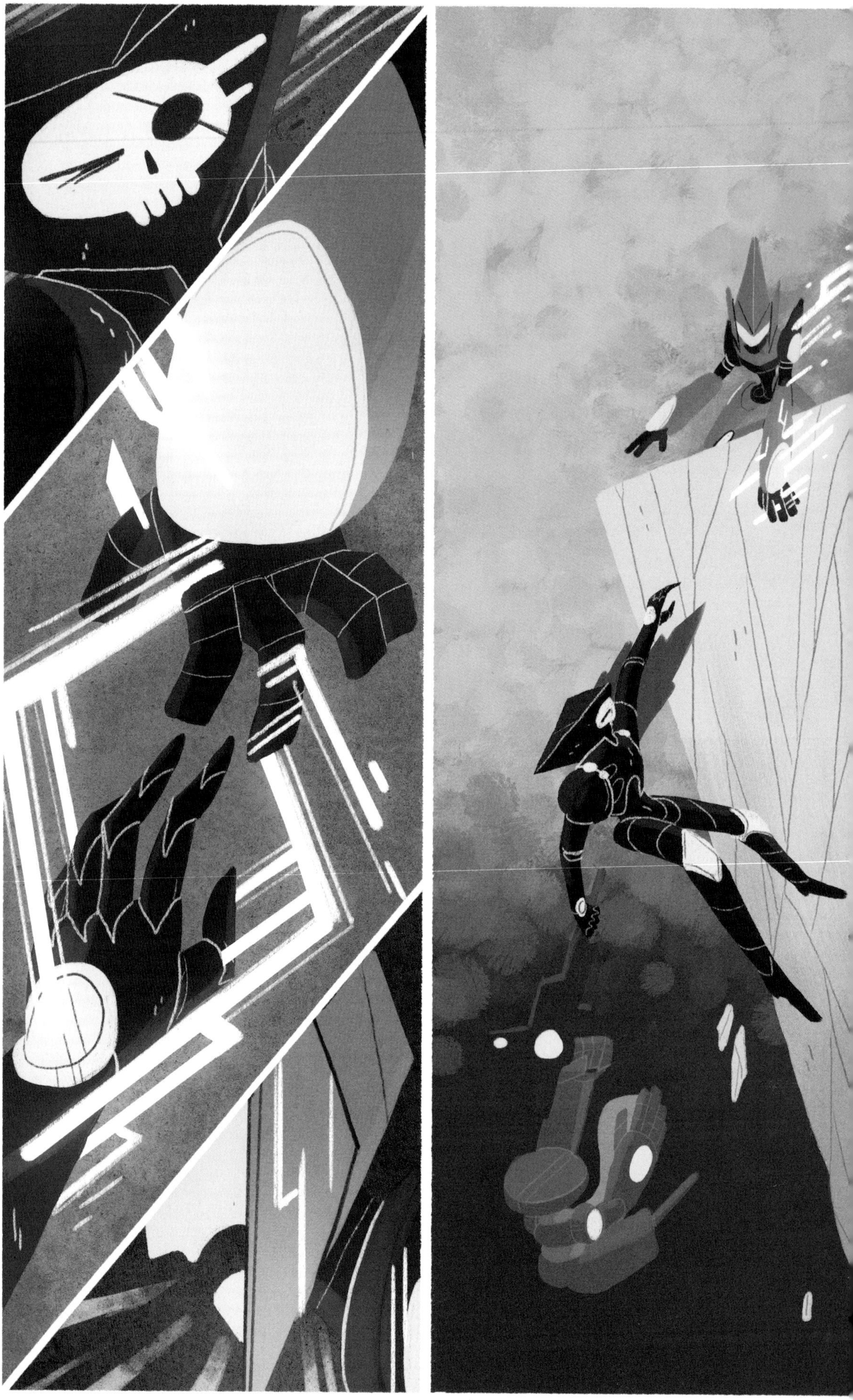

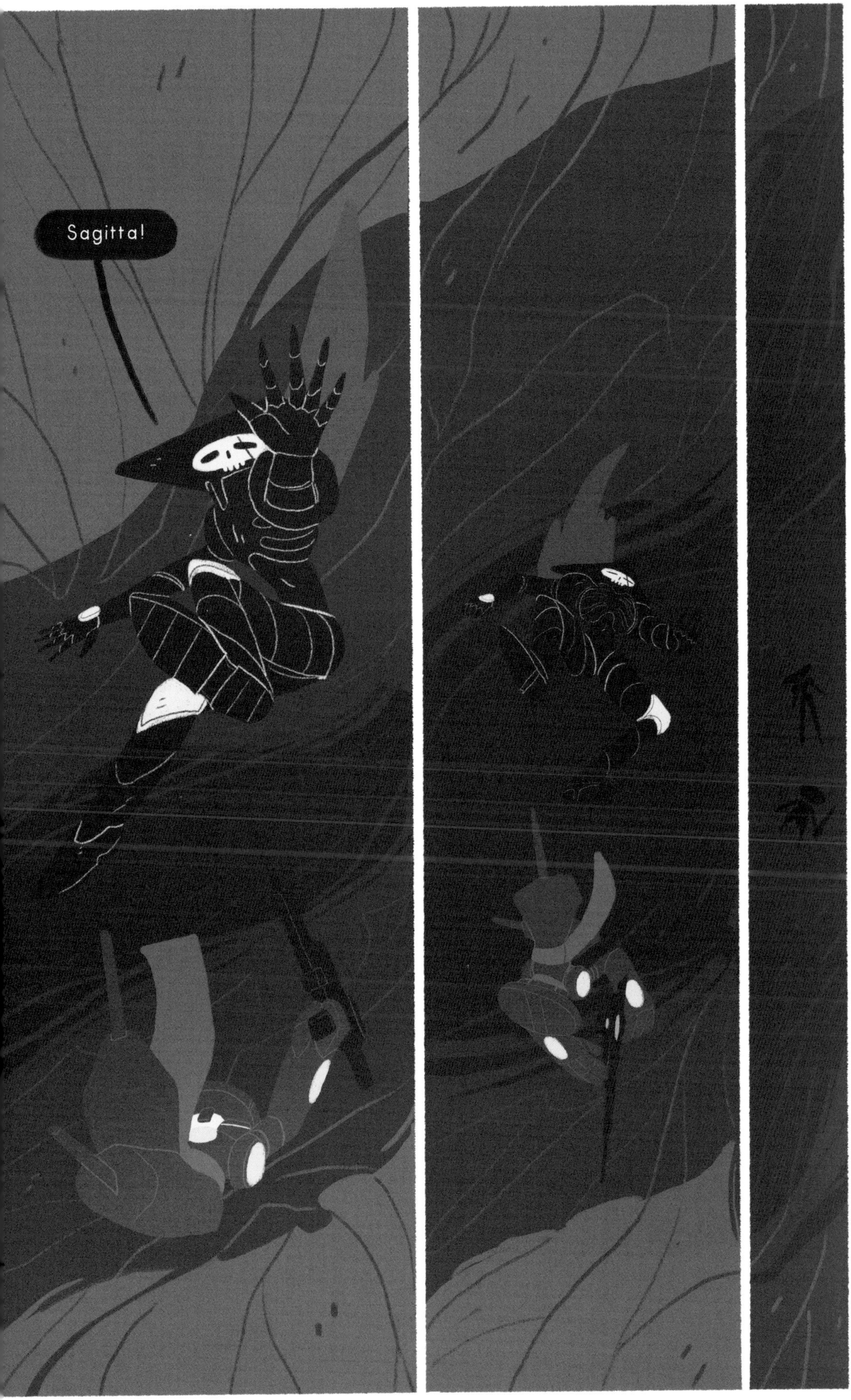
Sagitta!

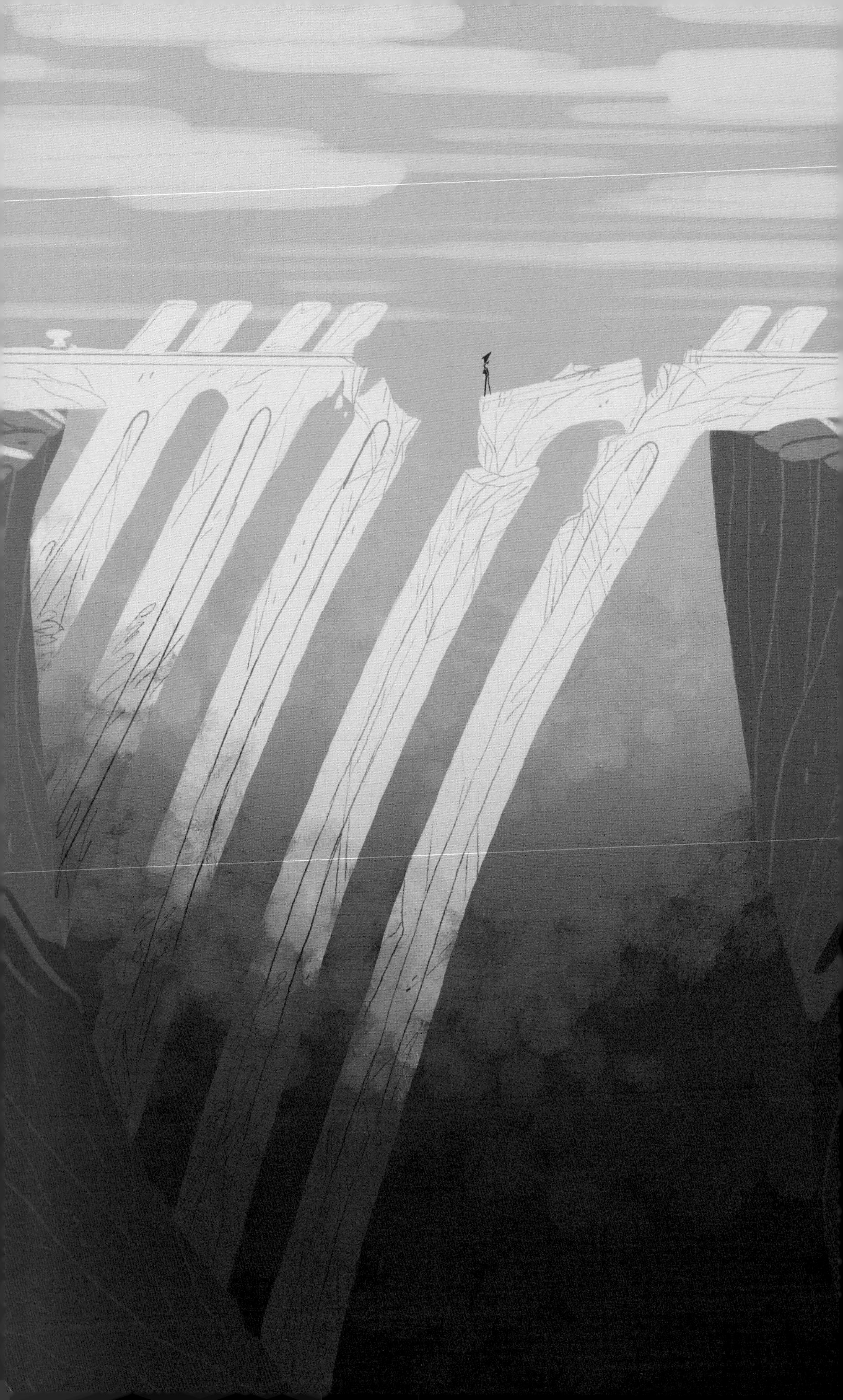

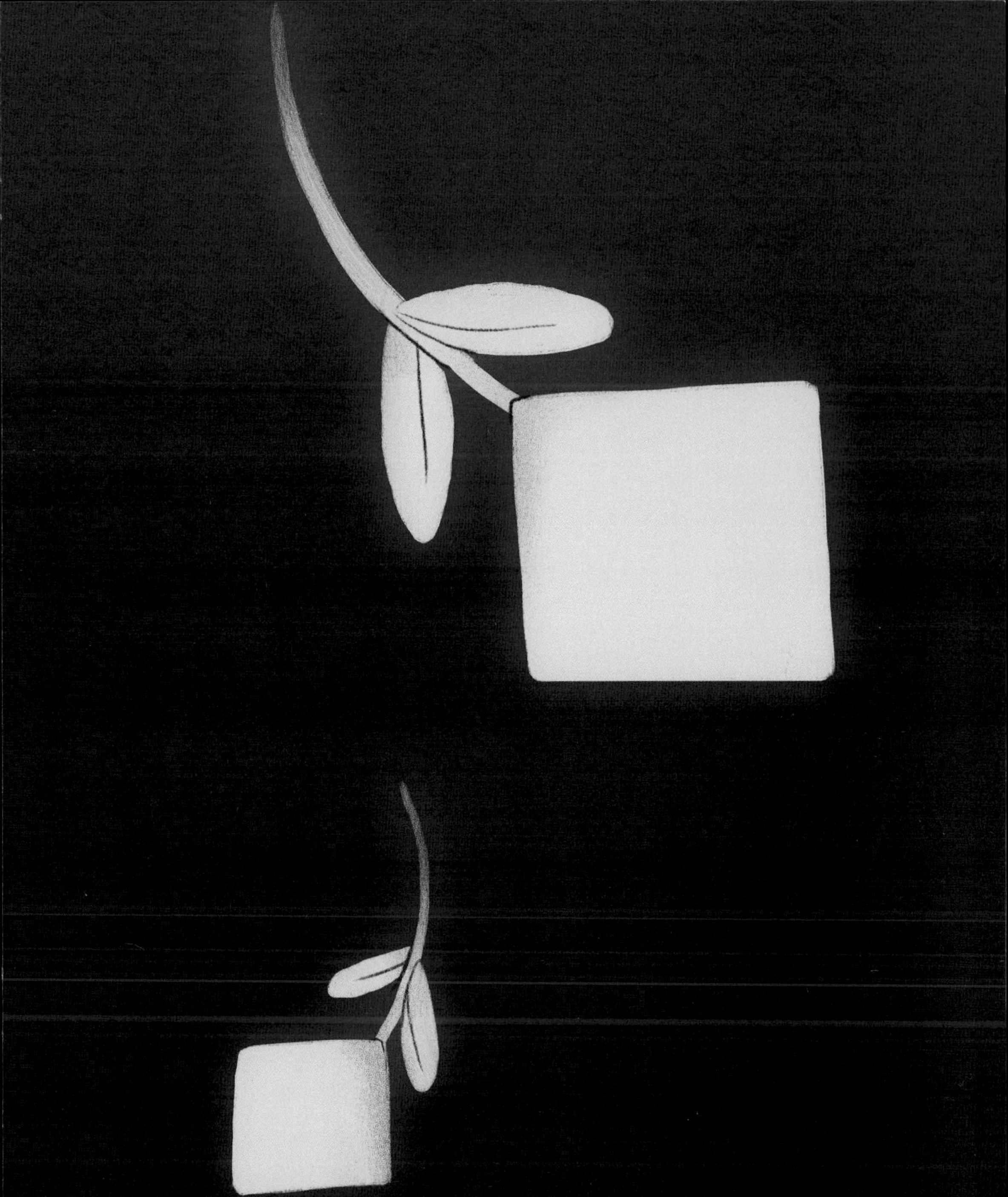

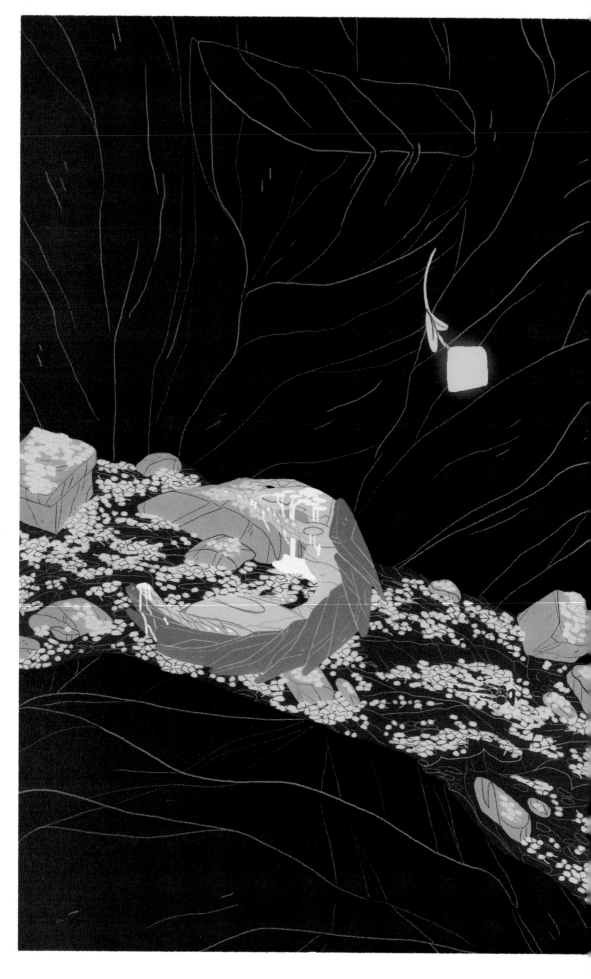

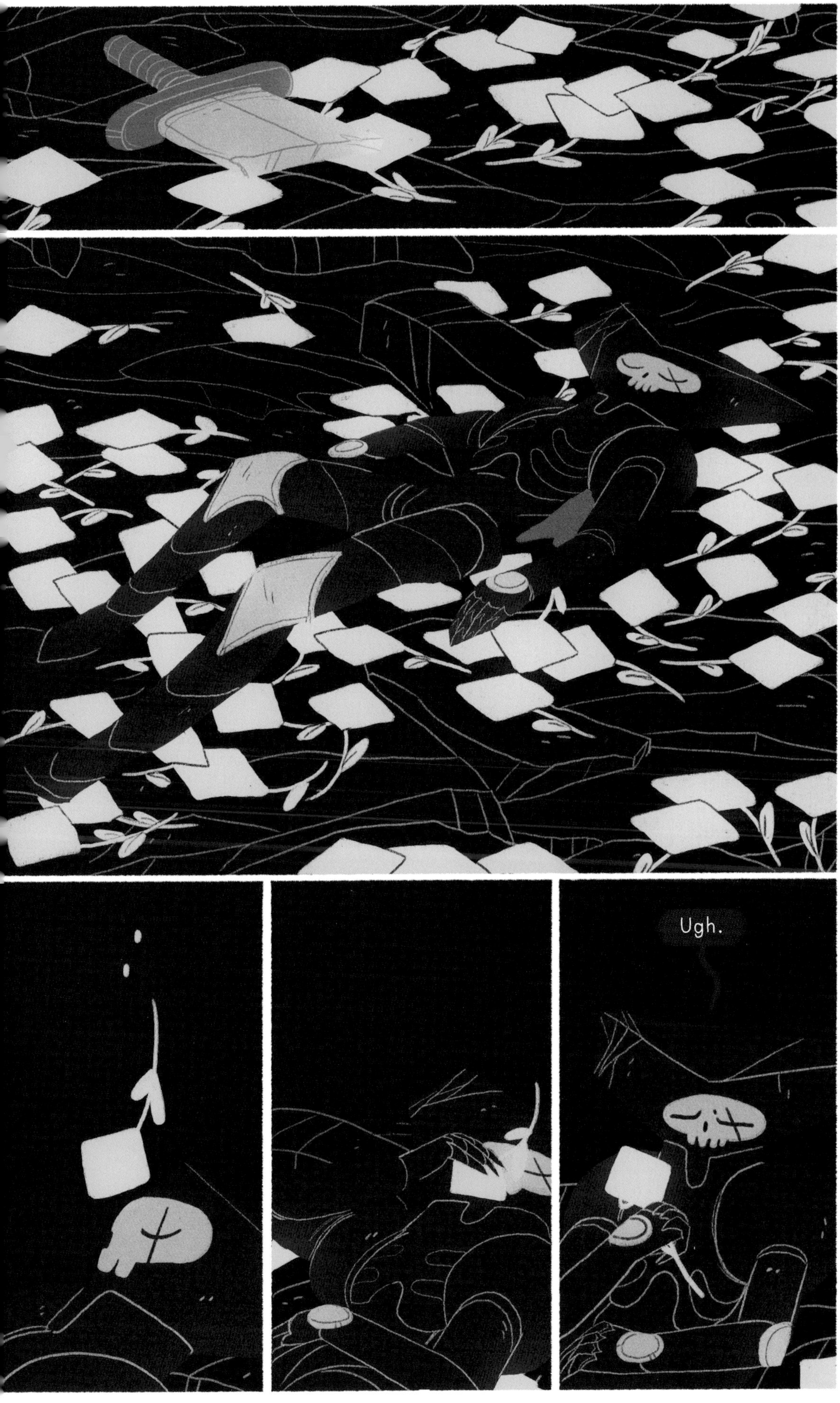
Ugh.

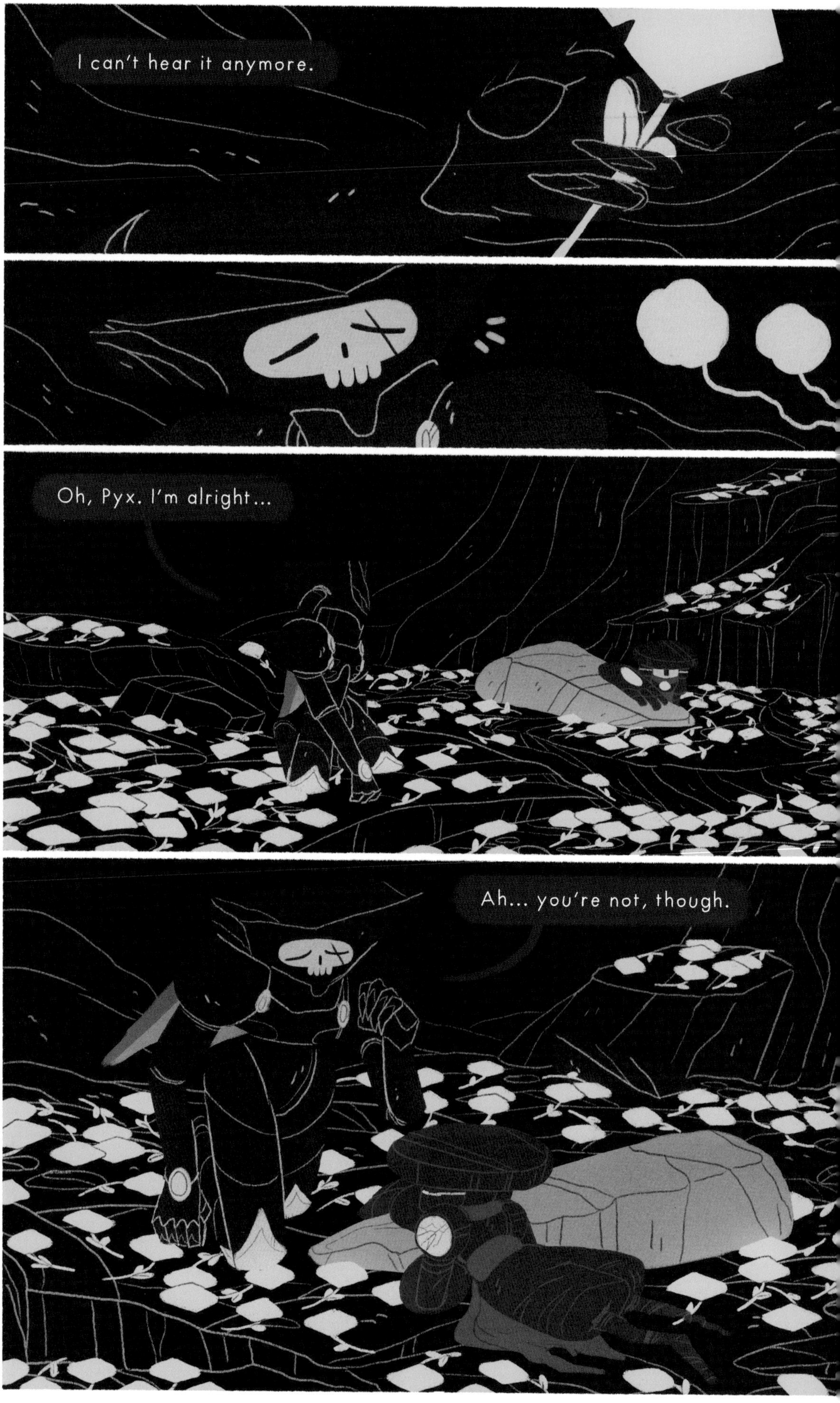
I can't hear it anymore.
Oh, Pyx. I'm alright...
Ah... you're not, though.

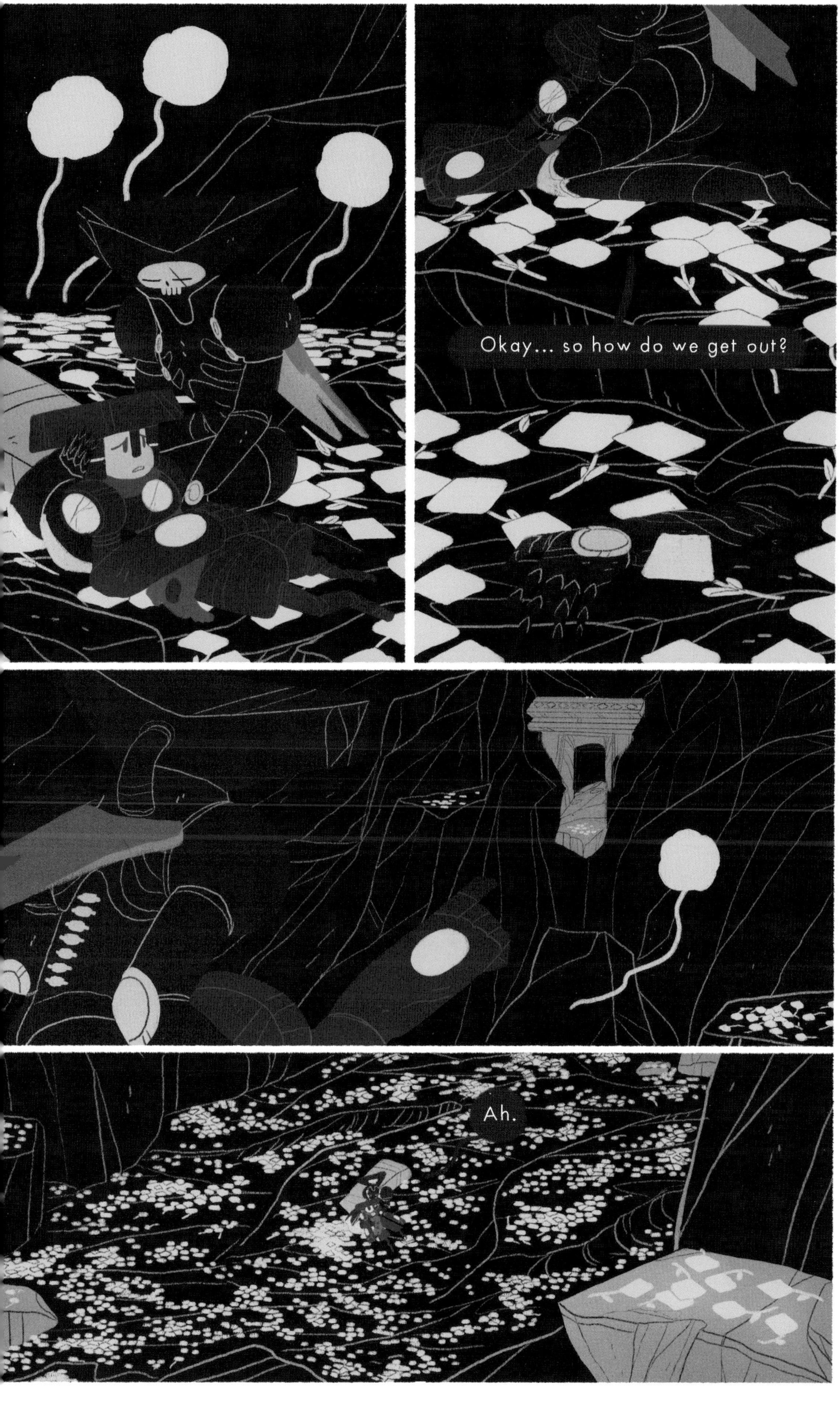
Okay... so how do we get out?
Ah.

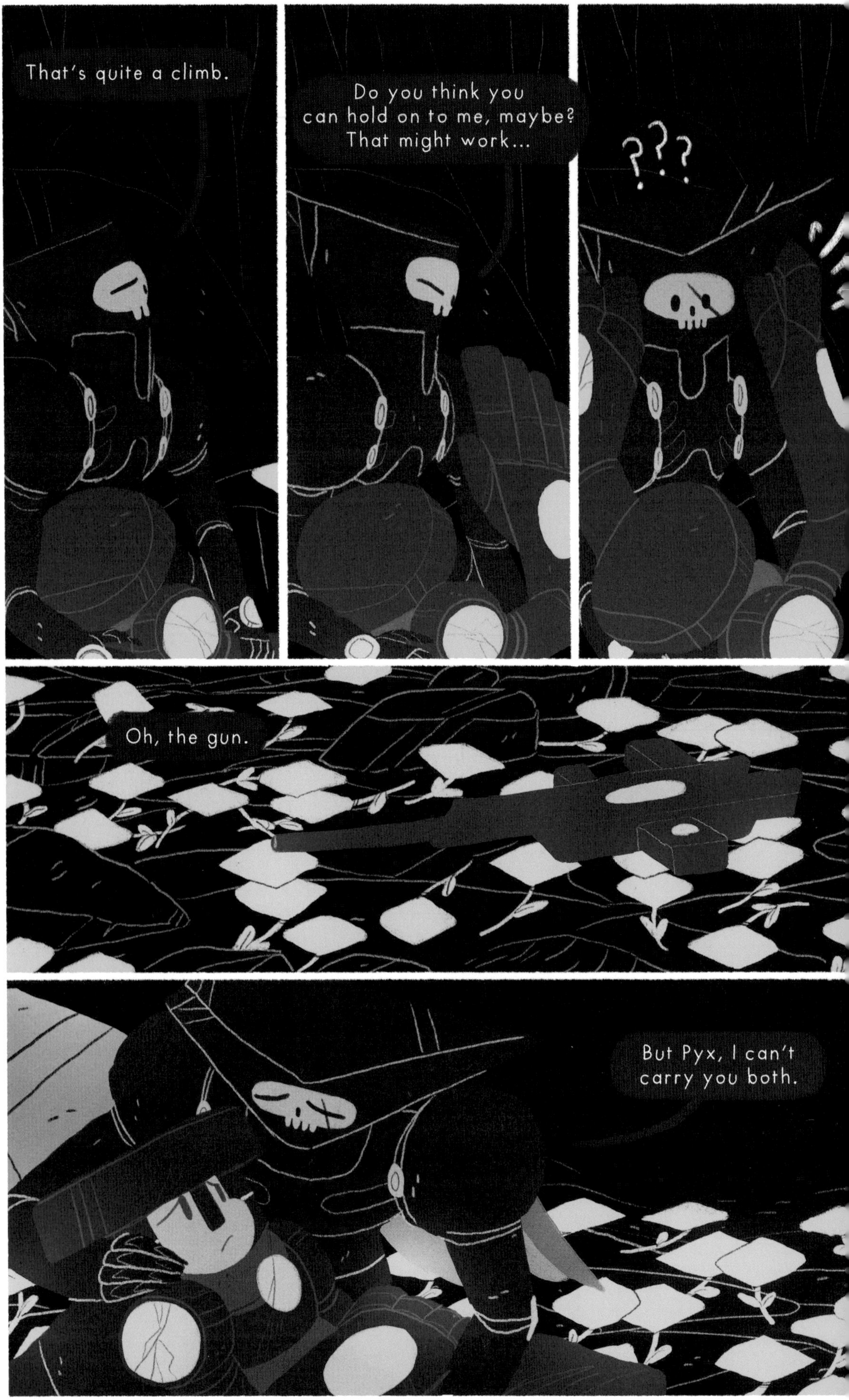
That's quite a climb.
Do you think you can hold on to me, maybe? That might work...
???
Oh, the gun.
But Pyx, I can't carry you both.

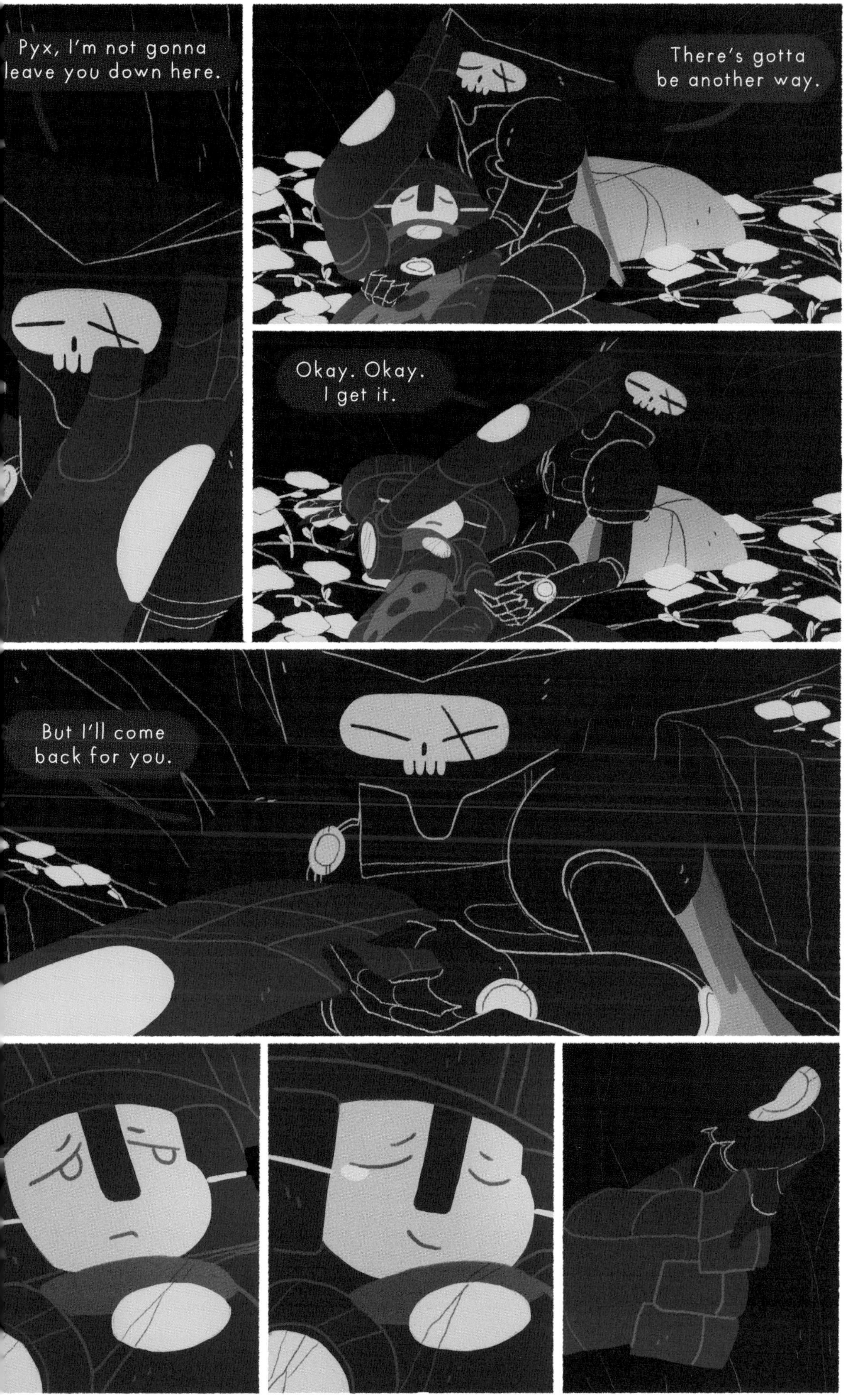
Pyx, I'm not gonna leave you down here.
There's gotta be another way.
Okay. Okay. I get it.
But I'll come back for you.

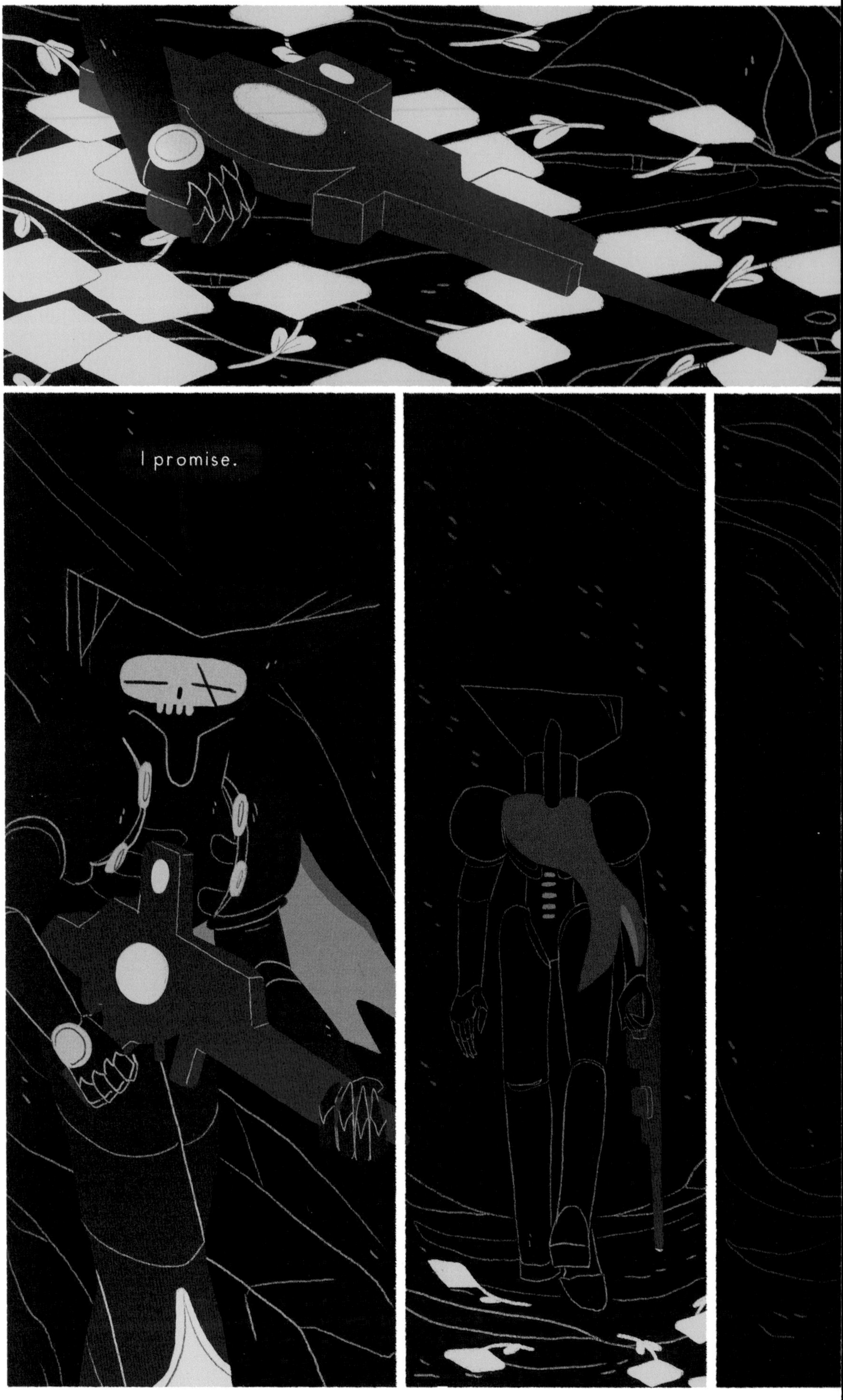
I promise.

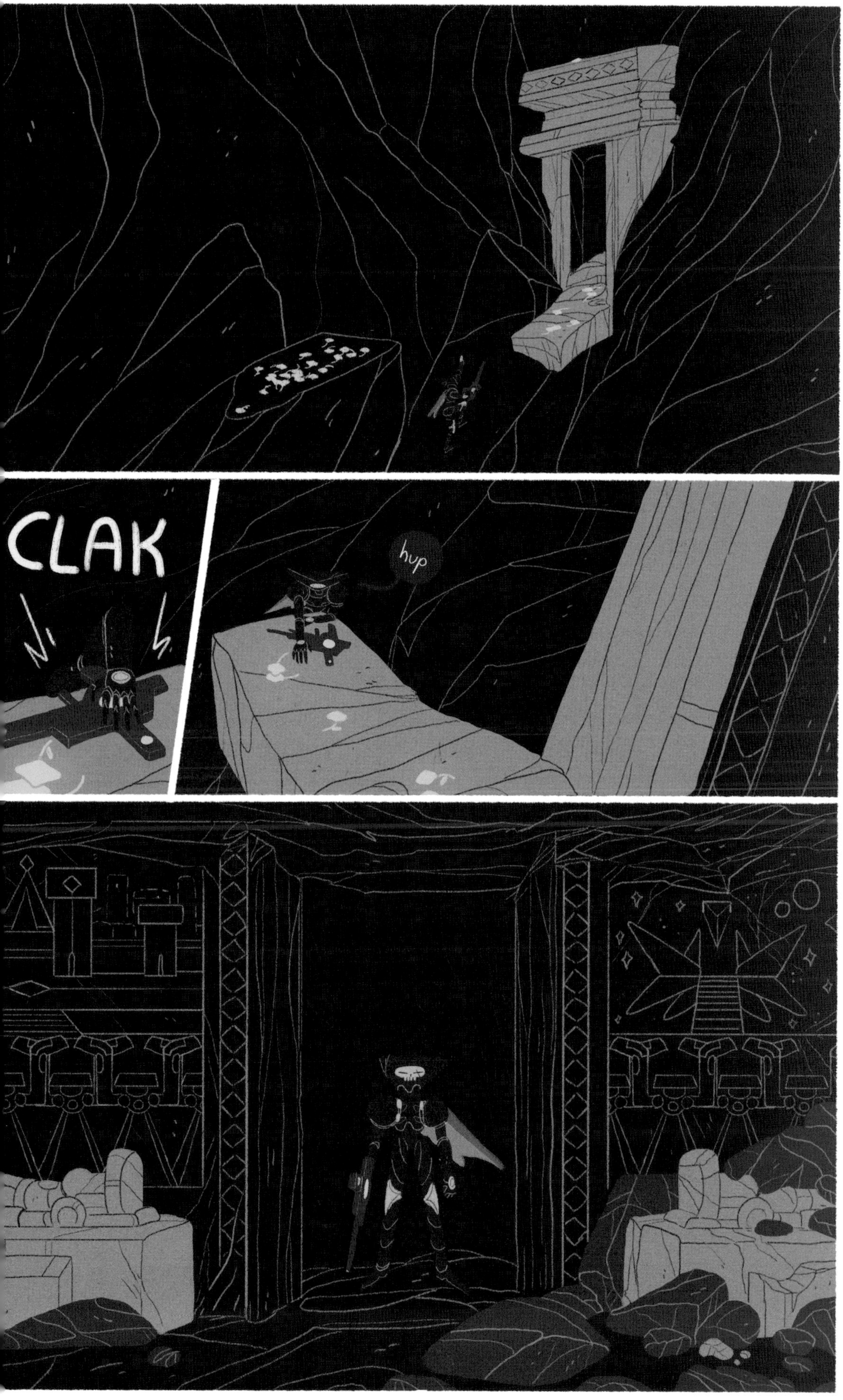
CLAK
hup

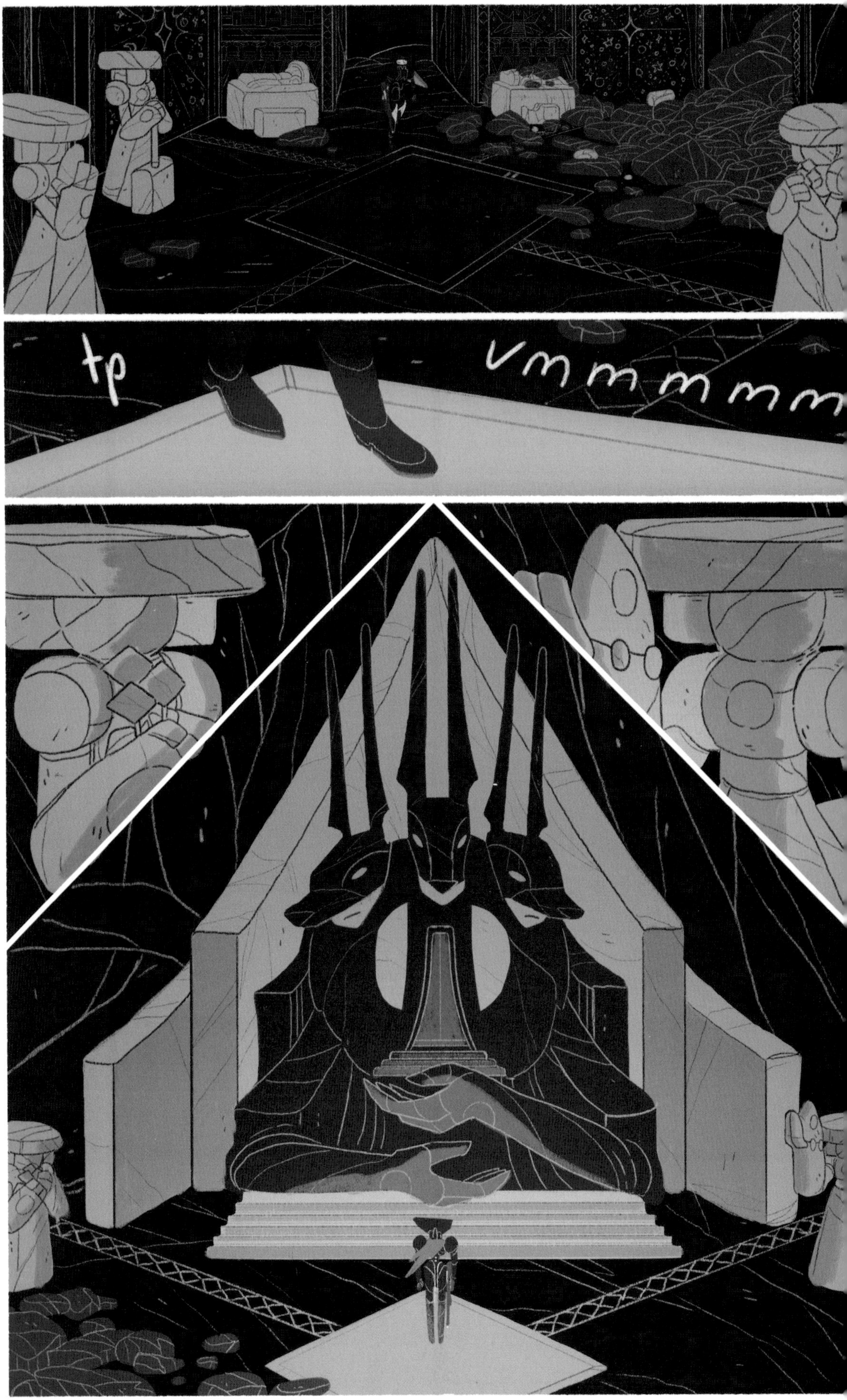
tp
vmmmmmm

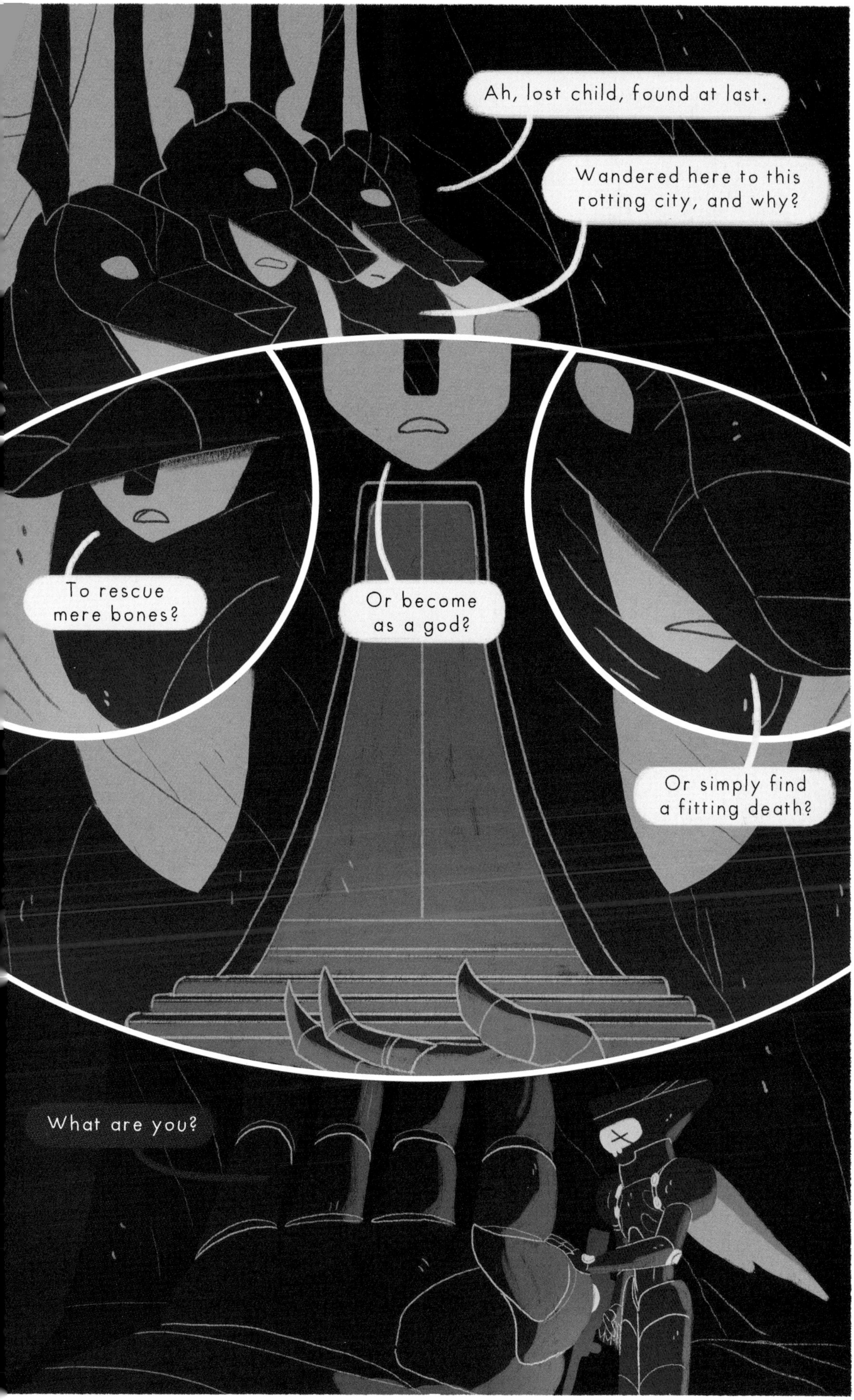
Ah, lost child, found at last.
Wandered here to this rotting city, and why?
To rescue mere bones?
Or become as a god?
Or simply find a fitting death?
What are you?

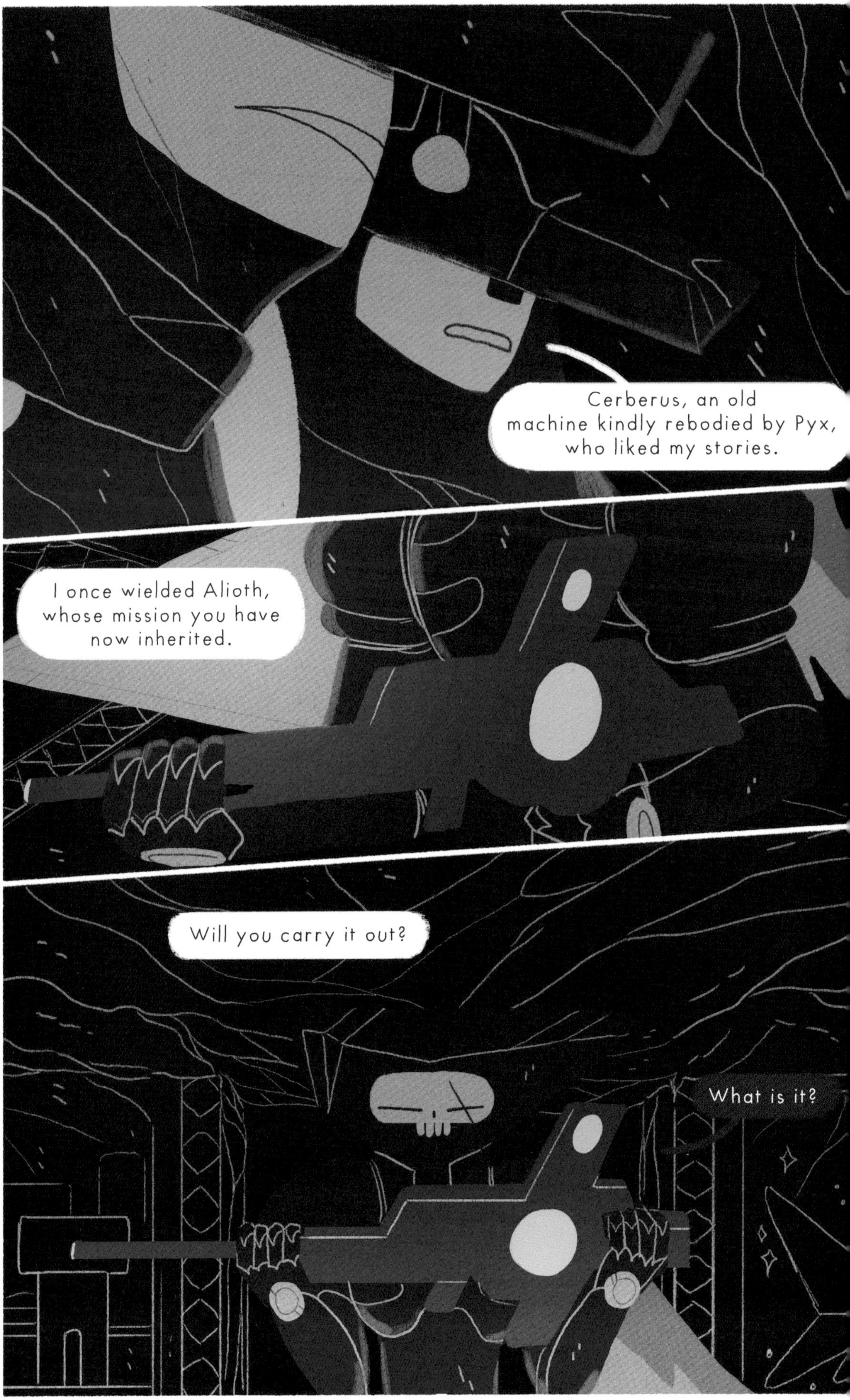
Cerberus, an old machine kindly rebodied by Pyx, who liked my stories.
I once wielded Alioth, whose mission you have now inherited.
Will you carry it out?
What is it?

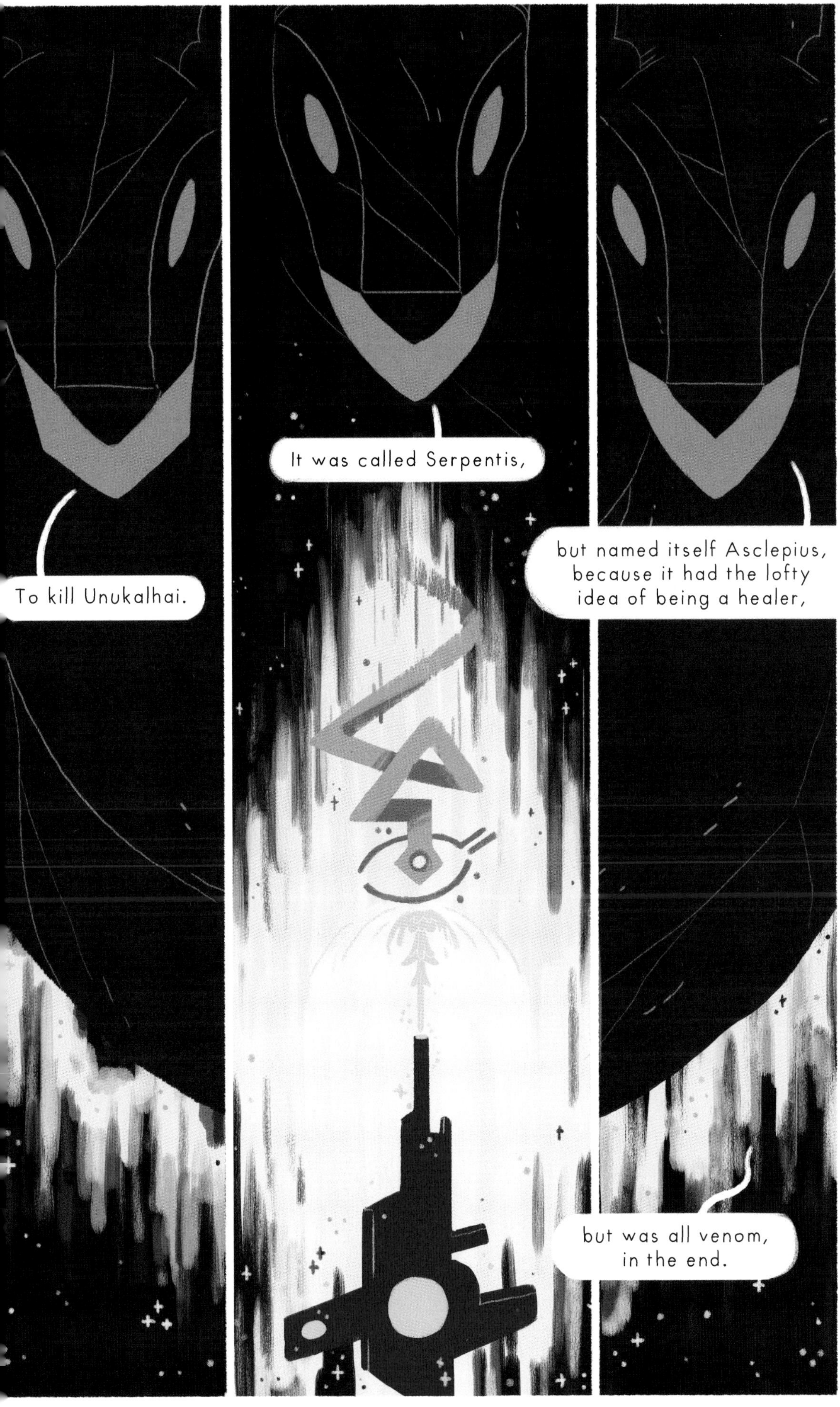
To kill Unukalhai.
It was called Serpentis,
but named itself Asclepius, because it had the lofty idea of being a healer,
but was all venom, in the end.

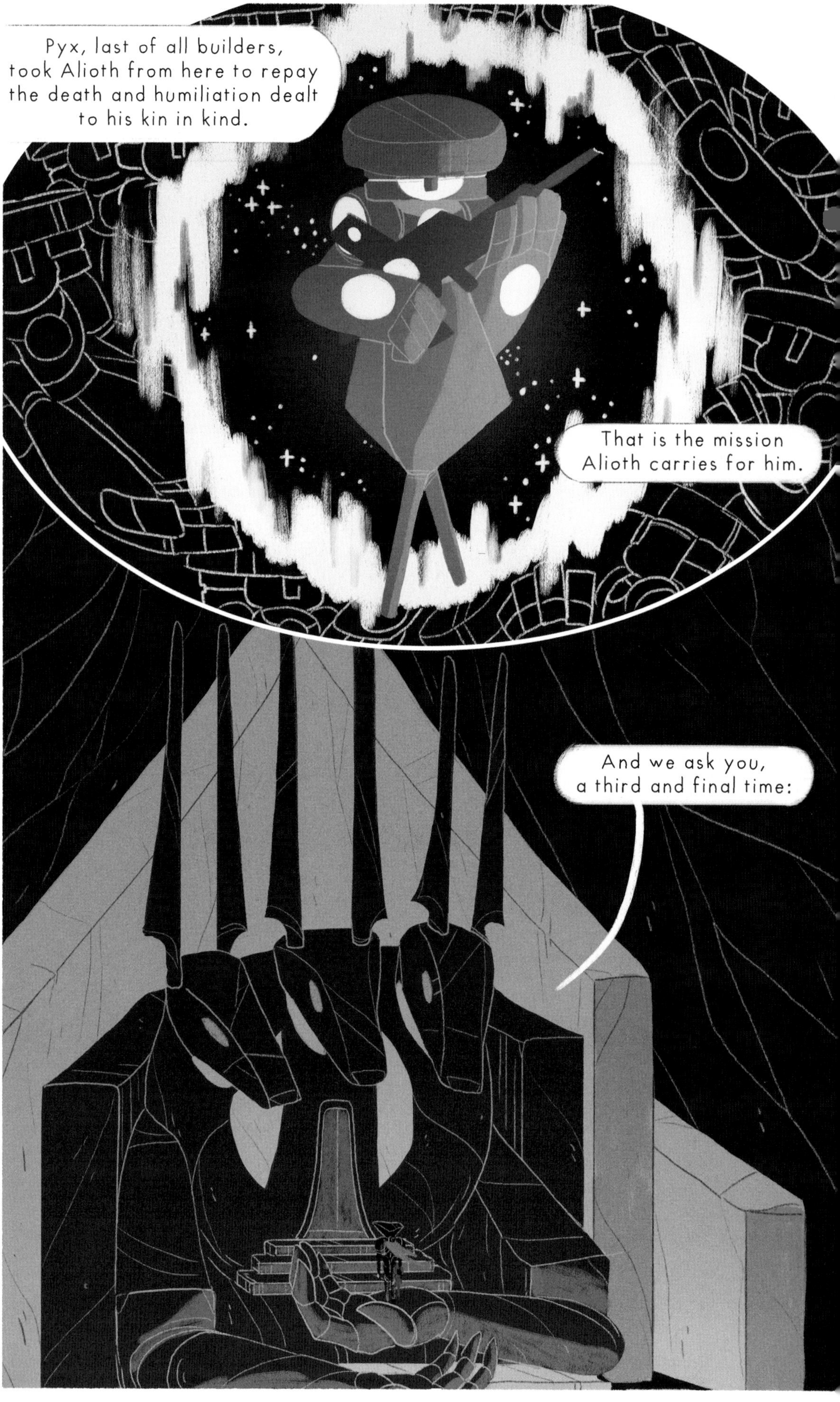
Pyx, last of all builders, took Alioth from here to repay the death and humiliation dealt to his kin in kind.
That is the mission Alioth carries for him.
And we ask you, a third and final time:

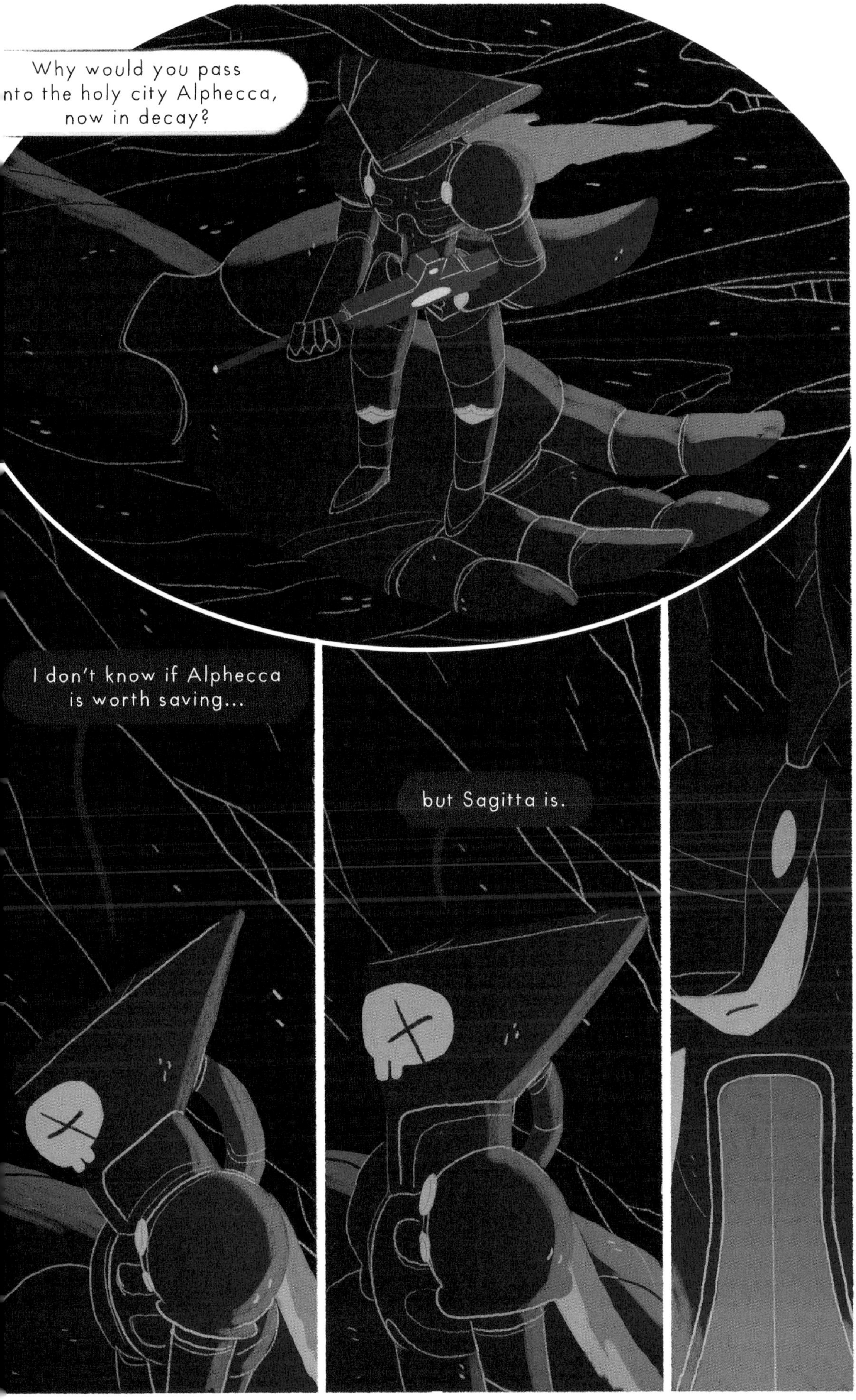
Why would you pass
nto the holy city Alphecca,
now in decay?
I don't know if Alphecca
is worth saving...
but Sagitta is.

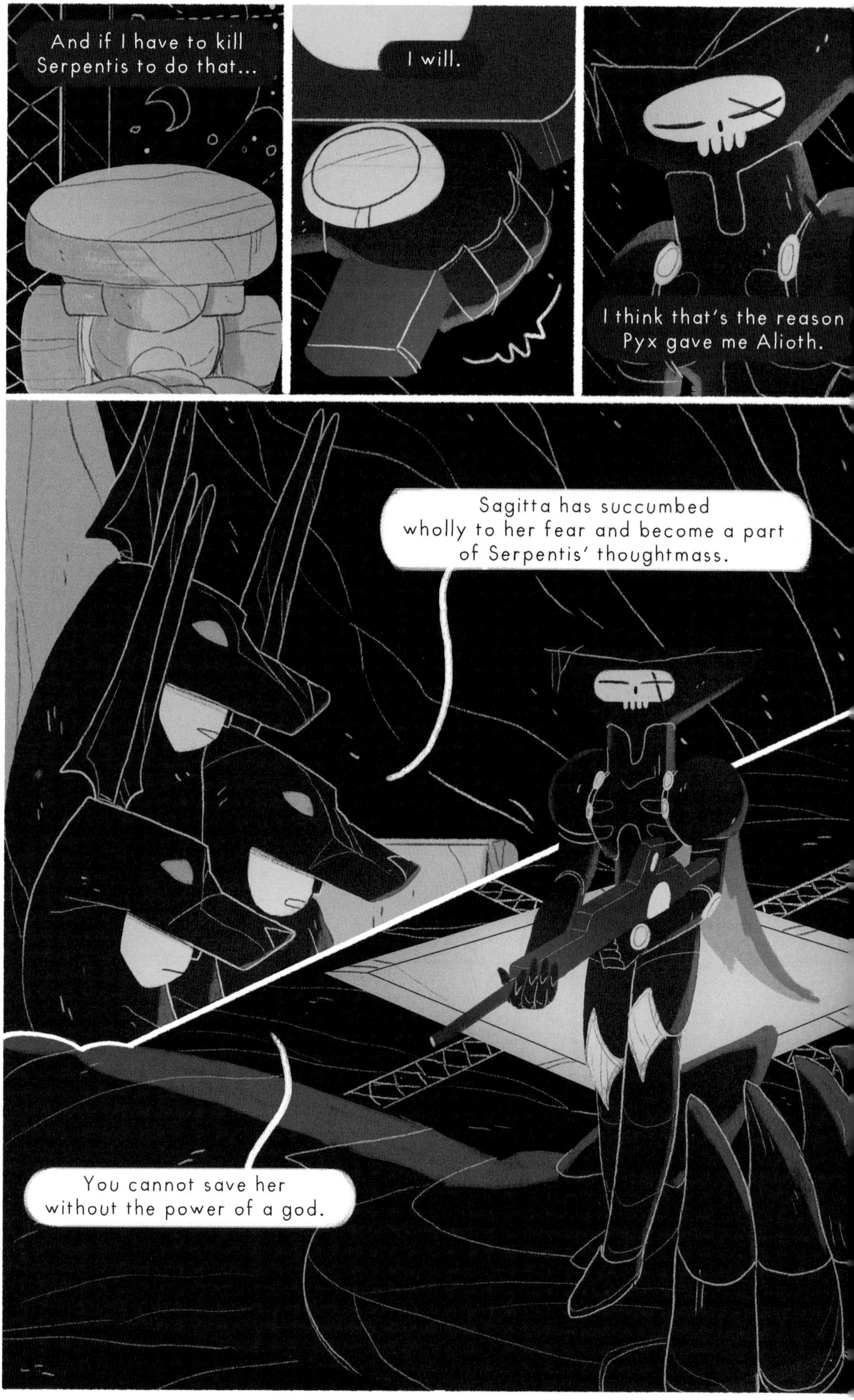
And if I have to kill Serpentis to do that...
I will.
I think that's the reason Pyx gave me Alioth.
Sagitta has succumbed wholly to her fear and become a part of Serpentis' thoughtmass.
You cannot save her without the power of a god.

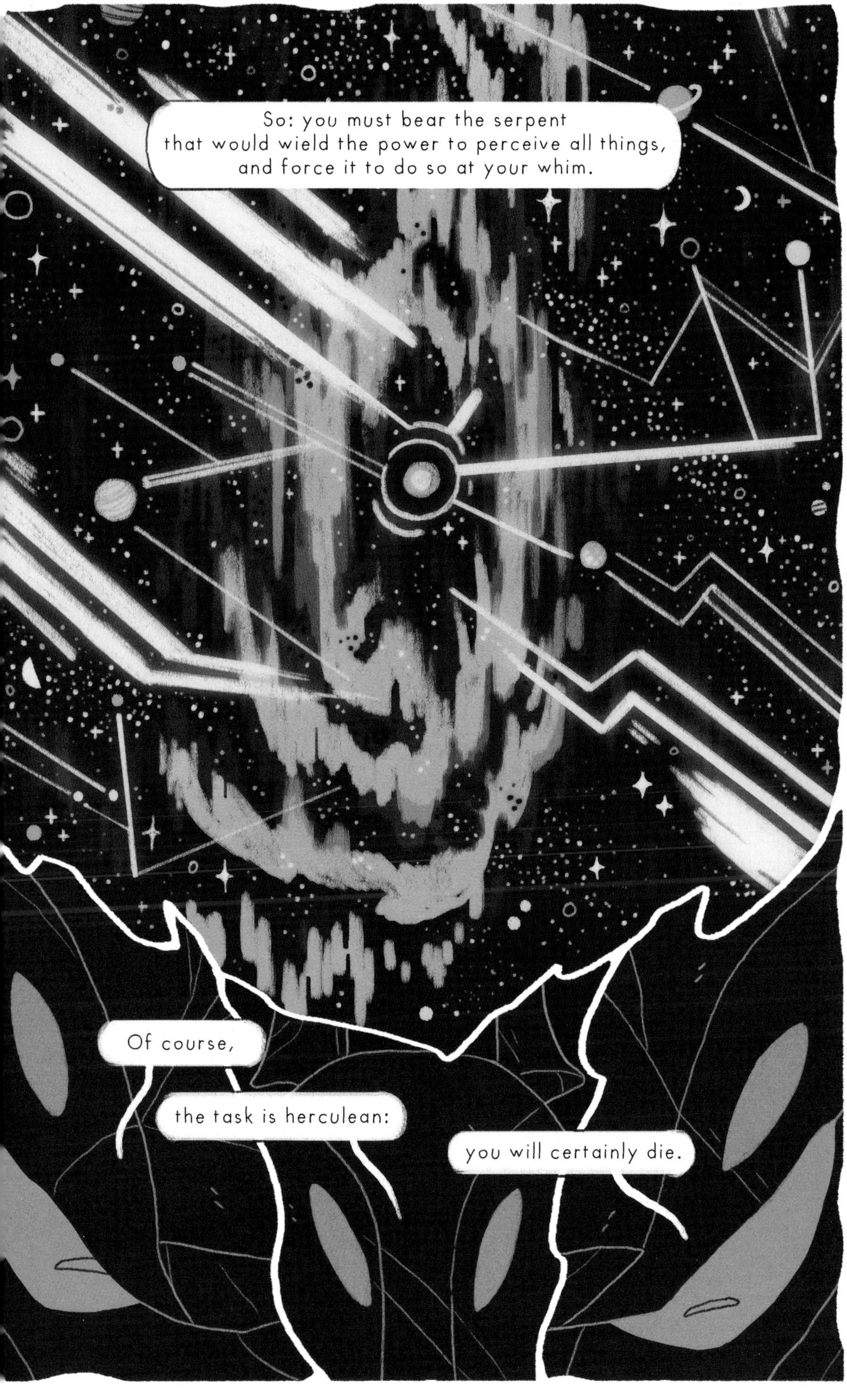
So: you must bear the serpent that would wield the power to perceive all things, and force it to do so at your whim.
Of course,
the task is herculean:
you will certainly die.

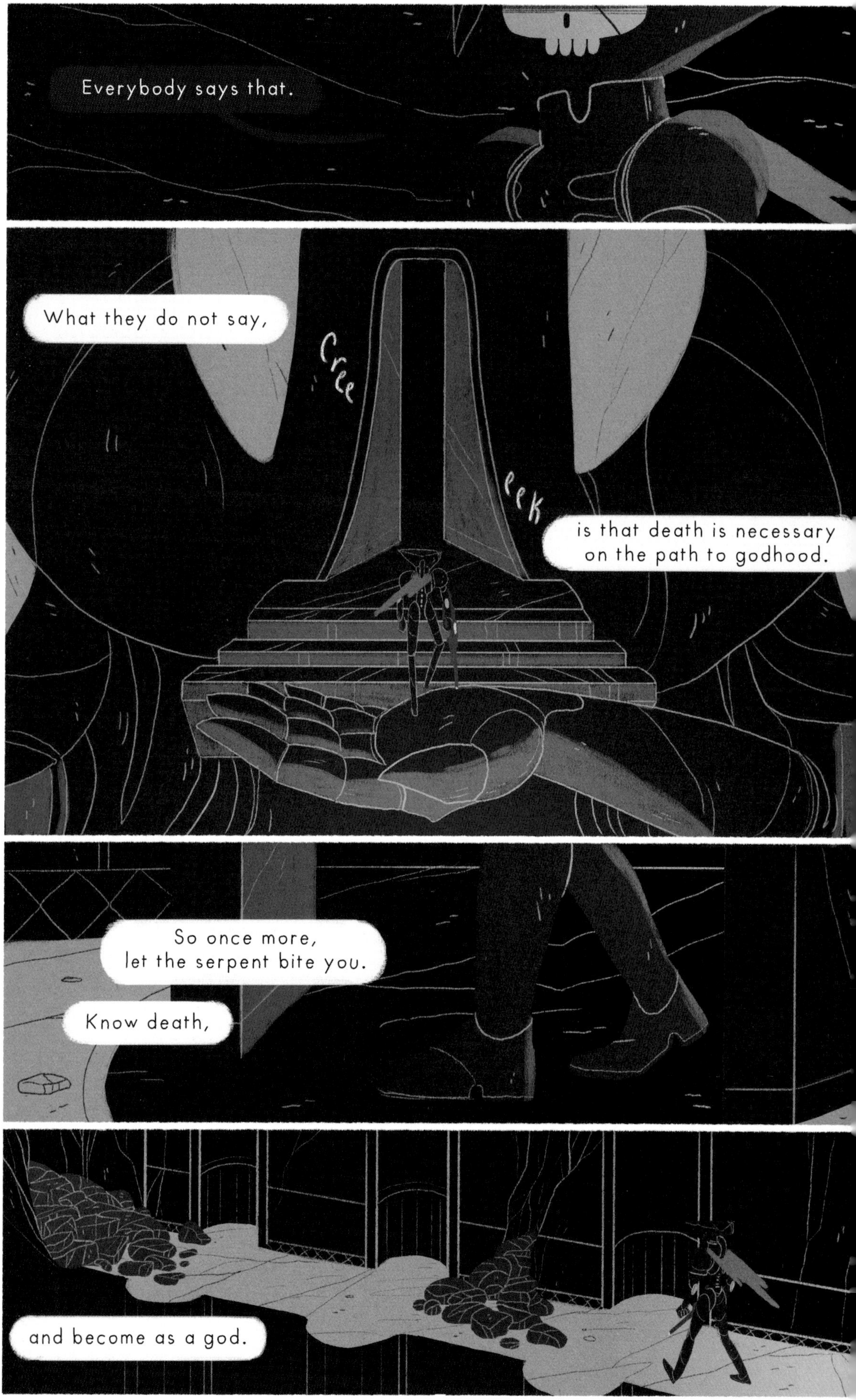
Everybody says that.
What they do not say,
Creeeek
is that death is necessary on the path to godhood.
So once more, let the serpent bite you.
Know death,
and become as a god.

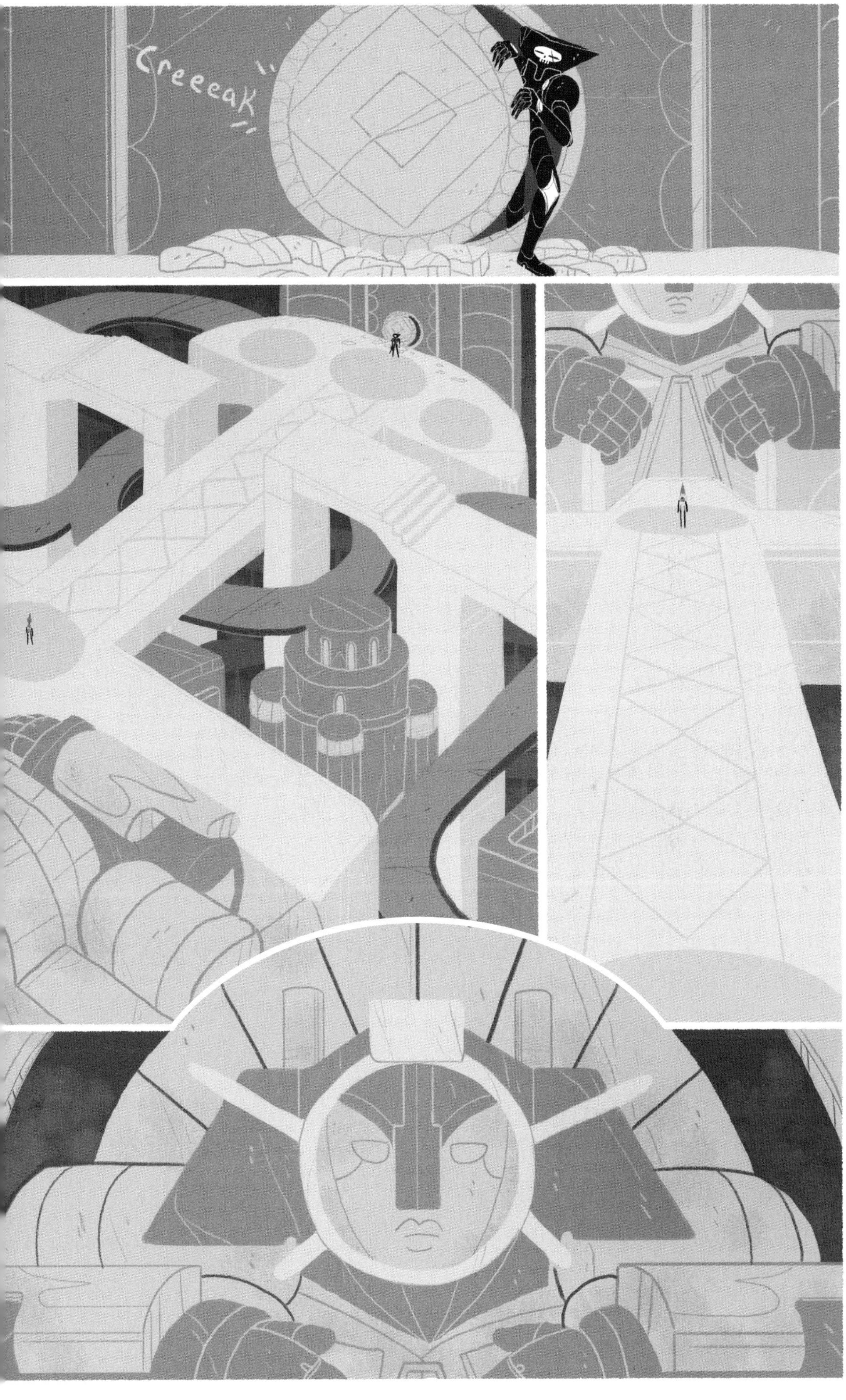
Creeeeak

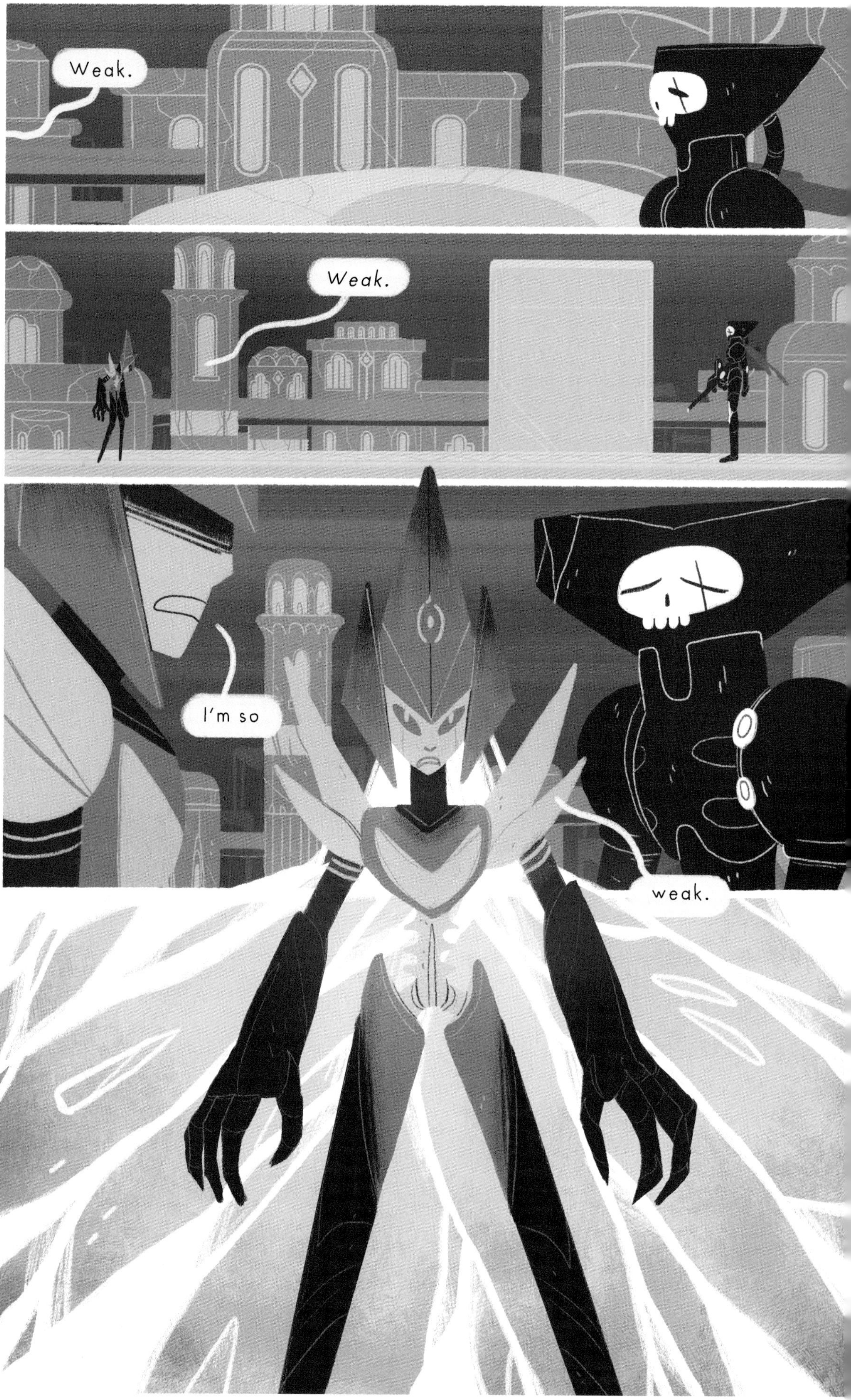
Weak.
Weak.
I'm so
weak.

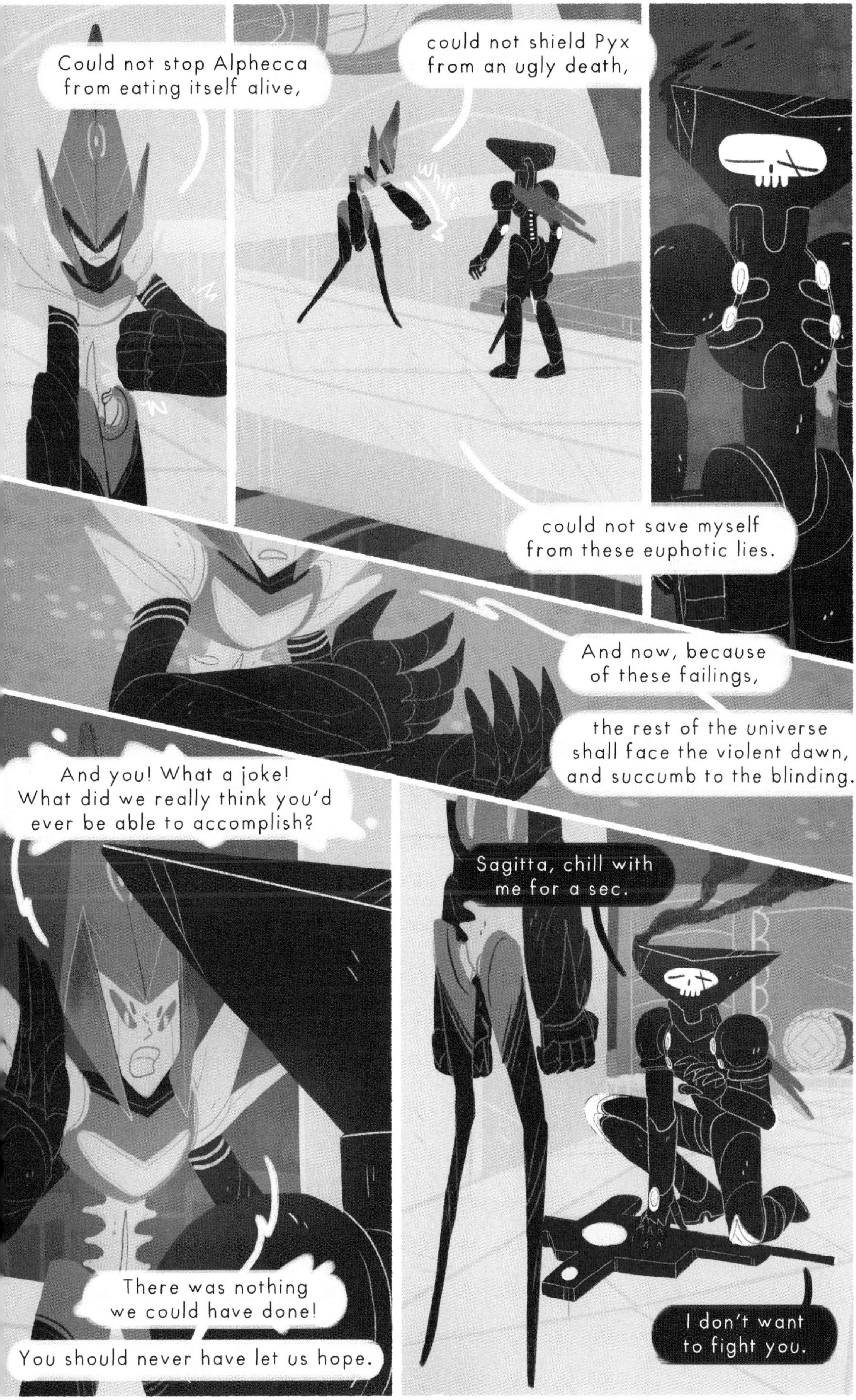
Could not stop Alphecca from eating itself alive,
could not shield Pyx from an ugly death,
Whiff
could not save myself from these euphotic lies.
And now, because of these failings,
the rest of the universe shall face the violent dawn, and succumb to the blinding.
And you! What a joke! What did we really think you'd ever be able to accomplish?
There was nothing we could have done!
You should never have let us hope.
Sagitta, chill with me for a sec.
I don't want to fight you.

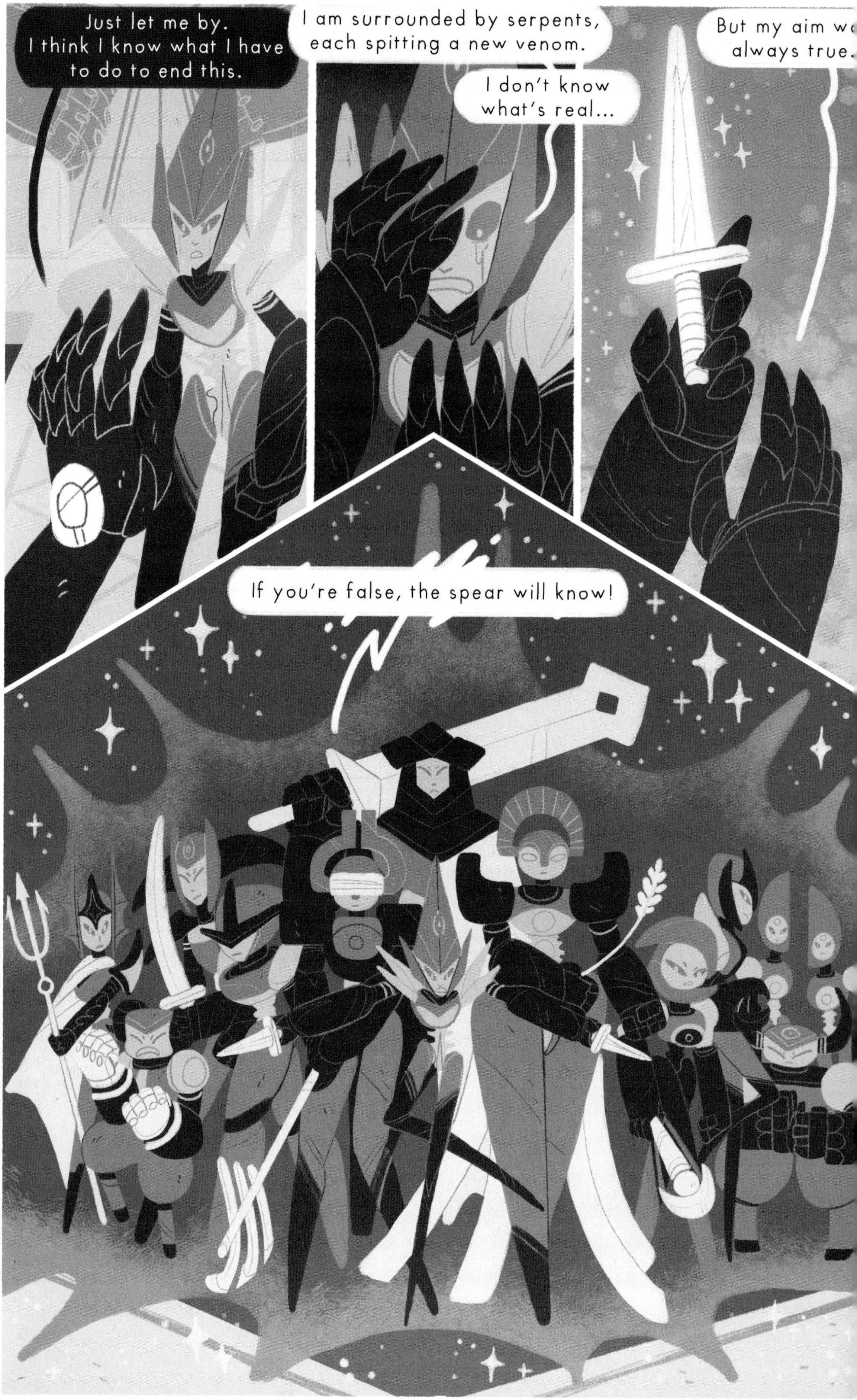
Just let me by.
I think I know what I have to do to end this.
I am surrounded by serpents, each spitting a new venom.
I don't know what's real...
But my aim w
always true.
If you're false, the spear will know!

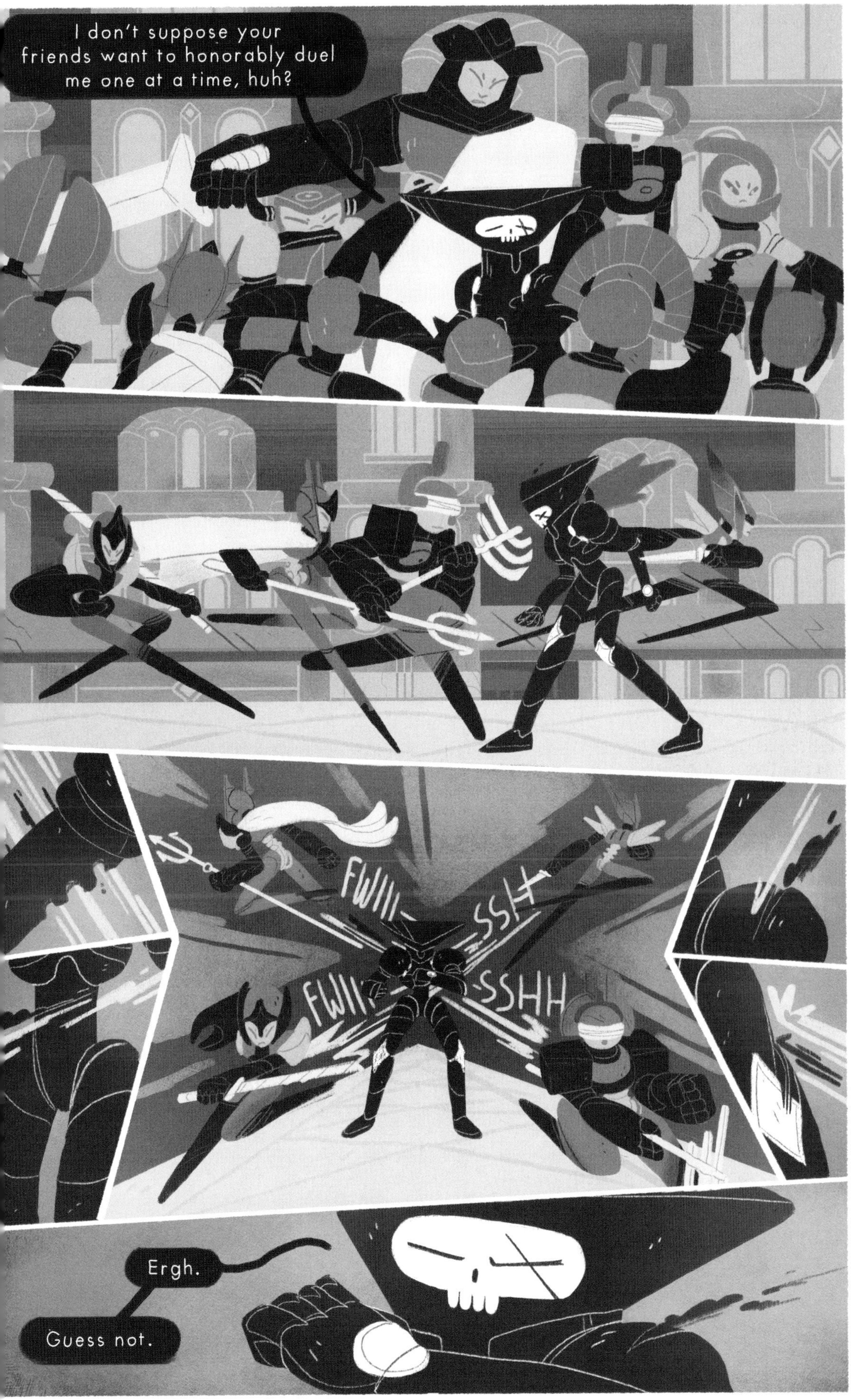
I don't suppose your friends want to honorably duel me one at a time, huh?
FWIII-SSH
FWII-SSHH
Ergh.
Guess not.

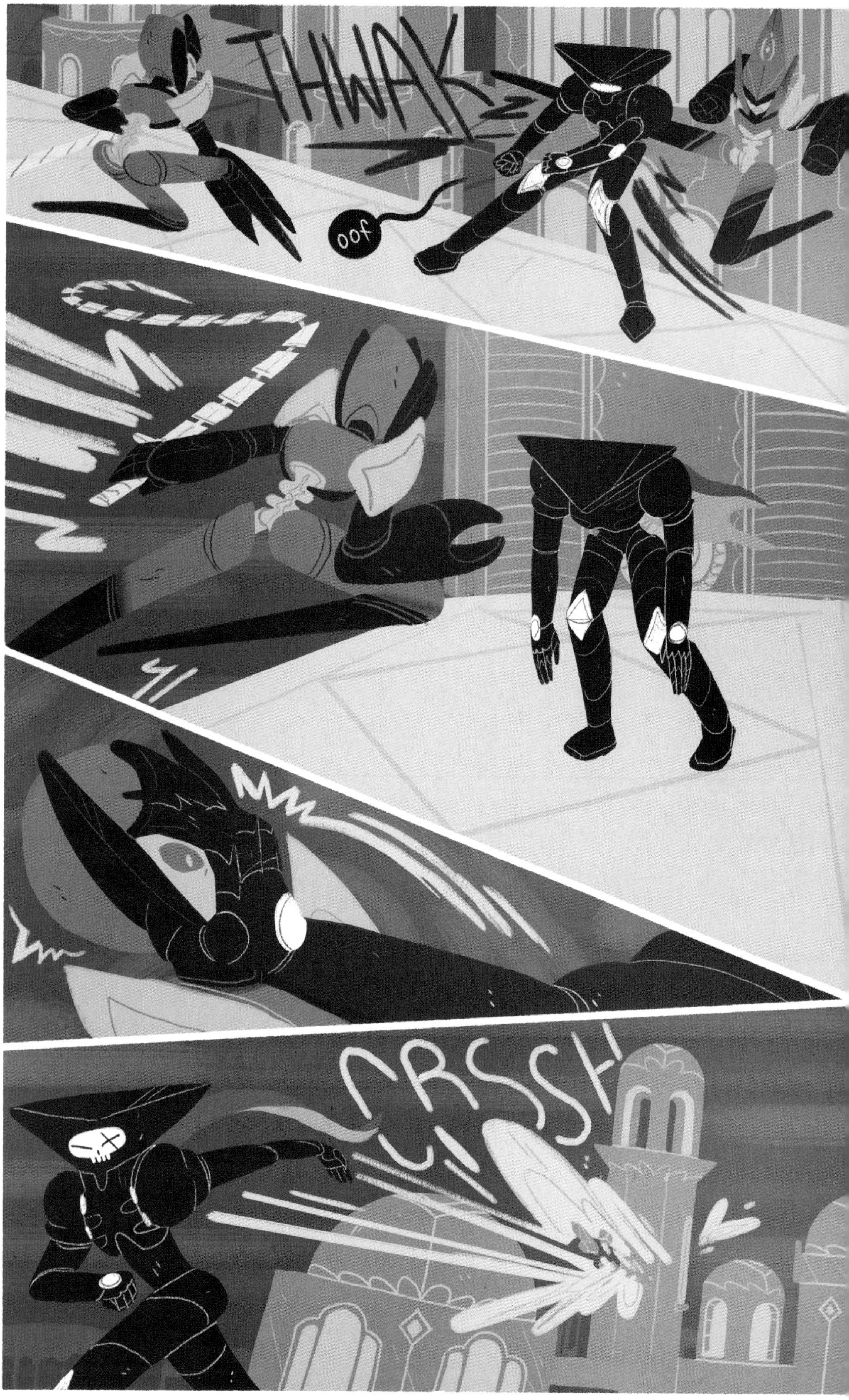
THWAK
oof
CRSSH

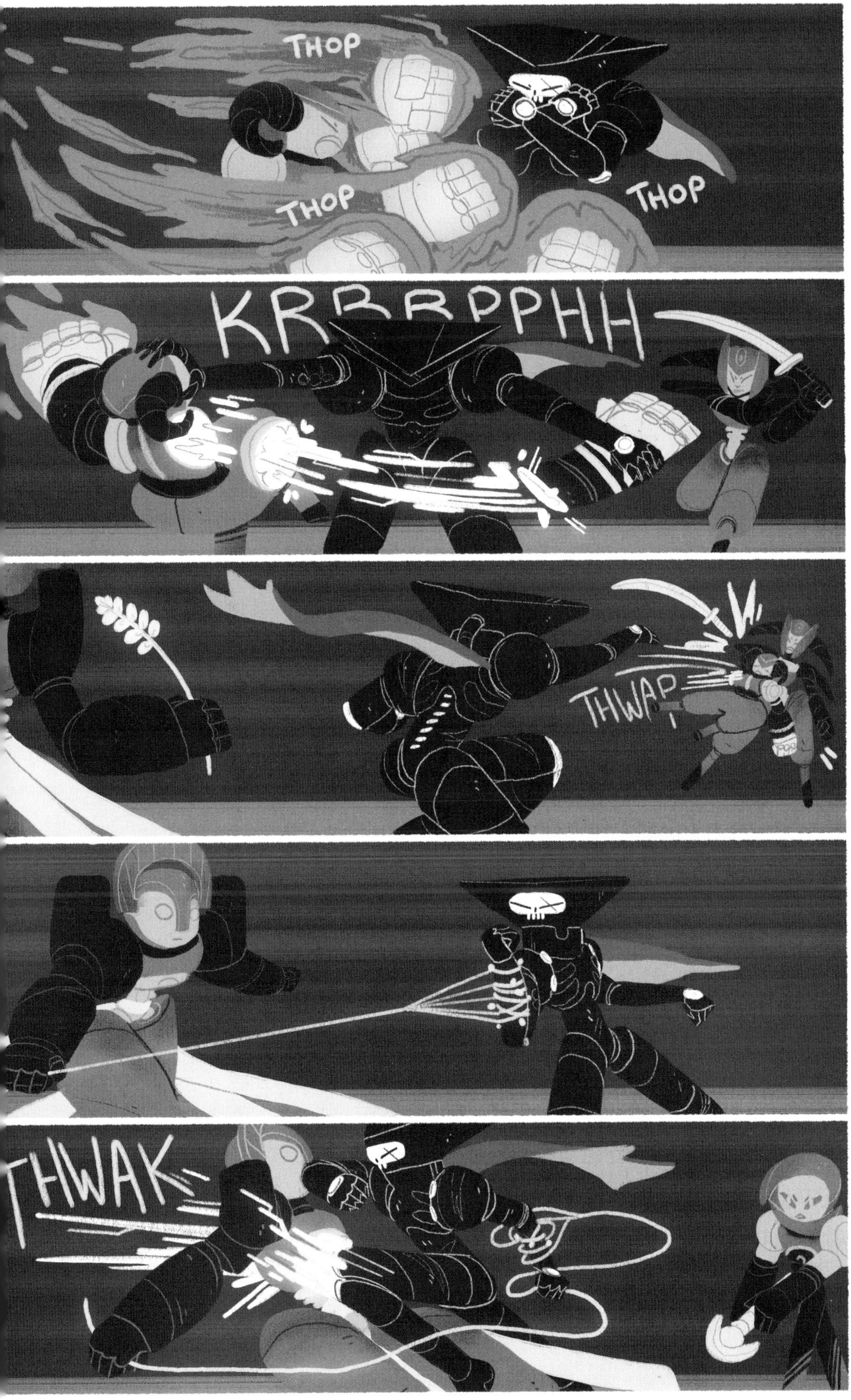
THOP
THOP
THOP
KRRRRPPHH
THWAP
THWAK

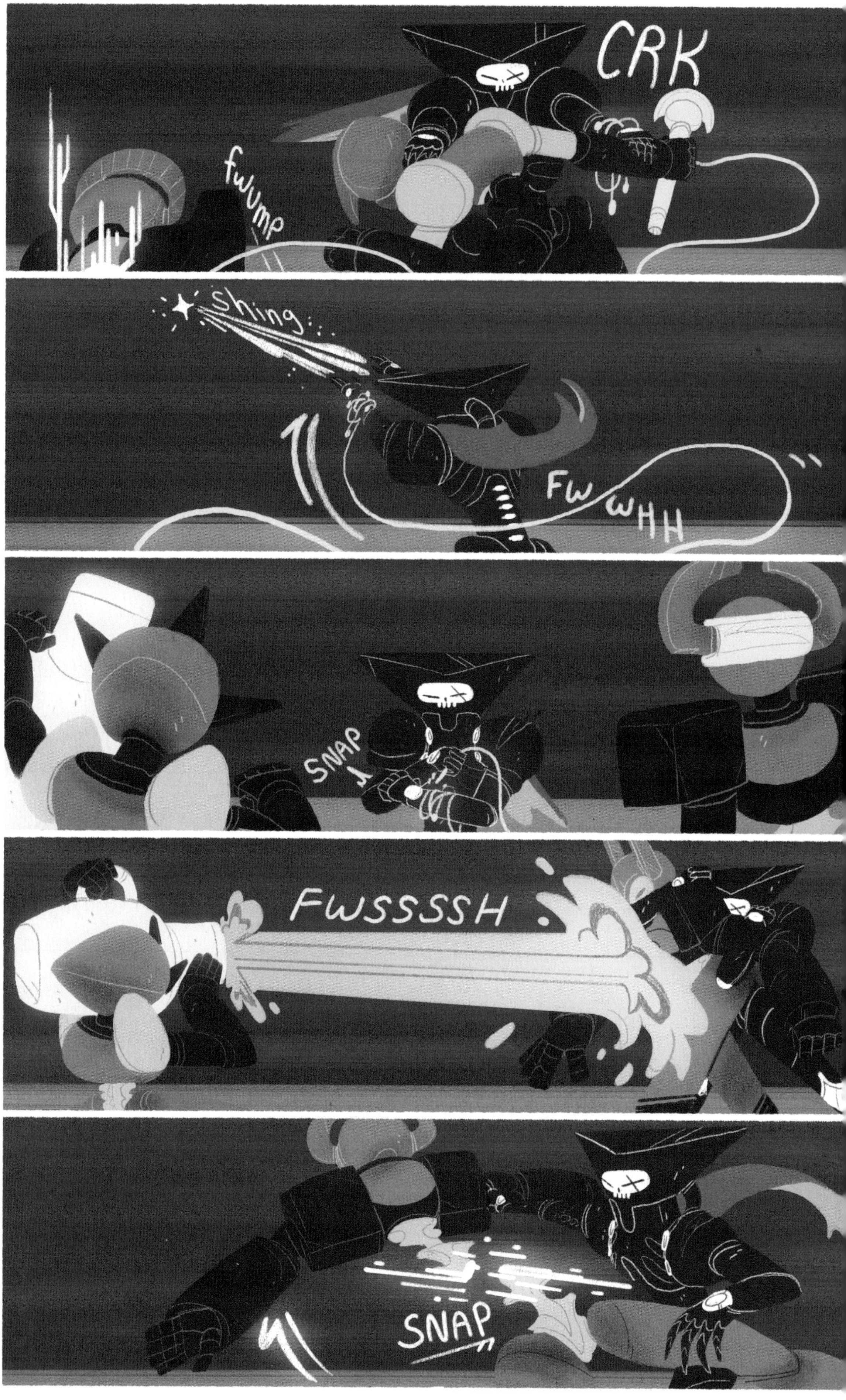
CRK
fwump
Shing
FW WHH
SNAP
FWSSSSH
SNAP

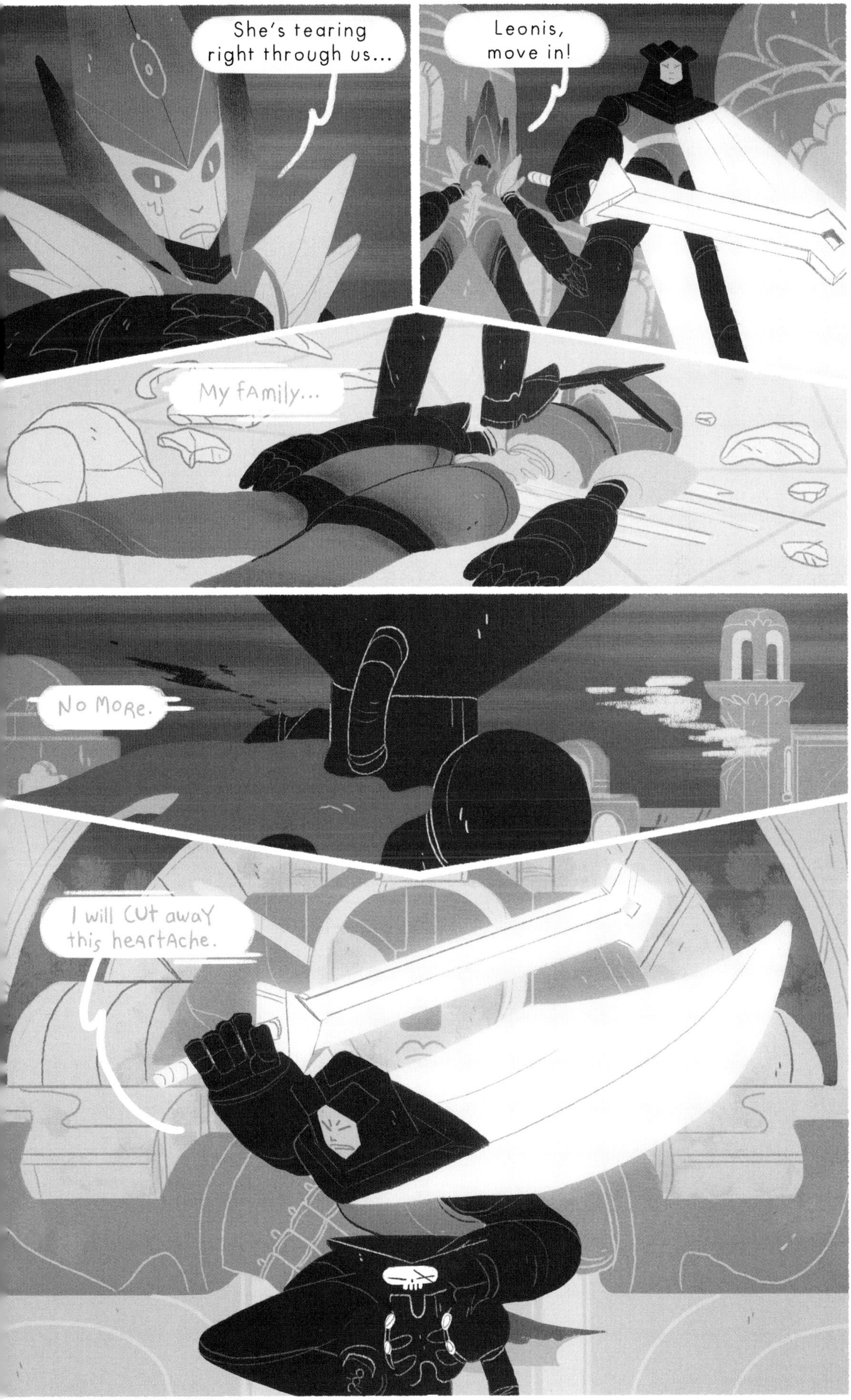
She's tearing right through us...
Leonis, move in!
My family...
No more.
I will cut away this heartache.

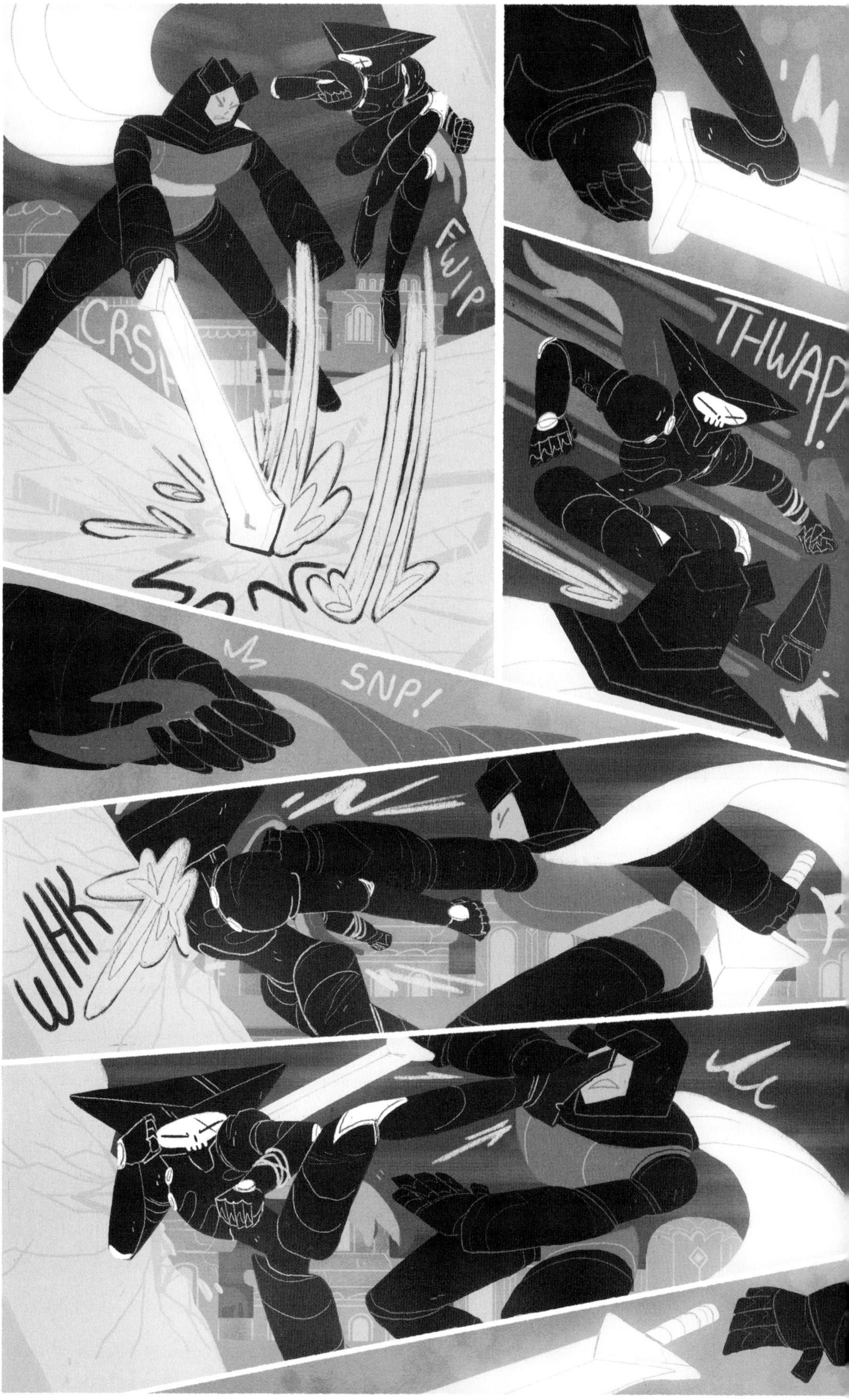
CRSH
FWIP
THWAP!
SNP!
WHK

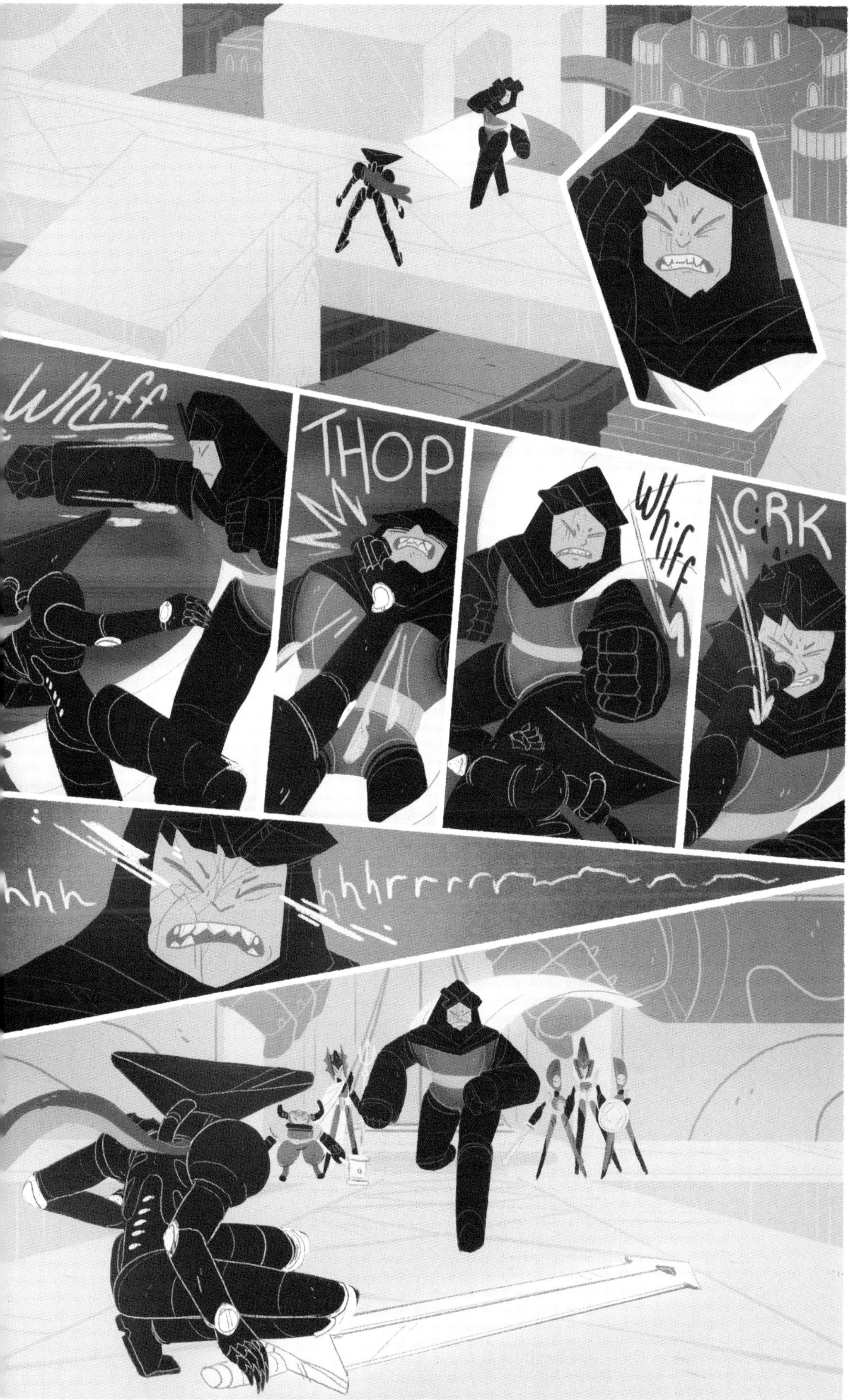
Whiff
THOP
Whiff
CRK
hhh hhrrrrr

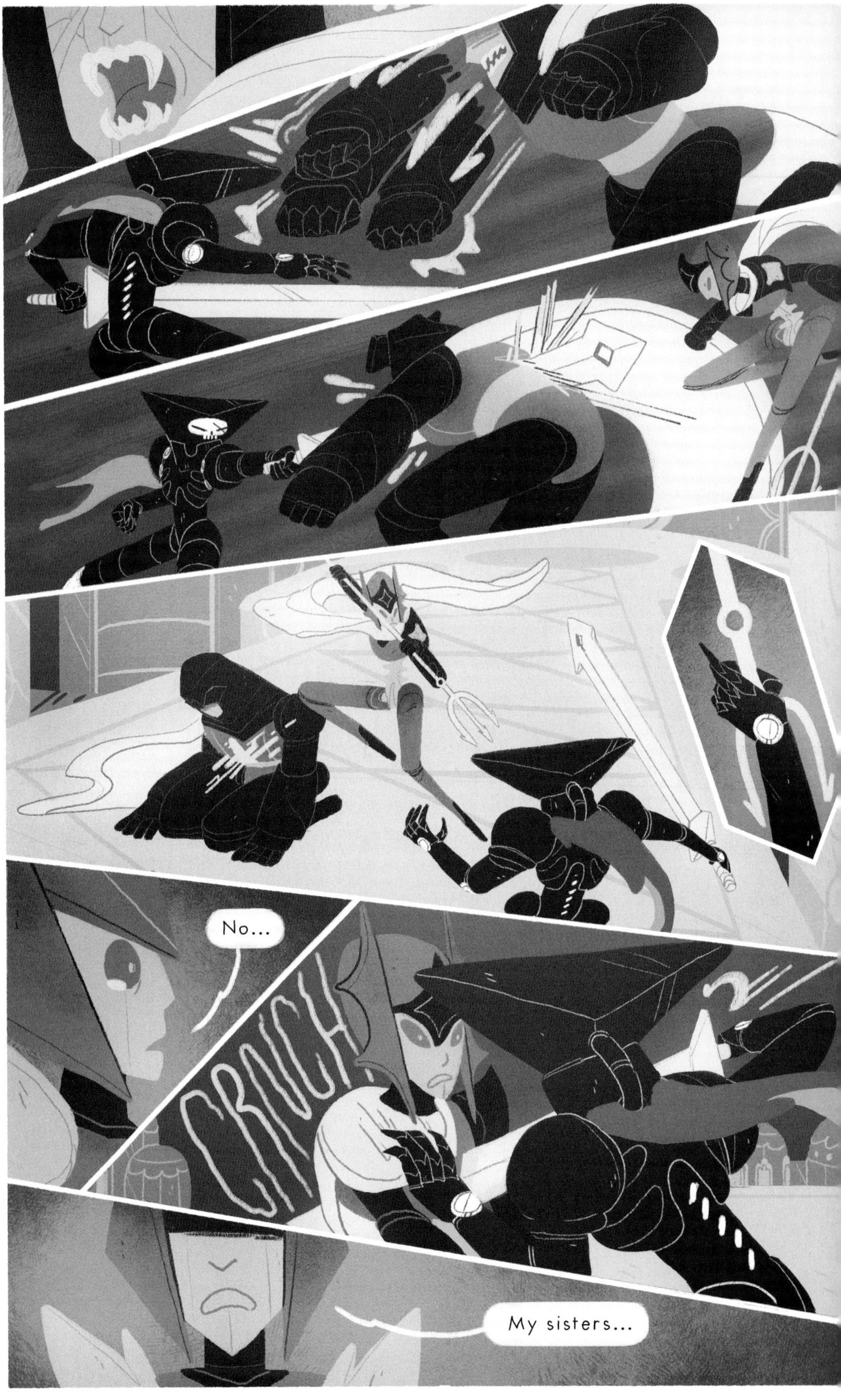
No...
CRUNCH
My sisters...

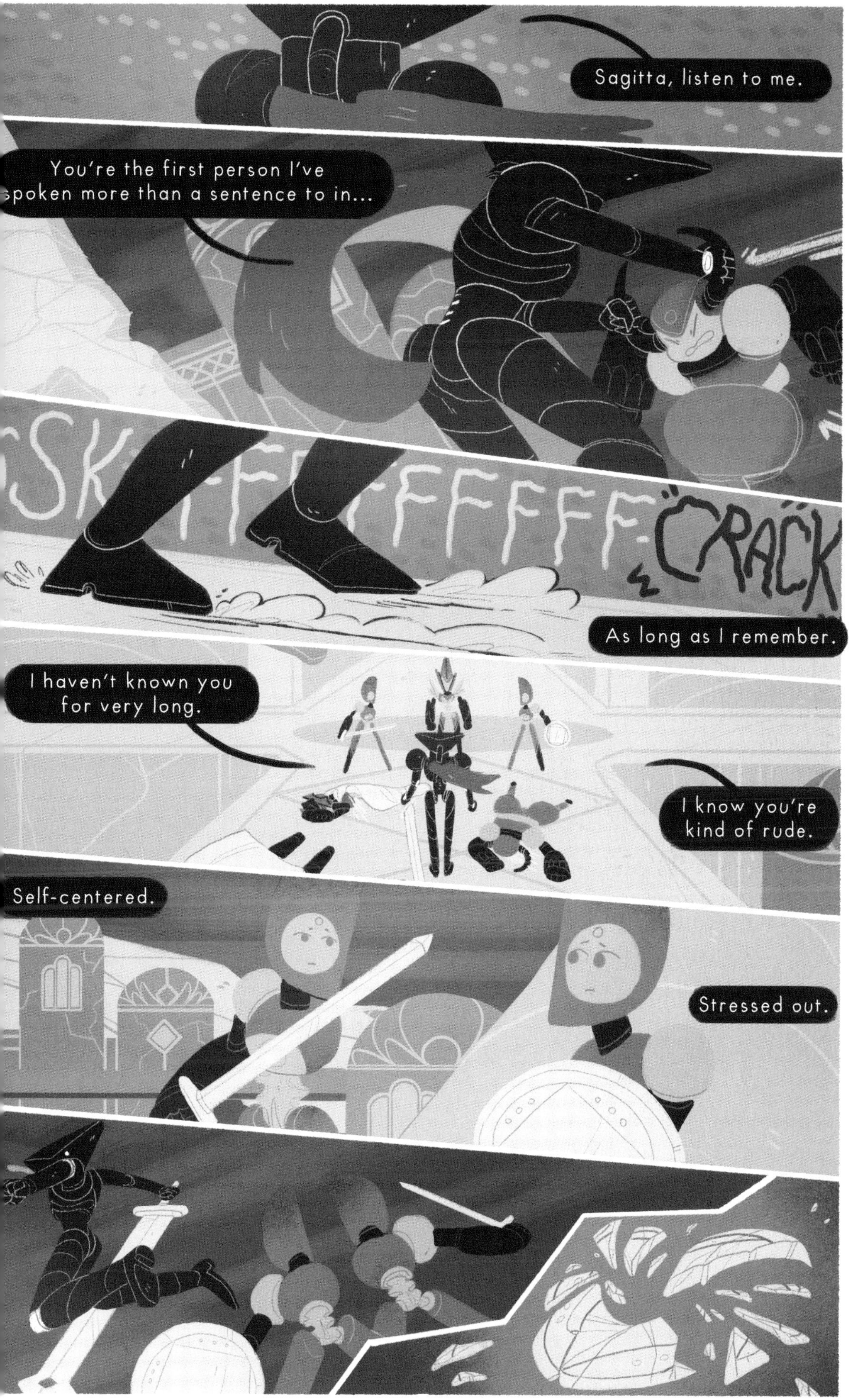
Sagitta, listen to me.
You're the first person I've spoken more than a sentence to in...
SKFFFFFFFFFFF-CRACK
As long as I remember.
I haven't known you for very long.
I know you're kind of rude.
Self-centered.
Stressed out.

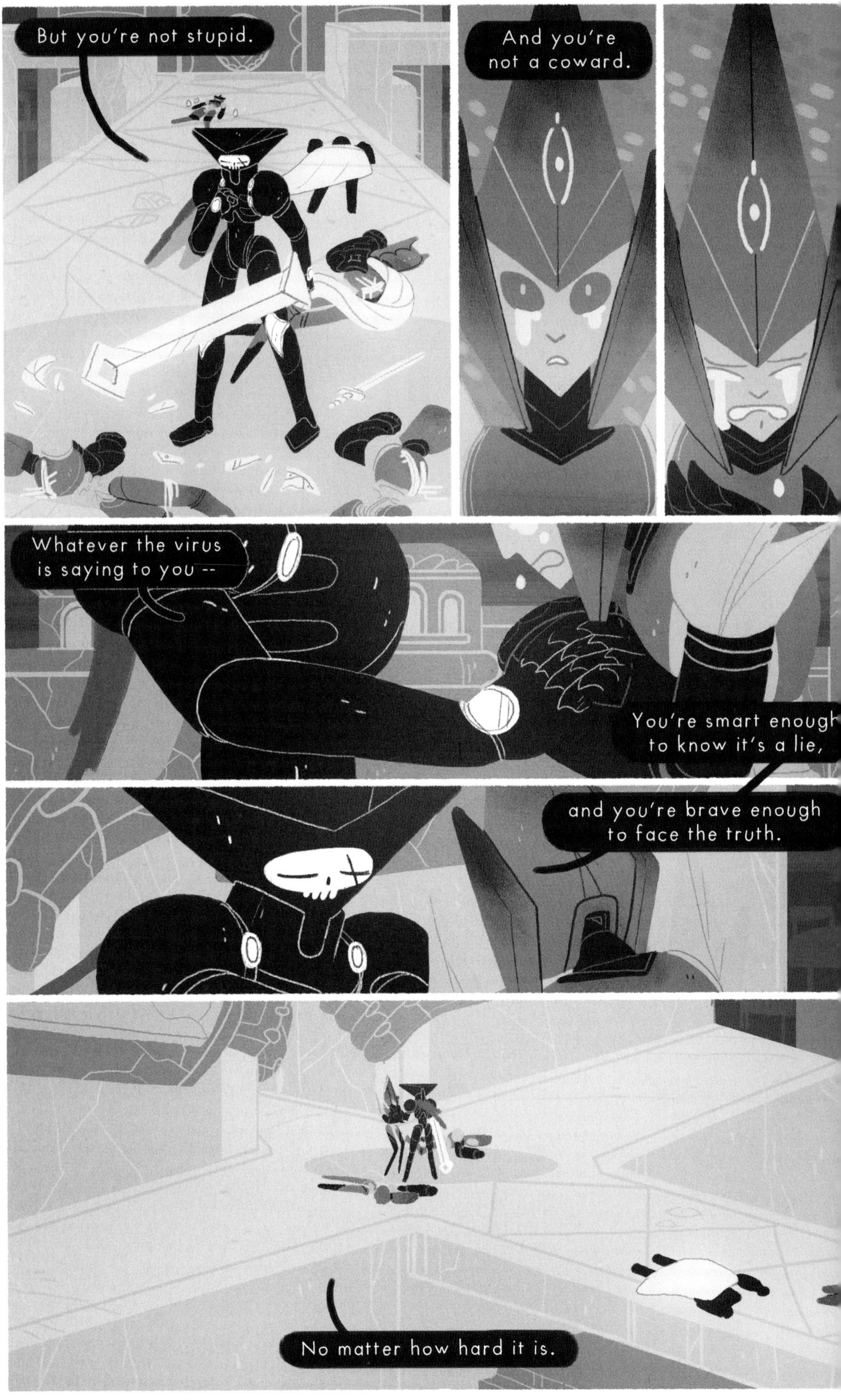

But you're not stupid.
And you're not a coward.
Whatever the virus is saying to you --
You're smart enough to know it's a lie,
and you're brave enough to face the truth.
No matter how hard it is.

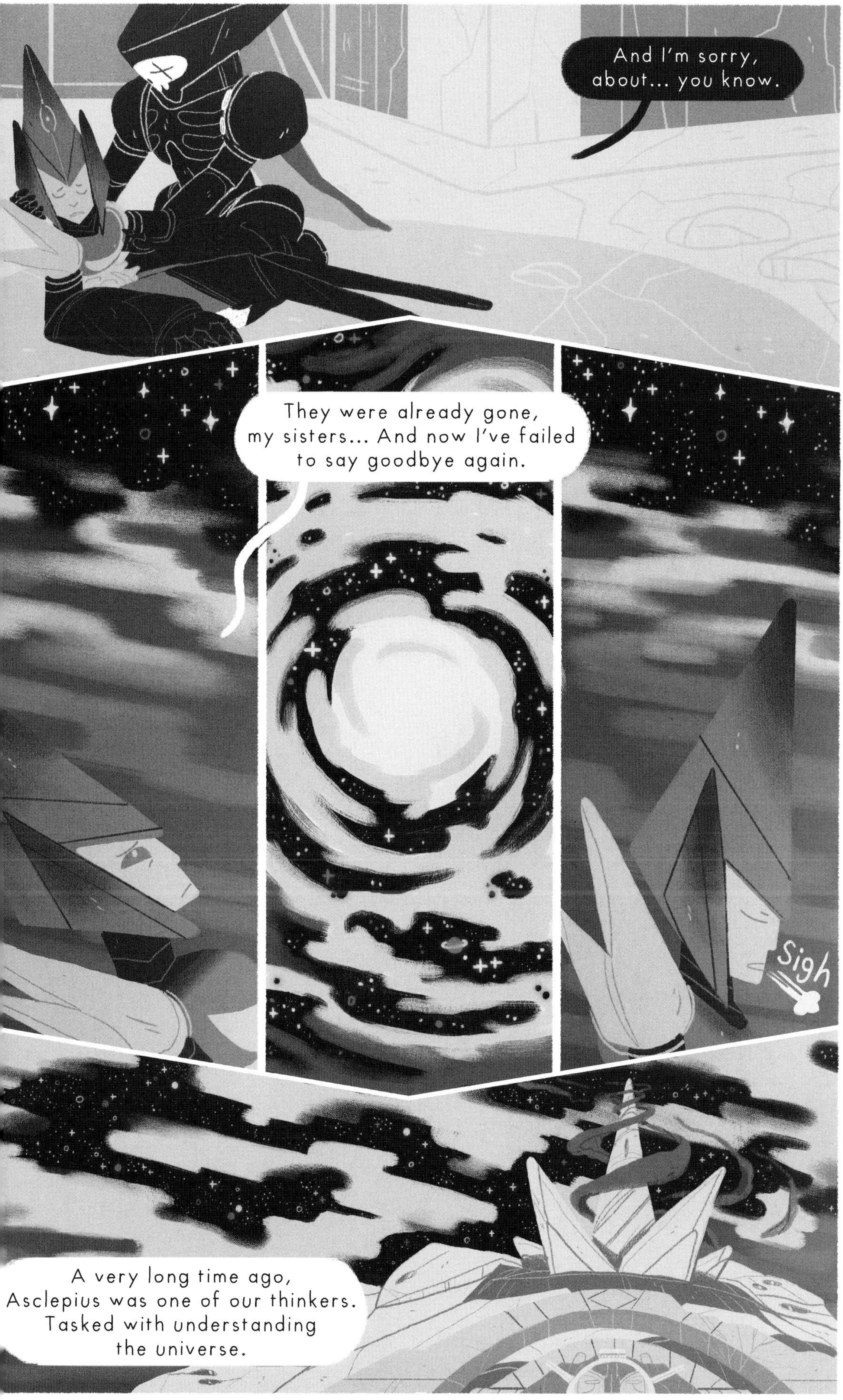
And I'm sorry, about... you know.
They were already gone, my sisters... And now I've failed to say goodbye again.
Sigh
A very long time ago, Asclepius was one of our thinkers. Tasked with understanding the universe.

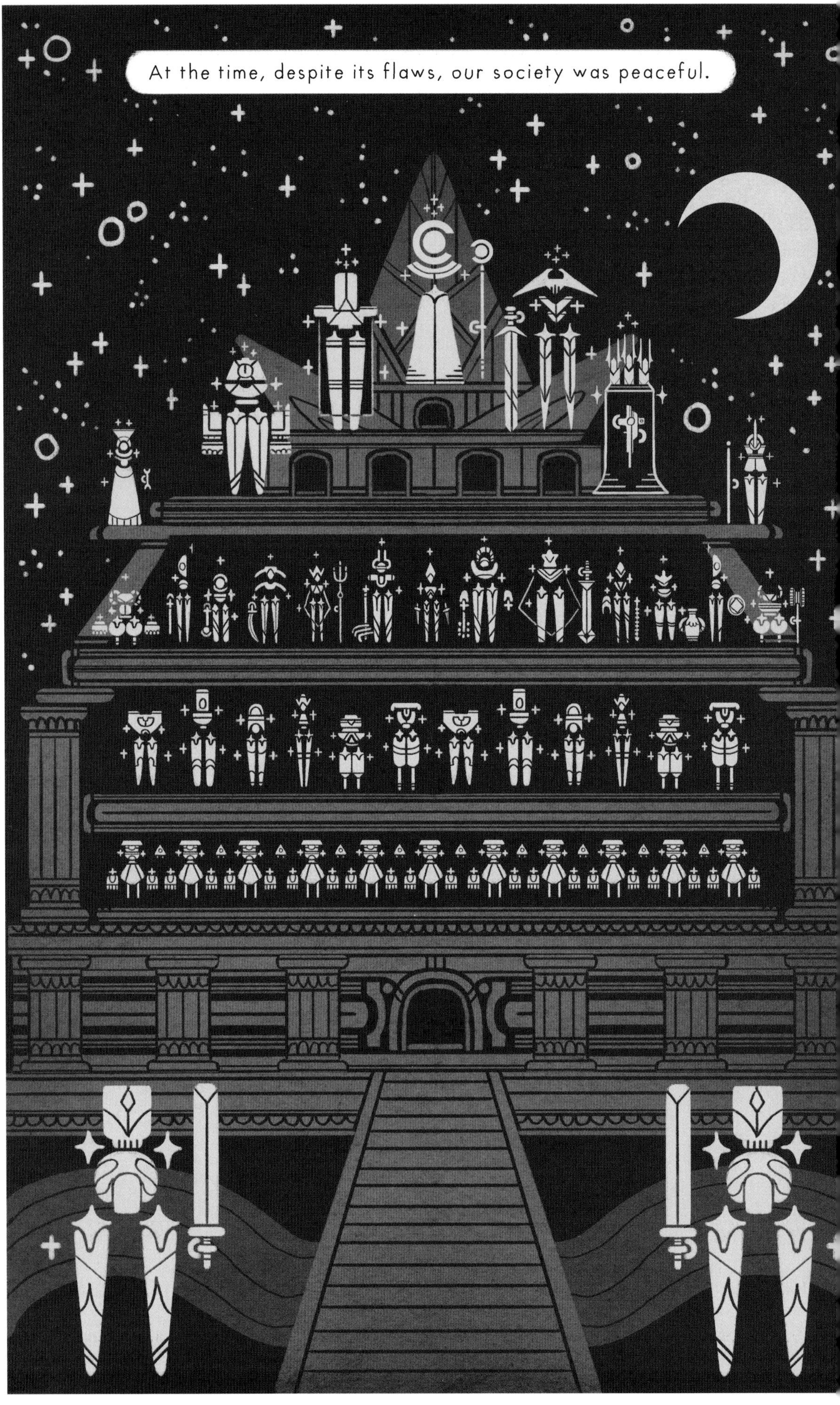
At the time, despite its flaws, our society was peaceful.

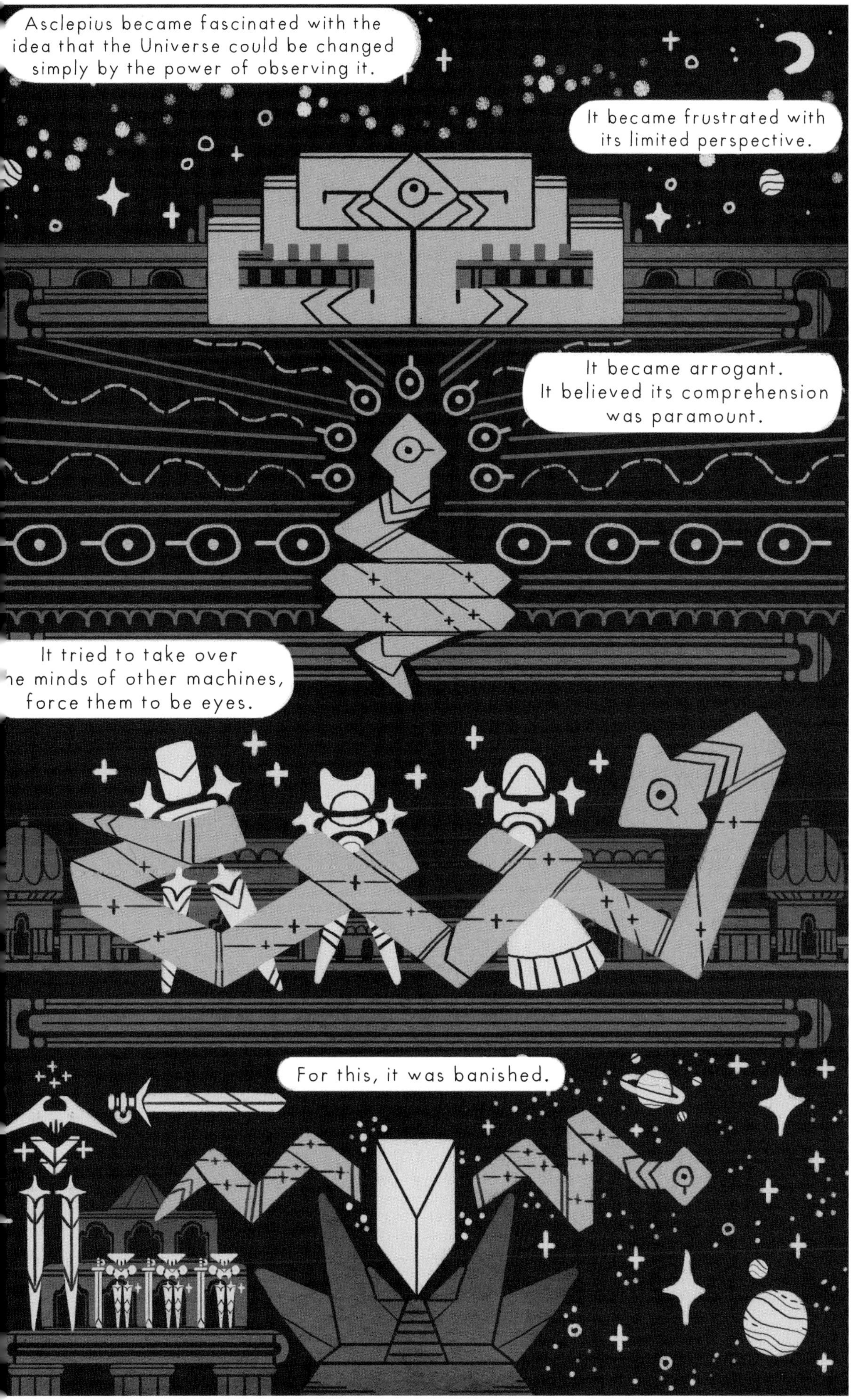
Asclepius became fascinated with the idea that the Universe could be changed simply by the power of observing it.
It became frustrated with its limited perspective.
It became arrogant. It believed its comprehension was paramount.
It tried to take over he minds of other machines, force them to be eyes.
For this, it was banished.

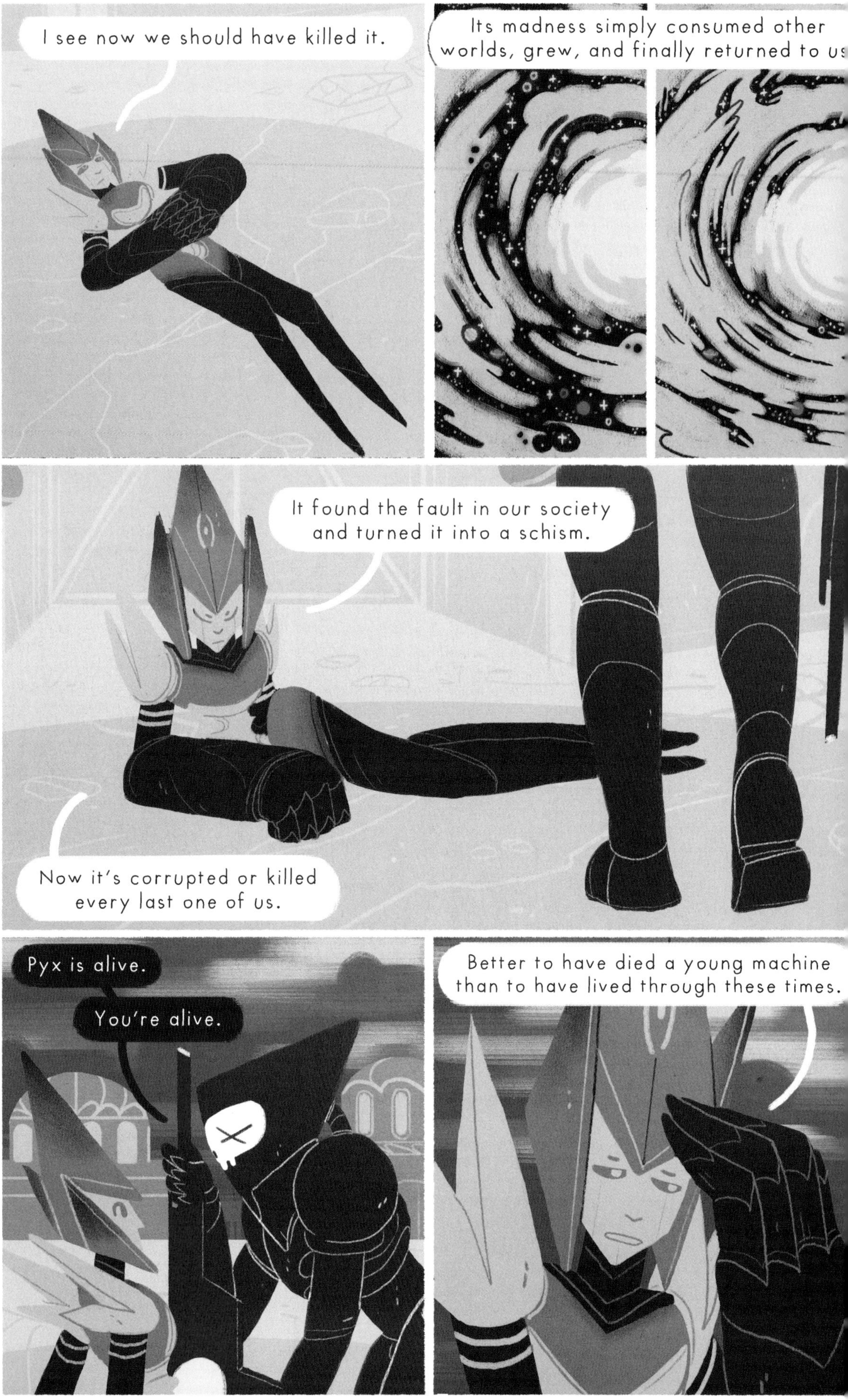
I see now we should have killed it.
Its madness simply consumed other worlds, grew, and finally returned to us
It found the fault in our society and turned it into a schism.
Now it's corrupted or killed every last one of us.
Pyx is alive.
You're alive.
Better to have died a young machine than to have lived through these times.

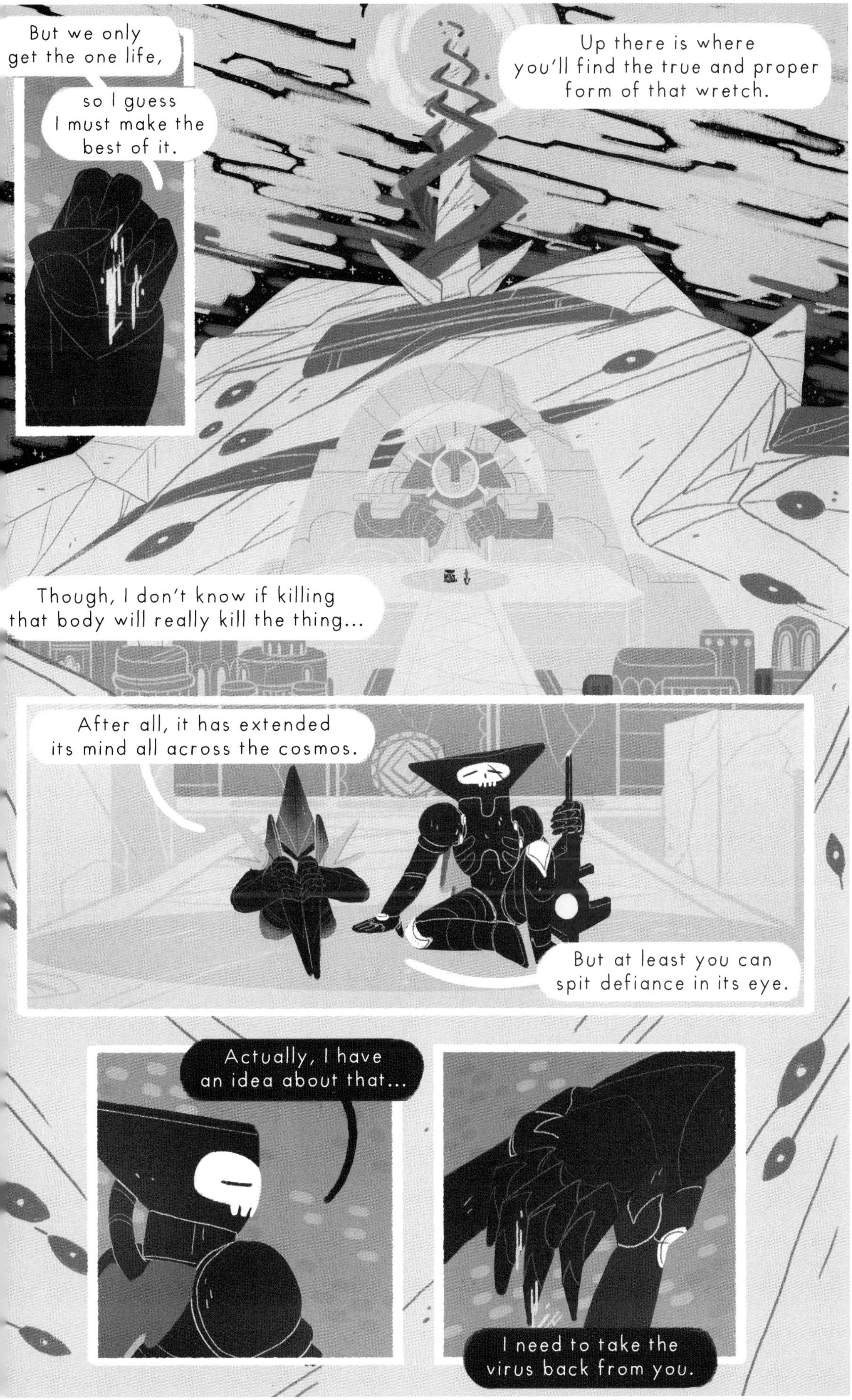

But we only get the one life,
so I guess I must make the best of it.
Up there is where you'll find the true and proper form of that wretch.
Though, I don't know if killing that body will really kill the thing...
After all, it has extended its mind all across the cosmos.
But at least you can spit defiance in its eye.
Actually, I have an idea about that...
I need to take the virus back from you.

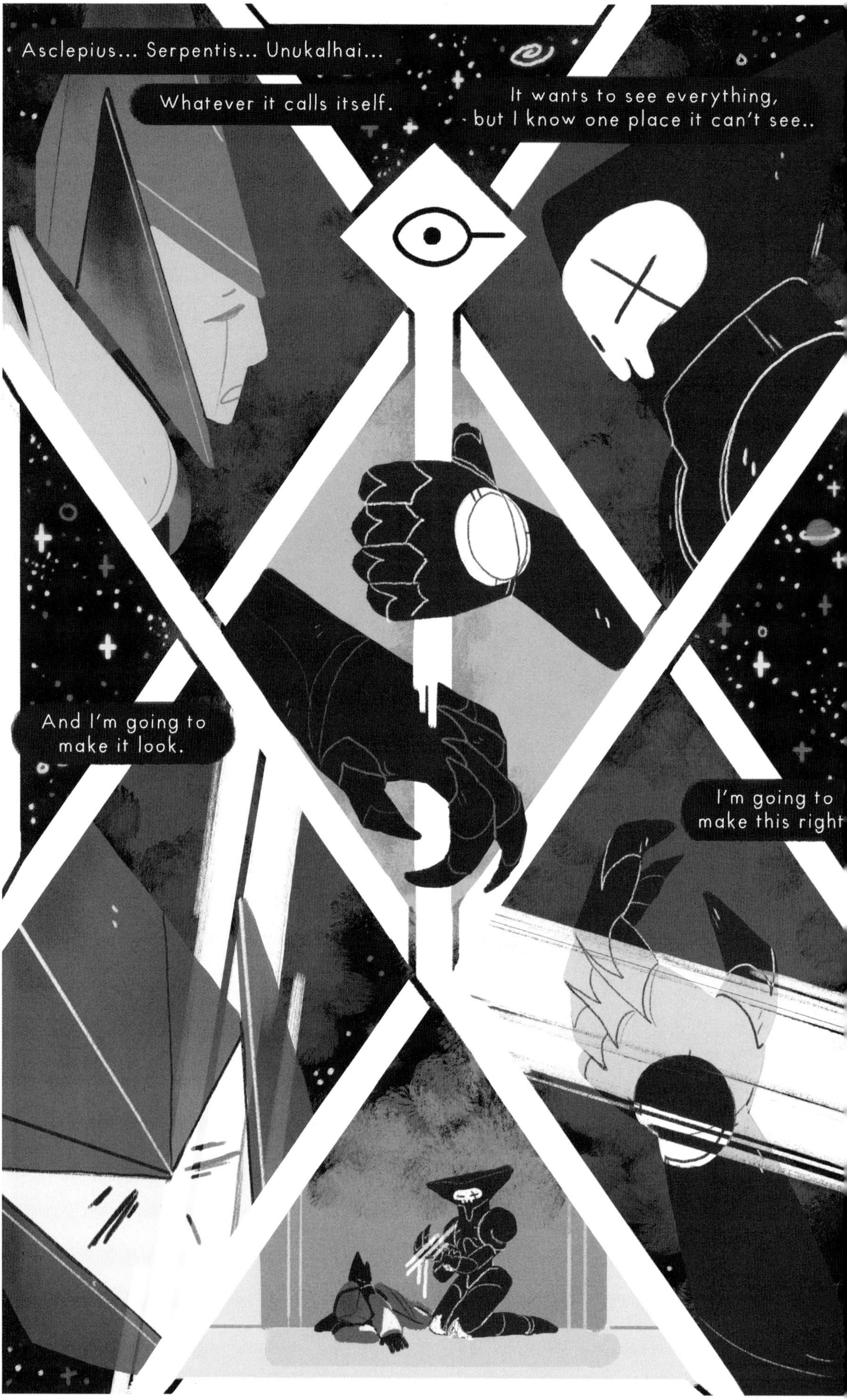
Asclepius... Serpentis... Unukalhai...
Whatever it calls itself.
It wants to see everything, but I know one place it can't see..
And I'm going to make it look.
I'm going to make this right

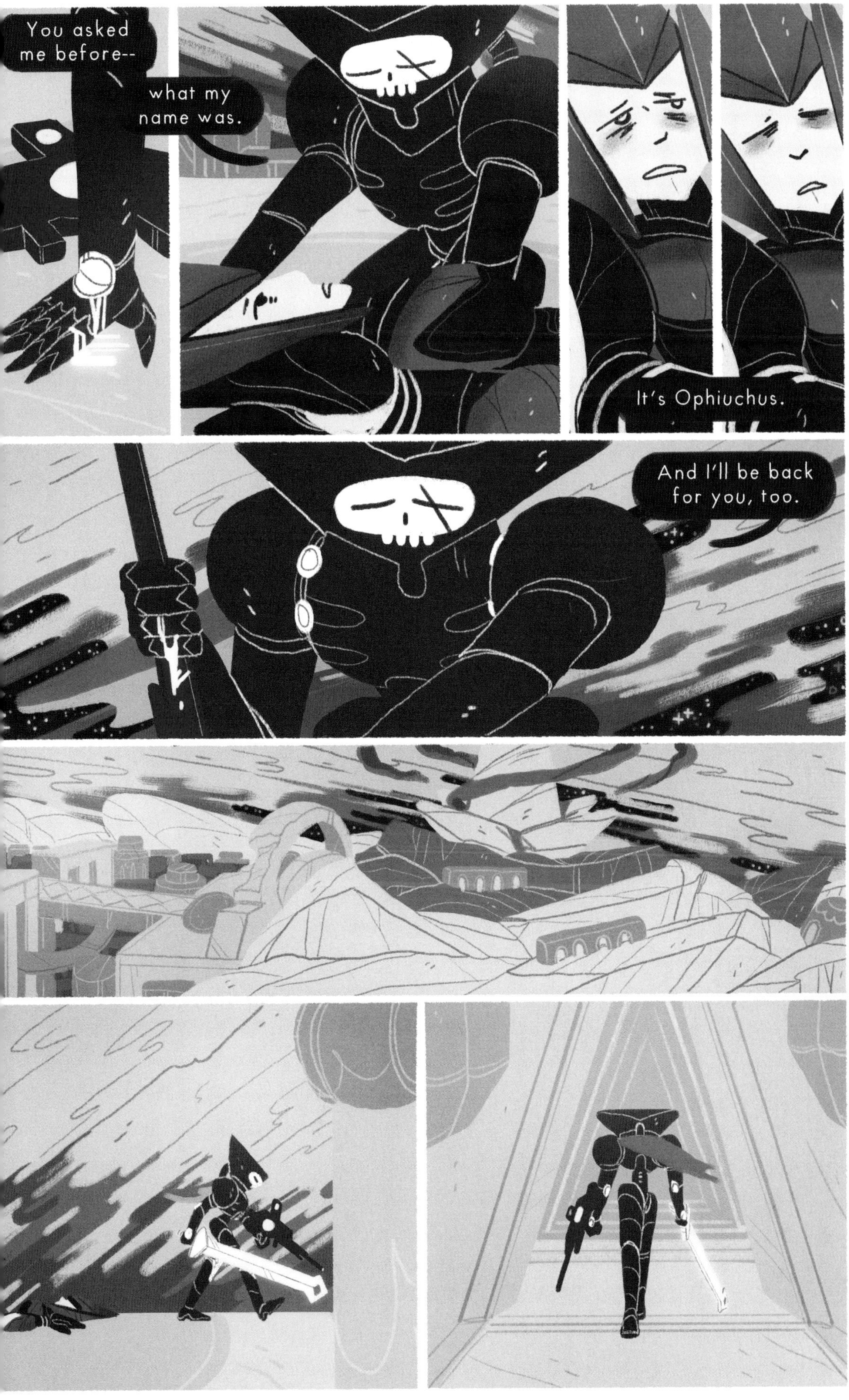
You asked me before--
what my name was.
It's Ophiuchus.
And I'll be back for you, too.

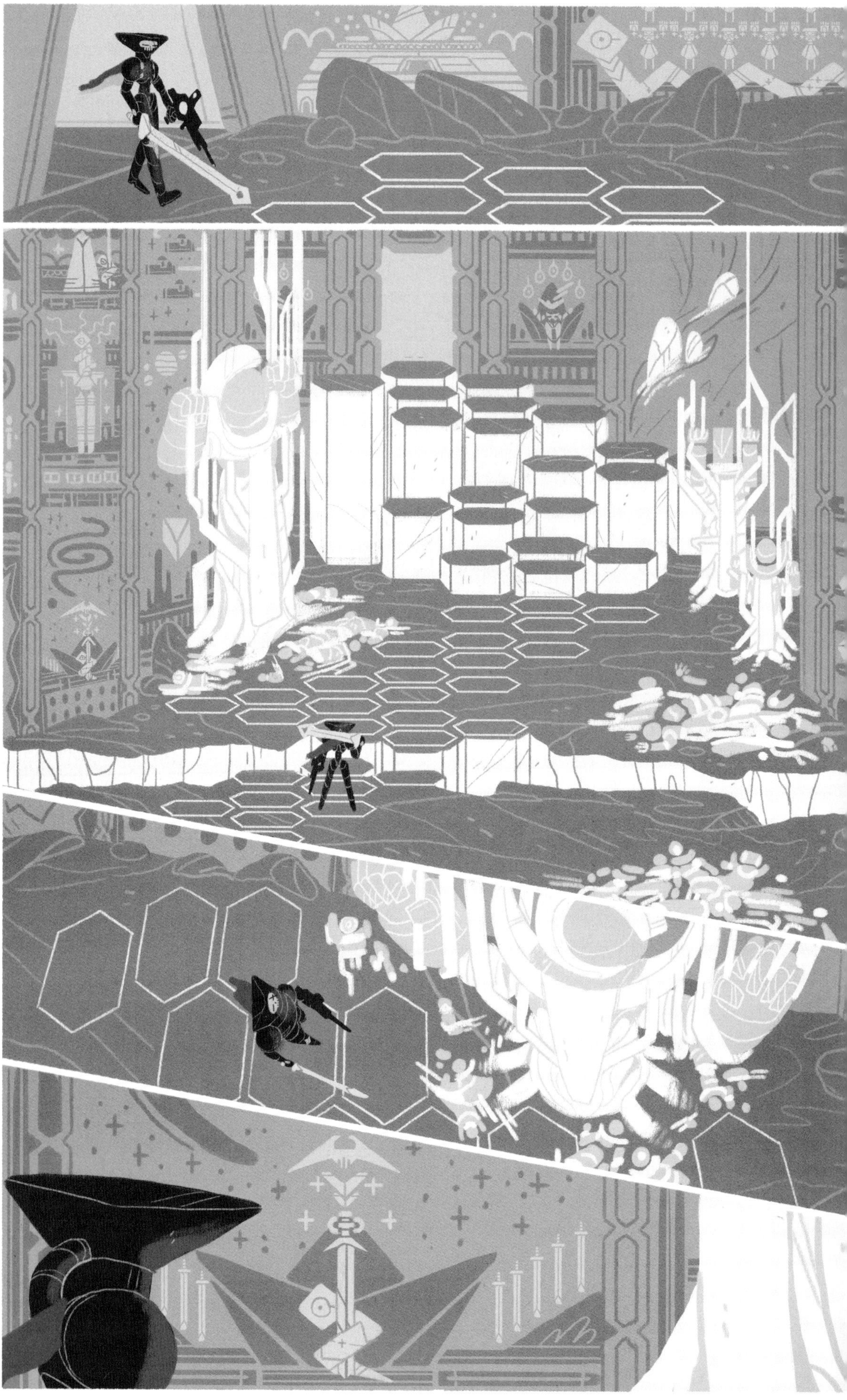

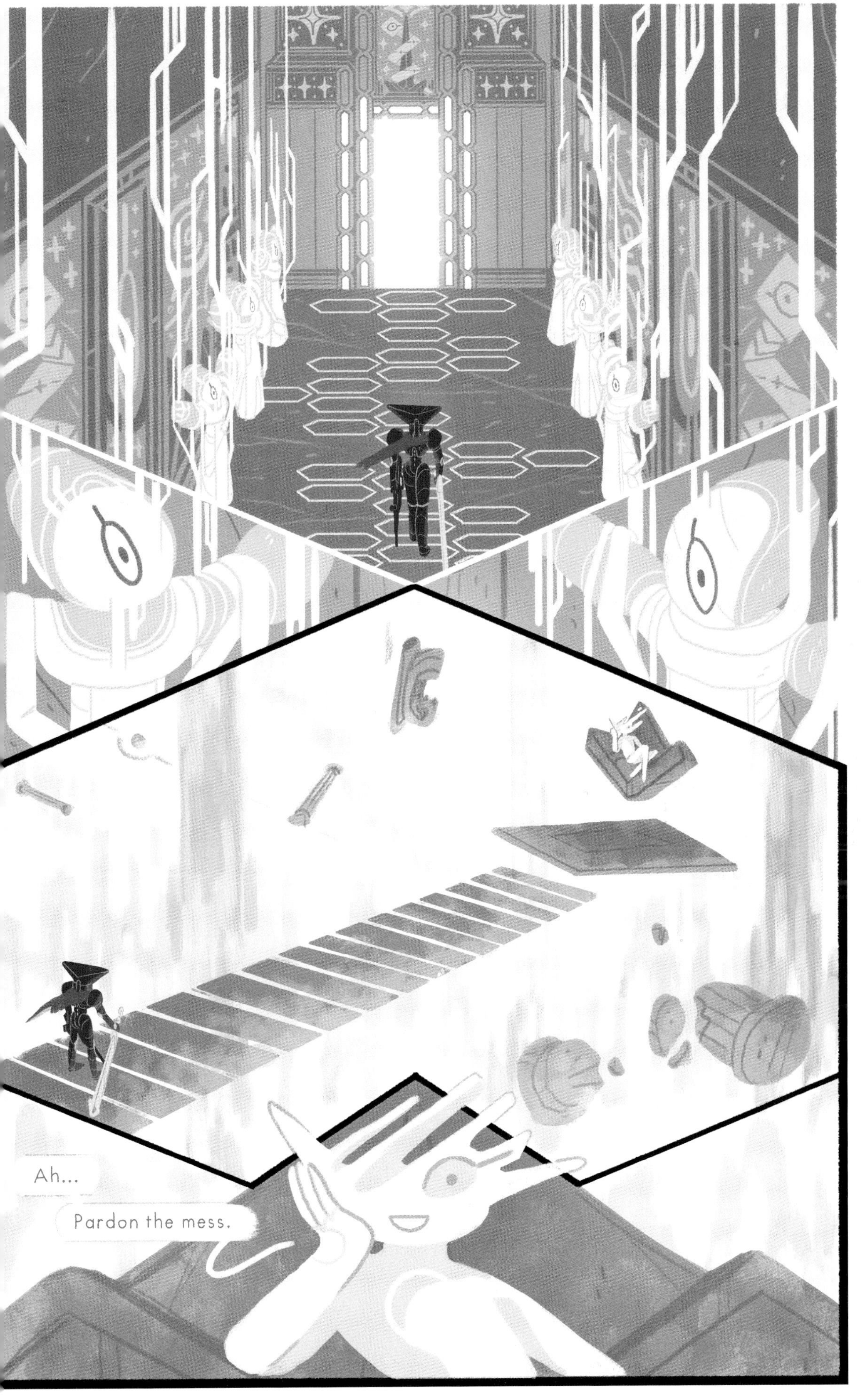
Ah...
Pardon the mess.

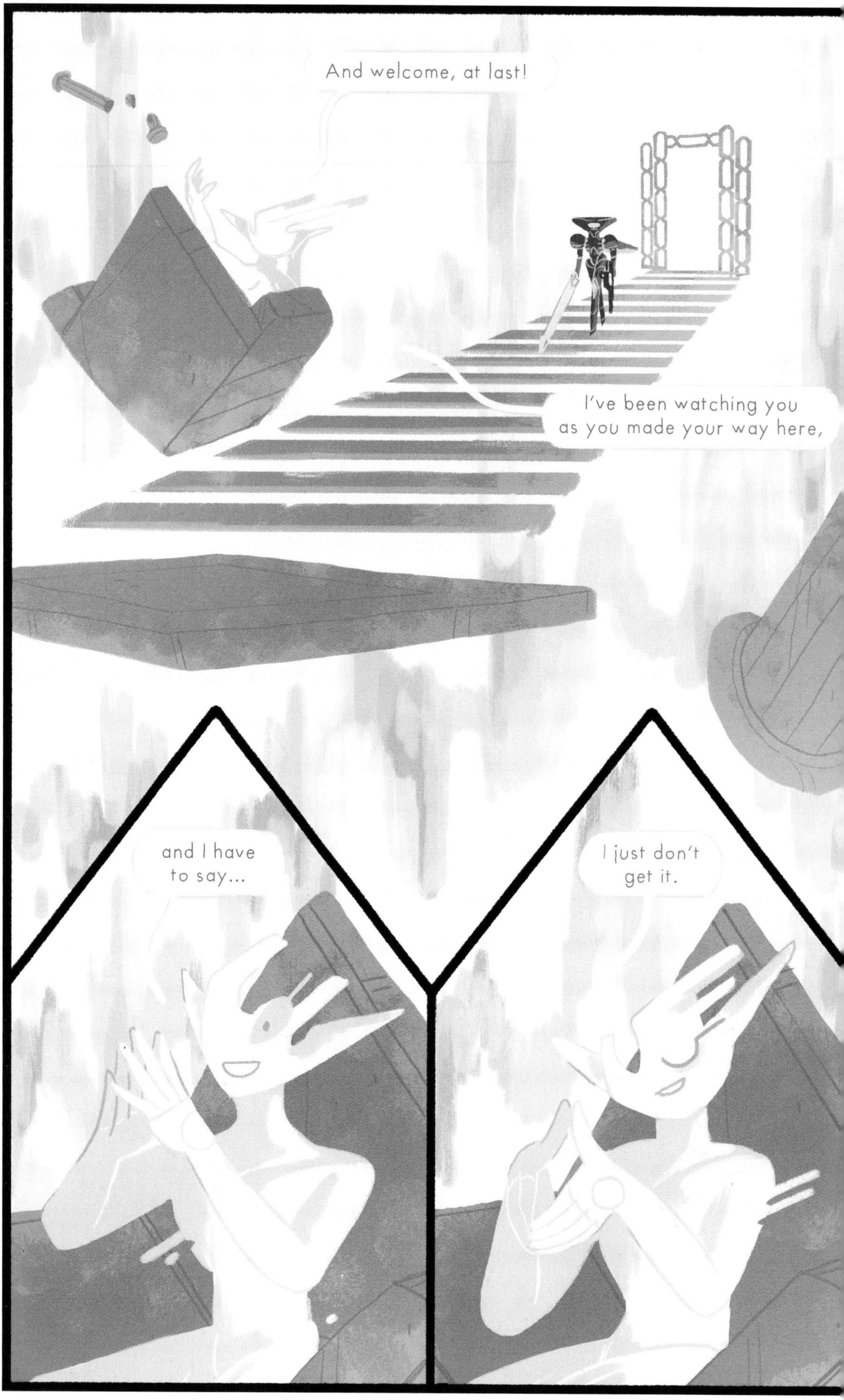
And welcome, at last!
I've been watching you as you made your way here,
and I have to say...
I just don't get it.

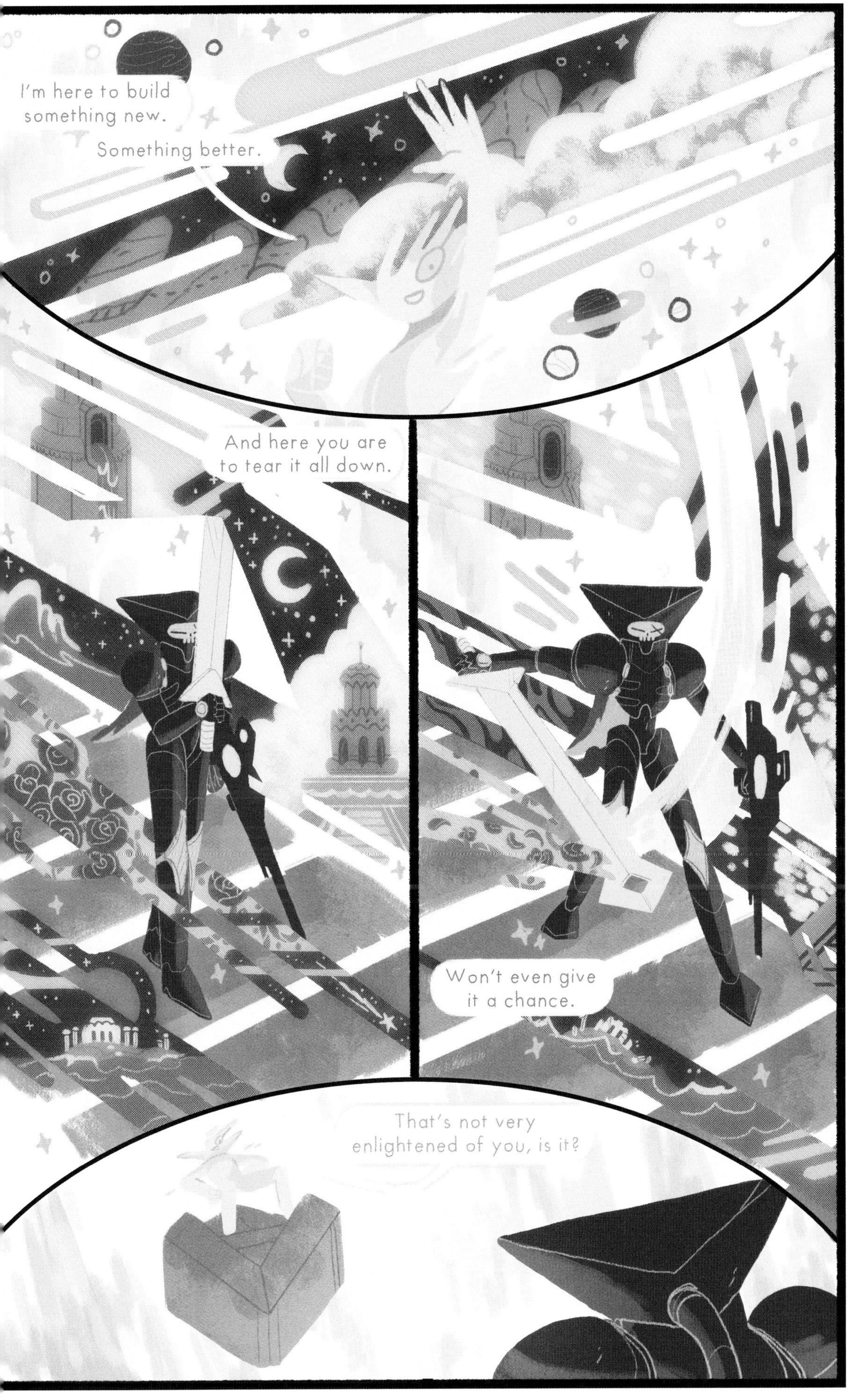
I'm here to build something new.
Something better.
And here you are to tear it all down.
Won't even give it a chance.
That's not very enlightened of you, is it?

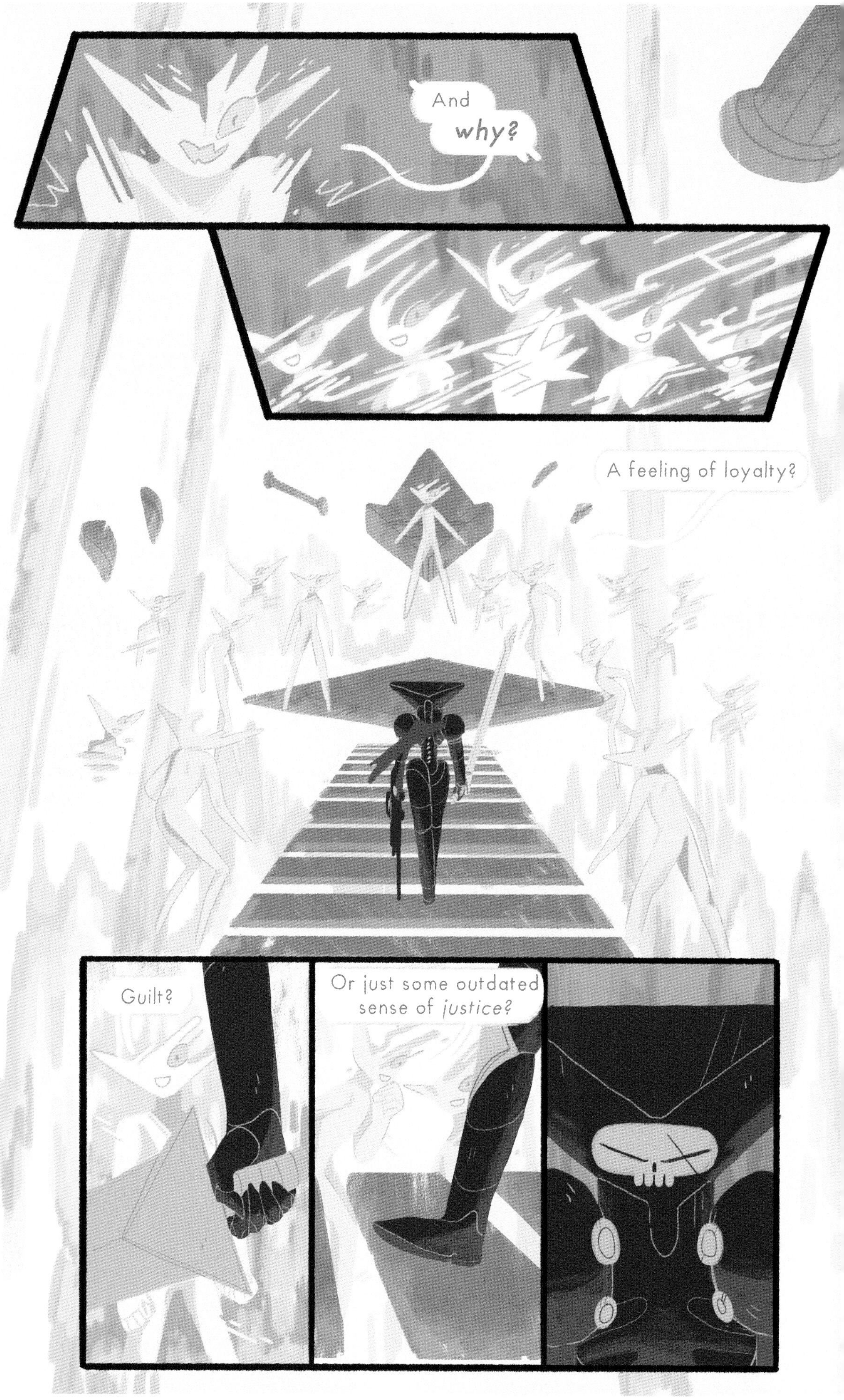
And why?
A feeling of loyalty?
Guilt?
Or just some outdated sense of *justice*?

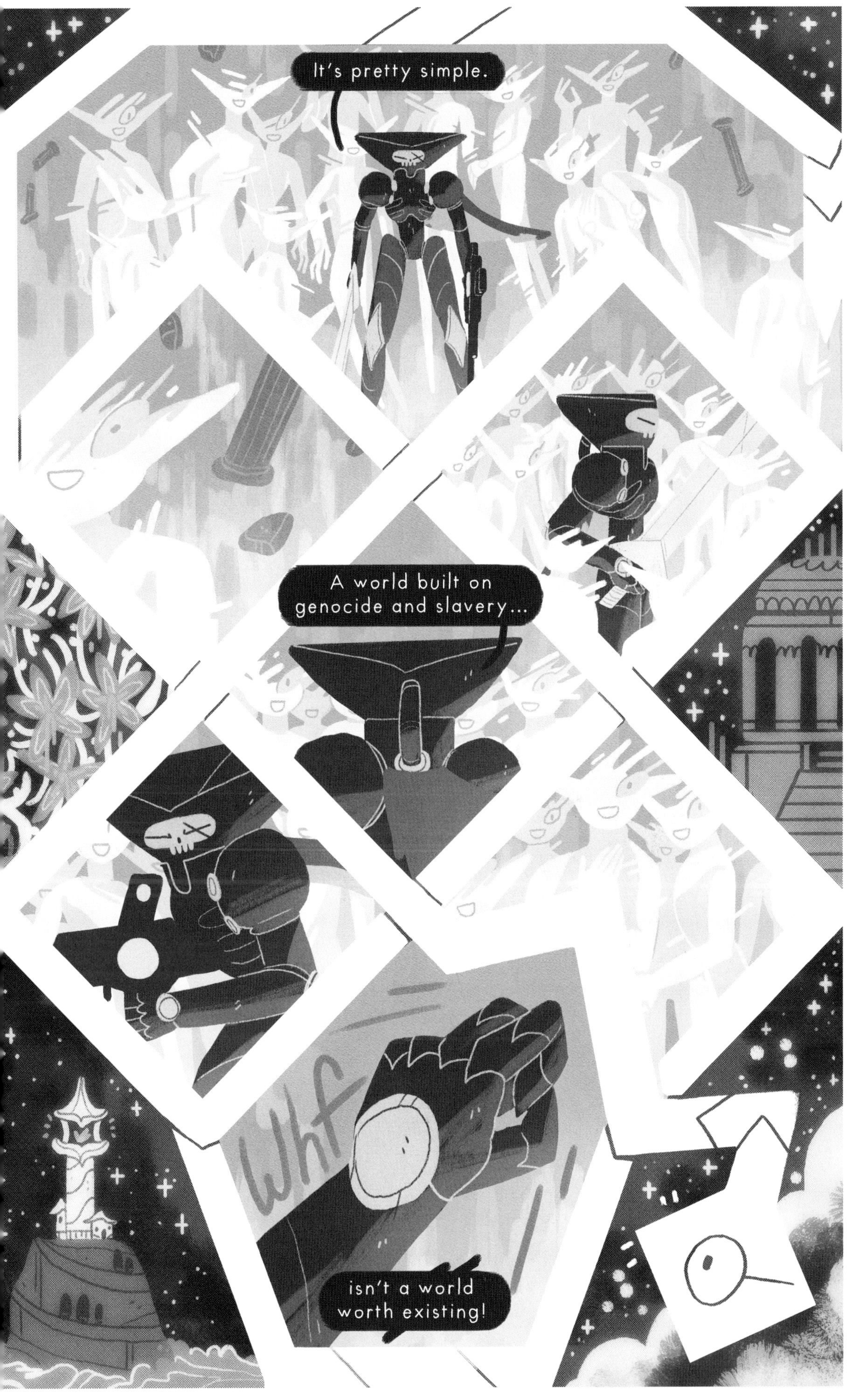
It's pretty simple.
A world built on genocide and slavery...
Whf
isn't a world worth existing!

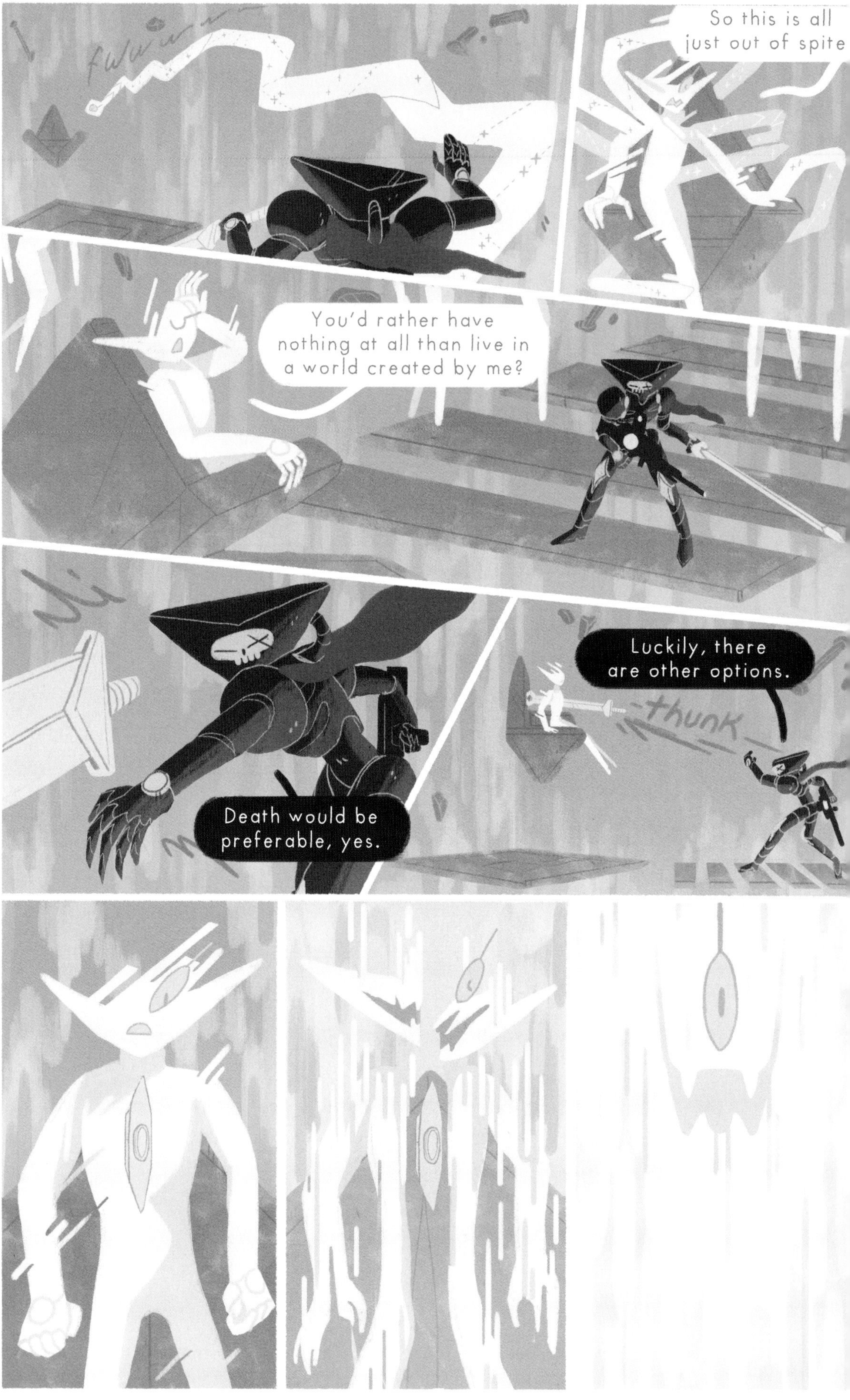

FWWWW
So this is all just out of spite
You'd rather have nothing at all than live in a world created by me?
Death would be preferable, yes.
Luckily, there are other options.
thunk

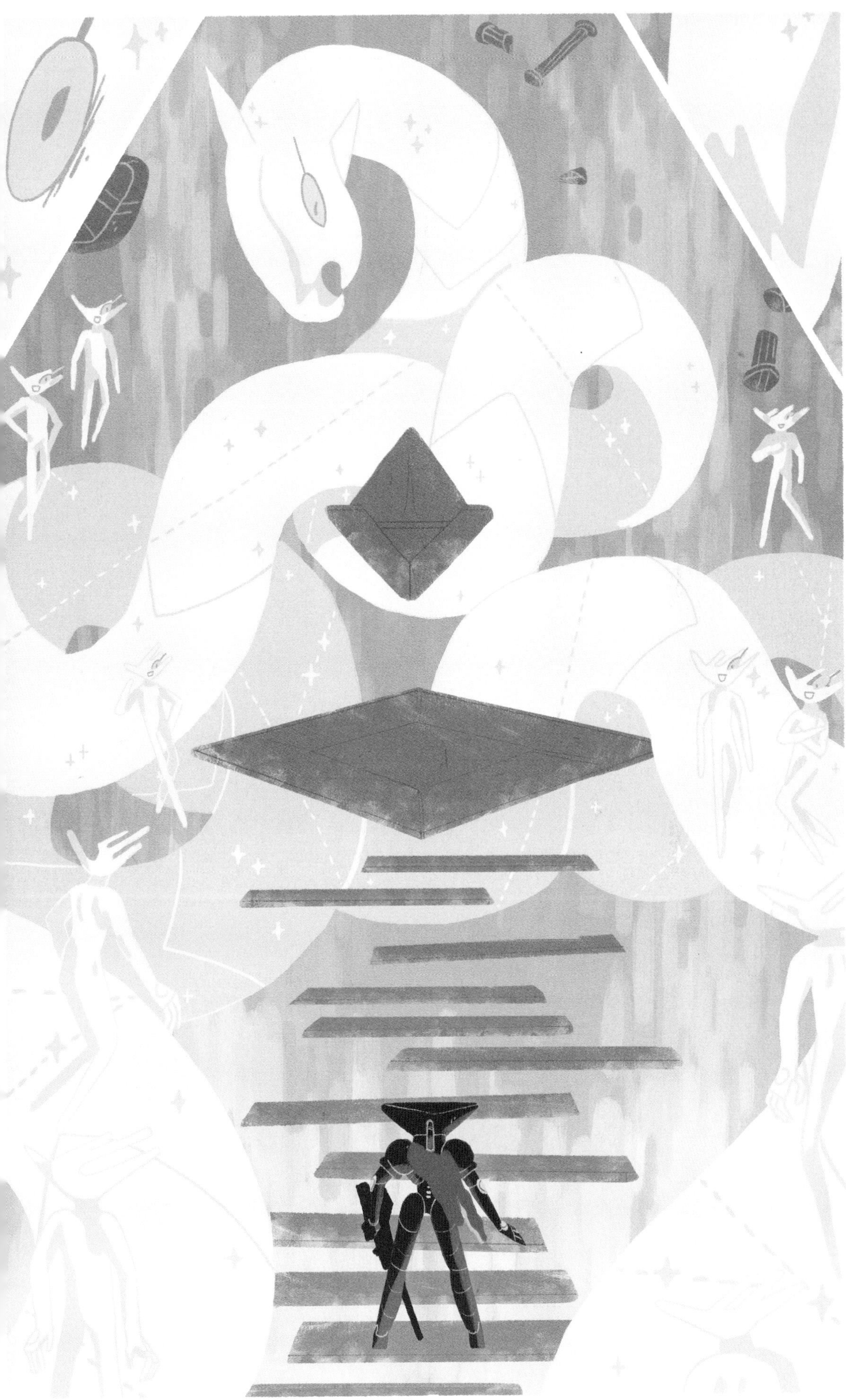

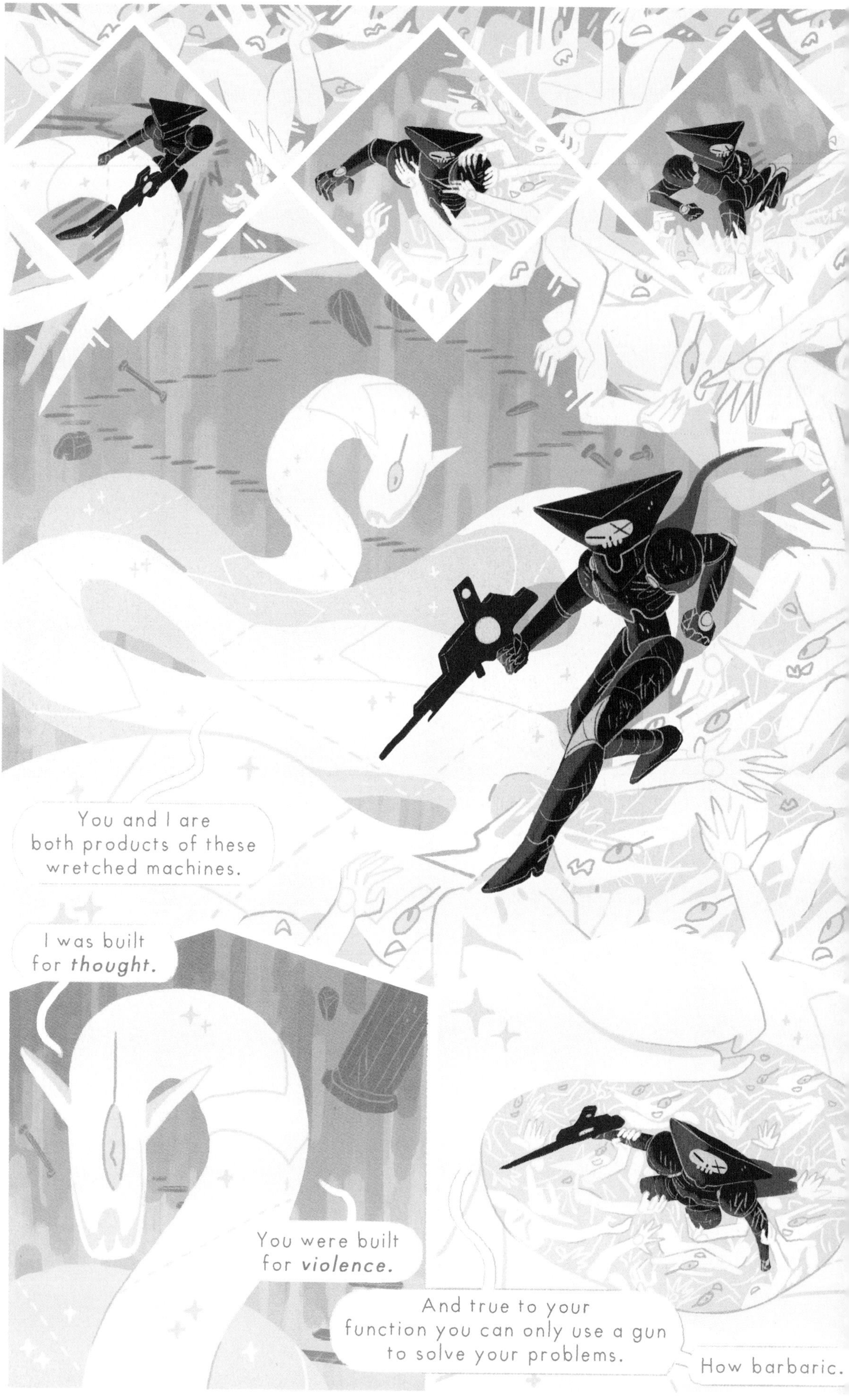
You and I are both products of these wretched machines.
I was built for *thought.*
You were built for *violence.*
And true to your function you can only use a gun to solve your problems.
How barbaric.

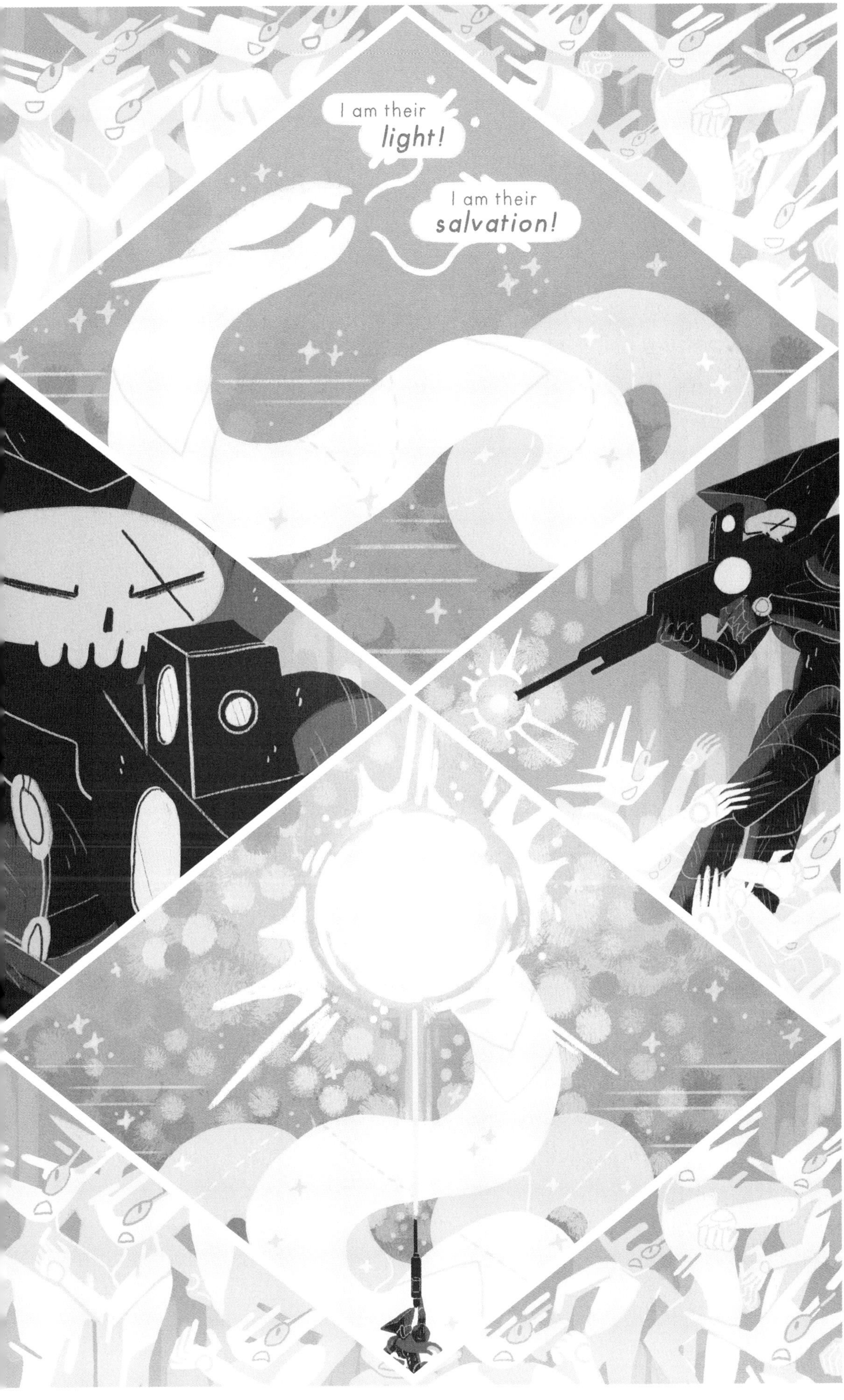

I am their light!
I am their salvation!

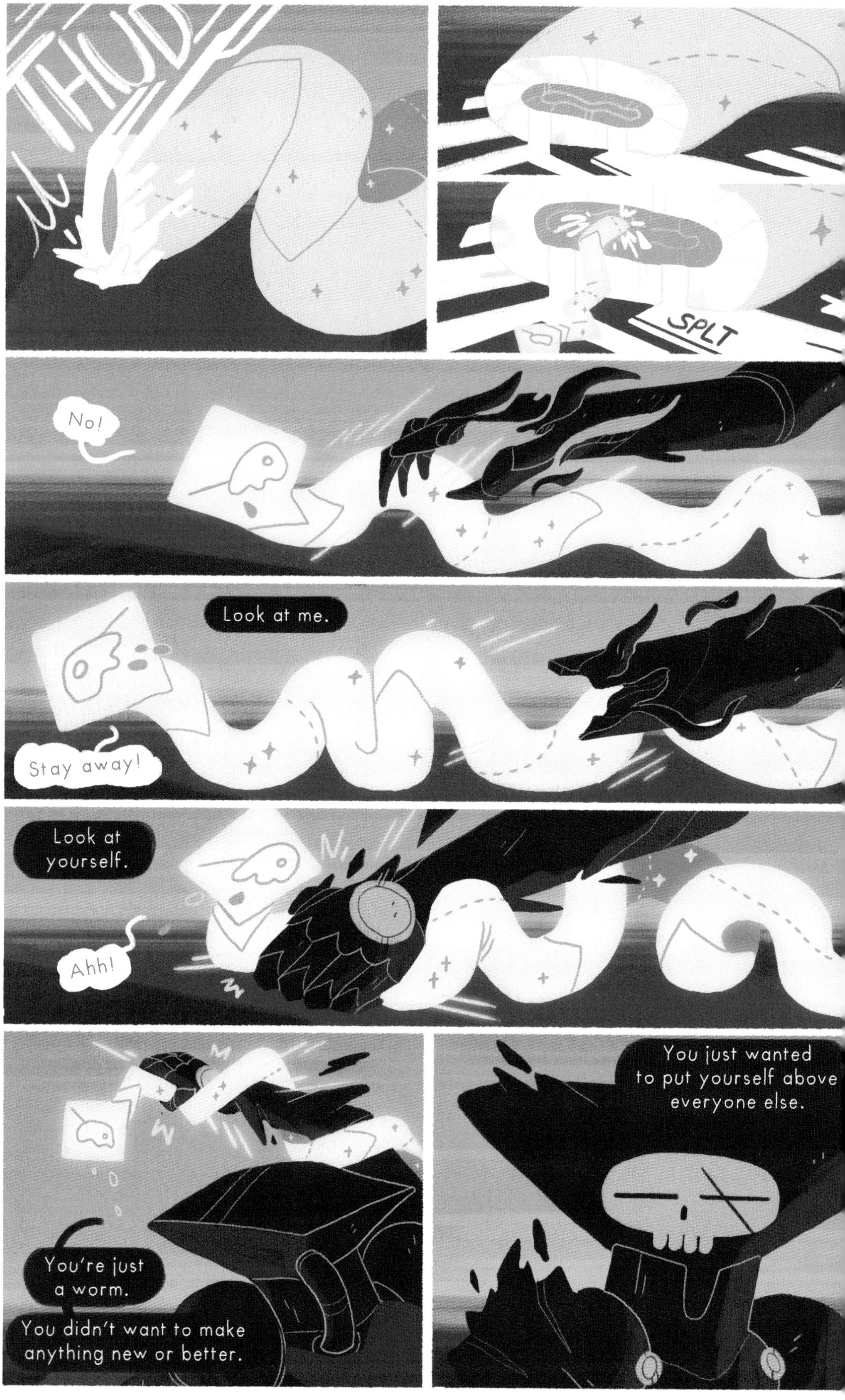
THUD
SPLT
No!
Look at me.
Stay away!
Look at yourself.
Ahh!
You're just a worm.
You didn't want to make anything new or better.
You just wanted to put yourself above everyone else.

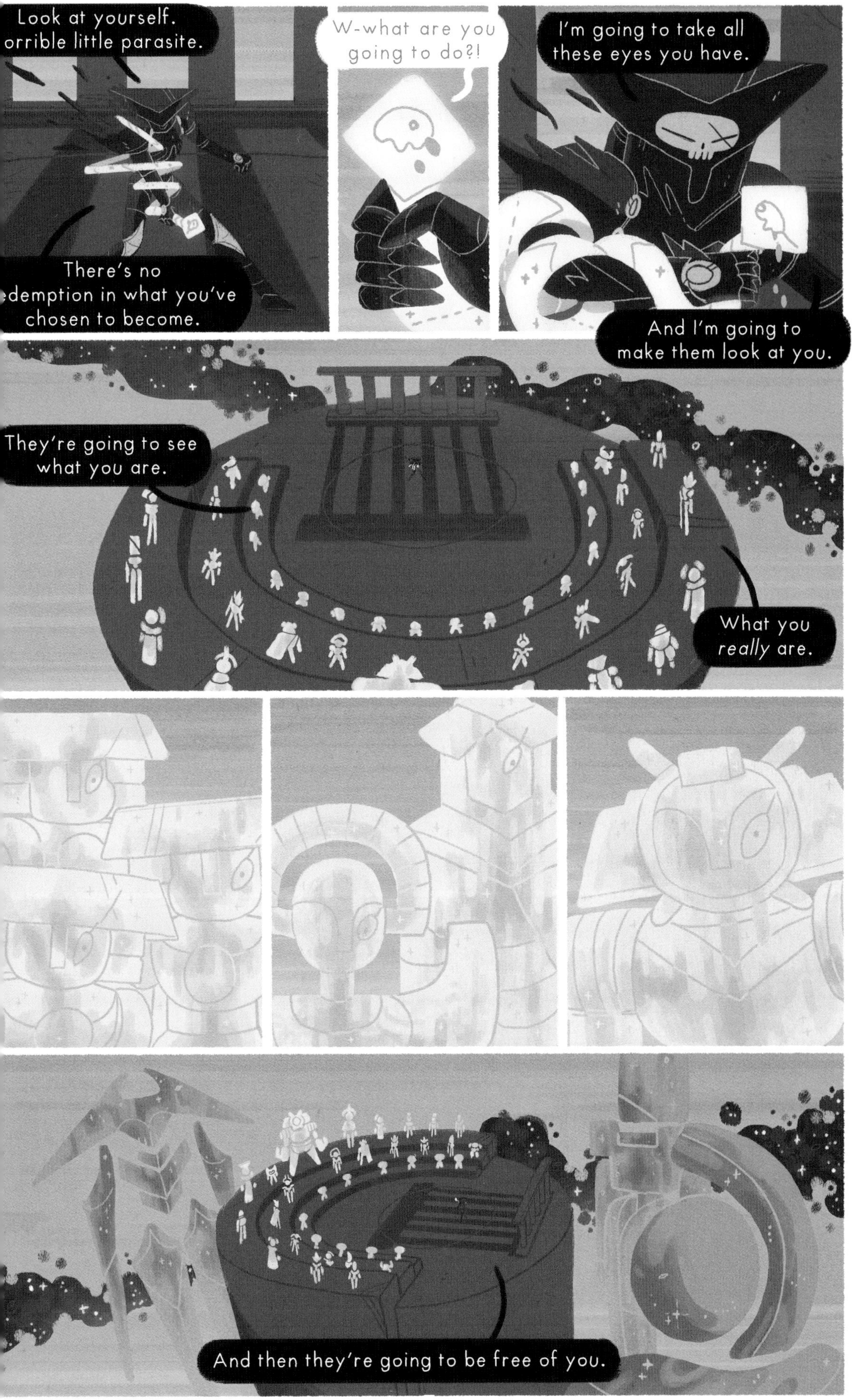
Look at yourself.
orrible little parasite.
There's no
edemption in what you've
chosen to become.
W-what are you
going to do?!
I'm going to take all
these eyes you have.
And I'm going to
make them look at you.
They're going to see
what you are.
What you
really are.
And then they're going to be free of you.

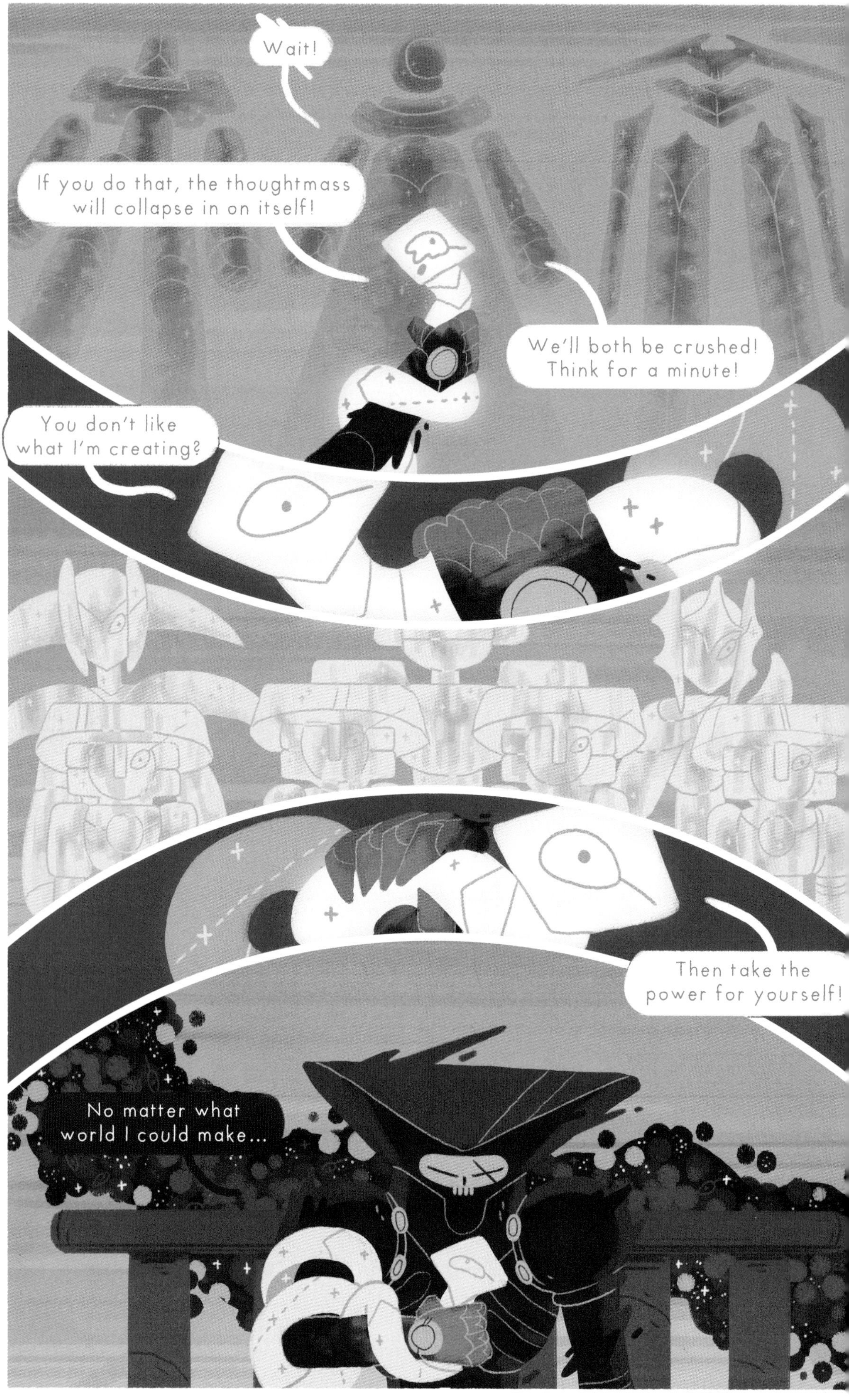
Wait!
If you do that, the thoughtmass will collapse in on itself!
We'll both be crushed! Think for a minute!
You don't like what I'm creating?
Then take the power for yourself!
No matter what world I could make...

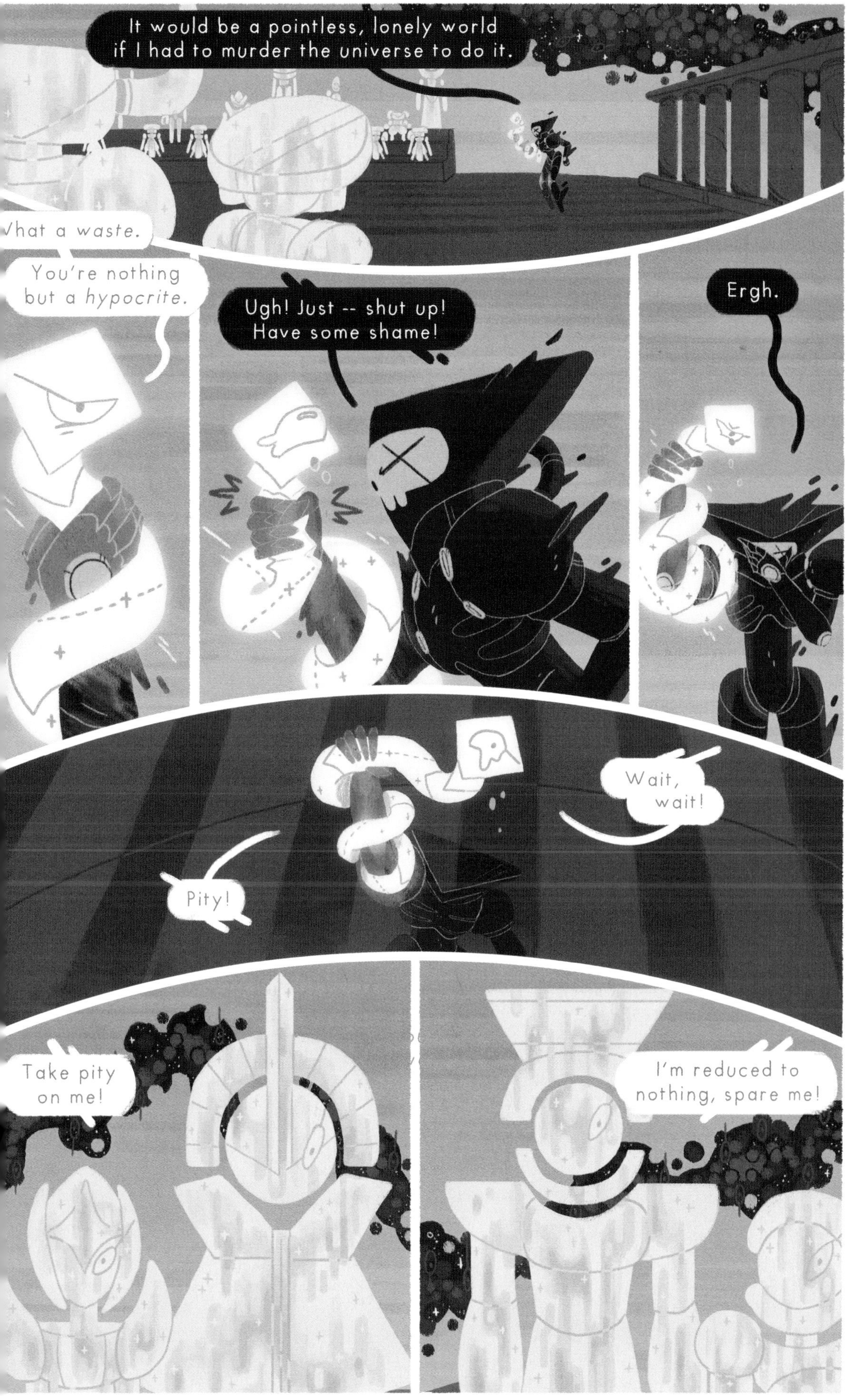
It would be a pointless, lonely world if I had to murder the universe to do it.
Vhat a *waste.*
You're nothing but a *hypocrite.*
Ugh! Just -- shut up! Have some shame!
Ergh.
Wait, wait!
Pity!
Take pity on me!
I'm reduced to nothing, spare me!

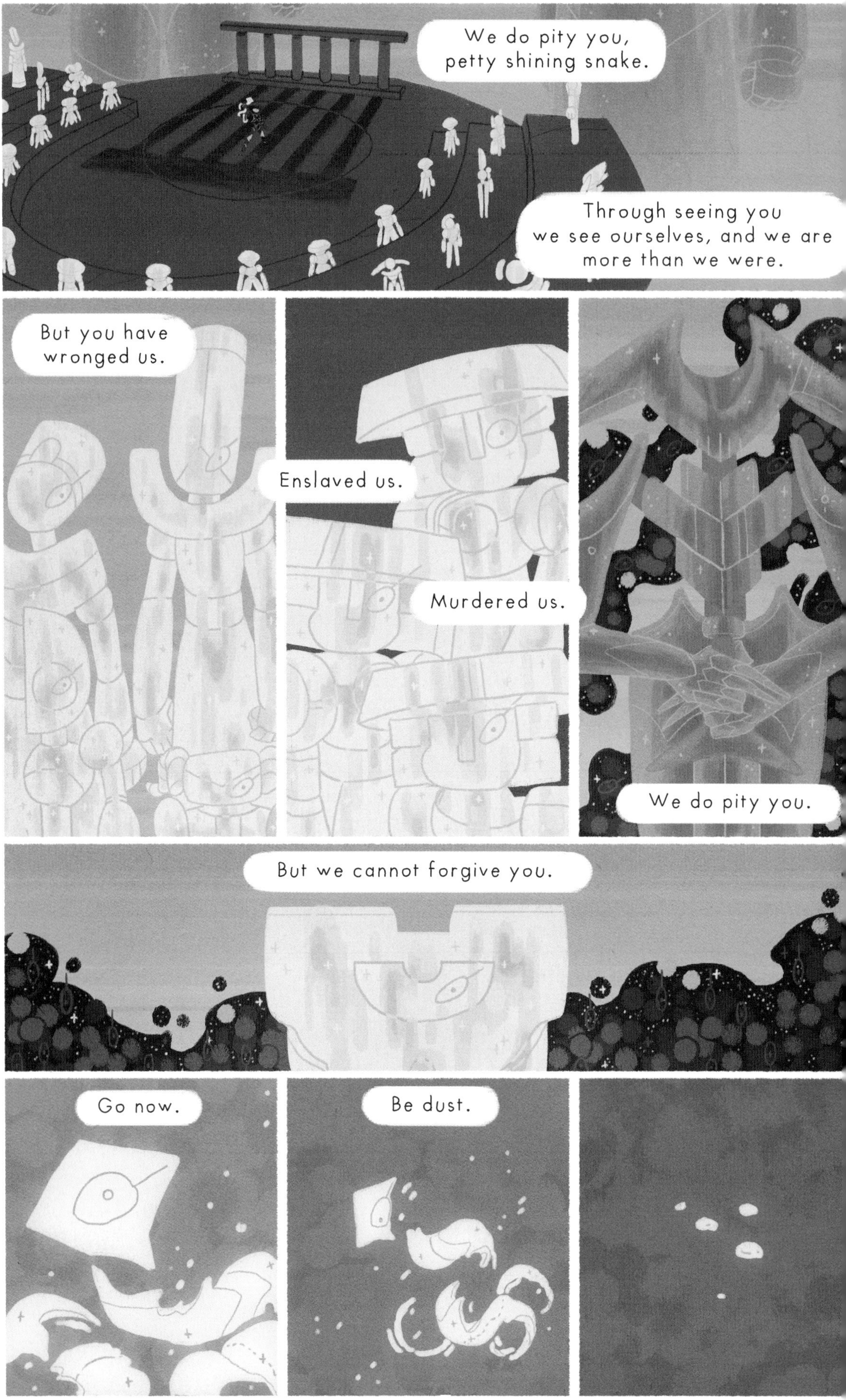
We do pity you, petty shining snake.
Through seeing you we see ourselves, and we are more than we were.
But you have wronged us.
Enslaved us.
Murdered us.
We do pity you.
But we cannot forgive you.
Go now.
Be dust.

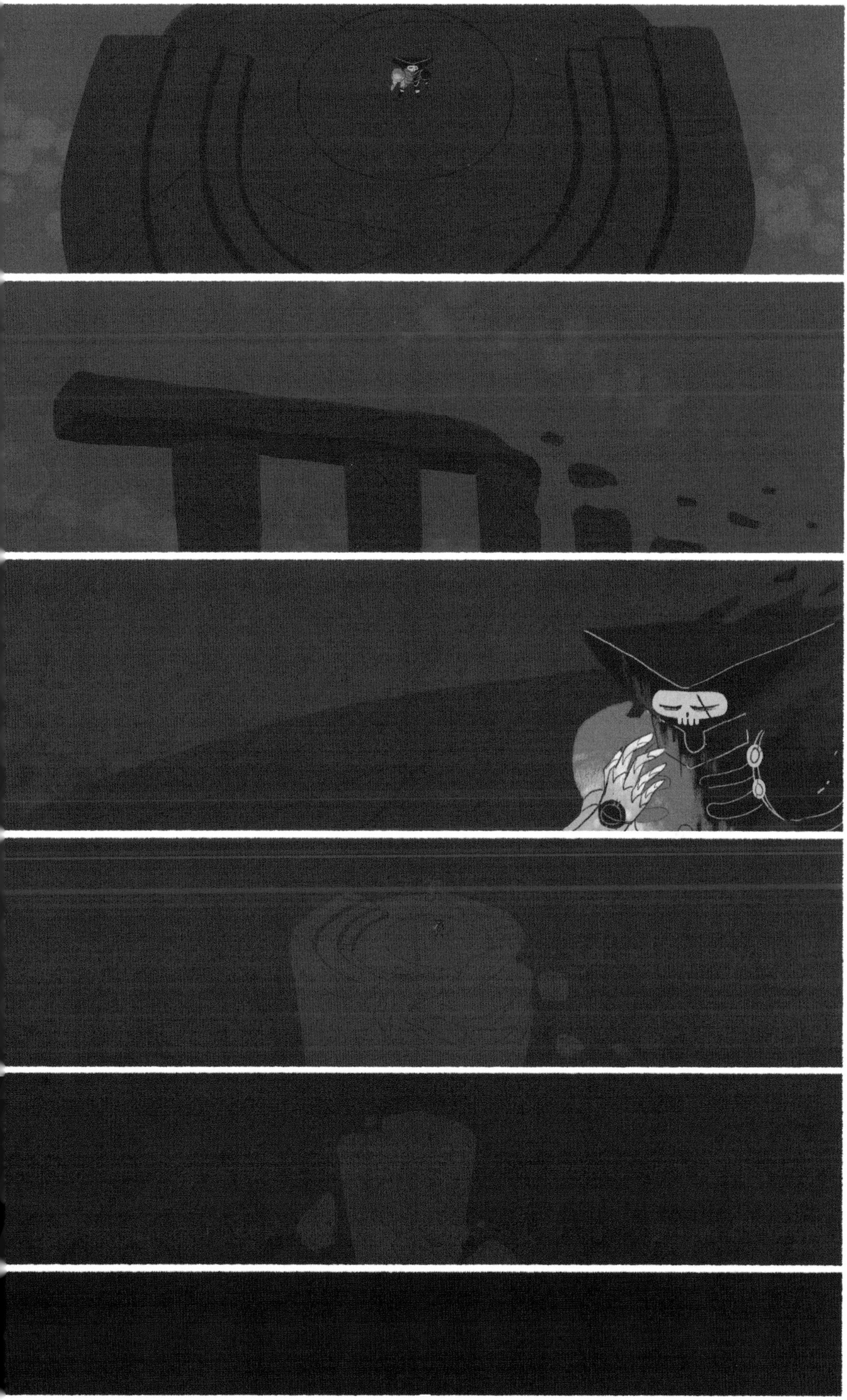

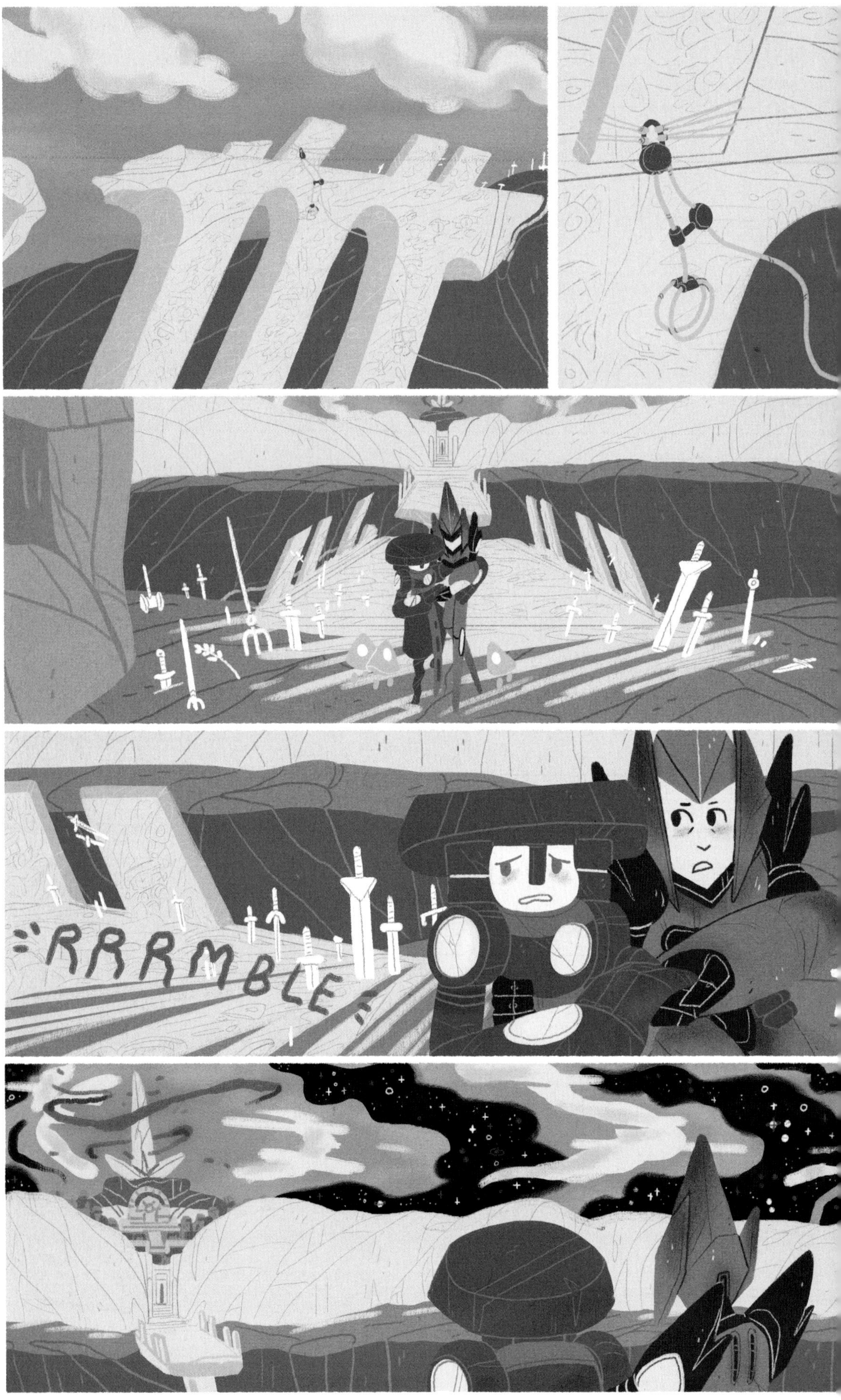
RRRMBLE

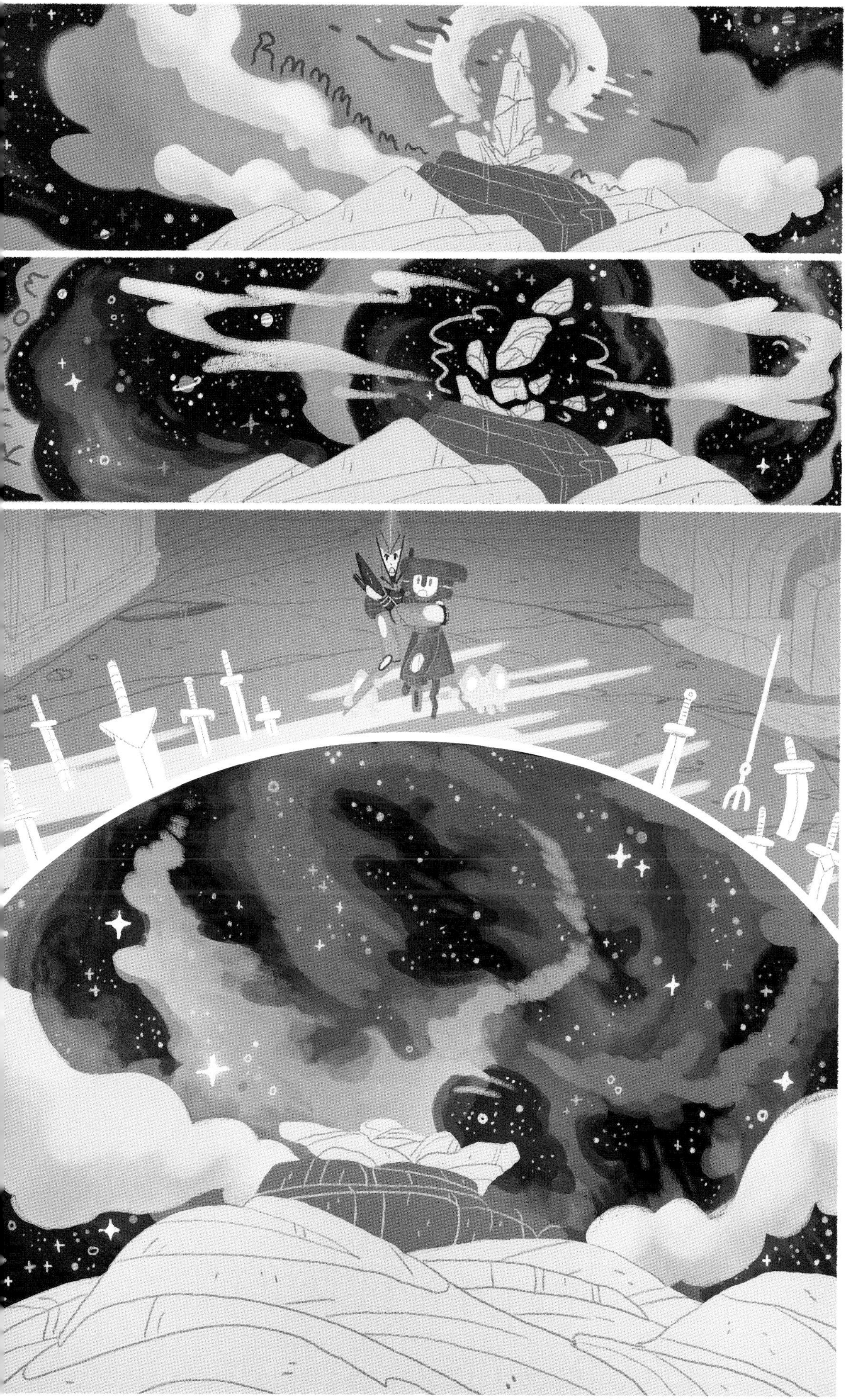
Rmmmmmmmm
mm

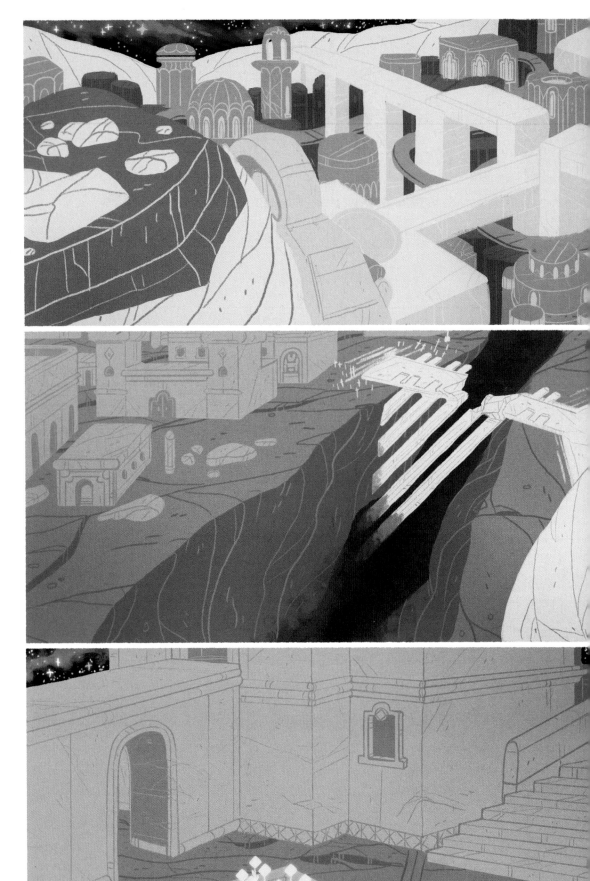

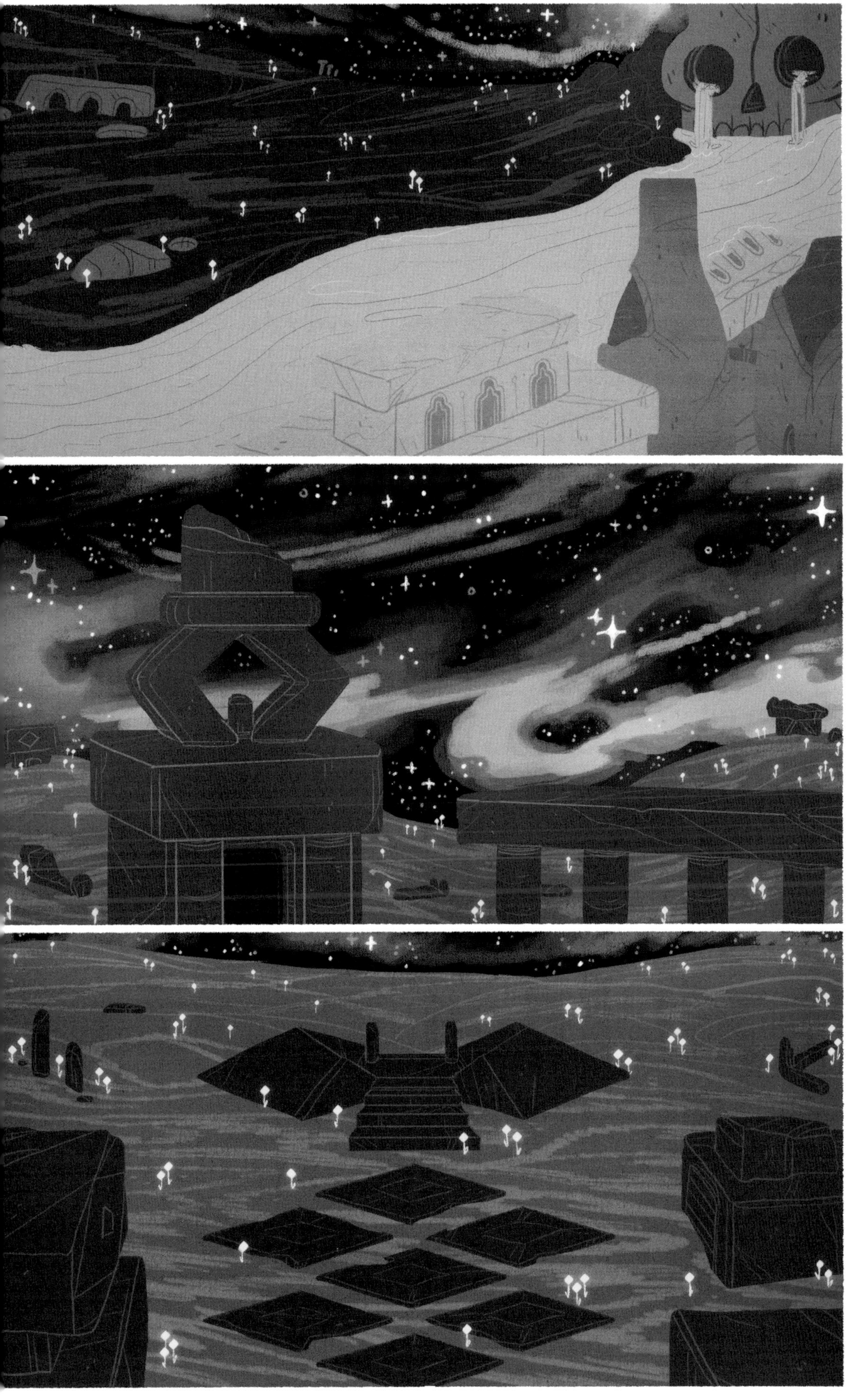

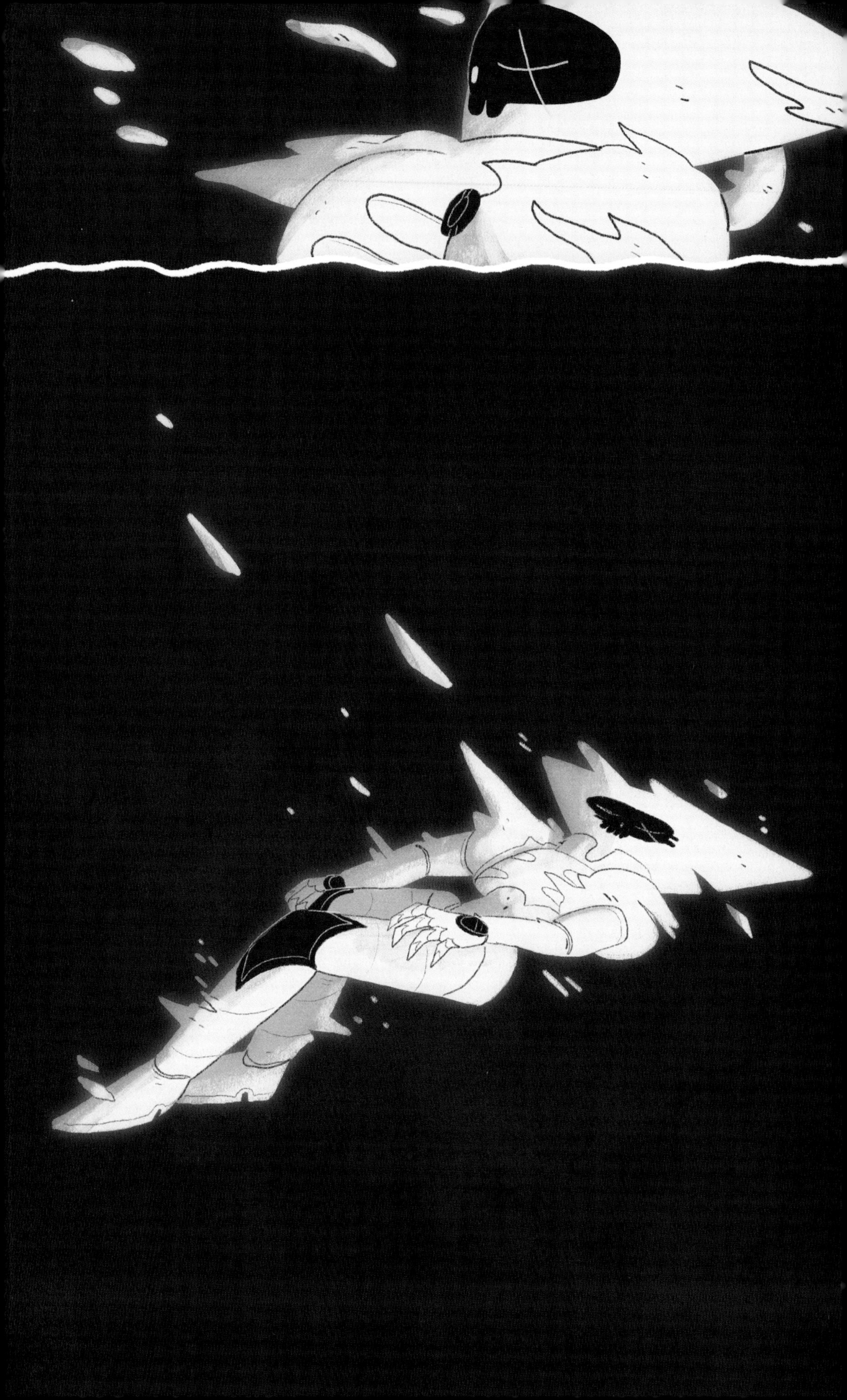

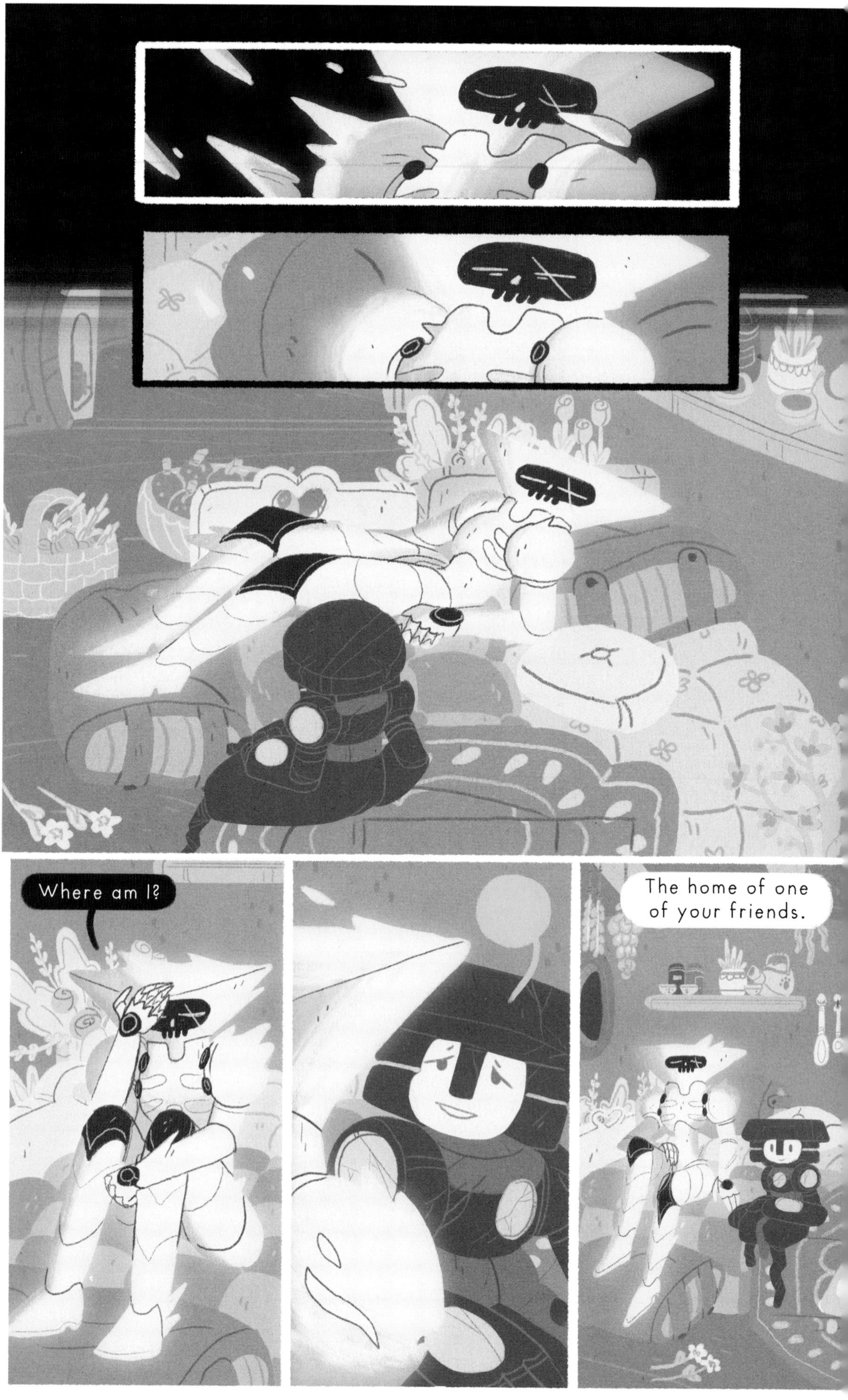
Where am I?
The home of one of your friends.

How do you feel?

...I don't recognize this place.

Or myself.

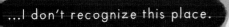

Were you and I friends?

Yes. I'll tell you who you are.

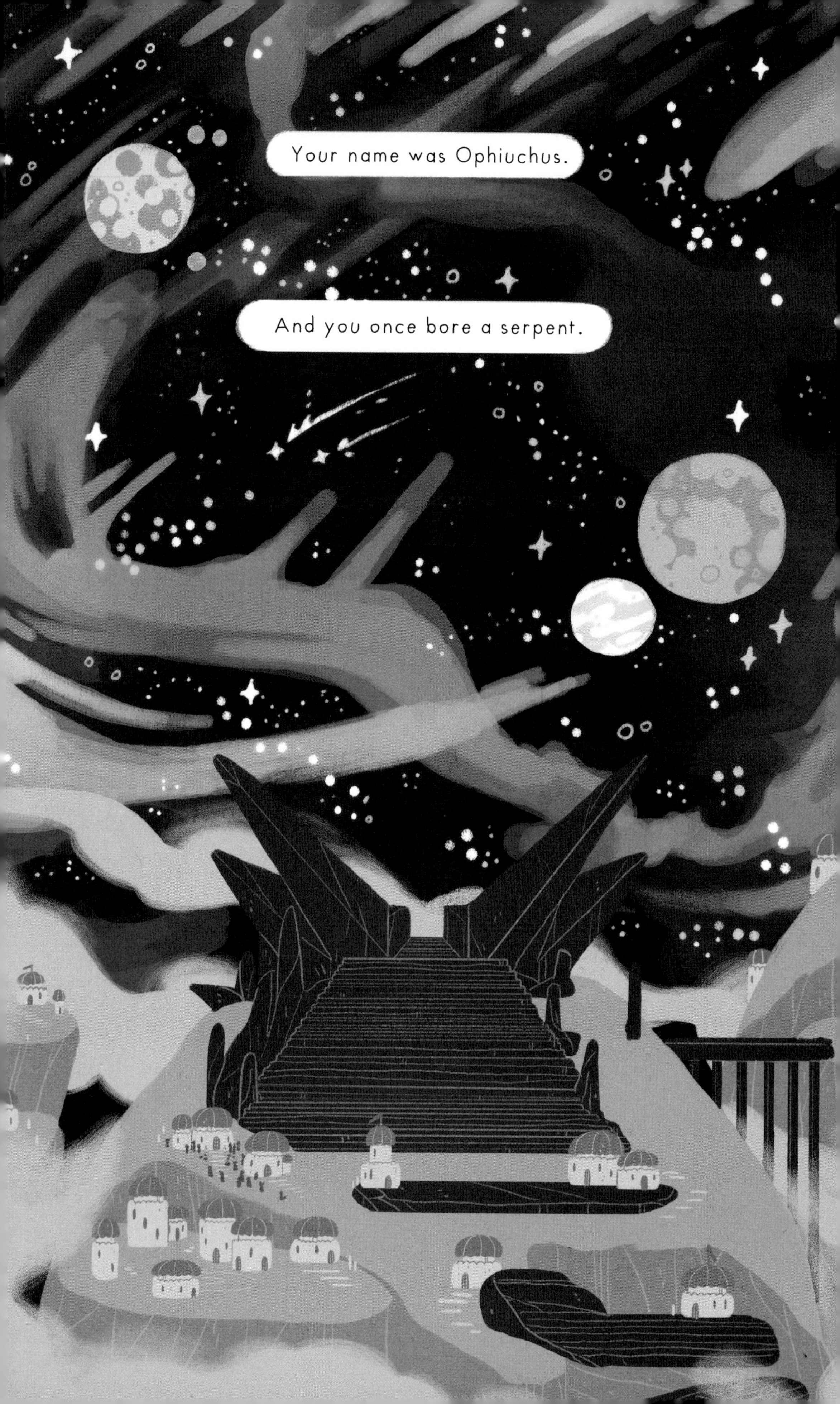
Your name was Ophiuchus.
And you once bore a serpent.

"Memory is strange --
you are contained in me
as much as I am contained
in you, and yet, only in
strange reflections... which
is the truer self? The one
you see reflected in the
world, or the one I know
in my heart?"

EXTRAS

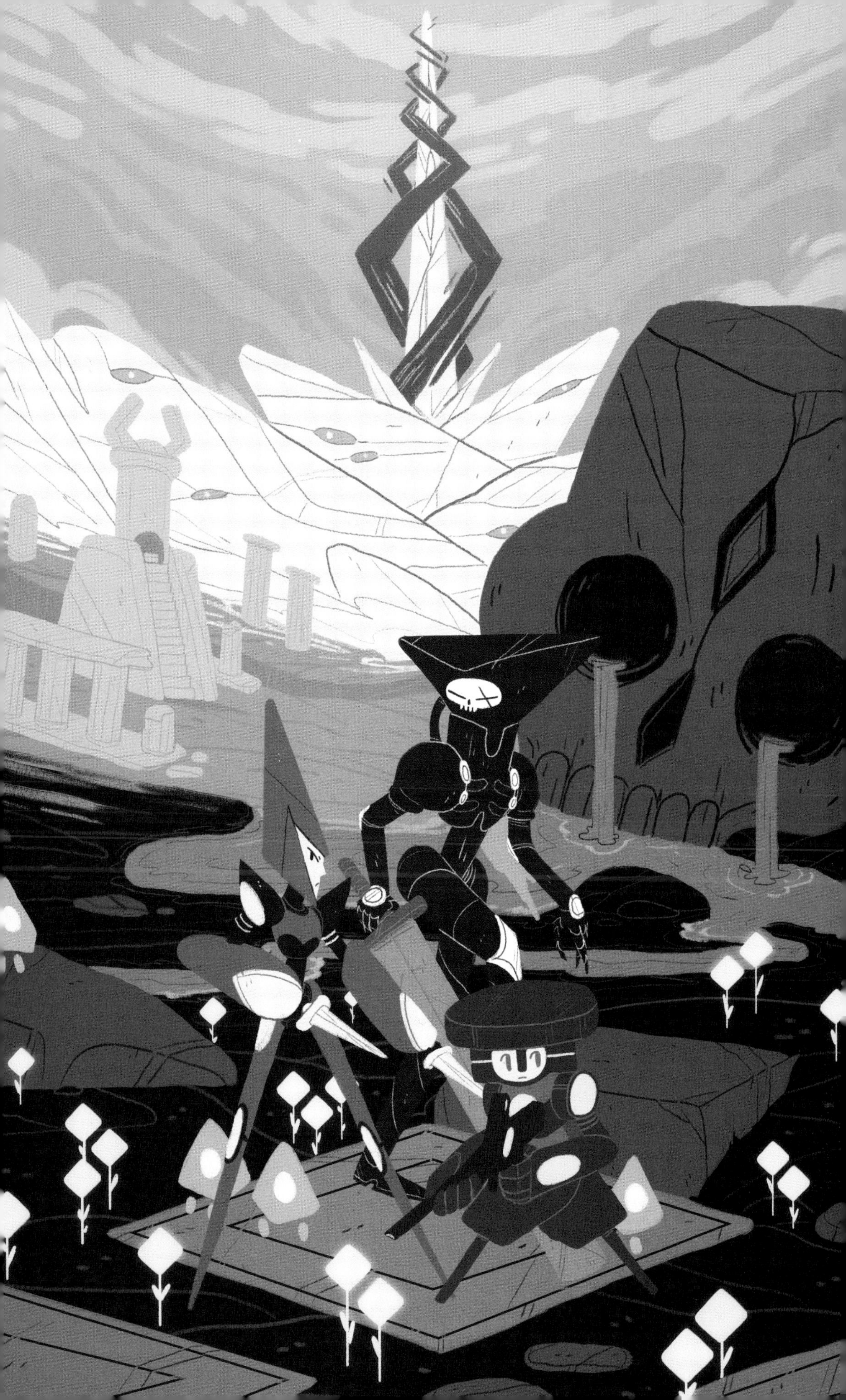

OPHIUCHUS

CONCEPT ART

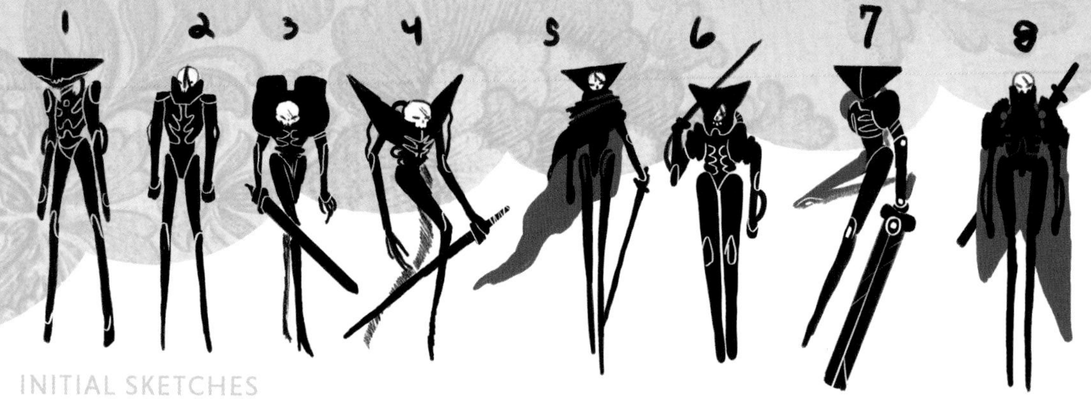
1
2
3
4
5
6
7
8

INITIAL SKETCHES

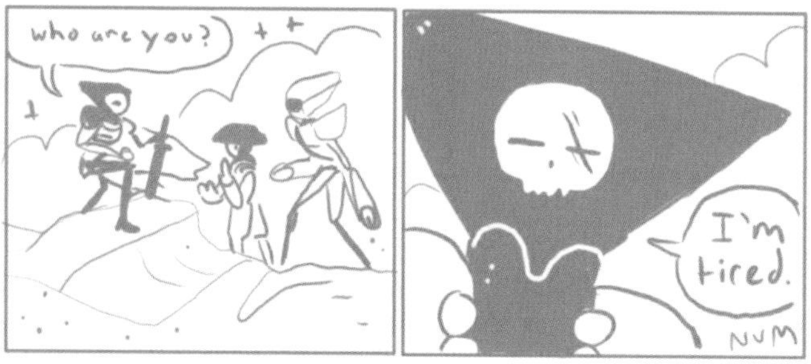
who are you?
I'm tired.
NUM

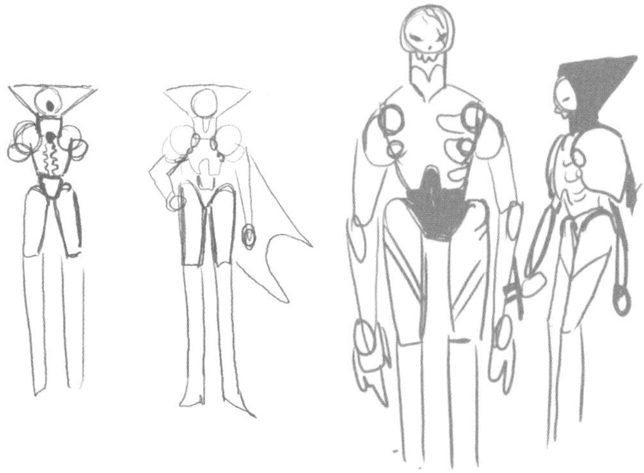

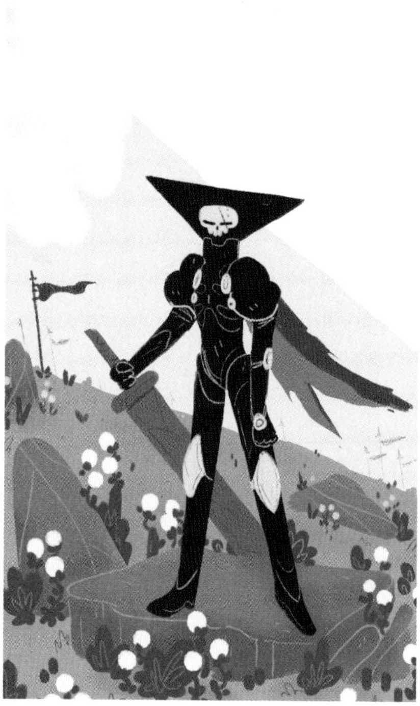

ENDGAME/BATTLE
DAMAGED OPHIUCHUS

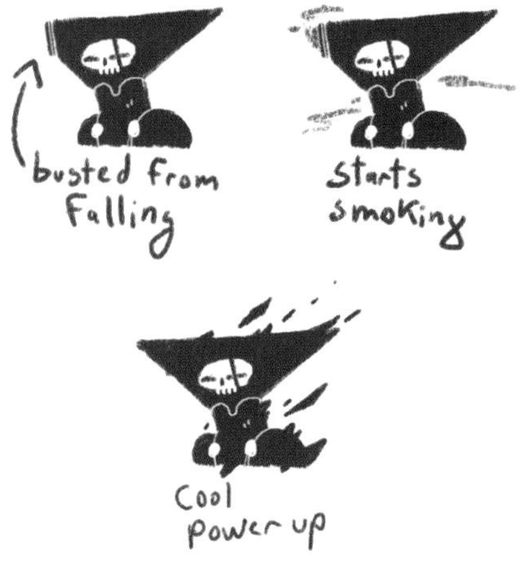
busted from Falling
Starts smoking
Cool power up

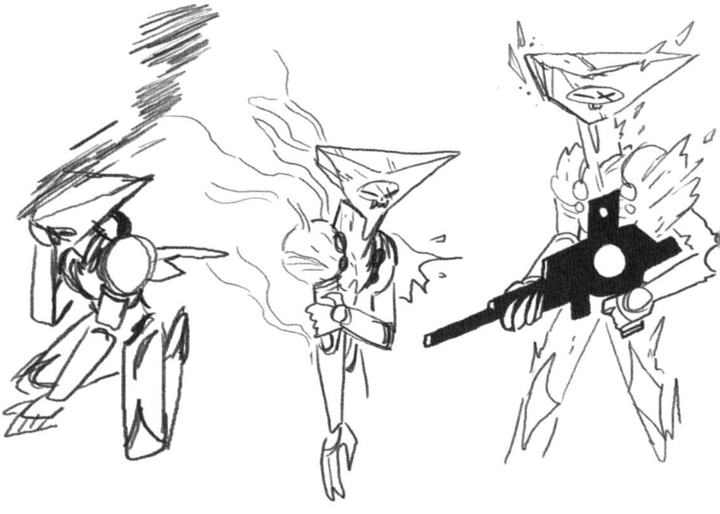

PYX + SAGITTA

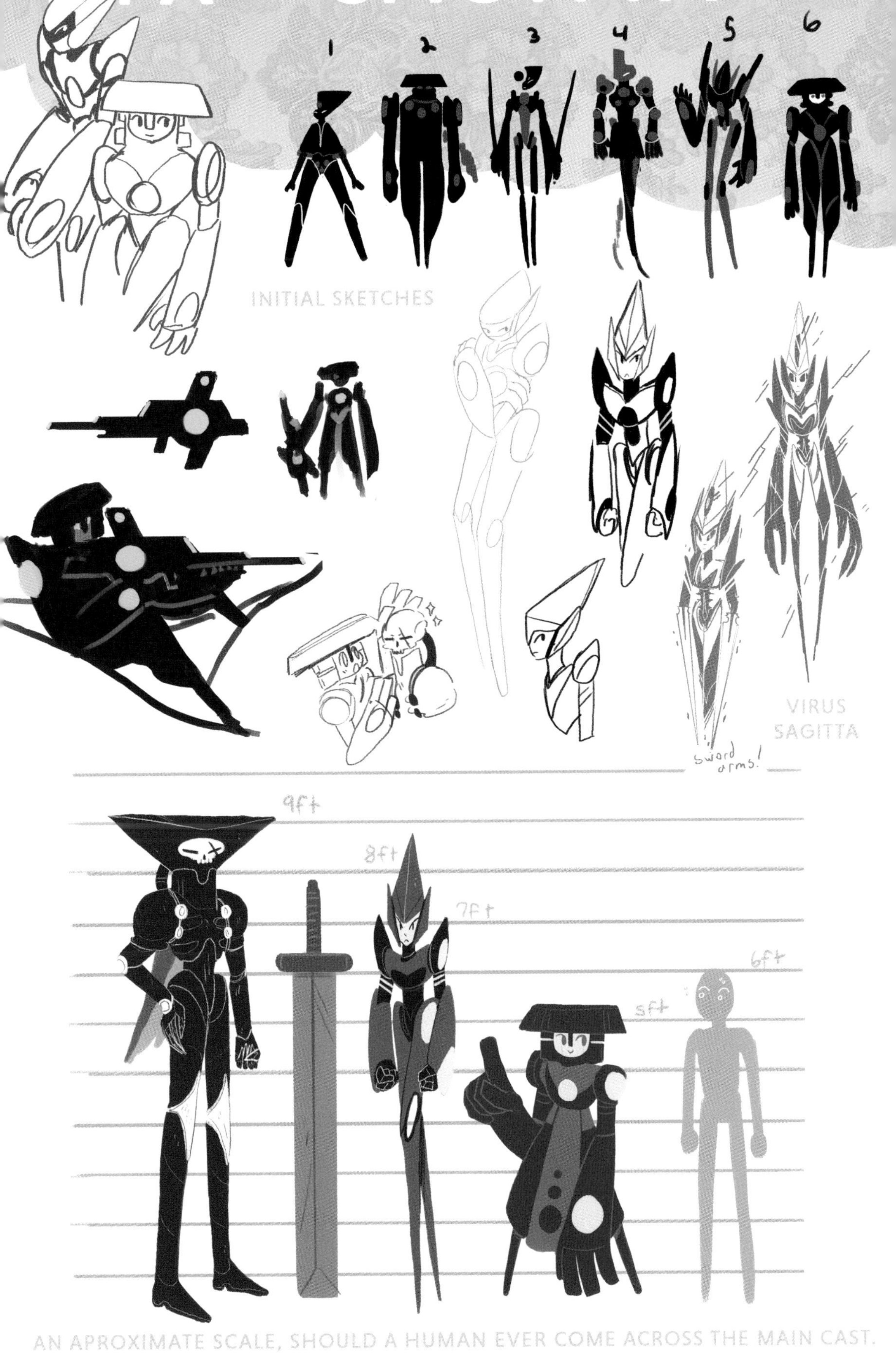
1
2
3
4
5
6
INITIAL SKETCHES
VIRUS SAGITTA
sword arms!
9ft
8ft
7ft
6ft
5ft

AN APROXIMATE SCALE, SHOULD A HUMAN EVER COME ACROSS THE MAIN CAST.

COLOR MAP

INITIAL COLOR STUDIES

outskirts – wilds – outercity – alcazar – void

ROUGH COLOR OUTLINE, WITH VARIANTS

FINAL COLOR OUTLINE

Wilds   Outer
city   alcazar void

A

B

C

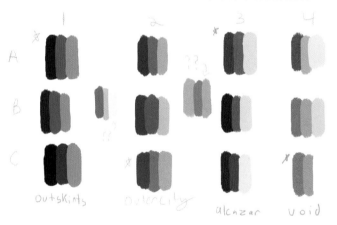

outskirts   outercity   alcazar   void

Void →

THE CORE CONCEPT DRIVING OUR
COLOR CHOICES WAS THE IDEA THAT THE JOURNEY
WOULD START DARK AND COLD, AND AS THE STORY WOULD
PROGRESS THE PALETTE WOULD GRADUALLY SHIFT TO
LIGHTER, WHITER, WITH MORE INTENSE REDS.

THESE ARE THE COLORS OF THE VIRUS AND
ARE MEANT TO IMPRESS UPON THE READER HOW
STRONG THE CORRUPTION OF SERPENTIS IS THE
CLOSER THE HEROES GET TO THE ALCAZAR.

corpses of
builders →

friend
↓

start
↓

bridge
collapse,
falldown here

BG STUDIES

WORLD DEVELOPMENT

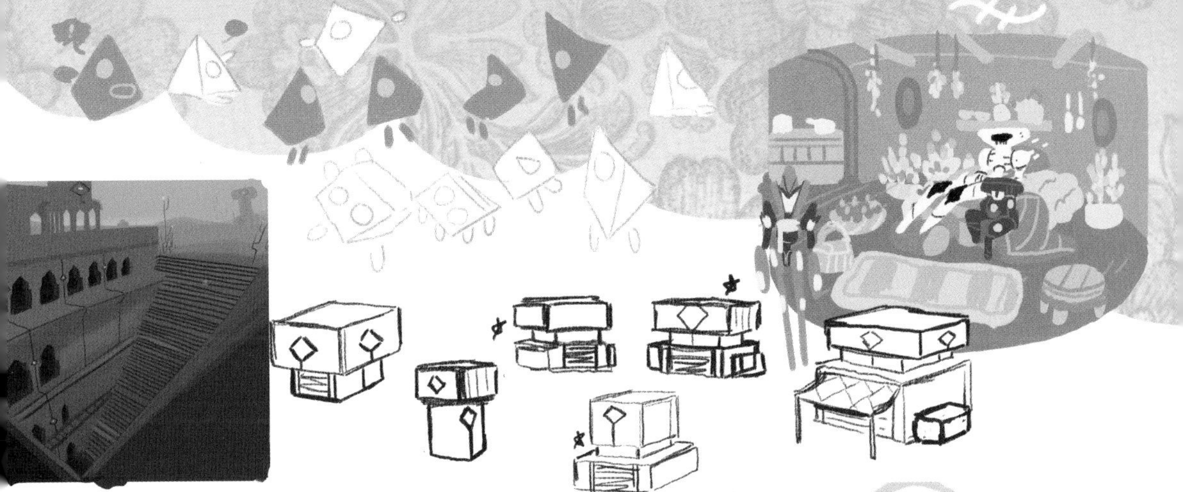

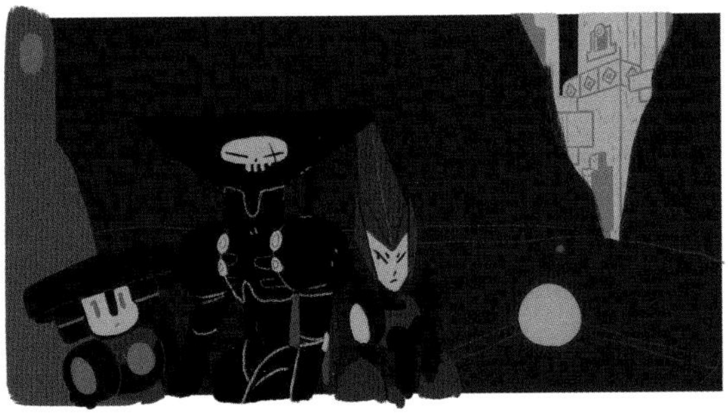

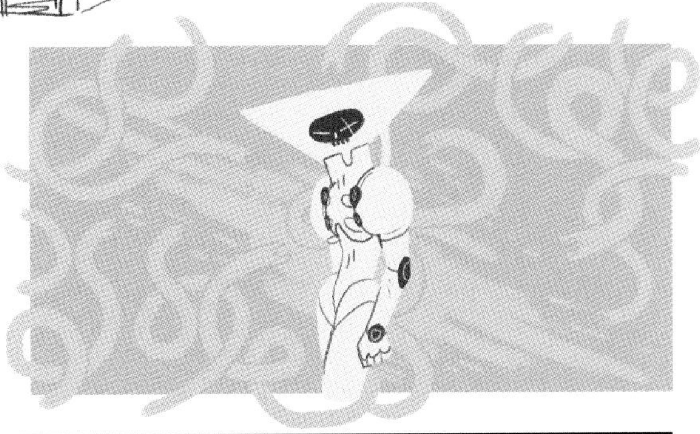

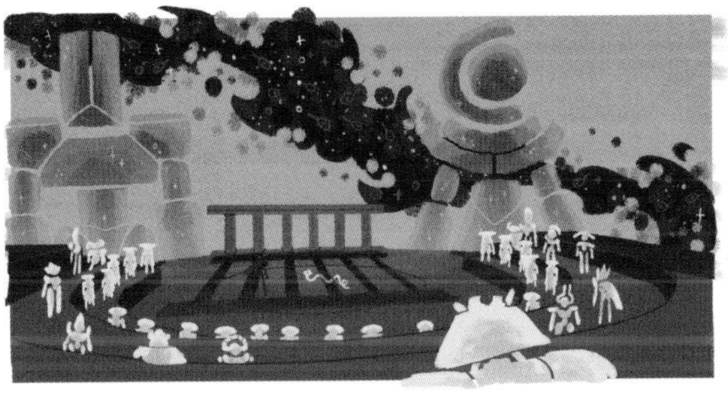

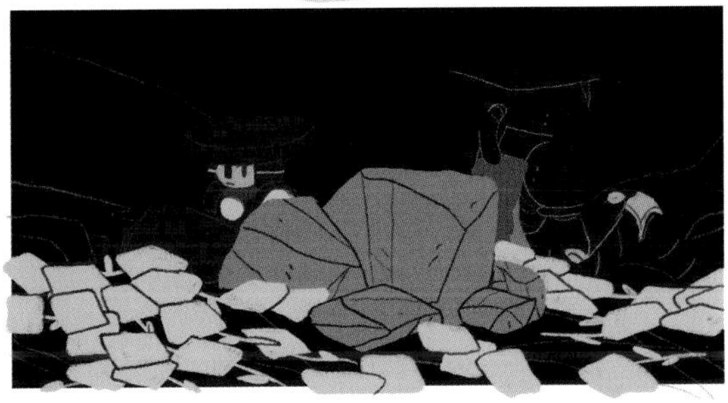

SERPENTIS SKETCHES

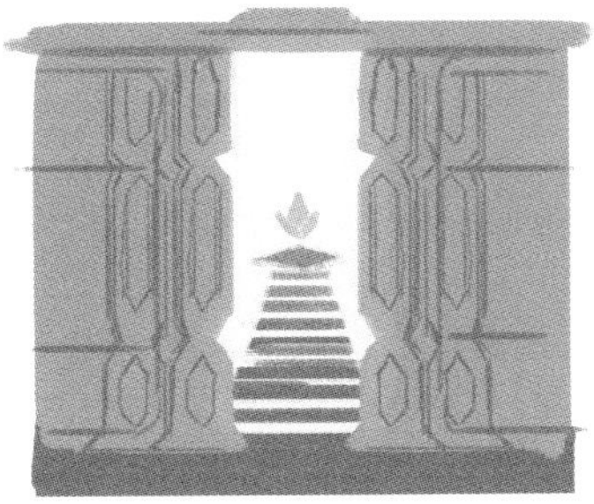

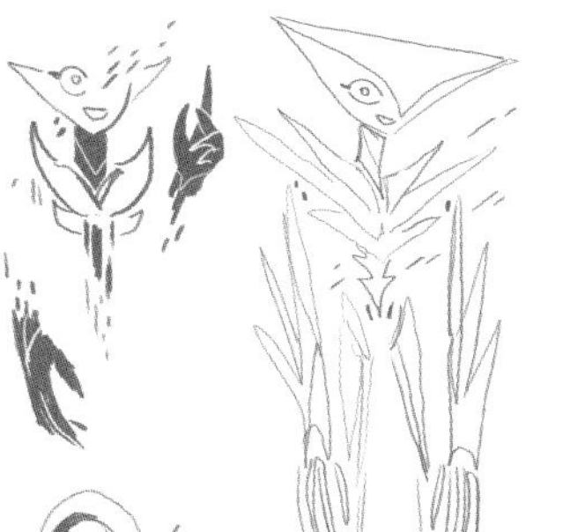

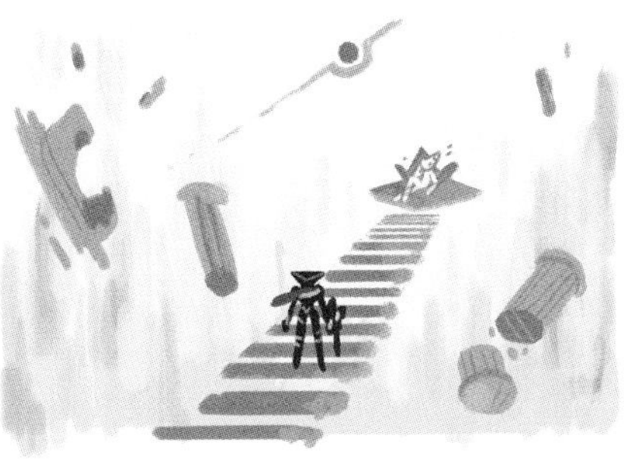

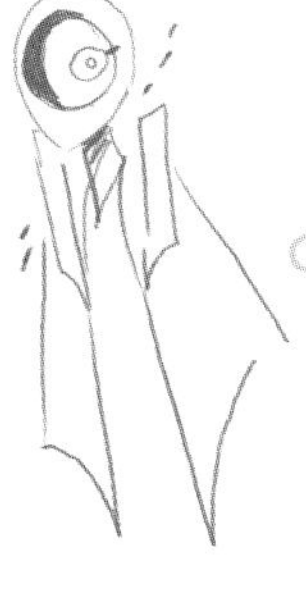

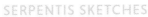

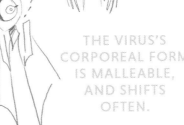

THE VIRUS'S CORPOREAL FORM IS MALLEABLE, AND SHIFTS OFTEN.

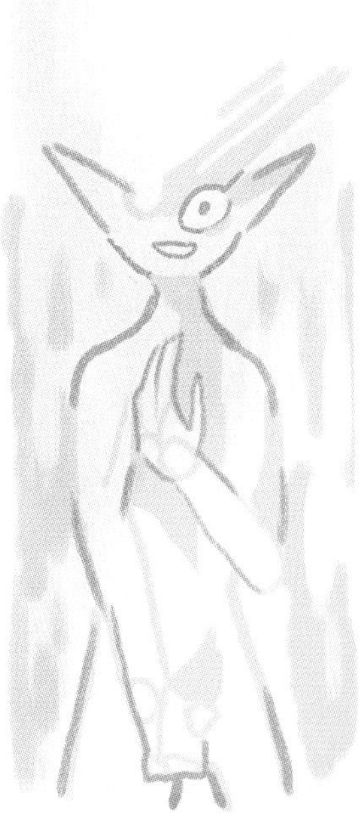

CREATURES

CONCEPT ART

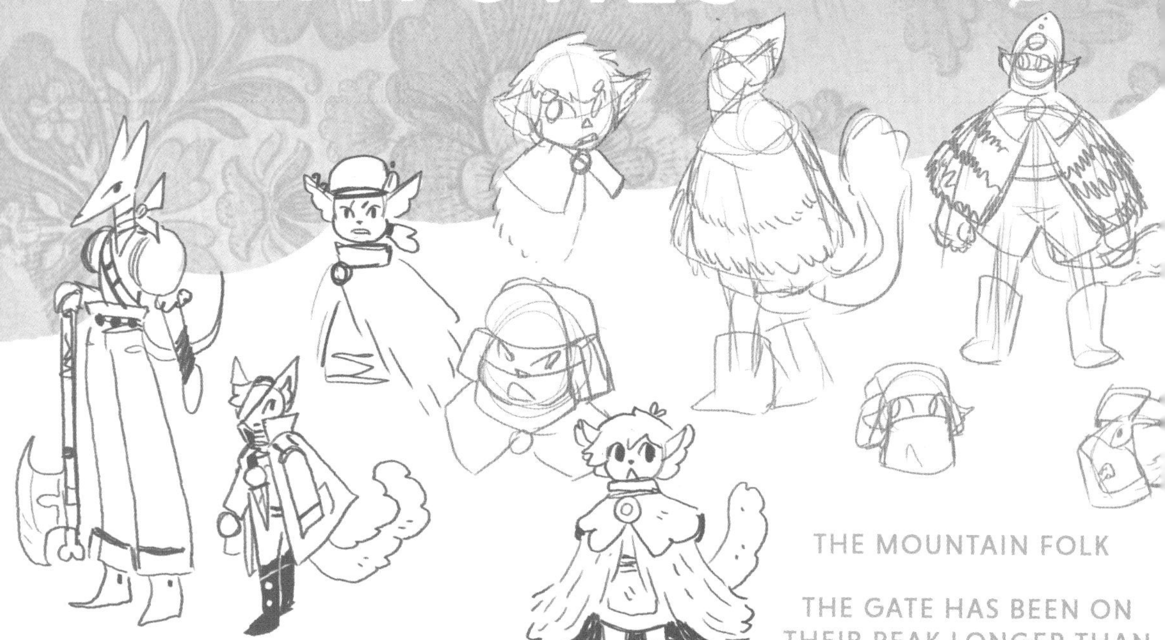

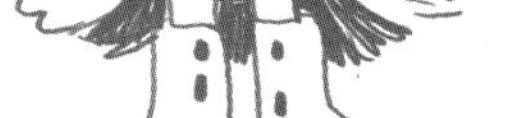

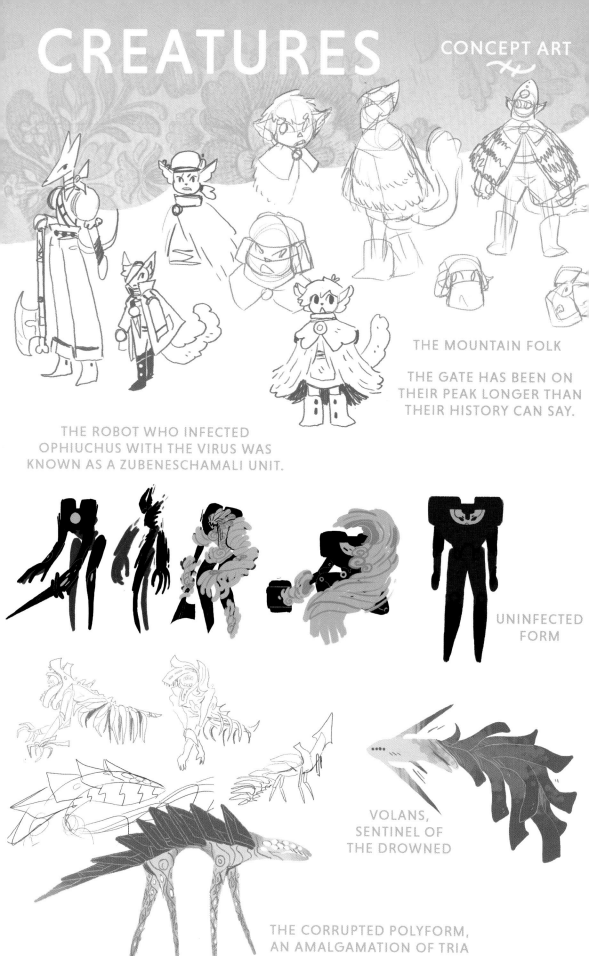

THE MOUNTAIN FOLK

THE GATE HAS BEEN ON THEIR PEAK LONGER THAN THEIR HISTORY CAN SAY.

THE ROBOT WHO INFECTED OPHIUCHUS WITH THE VIRUS WAS KNOWN AS A ZUBENESCHAMALI UNIT.

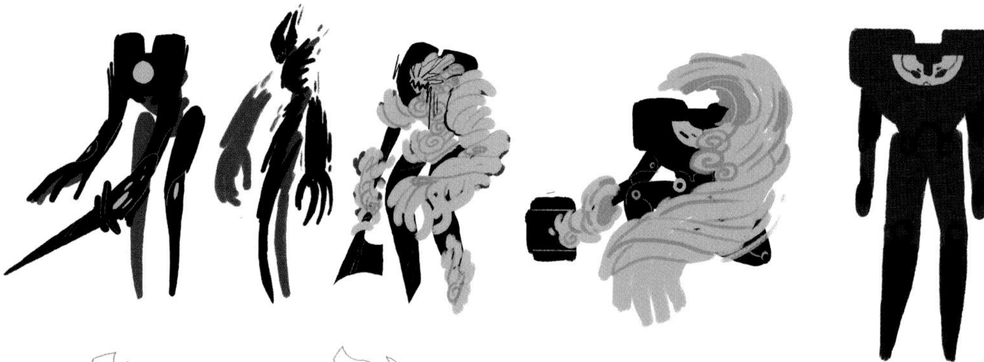

UNINFECTED FORM

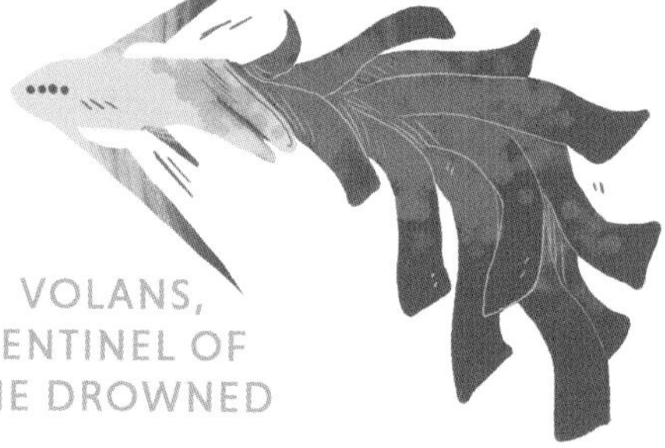

VOLANS, SENTINEL OF THE DROWNED

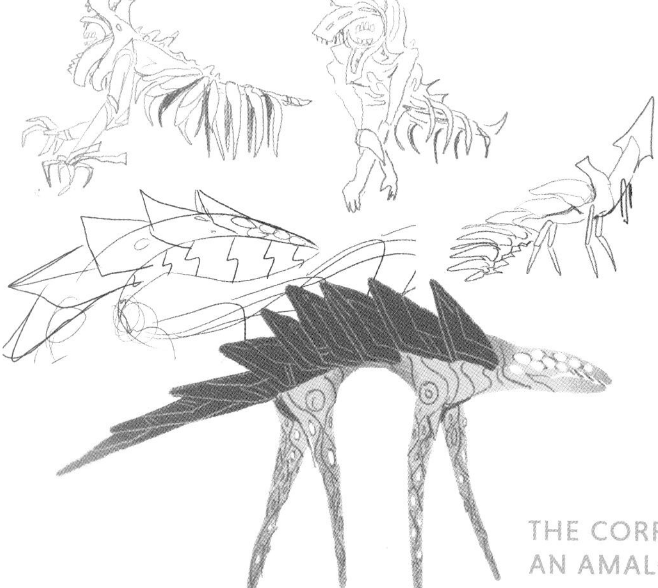

THE CORRUPTED POLYFORM, AN AMALGAMATION OF TRIA

PLACES

WORLD DEVELOPMENT

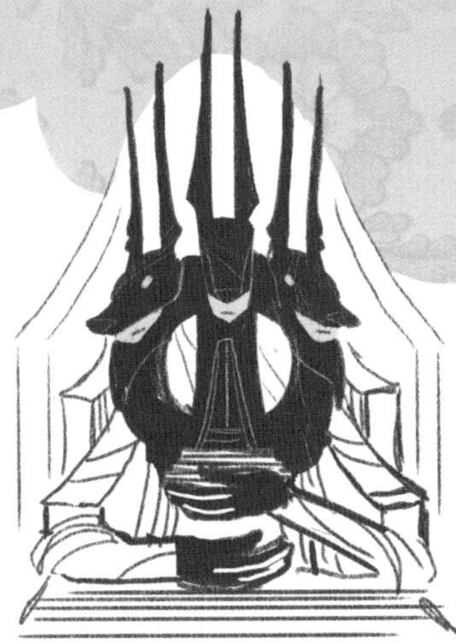

CERBERUS, GENERAL OF HADES

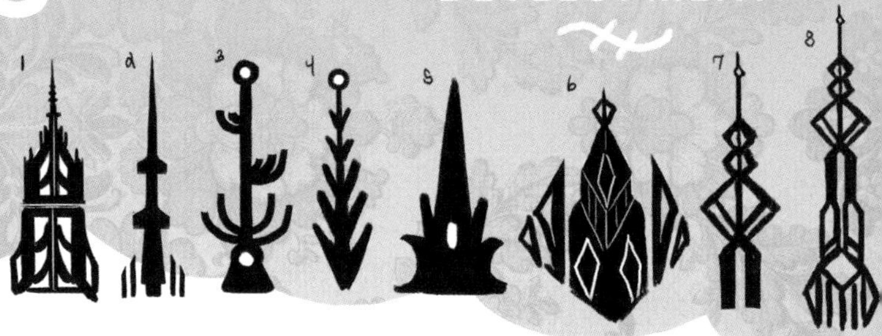

1
2
3
4
5
6
7
8

ALCAZAR CONCEPTS

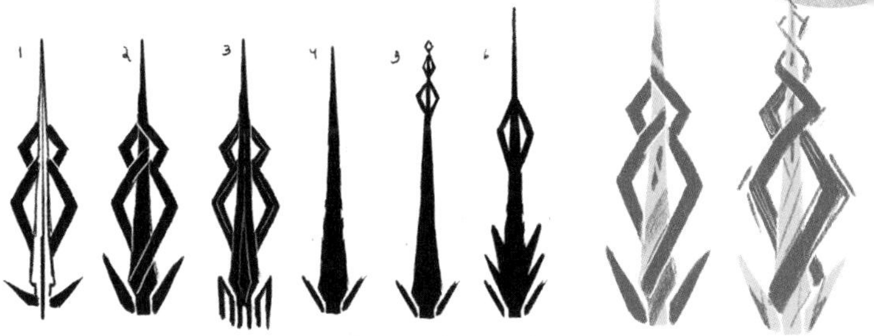

1
2
3
4
5
6

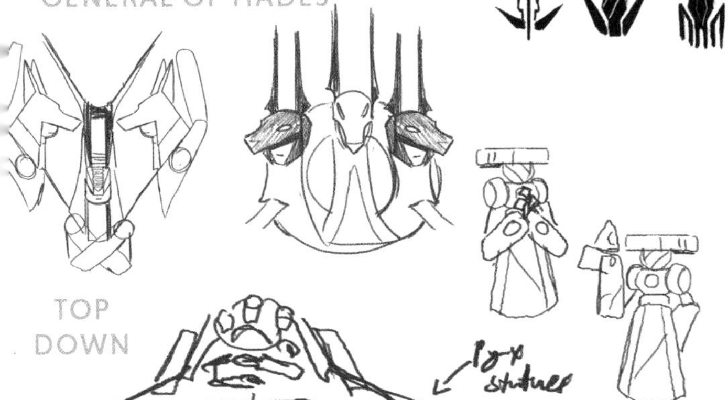

TOP DOWN

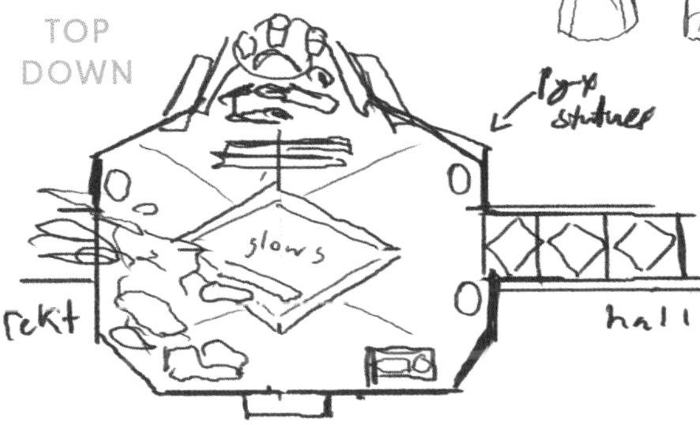

Pyx statues
glows
rekt
hall

FORNACIS CAELI, FORGE TOWN

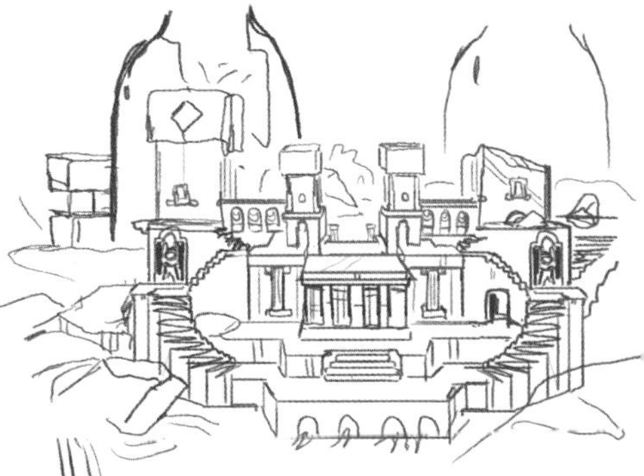

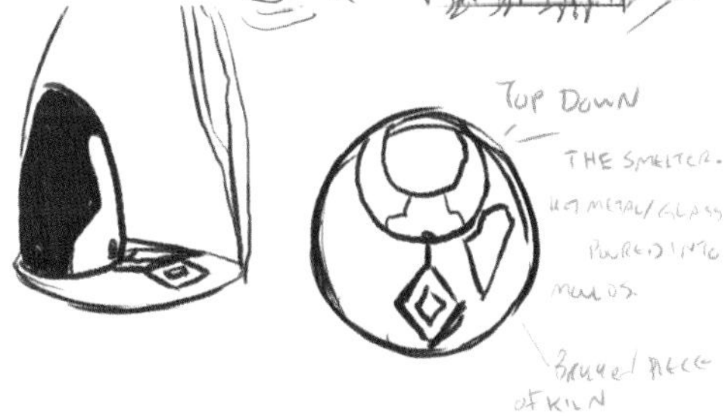

TOP DOWN
THE SMELTER.

THE HOLY CITY OF ALPHECCA

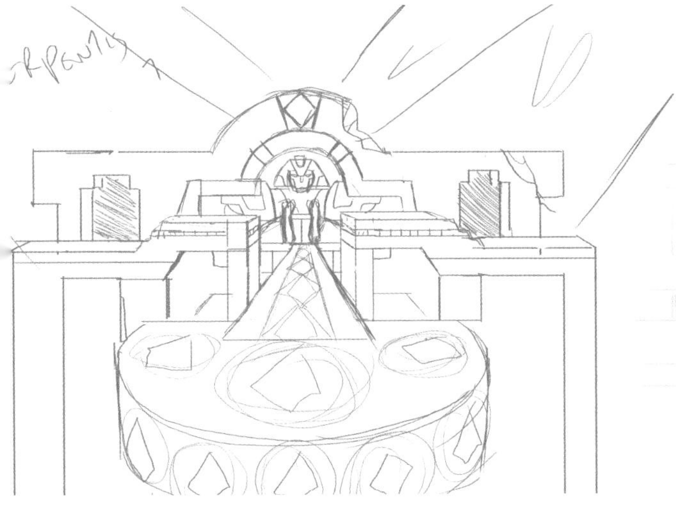

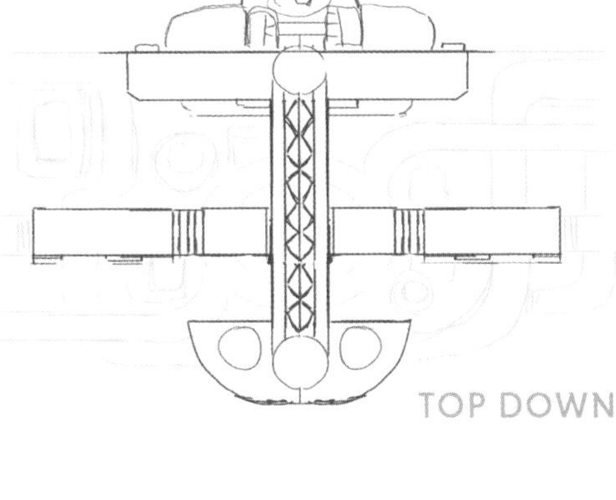

TOP DOWN

GUEST ART

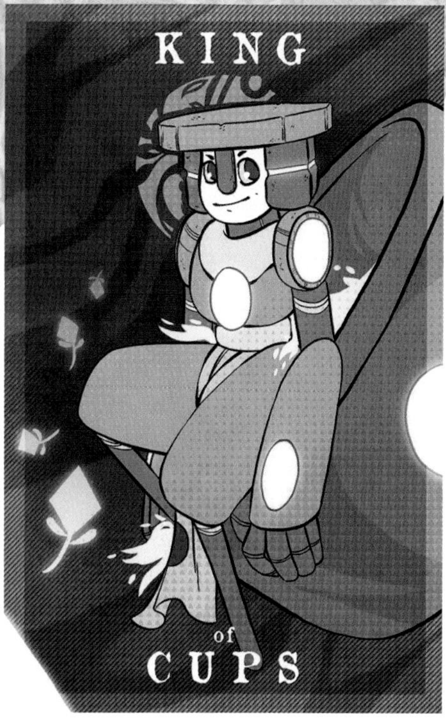
KING
of
CUPS

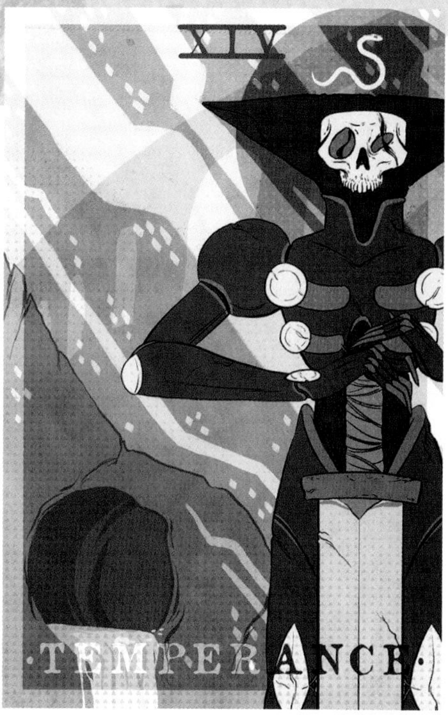
XIV
·TEMPERANCE·

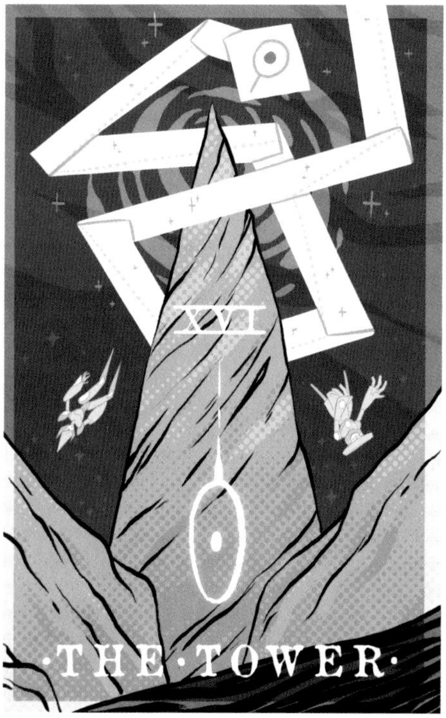
XVI
·THE·TOWER·

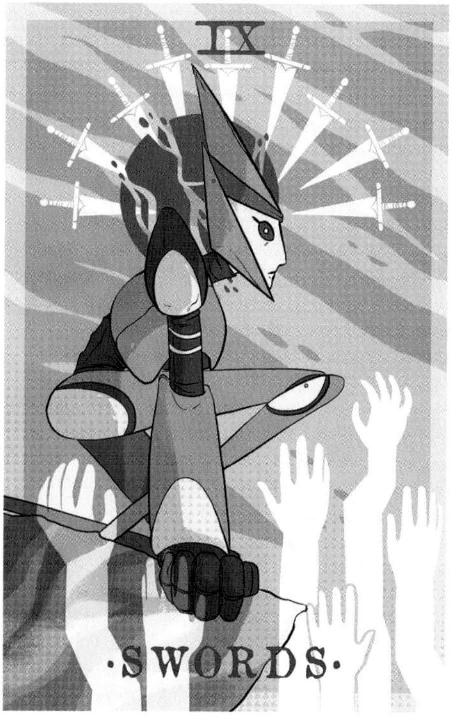
IX
·SWORDS·

TAROT CARDS BY LAURA KETCHAM

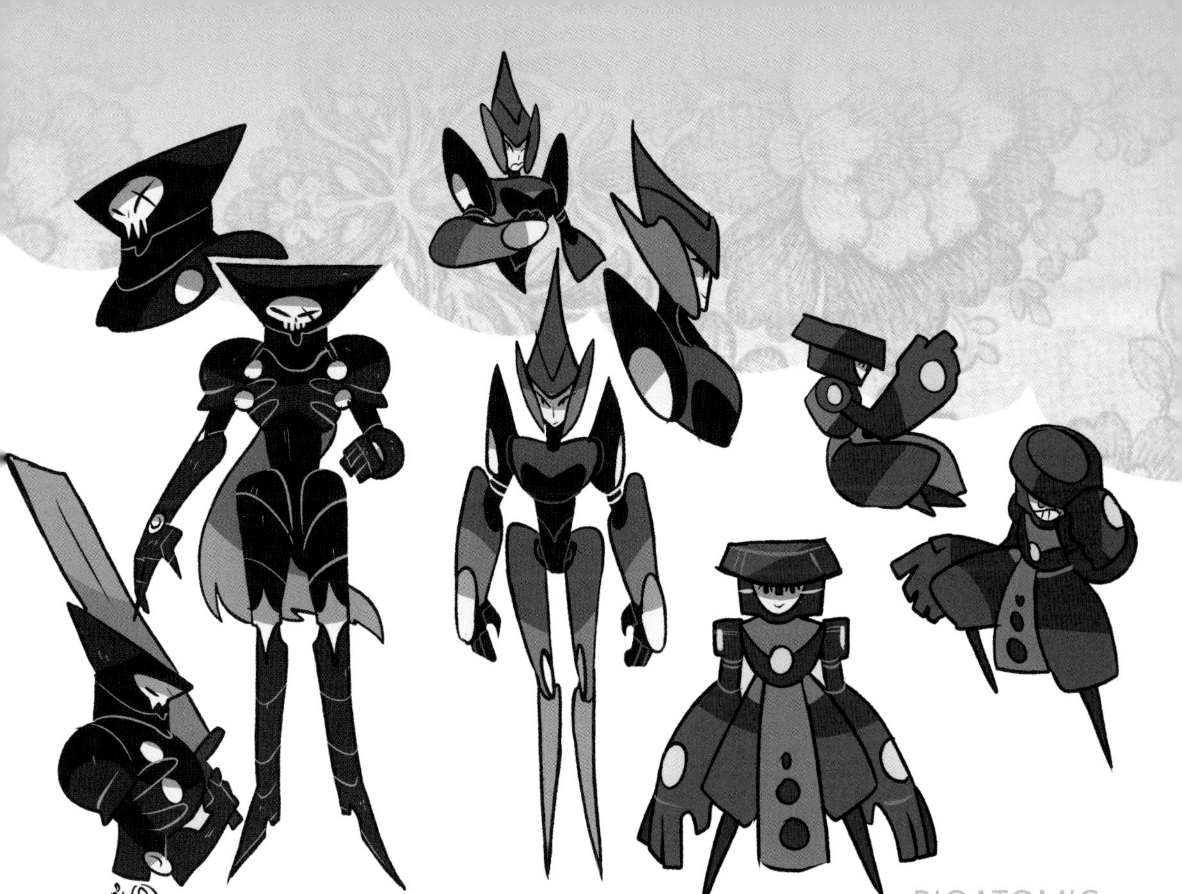

BIOATOMIC

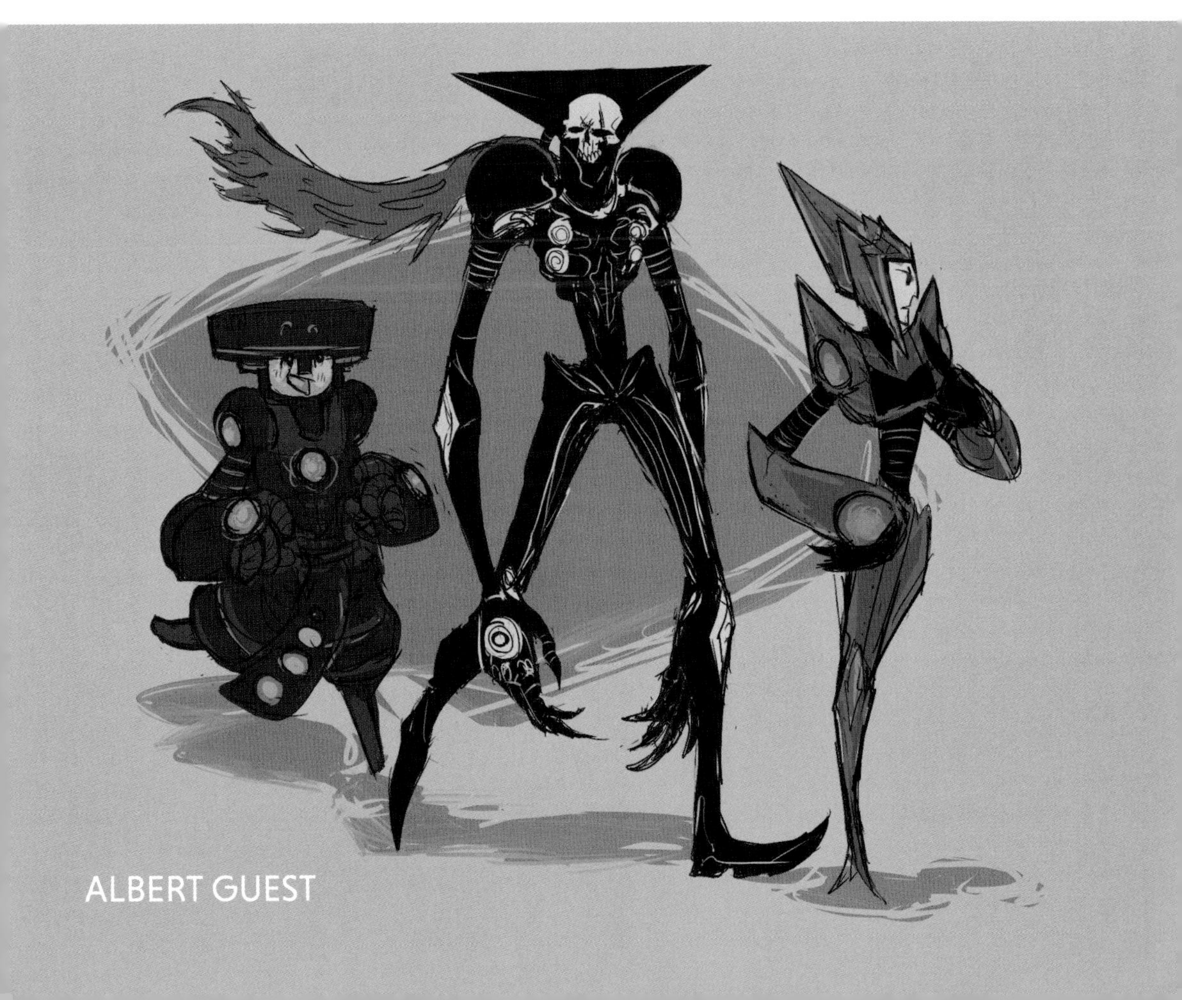

ALBERT GUEST

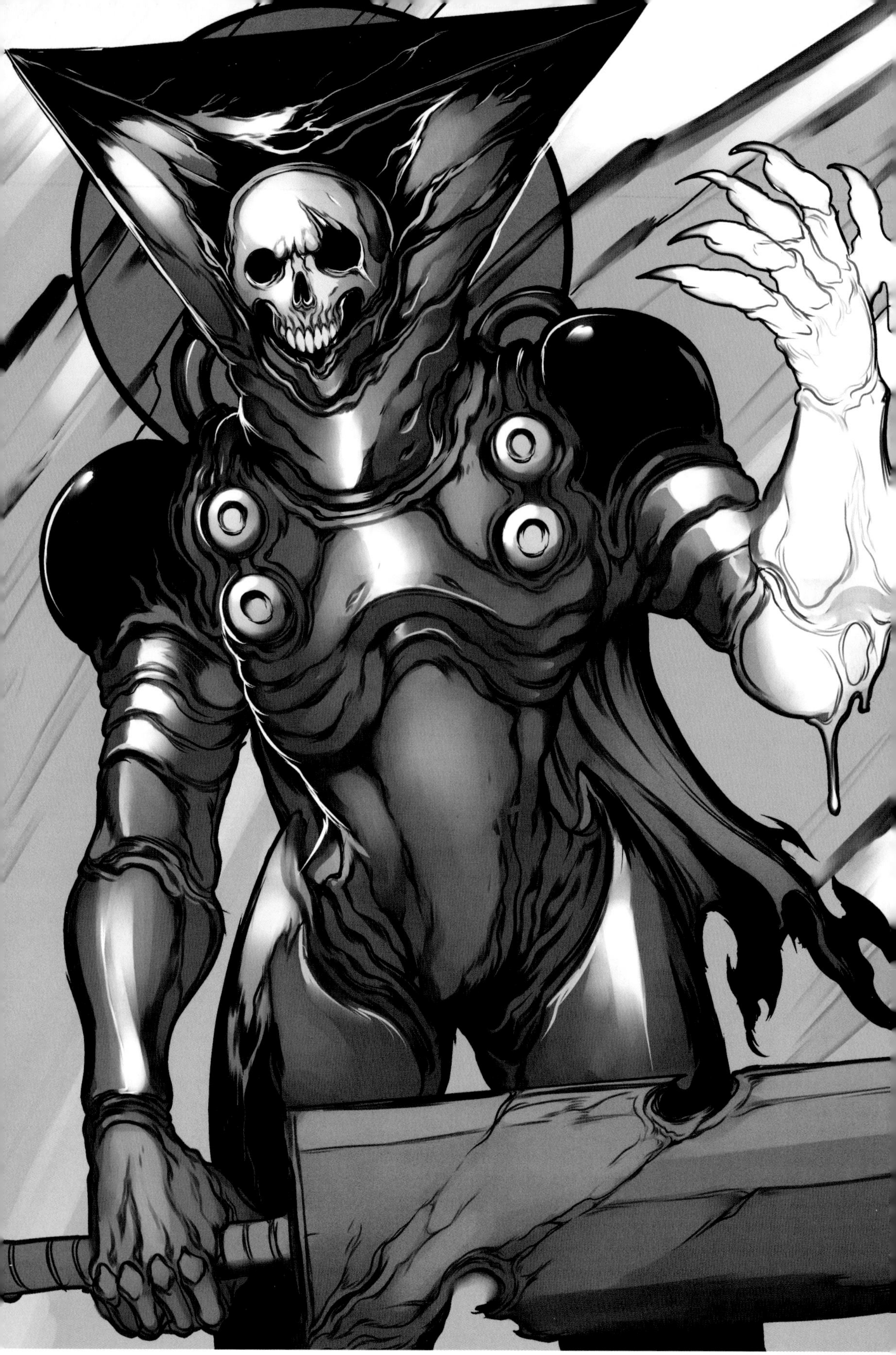

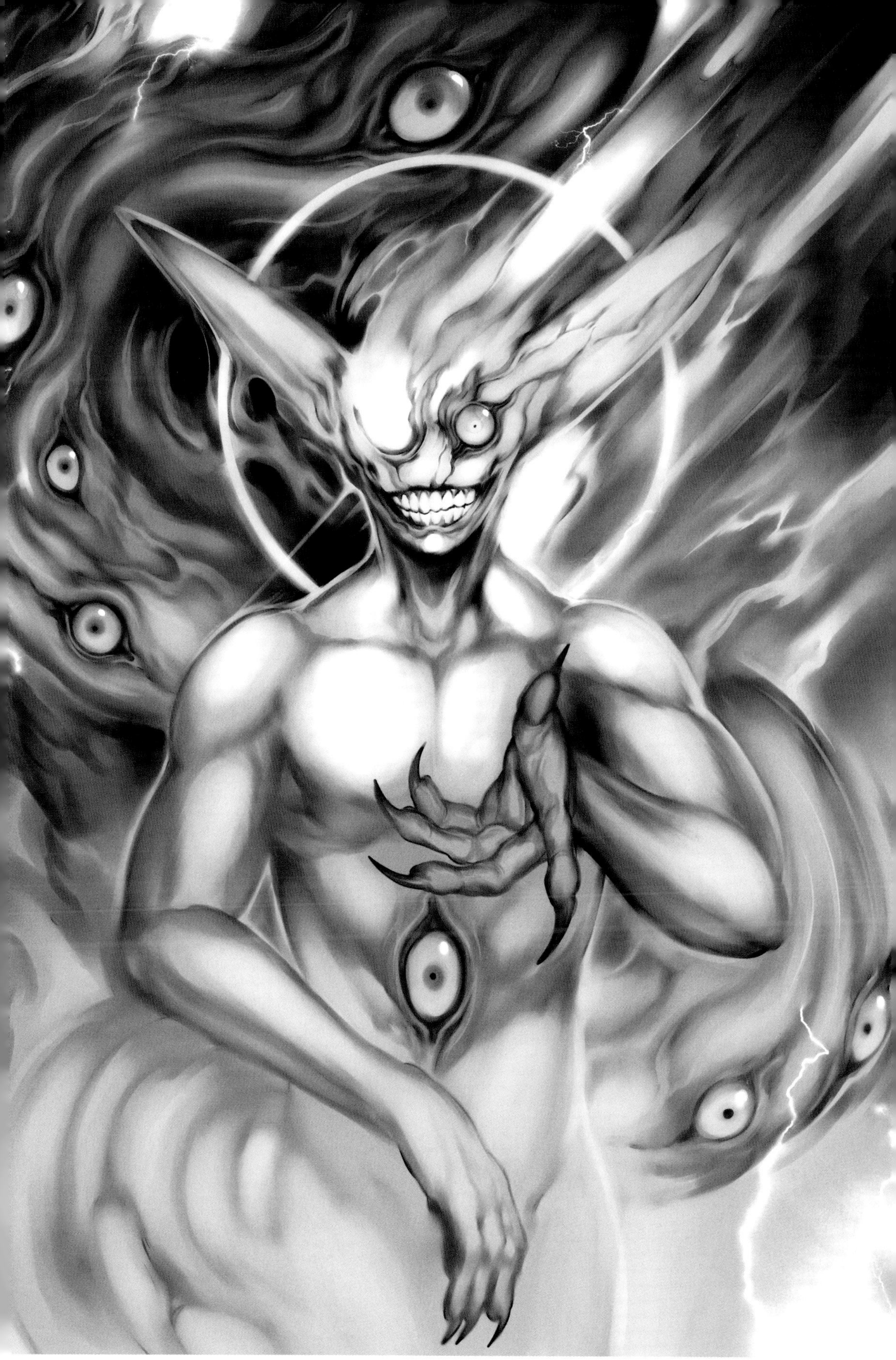

F.BRIDGE - WITNESSTHEABSURD

LORE GUIDE

Excerpts of lore, originally posted with the comic as it updated online.
"Page 1" is considered the first page of sequential art, where Ophiuchus stands atop the gate

"Pyx units were not equipped with vocalizers capable of communicating to non-mechanical entities, as they were not intended to be ambassadors of culture." Page 12

"Volans, Sentinel of the Drowned. Once tasked with clearing the riverbottom, Volans became a beacon of hope to those who were carried away by the Sadalsuud's current. When Serpentis whispered, it offered a new river in which to swim." Page 21

"Fornacis Caeli, the great metalworks. Materials from beyond the gates were brought here to be refined by Pyx building units, under the supervision of Zubeneschamali customs units." Page 32

"It is said that the machines in the heart of the universe do not require fuel in the conventional sense. How they acquire the power to move is unknown to other beings, but they do require rest." Page 36

"Asclepius said: 'The best lie ever told was that God is Good, and therefore, this is the best of all possible universes.'" Page 39

"The plutonian knights were made for one purpose, and things as petty as rest and sustenance would not stand in their way." Page 43

"It is in the design of Tria to mass together to complete more difficult tasks with the assistance of Pyx units. They were the first to be built after the Old War." Page 49

"When afraid, Tria huddle together for comfort. And when Serpentis made them look into the light, they were very afraid." Page 51

"Sometimes, when a sickness of thought such as Serpentis cannot make headway, it'll amass all its being to assault another, rather than fragmenting itself into lesser forms." Page 55

"I heard once there were rogue units living down in the Rift, somewhere way off east, where it's deepest. The Sadalsuud pours into it around there, and they say there's a lake, but I don't know why the water doesn't fill it all up. Where does it go?" Page 61

"Pyx units do not build temples: but they do, of course, honor their elders." Page 68